A Facade of Muscle

A Facade of Muscle

Brad Barham

Bridgeview Press
Philadelphia

Chapter One

The leak worsened, and water spewed everywhere. Joe thrust his hand through dense and sticky spider webs. In the ink-black darkness of the hole, his fingers searched for the shutoff valve. Having found it, he attached a wrench and gave it a sharp tug. It moved only a fraction of an inch, so he gave the wrench a stronger heave. Suddenly, the wrench slipped, slamming into another water line. It buckled and pulled free of its shutoff valve. "Damn!" Torrents of water gushed in all directions. Desperate, Joe tugged at the valve, but nothing happened. The deluge worsened. Water levels rose higher and higher by the second. Within minutes, he sat lap deep in water. Within minutes, water reached his belly. "Damn valve! Move!" Joe soon found himself in chest deep water as he fought the unyielding valve. "Help! Someone close the main valve at the street?"

No one responded.

The flow quickened, and in moments, water reached his nose. Panicky, Joe held his breath, plunged beneath the surface, and attempted to close the valve. It refused to budge. No longer able to hold his breath, he exhaled then coughed as water rushed in his nose and throat. Sinking, he felt he would drown.

Through the murk, Joe glanced right. A muscular man, wearing a leather thong and chest harness, swam toward him. The stranger smiled, grasped Joe's chin, and pulled him upward. Joe broke through the surface, and with an explosive gasp for air, bolted upright in bed and coughed water. "What the . . .!"

Joe's youngest son, Paul, stood beside the bed, giggling. Holding an empty water glass, he said, "Mommy says snoring means your throat is dry."

"Don't ever do that again!" Joe yelled. wiping his wet face and chest. *What a fucking dream. Gotta clear my mind of this shit.*

Once before, he had dreamt of a man in leather rescuing him from drowning.

Joe rubbed sleep from his eyes. With head dropped, Joe leaned against the headboard as though praying. He inched down onto the bed and pulled the sheet over his congested head, hoping to get more sleep. Snickering, he imagined Paul pouring water in his open mouth.

The alarm clock went off, startling Joe. It sounded more like a fire alarm than a time piece. He turned it off, then scratched his shaved head. *Maybe I should stay home and nurse this damn cold. Nah. I gotta go in.* He forced himself from bed.

Glancing around the room, he admired several photos of himself in football and band uniforms. *God, those were fun days.*

Born with the build of a linebacker, Joe excelled at playing quarterback for the Ohio Warriors and had lead them to a state football championship. When not playing baseball or football, he practiced playing trumpet or performed with the school band, dreaming of becoming a professional trumpeter.

Tottering past mementos, Joe walked toward the bathroom, adjusting his boxer shorts. After a pit stop in the smog of his wife's lilac potpourri, he headed for the kitchen and breakfast.

"How many times have I asked you not to walk around in your underwear," Maria yelled as Joe entered the kitchen. "It's not respectful."

"Woman, I'm not the president of the United States, and this ain't the White House. I'll do what I want in my house, and I don't feel like getting dressed this morning."

"Underwear," Maria said, shaking her head in disgust, "sets a terrible example for your sons.

Joe sniffled then kissed his young sons on the forehead, picked up the morning paper, and then took a seat at the breakfast table. "Morning guys," he said, sounding half asleep.

"Morning, daddy," the boys said as Maria prepared their school lunches.

"You coughed and sneezed a lot last night," Maria said, placing a cup of coffee before Joe. "You okay?"

"Gotta cold. I feel like shit."

"Maybe you should stay home?"

"I'm tempted, but dad needs me at the shop. Ted's out, so . . . I gotta go in. No work, no money."

"Take the cold pill I put on the table," Maria said, pointing to a white tablet.

"Thanks honey." Joe took a sip of coffee. "I had the weirdest dream last night. I couldn't stop a leak. The water rose so high I thought I'd drown. Turns out, *your* youngest son was pouring water down my throat."

"You know what they say about dreams. Water and floods are symbols of over-whelming problems that flood over you." Maria chuckled. "Better see a psychiatrist."

Joe turned to the sports page. "Gosh damn it. The Bengals lost again!"

"Which team?" Paul asked.

"A losing team," Joe said, folding the paper. "If that damn team doesn't start winning, I'm gonna write 'em off—for good!"

Maria stared at Joe. "Why get so upset over guys you never met, never shook hands with, never had a beer with or been closer than a country mile in some stadium?"

"Women. You don't understand these things—"

"That's my favorite song," Maria said. "Turn up the radio. Gosh darn. It's almost over."

A radio announcer said, "Presidential candidates will make campaign stops in southern Ohio in the coming weeks. Stay tuned to WBZI for schedules."

Joe looked up from the *Enquirer* then changed the station. "I'm sick and tired of hearing about politicians. It's time they listened to working guys for a change!"

"Yeah," Maria said, "all they wanna hear is that we're gonna vote for 'em. Oh. Almost forgot. Yesterday's mail is on the counter."

"All bills?"

"And flyers. Also a final, final notice about tickets to the Annual Bath and Kitchen Show. Anyone from the shop going?"

"Don't know. Why? You wanna go?"

"Can't. Your mother ain't well enough to watch the boys, and babysitters cost money."

Joe watched Maria, a former slim cheerleader, fuss around the kitchen, He grew pensive. *It's hard to believe we're married ten years. Look at her hair. It's is a mess, and she's gotten heavy.* "I hate spending money on the trip, but it's a chance to see new plumbing stuff. The shop sold all the crap from last year's show—at a nice profit I might add. Maybe things will be even better this year."

Joe looked at the wall clock. "Gotta go. I'll stop by the shop and then Mister Jack's place to check out his plugged drain.

Joe stood in his driveway and inhaled. The air seemed fresher here in the country. He admired the new ad on the company van.

Wertz & Son Plumbing
"Forty Years of Draining You Dry"
Smithville, Ohio.

The word *son*—a new addition—had been a recent birthday gift from his father.

Joe's parents, Don and Lois, were high school graduates. Don wanted Joe to learn, and one day take over, the family plumbing business instead of going to college.

The commute to Joe's shop took only minutes up Route 73 to what remained of Smithville, population 800.

Smithville, a rural one-traffic-light town, sat in the middle of southern Ohio's nowhere. Time and the nearby interstate highway had left Smithville in the dust of yester-year. Thirty-seven small storefront type buildings lined Main Street. Ten shops had been boarded up. Seven unboarded buildings' windows displayed fading *Going out of Business* signs or naked mannequins hiding behind *Everything Must Go* banners. One such mannequin leaned face first against one store's window.

A card shop, a gift shop, three Dollar type stores, and three "honky-tonks" (selling cigarettes, cheap beer, and in the past, cheap women), along with two sandwich shops, a hundred-year-old hardware store, a gas station (with one pump) and an assortment of antique shops were the only operating businesses. The antique shops sold local junk and dreams of hidden treasures.

The Wertz's upscale plumbing shop had off-street parking and a service counter that doubled as a hangout for locals who had nothing better to do than gossip, exchange the latest dirty joke, or brag about the fish that got away.

Joe parked in front of the shop, unlocked the door, and then entered the dark showroom. Someday the family business would be his, but he worried his sons might not be interested in plumbing. Would the business last? "Anyone here?" he yelled.

"In the back," Don yelled. "Turn on the showroom lights, will you?"

Joe switched on the lights then sat at the counter and scanned a plumbing magazine.

The door alarm sounded as Barbara, the fiftyish spinster secretary, waddled to her desk and dropped a box of doughnuts on a stack of papers. Her makeup leaned toward batter with

9

swatches of red rouge and wide swipes of bright-red lipstick that spilled beyond the borders of her lips—almost clown-like. She wore a floral-print dress that fitted like a circus tent. Her pumpkin shape had resulted from years of stasis and a morning diet of donuts washed down with creamed coffee and five sugars.

"Morning, Barbara," Joe mumbled, looking up from the magazine.

"How's your cold?"

"Horrible!"

Don entered the room, wiping his hands on a towel. "How you doing, son?"

"Got a hell of a cold. Better keep your distance. Other than that I'm fine."

"I had planned to go the bath show," Don said, "but mother isn't feeling so good. Barbara wants to know if she should change the hotel reservation to your name. You might learn or see something new."

Joe nodded. *Guess I'd better go.* "Okay, Dad." Joe put his magazine on the counter. "Barbara, make it for three days, okay? I have too many things to do at the new house so book me for Thursday through Sunday. There's always a free bar on Saturday night. If I stay until Sunday, I'll be sober and safe to drive home."

Joe glanced at his father. "I gotta go to Mister Jack's. Gotta clean out his pipes. He's forever putting crap in his drains. This'll be the *fifth* damn time this year."

"Don't get so upset, son. That old queer's business keeps this business going."

"Don't hurt anything," Don said, wagging a finger. "We can't have you out of commission. Ted is out for another week, so it's me and you."

"Don't worry. I won't."

Halfway out the front door, Joe heard Don yell. "Joe, be

careful if Sammy Schmidt is at the gym. Better shower with your clothes on. You don't want him sneaking peeks."

"Dad, why do you keep talking about queers?"

"Who?" Barbara shouted.

"Joe's queer classmate," Don yelled. "The guy got caught playing with another guy in the school shower when Joe was a junior. That old queer, *Mister Jack*, coached back then. He saw the kids but did nothing like in that Penn State scandal. Another kid came in, caught them, and told the principal. Mister Jack retired right after that."

"Joe!" Barbara yelled. "Don't forget women like small muscle butts. Biceps are a guy thing. Don't waste time growing them unless you're doing it for that Jack guy."

"Woman, you should feel how hard my ass is!"

"Don't you wish," Barbara said. "Remember, keep your plumber's crack covered. That's the reason Mister Jack calls you guys. Bet he puts junk down his drains just so he has an excuse to call us. At his age, you're the only excitement he gets."

"If that's the case, we'll charge an entertainment fee!" Don yelled from the back room.

"Barbara," Joe said, I can't believe you're thinking Mister Jack is a dirty old man,".

"He's not a dirty old man. Just a needy one."

Driving, Joe thought about the work needed at his new house. In a matter of minutes, he had arrived at Mister Jack's 110 year-old house. The Victorian home needed tons of loving care and paint. On moonless nights, the home resembled the Bates house in the movie *Psycho*, complete with rocking chairs on the front porch.

Mister Jack had inherited the house at age twenty-two, a month after he graduated college and the day his mother died. When Jack turned thirty, a "friend," George moved in. He lived with Jack for thirty-five years before dying. Rumors were he died of AIDS.

Joe knew the layout of Jack's house like he knew the way to his shop. The heritage home still had its original wooden-framed, slipper-shaped copper bathtub. The copper had oxidized to a green patina with the help of time, the county's hard water, and years of exposure to alkaline soaps. Joe had fitted the tub with faucets and a drain, so Jack could fill and empty it without using a bucket. However, despite having a totally functional tub, Mister Jack's friends believed he preferred Old Spice Cologne baths to water bathing.

Joe climbed the rickety steps and crossed the home's sagging wooden porch. The front door still had the original frosted-glass window secured with caulking that disintegrated at the slightest touch. He pulled a rope that hung from a hole in the upper-right corner of the doorframe. The tug caused a cowbell to ring on the other side of the door.

"Coming! I'm coming," a high-pitched voice called from inside.

Joe saw moving shadows through the door's frosted glass. The door squeaked open, the window rattled, and Mister Jack, looking old enough to have supervised construction of Noah's ark, stepped into view. A widening smile pushed years of sun-wrinkled skin toward his ears as his loose upper denture dropped into his gleeful smile. "Morning, Joe. Come on in."

"Morning, Mister Jack. What's the problem today?"

"It's my kitchen sink. I put corn silk in the drain, but it won't go down."

Following Jack into the simple 1940s kitchen, Joe pulled his pants higher. There would be no plumber's crack showing today.

Joe pushed aside the water-stained gingham curtain hiding the space under the sink. In no time, he had removed the elbow trap, extracted the corn silk, and dropped it into a waste can under the sink. He repositioned and tightened the elbow trap then pulled the gingham curtains shut. "Now, don't do that again."

"Bless you, Joe. Don't know what I'd do without you or your dad. You know, you remind me of George—when he was young—God rest his soul. He's been dead thirty-three years, but I still miss him. If I were fifty years younger, I'd give you a run for your money, young man."

"Guess what? I'm thirty-three. George must have died the year I was born."

"Well, I didn't know your age, but you don't think I'd be hankering after somebody my age do you?"

Mister Jack flashed an impish grin.

"Mister Jack—you're too much." Joe felt his face blush warm. "I've got to get outta here." *Hope to hell he doesn't think I'm gay.*

Mister Jack opened the front door then extended his hand. Joe shook it. As he turned to go, Mister Jack slapped Joe on the butt and handed him money. "God bless you—Joe."

For God's sake, leave the ass patting on the gridiron.

As Joe approached his van, a fellow Lutheran Church member, Irene, arrived to look in on the elderly man.

Many church women feared for his safety and often visited at the same time, making the house a hub of gossip. If anyone wanted to know the latest gossip and happenings in the community, they asked Mister Jack.

Chapter Two

Joe, a volunteer fireman, parked beside the frame structure that served as a firehouse. Outside, two friends were rolling hoses recently used to fight a fire.

"Twelve minutes," Buzz shouted, puffing his chest with pride.

"We saved Harriet Weller's house in twelve minutes," Big Boy said. "Fire started in the clothes dryer. Lint backed up to the heating unit and caught fire. Buzz and I are going back this afternoon to dissemble the exhaust duct. Wanna get the lint out to prevent another problem. Wanna come with us, Joe?"

"No can do. You know Harriet is blind? If the house had caught fire, she might not have gotten out. You probably saved her life. I just stopped by for a workout. You guys got time to join me?"

"Don't tell anyone, but we were gonna have a beer as soon as we stowed these hoses," Buzz said, "but we can work out first."

"I'll help with the hoses," Joe said, picking up a coiled one.

"Thanks," Big Boy said. "Make sure to change those work clothes. We don't want no plumber smell in our gym."

The firemen had created a makeshift gym in a back-room of the firehouse. Weightlifting provided a diversion for the firemen who often waited days between fire calls. It had an array of donated equipment. The ceiling and walls were covered with pictures from *Playboy* and muscle magazines. They provided equal representation of naked women and bodybuilders for inspiration.

"I'll change clothes while you guys finish here," Joe said, leaving for the gym.

Exercising with the guys gave Joe a chance to get out of

the house for male bonding, and Big Boy pushed him to lift more weight than if he lifted alone—a must if Joe was to get bigger.

Joe changed into gym shorts and a t-shirt and waited for Big Boy and Buzz.

Buzz entered and looked at Joe. "Wow, your cows are growing!"

"My legs have always been a strong point," Joe said, flexing his calves. "Never had to work them much."

Big Boy lay on the bench ready to press 390 pounds. Joe straddled the head end of the bench and prepared to spot him. Laughing, Big Boy said, "Joe, don't you ever wear a jock? I'm seeing right up your balls."

"Eat your heart out, pervert." Joe tucked his balls out of view. "At least mine are big enough to see."

Big Boy completed lifting. "You're next, Joe."

Joe did two sets of bench presses.

After rotating nine rounds of lifting, Big Boy said, "Guys, I have to go. Gotta do something for the wife, and then I'll go back to Harriet's house. Joe, increase your weight for the next set."

Big Boy and Buzz walked toward the door.

Joe called to the departing guys, "I'm finished. I'll rest a minute, shower, and then get out of here."

"Make sure the door's locked," Big Boy said. "You're the only one here."

Joe sat down on a bench. Back against the wall, its coolness on his sweat-soaked shirt felt refreshing.

Rested, Joe grabbed his sweat towel and headed for the shower. Soon, he luxuriated in the flow of a hot shower and lots of suds. Not long into his revelry, a ringing phone intruded on his bliss. *Damn. Better answer that. Could be a fire call.*

Grabbing a towel, Joe dried his feet. Wrapping the towel around his waist, he hurried to the phone.

16

"Smithville Firehouse, Joe speaking. Where's your fire emergency?"

"Oh! I'm sorry," a woman said. "I called the wrong number."

"Glad you didn't have a fire."

"Me too. Bye."

As Joe walked toward the locker room, his towel fell to the floor. He picked it up and continued walking toward the lockers. Glimpsing his reflection in a mirror, he stopped and eyed his image. His muscles were still pumped. *Not bad looking for a thirty-three-year-old guy.*

Joe scanned his pecs and belly before sucking it in. He bounced each pec a few times and smiled. He then struck his belly with a fist while tensing his abs. *Gotta work more on this six-pack.*

Joe admired the depth of his traps then did a double-bicep-pose. Tightening his glutes, he poked the left one with an index finger. *Gotta work this butt more if I don't want an ass looking like grandpa's.*

Joe pulled the towel back and forth over his back and watched various muscles contract. He stopped drying his back and tugged the towel in opposite directions, causing his chest muscles to bulge. *Looking good!*

After a last admiring glance, he dried his balls, buffed his shaved head, dressed, and then lest for the shop.

Chapter Three

"Back from the weightlifting wars?" Barbara asked, handing Joe an invoice.

"How'd you guess?" Joe handed her the money from Mister Jack's job.

"I bet you spent most of your time looking at those pictures of naked women plastered all over that gym. Whole town knows they're there."

Joe headed for the backroom. "Yep, but I always admire your picture more than any of the other women."

"Hi, son," Don said as Joe entered. "Did Barbara tell you about the president?"

"*No*. What about him?"

"He's coming through town in a few weeks and wants to visit a local business. We've been selected, but we have to be cleared by the Secret Service, so don't you get upset when government guys asks neighbors, the minister, school principal, and the banker about us."

"I'll be damned. Boy, can I give him an earful. Seems all he's interested in these days is gay shit while doing nothing for the economy—except make promises."

"Son, be respectful. The press and TV people will be with him."

"Shit. Wait till Maria hears this."

"Speaking of Maria, she called. Said she's coming to town." Don placed a faucet into a box then scribbled something on the top. "Thought we could all go to lunch. Your mom isn't feeling well, so she won't be coming."

"Sorry to hear that. Is it her chemo?"

"Yeah. Makes he pretty sick."

"I'll go see her tomorrow. Where are we going for lunch?"

Don shrugged. "Blue Bell Diner?"

"That's fine."

"Barbara, watch the shop while we're out, will ya?" Don yelled as he and Joe left the shop.

"Will do," Barbara yelled. "Joe, I changed the hotel reservation for the bath show!"

Opening the diner door for Don, Joe saw his sons and Maria sitting in a booth near the jukebox. Her hair, held with cheap silver clips, looked frightful. The absence of makeup magnified her harried appearance.

Maria looked up from a yellowed menu. "Hi, guys."

Don and Joe kissed her forehead.

Joe tousled the boys' hair. "How you guys doing?" he asked, sitting across from Maria.

"Good," the boys said.

"Guess what, Maria?" Joe asked.

"You won $500 from the lottery?"

Joe frowned. "No. The president wants to visit a local business in a few weeks, and we're it. Make sure you get a nice dress for the occasion."

"I'm not spending money on a dress just to see the president. No. thanks. I'll stay home. I don't care much for politicians."

"Maria," Don said, "it's not every day you get to meet the president in *our* shop. You should come."

"It'd be a waste of time and money," Maria said. "Hope the town enjoys the visit."

"Can Paul and me meet the president?" John asked.

"I'd guess the whole school would turn out," Joe said.

"Just wait till Paul and me tell our friends we're going to meet the real president," John said.

"Careful son. Don't expect too much."

Flo, Don's favorite waitress, approached the table, writing pad in hand. Fifteen years after moving to Ohio, she still harbored a Texas drawl. She brought with her a Texas-style beehive hairdo, reaching halfway to God, and a scoundrel of a husband whom she had since divorced. Her white orthopedic Frankenstein-like shoes squeaked on the terrazzo floor.

"How y'all doin'? she asked, popping gum. "I heard about the president. Are you excited?"

"God, word gets around quick don't it," Don said. "Everything's fine except for my empty stomach."

"Your usual, Don?" Flo asked.

"How'd you guess?"

"Let's say a fruit fly told me," Flo said, swatting at one.

"That's okay as long as it ain't a real *fruit*," Don said with bite in the tone of his voice.

Joe shuddered on hearing the word *fruit*.

"I'll have the chef salad," Maria said. "No cheddar. Give me blue cheese dressing."

Joe said, "I'll have the chef salad with oil and vinegar."

"Ya got it, honey," Flo said, straightening her starched-handkerchief crown.

Maria placed her menu behind the sugar container and looked at Joe. "After you left the house, I watched the TV news. The gays are gonna have a parade by the convention hall, during your bath show."

"Make sure you get to the hotel before the streets close for the queers' parade," Don said, disgust coloring his voice.

Joe leaned over the table and whispered, "Dad, please don't refer to people as queers and fruits. It's not nice. It ain't good for business, and your grandsons shouldn't hear you talk like that."

Don sneered. "Nice, smice—whatever. When I was your age, we called a queer a queer and nobody gave a rat's ass."

21

"Careful, dad, you never know when someone might be offend. It's not good for business."

"You referring to that queer sitting back there? The one who bought the Goldberger house."

"Shhhh, Dad. He's a good customer. Hell, we've redone all his plumbing. He's bought more expensive stuff than anybody in the history of Wertz & Son. We've made lots of money off that man, *and* he pays cash. Nobody else does that. Shit, he'll probably buy some of the new stuff from the bath show. Please, be careful what you say—for the sake of the business. It's not Christian."

"Guys, let's not argue, okay?" Maria said. "Our food's here."

Between bites, Maria said, "I stopped by Mister Jack's today."

"And what's the latest gossip?" Don asked.

Maria looked over her shoulder then whispered, "Susan, from my Sunday school class, has been seeing a Universal Packing truck parked behind Helen Miller's house. It's been there a lot of late. Turns out, the driver got Helen's granddaughter pregnant. Mind you, a black driver!"

Joe glared at Maria. "Stop the gossip."

"Half the town knows," Maria whispered. "Helen is fit to be tied. She wants Mary to get an abortion, but she insists the driver and her are gonna get married and raise the child."

"Great! That's all we need," Don said, slamming his fork on the table. "Another black in Smithville—living off our tax dollars,"

"Dad, he's working. Don't be so cruel. He's not on welfare."

"I'll bet the half-breed baby will be."

"Will be what?" Joe asked

"On welfare."

"Dad, don't you have any love in your heart? Neither you or Maria are sounding very Christian." Joe looked at his watch. "I gotta get to another job. Enjoy your lunch."

Joe stormed out of the restaurant. *I've never seen dad so worked up. Why now?*

Joe finished the last job of the day then headed home. Pulling onto his driveway, he heard yelling inside the house.

"Mommy. Mommy. It's daddy. Daddy's home," Joe's sons yelled and waved from the kitchen window then ran from the house and tackled his legs. In a mock fall, Joe rolled on the ground laughing while hugging his sons against his chest. The boys giggled and struggled to get free of the fatherly hug. *God, I love you guys.*

Joe kissed each boy on the forehead and then headed for the kitchen door.

Maria exited the house saying, "Hey, honey. How was your day?" She kissed him on the cheek.

"Oh, the same old crap," Joe said, entering the kitchen.

"The boys got their report cards," Maria said, smiling. "The time you've spent studying with them is paying off. Boys, get your report cards and show daddy how well you did."

"Did you pack my toilet things?" Joe asked.

"Not yet. I've been busy with your clothes," Maria said, looking sad. "Your travel bag is beside the kitchen table."

"Are you okay?"

"I'm okay . . . just wished I could go with you." She opened the oven door and peeked inside. "I made meatloaf. Want some before you leave?"

"Thanks, but I'm not hungry. I want to get started before the traffic gets heavy."

Joe rummaged through his suitcase. *I need a change of scenery.* He didn't know if the town, the people, or plumbing work bugged him, but he needed a break. Closing his bag, he looked at Maria. "I'll miss you and the kids. Want me to bring you anything special?"

"If you see something I'd like." Maria said, placing dinner plates on the table. "Did John mention wanting a trumpet?"

"No. Why?"

"He's been saying he wants a trumpet to learn to play like you."

"Well I'll be damned." Joe zipped his travel bag. "I had no idea. I'll see if I can find one, maybe a cheap one in a pawn shop."

Maria smiled. "That would tickle him pink."

"For God's sake, don't let Dad hear you mention the kids and the word pink in the same breath." Joe shook his head. "I don't want him thinking we're raising *fru frus*."

"After you left the diner the other day, Don went on and on about queers. I had to remind him that his grandsons were there."

"I don't know what has gotten into him, but I don't want the boys becoming bigots."

Joe perused his mail and remembered the hotel had a gym. *Better get my gym clothes.* He packed his gym gear then closed the bag. As he lifted it from the bed, his sons ran into the room.

"You guys wanna help daddy?"

John pushed up a shirt sleeve and flexed his bicep. "Look. I can help."

"No, let me!" Paul yelled.

Each boy jockeyed to share Joe's grip on the handle of the travel bag. With everyone's hand in place, the trio waddled

toward the door, half-dragging, half-carrying the suitcase.

Joe gave Maria a peck on the lips then kissed each boy

24

goodbye.

"You guys are in charge 'till Daddy gets back," Joe said. "Make sure you mind your mother and promise not to fight. Agreed?"

"We promise."

Looking at Maria, Joe said, "I'll drive up Route 52. It'll be slower, but it'll give me time to chill out. I'll stop at Burger House if I get hungry."

Joe pulled the boys against his legs in an arm length hug. "Now remember, mind mother. If you're good, we'll go fishing when I get back. How's that sound?"

"Yeah!" the boys yelled.

"Oh, that reminds me," Maria said, "Don said he'd take the boys fishing while you're away. Your mother's feeling better, so he wants to get out for a while. You have only one rod. Is it okay if I buy another one?"

"Sure," Joe said.

Joe would leave the family SUV for Maria and drive his 1975 Corvette to Cincinnati. After placing the travel bag in the trunk, he slid behind the wheel. As the family waved from the front porch, he blew a kiss and drove away.

"Boys, you ready?" grandpa Don asked, walking into their kitchen.

"Yeah!" they yelled.

"Well, let's get going. Maria, I'll have them home in a couple of hours."

"That's fine," she said, winking, "but watch who you talk about. Know what I mean?"

"Okay. Will you listen for the phone in case mother calls for help. There's no cell signal at the pond."

The pond, a sinkhole, had formed ages ago in the middle of a sixty acre tract of forest. Sixty years ago, the current owner had cleared trees from the pond's perimeter and added sand to make a small beach for sunbathing. The pond had been a private retreat for his family, but later, he opened it to the public.

As the owner aged and became disabled, trees and vegetation grew back. The area now resembled a deserted oasis. In exchange for feedback about the property's condition, the owner gave the Wertz clan permission to use it.

While driving to the pond, Don made small talk about the boys' school.

"John, is Mary Jones still your girlfriend?" Don asked.

Blushing, John said, "No!"

Stopped at a rural intersection with a four-way-stop, Don started across the intersection. Suddenly, a car from the left sped past—its driver ignoring a stop sign. "Damn!" Don said, swerving. He swung his right arm in front of John and stopped the car with a lurch. "God damn it!" Don shook a fist at the speeding car then asked "You boys alright?"

"Yep," the boys replied.

"Damn queer! Sammy Schmidt knows he should have stopped."

"Who?" John asked.

"A queer classmate of your dad's."

Don took a deep breath to calm his nerves then drove through the intersection

Appearing pensive, Paul asked, "What's a queer?"

Don thought for a second. "A queer is a son-of-a-bitch who does disgusting, nasty, horrible things with other sons-of-bitches. You don't want to be around them! They're evil. Even God hates them. Says so in the Bible."

"Grandpa, how do you know somebody's a queer?" Paul asked.

"Well, son, it's like learning to swim. Takes a little

practice, but you'll learn. When you're older, you'll know."

Paul said, "If God hates them so will I. You will too won't you, John?"

"If Grandpa and God hates them then we will too."

Chapter Four

Mark Hanlan, a twenty-nine-year-old bodybuilder, carried himself with the casual air of a California movie star. He exited a plane at the Cincinnati International Airport then headed for the baggage area. Having retrieved a leather bag, he headed for King's Cars rental agency.

At the rental counter, he handed a reservation form to the agent, leaned forward, and sucked air—liking what the agent and city offered. Nice, Mark said to himself, eyeing the agent's tight corporate shirt, baseball biceps, and deep pecs.

As Mark took the car keys, the agent smiled and let his fingers graze Mark's palm. He smiled then said, "Thank you, Mark, for choosing King's Rentals."

Mark scanned the agent's name tag. "You're welcome, *Roger*. May I have a map for walking tours?"

"Yes, sir." Roger handed him a map. "May I offer assistance in orienting you?"

"I'm a college graduate. I *think* I can figure out a map."

"Right. Sorry. What I meant to say was, if there's anything you need don't hesitate to call me—anytime."

"Thanks Roger. I will—if I need help."

Mark winked and walked toward the rental company's parking area.

Mark found his assigned car. "God damn it!" he yelled. "This is *not* the car I reserved."

He stormed back to the rental desk and tossed the keys to Roger. "I reserved a silver *Jaguar* convertible not a Cadillac. Is that so fucking difficult to manage?"

"Mister Hanlan, I'm so sorry." Beads of sweat formed on Roger's forehead as he scanned several computer screens. "Yes, sir, you *did* reserve a Jag."

"Are you calling me a liar?"

"No sir. Someone on the early shift failed to read your reservation. I'm very sorry. We have a silver Jag, and I'll have it prepped right away. Please have a seat."

"Well, get a move on, *Roger*. I'm already late."

"Sir, I'll have it moved to the head of the line."

Mark sat in a too-small chair, scanning magazines. Every thirty seconds, he glanced at his watch and shook his head.

Fifteen minutes later, Roger ran in, keys jangling from his outstretched hand. "Your car is ready, Mister Hanlan. Please follow me."

Roger escorted Mark to the Jag. "I'm sorry for the mix up. I've arranged a free day of rental for your inconvenience."

"That's the least you should do."

Mark started the car, typed Markham Hotel into the GPS, and then squealed off the lot. A mechanical sounding female GPS voice directed him to the interstate highway.

Sooner than expected, Mark arrived at his hotel two blocks from the convention center. A valet rushed to the Jag as Mark unfolded himself from the driver's cockpit. A cacophony of urban sounds replaced the car's awesome sound system.

"Make sure you park it in a safe spot," Mark admonished the valet. "No scratches. No dents!"

"I'll take care of it like it was mine," the valet said, burning rubber as he sped toward the garage.

The Markham Hotel had the grandeur and elegance of a bygone era, looking more like a bank than a hotel. Bronze capped black-and-white marble columns flanked the bronze lobby doors. Inside, a profusion of gold-fringed burgundy drapes defined the three-story-tall lobby windows. Oriental carpets decorated the black-and-white marble floors.

Mark knew this hotel from previous stays. He liked its proximity to bars, restaurants, and the city's business center. The layout of the lobby provided easy entry and exit without having to run a gauntlet of bellhops, security guards, and inquisitive doormen.

A desk clerk registered Mark then referred him to a bellboy who escorted him to a penthouse suite with a panoramic city view.

The bellboy explained the suite's amenities and recited the roster of guest services. "You obviously workout," he said. "Our gym is open from 6:00 a.m. to midnight. Are you attending the Kitchen and Bath Show?"

"No," Mark said. He knew of the bath and kitchen show, but he would not attend. However, its potential for male clients for him to escort had attracted him to Cincinnati.

Exchanging a ten dollar bill for the hotel key, Mark said, "Thank you."

"Thank *you* sir."

Mark decided to have a nap before going to the gym for a workout. He wanted to be pumped when he dined with a client at the Palms, one of Cincinnati's finest restaurants.

With the top lowered on his Corvette, Joe flew over Ohio's back roads. He stopped the car to remove his shirt and enjoy the afternoon sun on his bare chest. His stress melted away in the rush of warm air caressing his face held skyward for tanning. To prolong the enjoyment, he slowed the Vet to near speed limit, noting trees, old barns and wildflowers. He hadn't experienced such bliss in ages. *This is just what I needed.*

On the outskirts of Cincinnati, Joe pulled to the side of the road, donned his shirt then raised the Vet's top. Back in traffic, he scanned road signs for the proper exit then drove toward city center. Every lamppost had a sign advertising the Gay Pride Parade and the kitchen show. He chuckled. "Dad would shit if he saw these signs."

At the Markham Hotel, Joe drove into the garage, took a parking ticket from a machine, and then chose a parking spot in the back row of the fourth floor.

Once checked in, a bellboy escorted Joe to the elevators. The bellboy persisted in trying to take Joe's suitcase, but he refused the help. At the room, Joe handed the bellboy a dollar. He stared at it for a moment then sulked away.

Joe placed the travel bag on the bed, dug out his cell phone, and then called home. "Hi, honey."

"You in Cincinnati?" Maria asked.

"Yeah. Just checked in all safe and sound. How are you and the boys?"

"We're fine. I told the boys they wouldn't get gifts if they didn't behave."

"You didn't mention the trumpet."

"Of course not."

"I'm gonna shower, get something to eat, and then go to bed. I'll call in the morning."

"Fine. Sleep tight, honey. Love you."

Joe emptied the travel bag, showered, and then donned his snug, button-up, short-sleeve shirt. *Maybe the ladies will like the look.*

Joe ambled along Second Street, passing several restaurants serving ordinary food. Ten minutes later, he found a restaurant to his liking.

"Good evening, sir," the hostess said. "Table for one?"

"Yes. By the window, please."

"This way, please." The hostess pulled out a chair. "May I get you a drink?"

"I'd like a glass of one of Ohio's Merlots?"

As Joe scanned the menu, his eyes wandered over the top of the page. For a second, he peered into the face of a laughing man, one of four who sat at an adjacent table. The man smiled and nodded. Joe nodded and returned to his menu.

Minutes later, the four men paid their check then filed past Joe's table and headed toward the exit.

The man who had nodded to Joe paused at his table and said, "Try the lamb chops. They're wonderful."

"Thanks." *Why tell me that?*

After a few seconds, Joe sensed someone stared at him. He glanced out the window and saw the same stranger say something to his three friends who glanced at Joe, then ambled away.

Joe thought, *Why are they staring at me?*

After dinner, Joe strolled along Second Street and window shopped, but fewer and fewer shops had lighted-window displays. As the street became darker and darker, he thought, *Maybe I shouldn't be walking here.*

From the rear, Joe heard the animated voices of a group of men. He turned and saw eight guys crowding the sidewalk. They laughed and walked toward him. Heart racing, he moved to the curb to allow the men to pass. He prepared himself to run if the situation became threatening.

One man bumped Joe's left arm. "Sorry," the man said.

"No problem," Joe said, checking his left rear pants pocket for his wallet. *Whew. It's still there.*

Someone in the group dropped a booklet on the sidewalk. Joe picked it up—*A Guide to Cincinnati's Gay Life.* The cover featured a muscular man wearing a jockstrap. Joe could not help noting the model's muscularity. *God, what I wouldn't give for arms like that.*

Seeing no trash cans on the block, he stuck the magazine in a rear pocket.

Unsure of the safety of the neighborhood, Joe returned to his hotel. He put the *Guide* on the bedside table then took a shower.

Naked in bed, he turned off the lights, squirmed on the cool, crisp sheets and fell asleep.

Joe awoke at 6:00 a.m. He headed for the dining room where a hostess escorted him to a table near other diners. She held out a newspaper. He sat down then read the newspaper and ease dropped on neighbors' conversations concerning the kitchen show.

Joe folded the paper and turned toward a neighbor. "How's the show going?"

An older man answered. "There're all kinds of new kitchen gadgets I'm sure will be a hit with housewives."

"How about bath stuff?" Joe asked.

"Lots of new things," the man said, moving a bolus of food to a cheek pocket to speak. "Everything from vessel sinks, glass counters, chromo-tubs with TV sets and stereo sound, music-coordinated showerheads, tank-less toilets, motion activated toilet lids—you name it. It's all new this year."

"Sounds interesting."

"You attending the show?" the stranger asked.

"Yep. Arrived last night. I'm staying through the closing party. Leaving Sunday."

"Well, there's lots to do in your spare time," the stranger said and winked, "if you get my drift. Staying here?"

"Yeah?"

Lowering his voice, the stranger said, "We only wanted two but had to hire three call girls for tonight. Wanna drop by room 618 around ten? There'll be more than enough to go around. You'd fit right in."

"Thanks." *Why do they think I'd join in?*

Later that night, Joe became bored with television and

went to room 618. Hearing loud giggling inside, he knocked on the door.

Moments later, the door opened. A man wearing only boxer shorts peeked out. "Oh. It's you. Come in."

The only light in the room came from a TV screen. It displayed a porn film with several naked women entertaining one naked men. Joe scanned the room and saw three naked women.

Naked, the second host took his head from between a woman's breasts long enough to say, "Hi."

"What'll you have," the boxers-wearing host asked, holding out a half-filled glass. "We got scotch, bourbon, beer."

A well-endowed naked woman sauntered toward Joe as he said, "A beer would be fine."

"My, you are a big guy," she said, rubbing Joe's bicep. "I'm Clara."

Staring at the woman's breasts, Joe said, "You're kinda big yourself, Clara."

"I'll bet I can make you bigger," she said rubbing Joe's crotch.

"You move quick don't you," he said, taking the beer offered by the host.

"Sorry," Clara said. "I can take all night if you want. We're in no hurry are we girls?" The host, who had invited Joe, removed his boxers and sat down beside a woman on the sofa.

Joe stopped sipping the beer. *What the hell am I doing here?* "Ladies. Guys. I shouldn't be here. I'm married. Thanks for the beer, but I gotta go." *I can't get involved in adultery.*

Chapter Five

Joe went to the convention center, picked up his registration packet, and then entered the exhibition hall. He visited display after display, often stopping to inspect a gadget, select a sample pen, and accept a tote bag before resuming his search for the latest wonder.

After exploring several booths, he arrived at the back of the hall where convention sponsors had provided seven free booths for not-for-profit organizations. An Equality sign, rainbow flag, along with a gay pride parade banner, hung from one booth.

Joe turned to leave. A man at the gay-pride booth called out, "How was the lamb?"

Joe turned back and asked, "What did you say?"

"How was the lamb?"

Who the hell?

"Don't you want to know about the fun events happening in Cincinnati over the next four days?"

"No thanks," Joe said. He walked a few feet then paused.

That was the stranger in the restaurant.

Joe returned to the booth. "You're the guy who suggested the lamb last night."

"That's me."

"I loved them. Thanks for the recommendation."

"I thought you'd enjoy them. Are you coming to the parade?"

"I *don't* think so—"

"You don't have to be gay to enjoy the parade," the man said, extending his hand. "I'm Bruce."

Hesitating, Joe accepted Bruce's handshake. "I'm Joe. You from Cincinnati?"

"Born and raised here. And you?"

Lying, Joe said, "I'm from upstate. Just here for the show."

"Well, I hope you enjoy the city and the parade. I'll keep an eye out for you."

"Enjoy your parade."

Glad the first day of the show had closed, Joe lingered under the powerful flow of a hot shower. Maria would not allow him that pleasure at home because long showers wasted water and gas.

In the bedroom area, Joe turned on the TV, took a beer from the mini-bar and stretched out, naked, on the wide bed. He adjusted his balls, crossed his ankles and watched the evening news. *I can't believe how friendly that Bruce guy was or why I talked to him.* Joe surfed channel after channel. "Isn't there anything on other than this election crap?" He slammed the remote on the bed. "Damn election shit."

Bored, he turned to a sports channel and watched a game recorded a year earlier. In desperation, he turned to the PBS station and watched the New York Symphony Orchestra play Tchaikovsky's Fifth Symphony, one of his favorites. It had great trumpet passages. Joe lost himself in the music and fell asleep, but the symphony's climax awoke him with a start. "What?" *Must have fallen asleep.*

Joe debated whether to find something to eat or nap and then go out. A nap won out, but this time, he set the alarm.

The alarm, sounding like a firehouse bell, woke him. He pulled on his underwear then searched his limited ward robe. Friday night meant casual time—no long pants. He chose a pair of shorts, a t-shirt, and sandals. *God. This shirt is getting snug.*

Joe walked toward Fourth Street. There were more restaurants and better-lit shops than on Second Street. He

38

entered a restaurant featuring Greek and Italian cuisines.

"Table for one?" the hostess asked.

"Yep. Just one."

"Too bad," the hostess whispered. "There are many women, *and* some men, who would love to have dinner with you."

"Well, I'm not gay, and I'm married. I'll eat alone. *Thank* you."

Packed around small tables, diners could hear each other's conversation from across the room. Six men sat at a table inches from Joe's. *They have to be gay and drunk.* Several times, one of them referenced a bar and a jazz band. The word *jazz* attracted Joe's attention. A man said something about a trumpeter playing some-where that night, but the man slurred his words. Joe wondered if he knew the trumpeter whose name he had half-understood. Joe had never thought of his favorite player as being gay or would play in a gay bar. *Should I ask these guys about the band? Nah. Could lead to complications. I'll check that Guide book.*

Joe searched the *Guide*. On page 48, he found an ad for The Hang Out bar. The ad had a photograph of the band, Wicked Jazz. They would play there during gay pride weekend. Joe identified the face of one of his favorite trumpet players. *Damn!* Excited, Joe dialed the bar's phone number.

"The Hang Out. Bruno speaking."

"Do I need tickets to see the Wicked Jazz tonight?"

"Buddy, the music's free, but there's a $10.00 cover charge. It includes one beer but get here early. The place will be packed."

"Thanks, Bruno."

Joe hung up, looked at the address in the ad, then his watch. *It's only a few blocks away.* "I'm going, gosh damn it. I don't care if they are playing in a gay bar."

Joe hurried to the bar as fast as his thirty-year-old quarter-back legs would carry him.

Illuminated with black lights, the bar's sign glowed an eerie blue-green, making it hard to miss. Joe pushed open the door and entered. His heart raced, his gut knotted, and he trembled with anxiety, wondering what he might find inside. The musty, dimly lighted foyer had the smell of spilled beer and shook with boisterous laughter and chest-pounding bass music.

He paid the cover charge then entered the bar. He waited a moment for his vision to adjust to the dim lighting.

A man at the end of the bar placed a folded bill under his glass then left. *I've gotta get that stool near the bandstand.* Joe pushed through the dancing crowd, many of whom were shirt-less, then sat on the prized stool and smiled, feeling lucky.

After ordering a drink, Joe scanned the room and then the crowd. *Can't believe men kiss like that in public. What kind of place am I in?*

A sandwich board on the small stage read, The Wicked Jazz Band at midnight. The wall clock read 12:15 a.m., but Joe saw nothing resembling a band.

Joe tapped the shoulder of a drunken customer sitting to his left. "Has the band's starting time changed?"

"Nah," the man slurred. "These things never start on time. The owner wants everyone to buy as many drinks as possible before the show starts 'cause lots of guys leave when the music's over. Relax. They'll start—sometime."

At 12:37 a.m., the back drape of the stage fluttered then the band filed on stage.

Joe's neighbor muttered, "See, I told you."

The DJ stopped the recorded music, and the sweaty-chested dancers gathered around the stage.

An overweight drag queen, wearing a tent of floral fabric, swished to center stage and picked up a microphone. "Welcome to the Hang Out and Gay Pride Weekend. The owner hopes you fairies are buying lots of drinks; he's trying to avoid bankruptcy so suck up."

The crowd roared with laughter.

"Well, boys and hairy men, here's what you've been waiting for—Wicked Jazz."

The crowd clapped as the band leader took the microphone. "I want to say what a pleasure it is for me and the band to be in Cincinnati for Gay Pride Weekend. It's also great to be among jazz lovers, especially *gay* ones." The crowd clapped as the leader continued. "We want to thank the owners of the Hang Out for inviting us and hopefully, paying us." A ripple of laughter moved through the crowd. "We hope everyone has a fun, safe, and sane time. Remember, use condoms. Lots of them. Now it's time for some music . . . a one, a two, a three."

Joe eyed the band members. *Can't believe these guys are gay?* Each man wore either an open shirt, or leather vest, revealing a hairy chest. Many wore jeans worn thin and torn around their crotches. *I'd never thought they'd dress like that.*

The band played a spirited piece that sent Joe's feet tapping. He had difficulty containing himself, knowing he sat so close to a well-known trumpet player—something he still thought about becoming. He focused on the trumpeter's fingering and mimicked them. *Can't get any better than this.*

Joe's inebriated neighbor gave him a goodbye pat on the shoulder.

A second later, someone sat on the vacated stool.

Joe turned to see who had arrived. He needed to look skyward to see a man's face framed in long, light-brown hair. "My God, you're a tall one. How tall *are* you?"

"A hair over six seven," the man said.

"Yep, a tall one."

Joe turned toward the band. The music's rhythm became more complex. Each player did his own thing in a Dixieland Jazz kind of way. This struck Joe as true music—welcomed by his ears and tapping feet.

The stranger spoke into Joe's ear, "You enjoy jazz?"

"What about jazz?" Joe asked halfway facing his neighbor.

"You like this?" the stranger said, raising his voice.

"Oh, man, do I! Especially that." Joe pointed to the trumpet player. "I've played some, but not like that. He's a genius." Joe took a sip of his boiler maker. "I like classical music too *if* it's got strong trumpet parts." Joe's head movements matched the rhythm of the music. "Damn, these guys are good aren't they?"

"I have to admit, they're good. Get to hear them often?"

"No, damn it. Live too far away." Joe stood. "I gotta make a pit stop. Will you watch my seat?"

"Sure. What's your name?"

"Uh . . . Joe."

"Okay, Joe."

"Thanks."

Minutes later, Joe returned to his seat.

"Everything come out all right?" the stranger asked, grinning.

"Everything's okay," Joe said, waving to the bartender for another beer and a shot. "Can I buy you a drink for saving my seat?" *Shit! I just offered to buy a drink for a guy in a gay bar?*

"Sure. A beer," the stranger said.

"I'd like ta have a glass of Ohio Merlot, but they don't sell 'em here."

"I didn't know Merlots grew in Ohio."

"Ohio grows a *lot* of Merlots."

The bartender delivered the beers and a shot. Joe stood to get his billfold from a hip pocket. In doing so, his thigh brushed the stranger's hand.

"Sorry," Joe said.

"Oh I don't mind being touched with a well-worked thigh."

"They used to be bigger," Joe said, looking at and tightening his thigh, "when I played football, but I always had big legs and 'cows'. Sorry. I mean my calves. Uh, I mean lower legs."

"I understand *cows*," the stranger said. "I've done some working out. May I have a better look at those cows?"

Joe removed his foot from the footrest, moved his leg into the light, and then flexed his left calf. "There. How's that?"

"Damn. You got killer legs. Lots of lifters would kill for cows like that."

"Ha. I didn't kill for them. God gave 'em to me."

The stranger grinned. "Was God good to you in other ways?"

"You betcha! I have a *great* wife and *two* great boys."

"That's not what I meant."

"Okay, but I want to listen to the music." *What's with this guy?*

Joe mentally tapped into the rhythm of the jazz and continued to mimic the rapid fingering of the trumpeter. Soon, Joe's whole body reacted to the music's beat. He jerked his left arm backward and struck the stranger's belly.

"Sorry, man!" Joe exclaimed, touching the stranger's abdomen as if to soothe an imagined pain.

"Don't worry. You didn't hurt anything."

"I bet I didn't," Joe yelled over the loud music. "Those things are rock hard."

"Don't worry about hurting them. Give me your hand."

The stranger took Joe's hand, thrust it under his tight-fitting shirt, and then rubbed it over his six-pack. The man's ab muscles tighten under Joe's fingers.

"You won't hurt *that*," the stranger said.

Joe fingered the hard high ridges and deep valleys of the six-pack. "That's some set of abs, man. A *real* six-pack."

"I work my abs. You work your legs," the stranger said, gripping Joe's thigh. "Tighten it."

Joe looked the stranger in the eye as if to ask, 'Why?'

"Tighten it," the stranger said.

Joe tightened his thigh as the stranger grasped it with a beefy hand. "That's one hell of a leg."

Chuckling, Joe said, "I try to please."

"May I *please* see the other thigh?"

Joe sipped his drink. "A please here, a please there, and you'll want to see *all* my parts."

"That wouldn't be so bad would it? I'd let you see my six-pack, and plus, I have great hands for massaging thighs."

"I'm having another beer and a shot. Want one?"

"Sure, but I'm buying this round."

"Thanks. Hey, what's your name?" Joe asked.

"Mark."

"Mark, I'm Joe. Sorry, but the drinks have me feeling a little off. Gotta make another pit stop. Save my seat . . . will ya?"

"Will do. No ass will touch it until you return."

Minutes later, Joe staggered back. As he approached the stool, his feet flew out from under him, and he fell face first onto Mark's lap.

"Sorry!" Joe said, righting himself. "What's all that?"

"My crotch," Mark said. "Don't worry. You didn't hurt it."

"Sorry. I'm drunk. Please don't tell Maria. She'll kill

me."

"Is she here?"

"Nope."

"You staying downtown?"

"Yep."

"Where?"

"The . . . Markham," Joe muttered, "God, my boiler makers are catching up with me. My head is swirling."

"That's where I'm staying. Why don't we get you to the hotel while you can still walk."

Joe smiled then mumbled, "Okee dokee."

Mark helped Joe to the entrance where a bouncer called a taxi. Mark poured Joe onto the backseat and instructed the driver to take them to the Markham Hotel.

"Do you have your key?" Mark asked.

"Yep, in my pocket." Joe pulled out his key.

"Good," Mark said, sounding relieved. "I wouldn't want anyone see me searching your pockets for a key and suspect I'm a thief."

At the hotel, the driver assisted Mark in getting Joe out of the taxi.

"Thanks," Mark said, handing the driver a twenty.

"No trouble," the driver said, pocketing the bill. "Hope you guys make it in."

Joe looked around the hotel penthouse and shook his head. "This is *not* my room!"

"Shhh, Joe! This is my room." Mark patted Joe's shoulder. "We're staying in the same hotel. You're drunk, so I thought it best to bring you here. What if you fell in your room and hurt yourself? You're alone. What would you do? Spend the night here. In the morning, when you're feeling better, you can leave."

"Okay," Joe murmured. "Thank you."

Joe struggled to undress. He forgot to remove his sandals before trying to remove his narrow-legged shorts.

"Take your sandals off first," Mark said like speaking to a child.

"Okee dokee."

Joe removed his shorts then attempted to pull his shirt over his head, but it got stuck, leaving him blindfolded.

"For God's sake," Mark said, pulling free Joe's shirt.

"I sleep *naked* when I'm not at home," Joe whispered as though someone else might overhear him. "Maria hates me sleeping naked, but *I like it!*"

"Won't bother me. I always sleep naked."

"What! Your wife lets you sleep naked?"

"I don't have a wife," Mark said, undressing.

"You don't have a wife?" Joe asked as Mark dropped his trousers. "And I see you don't wear underwear either." Joe hiccupped. "Gosh damn man, did ya have a horse for a father? I've never seen anything like that—except on a farm."

"Nope, never wear underwear." Mark fluffed his crotch. "Too constricting for all this."

Mark scratched his balls then removed his shirt.

"My God. What a body," Joe said. "Spend all your time in the gym? And look at those biceps, those pecs. Gosh damn, you've got great abs."

Mark pointed both forefingers at his abdomen. "Have a feel if you'd like, but I promised you a thigh massage. Should I start on the front or the back?"

"What the hell." Joe sat down on the bed. "Start on the back."

Joe lay chest down and watched Mark approached the bed. He straddled Joe's left leg and rested his "package" on Joe's calf.

46

"Is that what I think it is on my cow?" Joe mumbled into the sheets.

"Yep. If it's a problem, I can move them."

"I've never touched, or been touched, by a man's package. Weird, I didn't know they could be so hot."

"Maybe I should move them. I don't want you getting burned."

"Whatever."

Mark started his massage at the back of Joe's left knee then worked his way up the thigh toward Joe's butt.

Joe moaned as Mark increased the intensity of the massage.

"God, I haven't had a massage like this since my football days. My trainer gave a good massage—damn good. He had strong hands, but he sometimes got *too* friendly if you know what I mean."

"Like this?" Mark asked, moving his hand onto Joe's glutes.

"No, not there. My privates."

"Lift your hips. Let's see if I can outperform your trainer."

Joe looked back. "Keep massaging my leg."

Mark finished with Joe's left thigh then straddled his right leg. Resting his crotch on the right calf, Mark massaged Joe's thigh.

"You take those *things* everywhere?" Joe mumbled through pillow-crushed lips.

"Sure. Do they bother you?"

"They seem . . . heavy. That's all. I never thought a man's *stuff* could be so . . . heavy."

"I've been told they're heavy." Mark continued to work his hands toward Joe's butt. "How am I doing? Want me to do your back?"

"That's great. Yeah . . . do the shoulders," Joe mumbled.

After massaging Joe's glutes, Mark stretched to reach Joe's shoulders but couldn't. He slid his legs forward until each rested beside Joe's hips then settled his weight onto Joe's butt. Resting his crotch on Joe's lower back, he massaged Joe's shoulders.

"Man, that package is heavy," Joe mumbled.

"Hope they're not hurting you."

"Hell no! Heat feels good on my back."

"Good," Mark said. "No charge for the heating pad."

Joe's hands felt numb and tingled. He shook each then extended them toward his feet, palms up. They rested on the bed along the outside of Mark's legs. Minutes after the right hand had been reposition, it became numb. Joe wiggled his fingers to get the blood moving. In doing so, he touched Mark's right thigh. Looking back at Mark, he asked, "Stubble? You shave your legs?"

"Yep. Some people don't like body hair. I shave *most* of my body. A few times I've shaved everything."

"Everything?"

"Everything but my head."

"Doesn't it itch?"

"Nope. You shave your head, and you shaved your ankles, when you played ball didn't you?"

"Yeah, but I never thought of a guy having a five-o'clock shadow on his body."

Mark chuckled. "Well, it's possible."

"You moved the heating pad didn't ya," Joe murmured.

"Didn't want you getting burned. Okay. It's time for your front. Turnover and I'll start with the shoulders."

Mark got off the bed, allowing Joe to turn onto his back.

"Would you turn off that overhead light?" Joe mumbled, blocking the light with his forearm. "It's blinding."

Mark switched off the light then returned to the center of the bed where Joe lay, face up, eyes closed. Mark straddled Joe's pelvic area, resting his crotch on Joe's abdomen.

Eyes closed, Joe said, "The heating pad's back."

"At your service," Mark said, his package spread over Joe's lower belly. He massaged Joe's shoulders and said, "You have chest hair but none on your abdomen. Do you shave your belly?

"Nope." Joe rubbed his abdomen with his right hand. "Never had hair here. Crotch, yes. Belly no."

"Am I being too rough?" Mark asked, pausing his massage as Joe jerked. "Hell no. Feels great."

Joe's body stiffened.

"Something wrong?" Mark asked.

"I wonder what Maria would say if she saw me now?"

"Your wife?"

"Yep. For twelve . . . fourteen years—whatever."

"Well, Maria isn't here, so she can't see you; she can't hear you, and I won't tell."

"Damn right," Joe whispered, squinting at Mark. "Fuck, you have a huge chest—and monster biceps. Shit—*big fucking biceps.*"

Mark raised both arms and flexed his biceps. "Not bad, huh?"

"Hell no." Joe gripped each cantaloupe size bicep. "Those suckers are hard as rocks."

Mark flexed his right pec then the left. Alternating contractions in rapid succession, his pecs moved like waves on the sea.

"I can do that," Joe said, mimicking Mark's actions. "See."

Mark gripped Joe's pecs. "Not bad for an *old* football player. Flex them."

49

Joe complied. "They're not as big or hard as yours, but they ain't bad, but who are you calling old? I'm thirty-three."

Mark flexed his pecs.

For a moment, Joe stared in admiration at Mark's chest muscles. *God those things are huge.* Suddenly, he gripped them. "God, you have chest stubble. You shave it too?"

"I told you some people don't like body hair."

What does he mean some people don't like body hair?

Joe fingered Mark's chest, first noting the prickliness of the stubble, then gripped Mark's pecs as if to prevent their escape. "Got 'em," he said.

"So . . . ? You got them. What now?"

For a second, Joe just stared at Mark's chest, and then he sat up. He squeezed Mark's pecs then explored the right nipple with his tongue. Moments later, he looked into Mark's face. "What the hell am I doing? Shit! I'm feeling up a guy's tits. I ain't never touched a man's chest. Never! What the fuck came over me."

"You're doing what you wanted."

"Not with a man."

"Well then. Did it give your woman pleasure . . . Did it give *you* pleasure when you pleased her?"

"Yeah, she loved it, and I loved it . . . but a woman—not a man."

"When you were licking my chest, you had your eyes closed. Right?"

"So?"

"Maybe you *thought* I was a woman, or you enjoyed licking a *man's* pec—*my* nipple. I know I enjoyed the attention."

"I don't know what I was thinking. Shit! I don't know what came over me. Sorry, man. Guess I'm drunk."

Mark pulled Joe's head close to his right pec. His lips touched Mark's nipples, but his lips were still.

50

Mark whispered, "My nipple belongs to whatever sex you want. Male or female. Make love to it. Pleasure it. Enjoy it. Let it pleasure you."

Joe's breathing quickened, and his hands twitched on the bed.

Still holding Joe's head, Mark remained motionless, waiting to see if Joe could muster his courage.

Suddenly, Joe grabbed Mark's pecs and squeezed them. He took the right nipple into his mouth and tongued its every millimeter. Feeling no shame, he sucked it, attempting to ingest the entire pec. He moaned with excitement, moving his mouth from nipple to nipple as if one would escape to some nether place never to return.

Mark, head back and eyes closed, seemed lost in sexual revelry. He tried to hold Joe's mouth against one nipple, but hunger for Mark's chest obsessed Joe. Mark's moaning mingled with Joe's, producing a symphony of sexual delight.

Each man stimulated the other's cock as it moved in sync against the other's body.

Mark surrendered his tussle to lodge Joe's mouth on one nipple then tweaked one of Joe's nipples. Joe's appetite for chest flesh reached a momentary level of satiety as he succumbed to the ecstasy produced by Mark's manipulations.

Joe wondered what had happened to him. He recalled how Maria had sucked his nipples, but she never tweaked them. Her pleasure-developing ability could not compare to Mark's expertise.

Frozen in a half sit-up position, Joe enjoyed these new erotic sensations.

Mark grabbed Joe's other nipple and tweaked it.

Joe moaned with unparalleled ecstasy and slumped, submitting to the incredible sensations that electrified his body. One sharp, nipple pinch had transformed itself into a pleasure that left him breathless. Joe clasped his belly as unbelievable pleasure spread through his abdomen into the crotch. He grasped Mark's pinching fingers and squeezed them tighter. Mark, wanting to accommodate Joe's desires, maximized his pressure. Joe's ecstasy rose to new heights. He dropped his head as if unconscious, arms hanging by his side. Only the determined strength of his abdominal muscles kept him upright.

Mark whispered, "You okay?"

"No," Joe moaned. "It's . . . don't stop. Ahhh."

Joe gripped Mark's nipples and mimicked his squeezing. Mark's head snapped back, and his jaw dropped with the soft utterance, "Oh, my god."

Each man enjoyed and reciprocated the others pleasure. Mark kissed Joe on the forehead. He moved his head closer to Joe's until their lips met. Stunned, Joe froze for a second then kissed with the abandonment he had given Mark's nipples. Their nipple play continued as they kissed. Each kiss grew stronger and lasted longer until the men were anoxic. They pulled apart and smiled. Mark winked. Joe winked and gave Mark's nipples a hard squeeze.

"Better not quit that," Mark said.

Joe smiled and began a twisting, squeezing twirl of Mark's nipples.

"Oh, my God. You're a fast learner," Mark whispered, his eyes rolling back in his head.

Joe whispered, "I know how to control you."

Joe liked Mark's pulsating cock against his abdomen as he continued twisting Mark's nipples.

Mark abandoned one of Joe's nipples.

"Don't leave me," Joe said, shifting his head on the pillow and staring into Mark's eyes.

Mark whispered, "Have no fear. I'm not leaving."

Mark reached behind his back and caressed Joe's thigh.

52

His fingers moved up the thigh until they reached Joe's cock.

Joe's breath caught then fled his chest in a moan.

Cock in hand, Mark smiled. "Just checking your directional pole."

Joe grabbed Mark's left arm. "That's my cock, man—not some pole."

"Oh yes it is."

"If it's a pole, it's my private pole."

"I can tell it's a directional pole by the direction it's pointing."

"Which way?"

"The right way—up." Mark moved Joe's balls to get a better grip on his cock. Mark's thumb gyrations on Joe's cock caused him to moan and say, "God, you've got good hands."

"You better watch out," Joe said, grabbing Mark's cock and stroking it. "I can outdo your thumb."

The pace quickened until Joe pleaded, "Slow down. I don't wanna cum—not yet."

Mark released Joe's cock and assumed a "push-up" position over Joe's shorter frame.

Joe smiled and resumed his twisting of Mark's down-ward pointing nipples.

Mark lowered himself onto Joe's torso.

"You're heavy, but it feels good," Joe said, catching his breath.

Rolling off to Joe's right, Mark stretched out on his left side. His index finger roamed from Joe's eyebrows to the tip of his nose and then paused on the lips. Joe kissed the finger before it resumed its journey down his neck and onto the chest. The finger toyed with Joe's chest hair and cleavage before redis-covering his nipples. Mark tweaked the left one and provided oral service to the right one. He started with a nibble, but incisors soon joined the party, bringing a new sensation to Joe's chest.

Despite feeling like being eaten alive, Joe surrendered his nipples. Mark's teeth and fingers had him squirming.

Mark and Joe stroked each other's cocks, but Joe's hand got pushed to Mark's balls. Joe assumed Mark wanted his balls to be the center of attention. Mark closed his forefinger and thumb to encircle Joe's balls.

Freeing Joe's nipple, Mark whispered, "Now I've got you." Shaking Joe's encircled balls, Mark said, "Take my balls like I have yours."

Returning to Joe's nipple, Mark's grip became a fist first engulfing Joe's balls and then pulling them away from their roots. Joe moaned with pleasure.

"Too hard?" Mark asked.

"No. I've never had that done. It's weird, but I like it. Don't stop."

Enjoying an unexpected erotic high, Joe wanted to return the pleasure and tweaked Mark's nipple.

Mark assumed a push-up position over Joe then lowered his left nipple into Joe's waiting mouth.

Moaning, Mark said, "Use your teeth."

"How's this?" Joe asked, heeding Mark's request.

"A little harder. That's it. Oh . . . God."

Joe smiled. He knew how it felt to receive pleasure by giving it. Using his teeth, Joe tugged on Mark's nipple.

Shaking his head, Mark moaned, "Oh God."

"Sorry. Too rough?" Joe asked. Marked stared into Joe's eyes. "Don't worry about being rough. I'll let you know if it gets to be too much."

Mark lowered his nipple into Joe's mouth where it remained for a few seconds. Abruptly, Mark pulled away. "Let's do a titty 69."

"What?"

Motioning for Joe to slide farther down the bed, Mark

said, "Roll on to your right side."

"Oh. We're going to suck nipples."

The men lay head-to-toe, their nipples providing a meal for the other's incisors.

Mark muttered, "This leaves hands free for other things."

"I get it. Jerk each other."

Mark resumed nibbling Joe's nipples and stroking his cock. Joe squirmed, abandoned Mark's chest, moved onto his back, and lifted his hips off the mattress. Joe's heavy breathing morphed into grunts. Body trembling with heat, his heartbeat pounded and groin muscles contracted in waves of pleasure. His moans reached a crescendo.

"Quiet," Mark whispered, "we're in a hotel, damn it."

Joe sensed he should follow Mark's lead and increased the speed with which he stroked Mark's cock. Responding to the other's handy work, their pace quickened. They intensified their nipple play as the speed of hand strokes brought them closer to climax.

Suddenly, Joe yelled, "Oh . . . God." He almost convulsed and panted like he had completed a marathon race.

Coming in second place, Mark's race concluded with thunderous moans and shaking relief.

Exhausted, the men had drowned each other. They collapsed side-by-side, sounding like a broken calliope.

Joe had begun a new journey of discovery.

Chapter Six

The hallway outside Mark's room echoed with the sound of guests conversing as they waited for an elevator.

Eyes half-open, Joe turned his head toward the noise, listened, and then stared at the large windows overlooking the skyline. Anxious, almost panicky, he yelled, "This isn't my room." He bolted upright. "This isn't my room!"

Shocked, he looked to his right. There lay Mark. Face half-buried in a pillow, the sheet rested below his butt.

"Good morning, tiger," Mark said, flashing a sheepish grin.

"What the hell? Where the hell am I?"

"You're in my room—at the Markham. Don't you remember?"

"Oh god. What time is it?"

Mark looked at the bedside clock then said, "10:37."

"Shit!" Joe said. "I was supposed to meet a guy for breakfast at eight."

"I don't think you'll make it, sport."

Joe held his head with both hands and moaned.

"Hangover?" Mark asked.

"A little. God, what did I do?"

"You had a *good* time."

"It's all a blur," Joe moaned, rubbing his forehead. "I don't wanna remember."

Mark propped himself up on one elbow and stared at Joe. "Well, I and the *heating pad* had a good time— a night with memorable qualities." He rubbed his chest. "My nipples remember it too."

"Mine are sore," Joe said, touching them. "God, forgive me. What did I do?"

Mark smiled. "You had a great time as far as I can tell."

Head in his hands, Joe mumbled, "I've never done anything like that—not even with Maria. I've really fucked up."

"There's no reason to be unhappy. You made me happy, and I made you happy."

"Yeah, but with . . . you—a *man*. Shit. I've never had sex with a guy, not even as a boy—never. Not even to experiment?" Mark grasped Joe's hand and thrust it onto his crotch then clamped his thick thighs over it. "This is happiness, my friend. Don't tell me you're not happy with this."

For the first time, Joe noted the hot, soft smoothness of Mark's cock and shaved balls now compressed beneath his hand.

"Now you're struggling to get free, but you didn't last night."

Joe stopped struggling.

Mark's index finger explored Joe's pubic hair.

Mark smiled then said, "And this finger is pointing the way to happiness. See, it's moving to the South Pole. It must be cold down there because everything is frozen—*hard*. Is that a morning woodie or anticipation?"

Joe pushed Mark's hand away. "I can't do this. I'm not gay! Hell, I have children! I'm a straight guy! You hear—straight!"

Mark patted Joe's hand. "You are what you are. I think you're a nice guy; a great looking dude with a super bod and killer legs. You know how to work nipples and please someone. That is rare these days. Most people take. You take *and* give. And wow! Can you give?"

"Give? I've given myself a headache, that's what I've done."

Mark frowned. "Don't be so hard on yourself. Learn to be *you*. You may be straight, gay, or . . . Hell, you might be bi, but you're a great guy—that's what matters."

"Shit. How do I deal with this? My mind's going a mile

a second. Things aren't computing."

"You're not entitled to answers for all of life's questions," Mark said. "That's a luxury. Just file away the experience. Revisit it when you have time to negotiate with yourself." Mark glanced at the bedside clock. "I hate to do this, but I have to kick you out. I have an appointment at one o'clock. Why don't we meet for a drink at five? The kitchen show will be closed, and you'll feel better. By the way, do you need an aspirin?"

"Mark, we can't meet again. It's hard to explain, but you can't imagine how I feel lying in bed with a naked man. Guys like me don't do—"

"There's no one else like you, Joe. You're unique, but I won't push you to do something you don't want to do."

At the desk, Mark wrote something on a piece of paper. "Here's my number." He then pushed the paper into the pocket of Joe's shirt, which hung over a chair. "If you want to meet for a drink or talk give me a call."

"Damn it," Joe said.

"What's wrong?"

"I shouldn't have, but I couldn't help it. I looked."

Mark appeared to be puzzled. "Looked at what?"

"At your fucking body while you stood there writing your number. What the fuck has come over me?"

"Joe, you're like Adam after eating the apple in the Garden of Eden. Your mind has been opened to another world. Another way."

"Yeah, the apple of sin, and I'm about to be kicked from the garden and this room. I can't promise anything."

"I hope you're wrong, but if you can't, I'll respect it. You be what you're meant to be. Now get dressed and get out of here. We both have things to do."

In his room, Joe thought, *What have I done? I Don't*

59

wanna think about it. It didn't happen. I didn't do that. Not me. I'll never get in that situation again. Never. God, forgive me. Gotta put it out of my mind.

Chapter Seven

For two nights following his affair with Mark, Joe had difficulty sleeping. He could not rid his mind of the events.

Shaving, he stared into the mirror and frowned. *What the hell did you do? I'll never let myself get in that predicament again.*

Joe wandered the aisles of the exhibition hall, exploring booths he had not visited. At several exhibits, he placed orders for the newest faucets and showerheads. In aisle four, he met an old acquaintance, Matt, a man in his mid-sixties.

"Well bless my soul. It's Joe," Matt said, shaking Joe's hand.

"Matt, nice to see you. You're the only guy I know here. Seen anyone from our part of Ohio?"

"Yeah, a few," Matt said, removing his ball cap to smooth his thinning gray hair.

"How's business?"

"A little slow but how're things with you and yer dad?"

"Dad's fine. He stayed home to look after mom. She's not doing well. Her cancer came back, and the chemo's left her weak."

"Sorry to hear that."

"Let's change the subject," Joe said. "We enlarged our shop and sell the fancy stuff you see here. I'm surprised people in Smithville go for it, but if they got the money, we're happy to sell it."

"I've been thinking about retiring," Matt said, shrugging. "Wanna buy another shop?"

"That's something I'd have to discuss with Dad, but it sounds like a good idea. After all, our service area overlaps. How many men are you working?"

"There's four counting me, but I'm too old and stiff to crawl around anymore."

"Let me talk to dad. See what he says. Still have the same phone number?"

"Yep. Say, what are you doing for lunch?"

"Nothing. Why?"

"Me and four guys are meeting for lunch in the café up there." Matt pointed to the balcony. "Join us. We're gonna watch the queers' parade. It passes here at one o'clock.

Ill at ease, Joe chuckled. "Didn't know plumbers had an interest in gay things."

"Saw it last year. I'd never seen guys dressed like women—I mean *hot* looking women. I mean men. You wouldn't suspect they weren't what they seemed. Hell, I considered asking one out 'till I found out *she* was a he."

"Just goes to show you, you can't tell a book by its cover. Sure, I'll meet you guys. I wouldn't wanna miss the *women*."

First to arrive at the cafe, Joe asked the hostess if he could have the table for six beside the window overlooking the parade route. She nodded and handed him six menus. He seated himself.

Soon afterwards, the other guys wandered in. Matt introduced Joe to his friends.

A young waitress approached Matt. "Which of you guys do I take first?"

Matt grinned. "Start with my friend, Joe. He's the youngest and best built. We older guys gotta wait 'til our Viagra kicks in."

The waitress rolled her eyes and frowned. "You guys are toooo funny."

"Well, don't renege, sweetheart," Matt said. "Joe's about

to take you up on your offer."

The men laughed.

"Come on guys," Joe said, "give the girl a break. She's trying to do her job."

"Miss," Joe said, "I apologize for my friends. They should know better."

"Apology accepted. Now, may I take your orders?"

Drinks, food, and conversation were accompanied by mutual ribbing: Henry for getting drunk the night before; Harry for picking up a prostitute; Matt for discovering, at the last minute, that his new girlfriend was a drag queen; George for sleeping through an important appointment, and Jim for tripping over a temporary electrical line that served one of the show's displays, causing it to fall on him, cutting his leg.

Matt smiled at Joe. "What kind of mischief have you gotten into?"

"Well, I had sex with an Amazon last night—in my dreams."

"Sure it wasn't one of them tall drag queens?" Matt quipped, slapping Joe's shoulder.

"Look!" Joe said, pointing out the window. "The parade's coming. See there."

The parade marshal's car was less than a block away.

After ordering another round of drinks, the men moved their chairs closer to the window. The guys displayed the anxiety one sees as men wait for a field goal at a football game or a stripper about to remove her thong.

Parade Marshall, Kathy Griffin, the comedienne popular with the gay crowd, rode in a convertible. She waved and blew kisses to the men sitting at the café window. A group of flag throwers followed the convertible.

Three of Matt's group became bored and chanted, "Bring on the queers. Bring on the drags."

Joe wanted to lecture the guys about their behavior, but given recent events, he held his tongue.

The café windows rattled with each deafening bass note emanating from thirty-six-inch woofers on the first float. It carried a troupe of drag queens, executing the royal wave perfected by Queen Elizabeth, and ten muscular young men wearing G-strings. They flexed and posed for the crowd. Each man tried to outdo the other in shaking his bubble-butt, humping his crotch, and flexing oiled muscles.

"Joe, you oughta be out there," Matt said. "You could give those muscle guys a run for their money."

"Yeah!" Henry mumbled. "Give 'em some competition!"

Joe smiled and scrutinized the guys on the float. One of them looked like a guy Joe had seen in a magazine picture stapled to his gym ceiling. *Don't tell me he's gay?* Joe scanned the man's body. *He's wearing the same skimpy blue posing trunks as in the gym photo.* Joe could not stop staring at the man's crotch. *Is that real or a zucchini?*

Matt said, "You think those guys work out, Joe?"

Joe chuckled. "At least once a month."

Several floats and a group of dykes on motorcycles passed, revving their engines.

George yelled as though the dykes could hear him. "You gals need men like us. We'll make women out of you. I'm sending down a real man. Take good care of him."

George slapped Joe on the shoulder. "Go get them, tiger."

Joe smiled. "No thanks. I prefer my women to be a little more feminine."

"Look at that huge gal on the big Harley," Henry said. "She could beat you to a pulp then eat you."

"Or, squeeze you to death with those thighs," Harry said.

"Anyone of them could eat me," Henry chuckled.

Another float, carrying drag queens and guys clad in scanty trunks, passed the window. Harry commented on one "woman" who displayed D-cup breasts exposed beneath a dress whose neckline plunged to her knees. "Now there's a set of tits. God, what I wouldn't do to get ahold of a pair like that. Hell, I'd pay five bucks to touch 'em!"

"Joe, are you a tit or leg man?" George asked.

"You forgot to include butts," Joe said, "but are those tits real?"

Laughing, Matt said, "You betcha! I almost took a pair to bed. Thought he was a she. Those guys take hormones to grow those boobs. I know they're on a guy, but damn, they look good."

The next float flew banners advertising several gay bars. The *Guide* had ads for several of them. One banner advertised a wet underwear contest Saturday nights.

Near the back of the float, Joe noticed Bruce, the man who had recommended the lamb and worked in the not-for-profit booth at the kitchen show. Joe had not noticed the man's body earlier, but now, Bruce wore posing briefs that displayed everything. Joe scanned Bruce's well-defined muscular frame that fell somewhere between a swimmer's and a powerlifter's build. He had thick, hairy, and broad pecs partially framed by a remarkable six-pack. His arms were proportional to the rest of him, but his thighs were huge.

What a body. How did I overlook that?

Joe pointed at the drag queen beside Bruce. "I can't believe those guys have tits—I mean *real* ones! They look too big to be real. Think I'll get a better look." *I want to see Bruce up close*

"Joe," Harry yelled, "ask if I can touch those tits."

Harry's yelling drew the disdain of nearby female

diners.

"Hey guys, cool it," Joe said.

"I'll pay five dollars," Harry said.

Joe pushed through the crowd to get to the curb. A drag queen with big tits stood at the head of the float labeled Hang Out Bar. It had stopped in front of the convention hall and Joe. He waved and motioned for the drag queen to bare her tits—Mardi Gras style.

The drag queen beamed at hearing the request. She pulled her dress open and shouted, "Enjoy, honey. Come see them up close at the bar tonight."

Joe knew the guys in café watched him, so he turned toward them, waved, and mouthed, 'How about them apples?'

The guys gave Joe a thumbs-up salute.

Joe turned his attention to Bruce who stood at the rear of the float beside a drag queen. He waved to Bruce, but the drag queen waved back. *Shit!* Joe thought. He hoped the café guys thought he had flirted with the drag queen.

"Bruce!" Joe yelled, hoping Bruce would hear him over the din of the float's sound system.

Bruce grinned and waved back.

Joe shouted, "Looking good!"

As luck would have it, the drag queen blew kisses to Joe and Bruce waved.

Bruce pointed at the float sponsor's sign and yelled, "Meet me tonight."

"Maybe."

Joe turned toward the guys in the café, hoping they believed he had taunted the drag queen.

Joe returned to the café where the group cheered his *chutzpah* and congratulated him on his uninhibited tack with the drag queens. The men took turns buying him beers for having the balls to confirm the drag queen's tits were real.

After the parade ended, Joe headed to his hotel. Images of Mark intruded on his thoughts. *That was a mistake. A drunken experiment. Gotta forget the whole thing—move on. I'm not that way. I regret what I did and I hope God forgives me.*

The clock on the corner bank tolled six times. Joe's anxiety had him shaking as if a catastrophe would strike him at any minute. He looked at his shaking hands. *Why am I sweating this? I'm not gay. I'll call . . . tell him we can't meet.*

Joe took out the paper with Mark's number then dialed his phone. Mark's phone rang several times before going to voice mail. *Thank God!* Joe waited for the beep then started his message. "Mark, this is Joe. We can't meet again. Have a great life." With his anxiety waning, he hung up.

Within seconds, Joe's phone rang. *Who the hell?* Joe looked at the caller id. "Who is that? Hello."

"Joe, this is Mark. Don't hang up! I just got your message. Thank you for a great time. I don't often meet a guy like you. I'm not a happy camper when I don't get what I want, meaning you, but I wish you and your family all the best. But hey, you never know. Our paths might cross again."

"Thanks, but I don't think so, Mark. Bye."

Joe hung up. His shoulders sagged. His arms fell to his sides, and he sighed. "Thank God that's over."

Joe showered then threw himself naked and "spread eagle" on the bed. He closed his eyes and tried to get comfortable. He couldn't help thinking about being in this same position with Mark. *I gotta forget about . . . it was a drunken mistake.*

Surfing several TV channels, Joe found nothing of interest. He turned on the radio and searched until he found a station broadcasting a symphony with an amazing trumpet passage. He got lost in the music and fell asleep.

Noises outside Joe's door startled him awake. Joe tossed and turned but couldn't go back to sleep. He looked at the clock—9:07. He turned on the bedside lamp, took out the telephone directory, and thumbed through the yellow pages, looking for pawn shop listings. On page 478 was an ad for a nearby shop open twenty-four hours a day. He called the shop to confirm its hours of operation.

"Good evening," a man said in an elderly sounding voice.

"Hi. I wanted to make sure you're open tonight."

"Yep. Open twenty-four hours. Drop by any time."

Joe entered the shop, triggering an entry alarm. The showroom, lit by too few fluorescent bulbs, had a worn black and white checkerboard floor and the strong odor of pine oil. He sensed the room held immeasurable quantities of sadness and despair. Black and white TV monitors, displaying flickering images of various sections of the store, lined the back wall. Joe glimpsed himself on monitor three. He stood tall, flexed his pecs and smiled.

From a backroom, a voice called out, "Be right there. Look around."

Joe scanned several show cases. He eyed a gold Rolex watch, an assortment of rings, canes, bracelets, crutches, lawnmowers, an artificial leg, fishing gear, several guitars, a violin, and several brass musical instruments.

An elderly hunched man, looking like Doctor Brown of *Back to the Future,* entered the room. Staring over his glasses, he said, "Good evening, young man. What do you have to pawn?"

"Oh, I'm not here to pawn anything. I'm looking for a trumpet or coronet . . . for my kid."

"Plays a horn, eh?"

"Not yet, but he wants to."

"What's his inspiration?"

"We listen to lots of trumpet playing at home. I used to play some . . . back in high school. I often dreamed of playing jazz like Wynton Marsalis or playing with a symphony, but life took me on a different course."

In his car, Joe had several CDs containing jazz and symphonic music. All of the classical pieces were replete with rousing trumpet passages. His favorite—Respighi's *Roman Festival*. That disc had almost burned through due to repeated playing.

The shop owner smiled. "Well, that's a good place for a kid to start—having a dad who plays."

The man led Joe to one side of the room and gestured toward several instruments in a display case. "Have a look at these. Do you want a coronet, trumpet, or a trombone?"

"I think his heart's set on a trumpet."

"There're several here and more in the back. Seems everybody's giving up horn playing these days. I take them in, but nobody is buying. I can make you a good price." The shop owner held up a coronet with several small dents in the bell. "How about this one?"

"That's a little beat up," Joe said, eyeing the dents. "I'd like something in better shape."

"Do you want a case?"

"That'd be nice, but . . . it's not necessary."

"I have a horn in the back that's a beauty, but the case is kinda beat up. Be right back."

Within seconds, the owner returned carrying a black horn case with frayed edges. He handed it to Joe. "The case's worn, but the horn has been well cared for. The owner once played with the Cincinnati Symphony, but he died a few years ago. His family recently cleared out his things so here it is."

With reverence and some anxiety, Joe fingered the case's pitted chrome latches then released them. Snap. Snap. They sprang open. He raised the lid with care. "WOW."

Inside sat a gleaming brass trumpet nestled on its original royal-blue velvet lining. "Owned by a professional musician, huh?"

"Yep. Somewhere, I have some $33^1/_3$ records with the owner playing this horn."

"Gosh," Joe said, removing the trumpet and fingering the valves. "A player never forgets the feel of this cold metal."

"You still play?" the owner asked.

"Some but not like when I was younger—before the kids."

"I know. I have children. Go on. Try it, son."

Joe blew into the mouthpiece, fingered the valves, pursed his lips, and then paused for a moment.

The owner frowned. "What are you waiting for?"

"I'm trying to remember a certain piece." Joe glimpsed himself in a mirror. *Wow. Can't believe I'm holding the horn of a professional player.*

With repressed excitement and shaking hands, Joe raised the horn to his lips, repeated his fingering ritual, and then began to play. After a slip of the lip, he made the horn sing.

Enraptured, the shop owner slumped onto a stool. "That horn hasn't been played like that since its owner died. Are you sure you don't wanna play professionally?"

"That'd be nice, but it's hard to make a living as a musician. I have a family to support plus I help my dad run our business."

"What kinda business?"

"Plumbing."

"Well, you're into pipes." The owner laughed. "Either it's plumbing pipes and shutoff valves or horn pipes and spit valves."

"How much?" Joe asked, admiring the horn. *God, I want this!*

"You noticed it's a Selmer? I'll let you have it for . . . $100.00."

"Are you sure? $100.00?"

"Yep. $100.00. Between your playing and its pedigree, maybe your son will be inspired. If he makes something of it, I'd like to think I helped . . . The case is free."

Chapter Eight

Horn and case in hand, Joe headed for his hotel. The streets were quiet except for the sounds of an approaching street sweeper.

Joe fingered the case, marveling at its contents and the fact he owned it. He tried to imagine what it would have been like to play the horn with the symphony where it had spent so many years. Suddenly, reality returned. He heard sounds of music and laughter in the distance. They alternated between loud and muffled.

Joe walked toward the sounds and discovered they emanated from the Candy Bar whose ad he had seen in the *Guide* and on a parade float. The sounds waxed and waned as customers opened and closed its doors. The music and laughter created a festive atmosphere that beckoned.

Standing at the bar door, Joe wondered what would happen if he had a drink. He reached for the door handle, paused, and remembered Bruce. *This is the bar where he wanted to meet me. Is my being here an omen?*

Taking a deep breath, Joe entered the low-lighted, pulsating bar. He pushed through a sea of dancing bare-chested men and headed for the bar. Inserting himself between two short guys, he called out his order. The bartender, looking about twenty-five, sported a leather harness over his bare, muscular chest. *Looks like this kid shaves his chest too.*

Joe reached for his beer mug and handed over some bills. "It's easy to see why you were hired."

"Oh, you like my harness." The bartender tugged at a chest strap.

Joe grinned. "I was referring to your pecs."

"Like them do you?" the bartender said, flexing and smiling.

"I can tell you've worked them long and hard."

"Thanks. Yours don't look too bad either." The bartender said, staring at Joe's case. "What's that you're wrestling with?" "

"A horn case."

The bartender chuckled. "Blow your own horn, huh? If you'd like, I can put it behind the bar until you're ready to leave. You'll be free to do . . . whatever. Who knows, you might need empty hands tonight."

"Thanks. It'd be nice not to bother with it for a while."

"Okay," the bartender said, taking the case. "It'll be here when you want it. We close at two so don't forget it."

"One more thing? What's with all the various colored bandanas hanging out of everybody's hip pocket?"

The bartender gave Joe a curious glance. "Each color represents a sex . . . thing. It's a kind of hassle-free sex advertising. They were common everywhere years ago, but Cincinnati still uses them."

"So. What does your color represent?"

"I like everything, everywhere, with everybody."

"Really? I bet that gets you into lots of trouble or fun, depending."

The bartender wiped the bar, saying, "Sometimes both." Scurrying away to take another order, he said, "Have fun but don't forget your case."

Joe scanned the crowd. Most of the guys were bare chested. Several wore nipple rings. Most of the guys wore jeans, but some wore leather chaps over a jockstrap. More than a few were well-built.

What kind of a place have I gotten into?

A six-foot shirtless, hairy-chested guy, wearing chaps that revealed his bare butt, pushed his way to the bar. Joe made room for the man to place an order.

74

The bartender handed the man a beer, stared at him and then Joe. "Do you guys know each other?"

"No," the man said and extended his hand. "I'm Butch."

"Glad to meet you, Butch. I'm Joe."

The bartender smiled. "It's my job to introduce strangers. We're a friendly bar. Have fun."

"Come here often?" Butch asked.

"First time. In town for business." Joe went silent for a moment. "Butch, may I ask something kinda personal?"

"Try me."

"I see lots of guys here with shaved chests. Hell, the parade had a lot of guys with shaved bodies. You're a built guy. How come you haven't shaved your chest?"

Butch grinned. "You're not wanting to shave me are you?" Before Joe could reply, Butch said, "Well, I, *and others*, have shaved it, or all of me, at one time or the other. Can't say I hated it, but I kinda like body hair and so does my lover. I keep most of it, except for around my cock and balls."

"You let other guys shave you?"

Turning to leave, Butch said, "Sure. It's fun. You outta try it sometime. It grows back. From all the hair I see sticking out of your shirt collar, a lot of guys here would like to shave you."

Suddenly, a recorded drum roll screeched from the bar's cheap audio system. A tall, bare chested muscular man wearing leather chaps over a stuffed jockstrap walked on stage. "Good evening, tops and bottoms. It's time for our wet-briefs contest. Tonight's prize is $500. With that kind of prize money, I'm sure we've attracted the biggest cocks in Ohio for tonight's contest. If any of you wanna compete and haven't registered, see George at the bar. Don't be surprised if he asks for proof of eligibility." The crowd laughed. "But first, we'll have a drawing to select tonight's water boy."

A few guys shouted their availability.

The emcee continued. "I want you to look under your paper coasters. You know those little round paper thingees we put under your beers. Let me know if you have number 207."

In a heart-stopping surprise, Joe discovered his coaster had number 207. He pushed it toward the kid on his left. "You take it."

"Thanks, but I don't want it," the kid said. "I'm into older guys." The kid picked up the coaster then waved it in the direction of the emcee and yelled, "Here! This guy has number 207!"

"No," Joe said. *Shit!*

"Congratulations, sir!" the emcee said. "Come on up and let me present you with a bucket."

Joe shook his head. *What the hell is this about?*

"Don't be shy. We won't eat you . . . not yet. Come on up."

"Damn," Joe said, feeling his face warm with a blush. He pushed his way through a sea of naked chests on his way to the stage. Many of the customers extended their congratulations and slapped him on the back or butt as he passed.

On stage, he shook the emcee's hand and felt his face warm as he blushed again when asked, "What's your name and where are you from?"

"I'm Joe, from upstate."

"Are you a top or a bottom, Joe?"

Joe's face warmed more. "Uh, not sure."

"Anyone here want to help Joe decide?" the emcee asked, sizing him up.

The crowd erupted with shouting and cat calls.

"He looks like a top to me," the emcee said.

A man near the stage yelled, "He can top me anytime."

Joe knew his face had to be scarlet red. *This is embar-*

rassing.

"Well. Welcome, Joe-from-upstate," the emcee said. "Here's your bucket. There's water in that barrel at the edge of the stage."

"Uh, what am I supposed to do?" Joe asked, voice breaking.

"You've never been to one of these contests?"

"Nope." *What the hell am I doing here?*

"Well," the emcee said, pointing to a barrel. "First, you fill your bucket with water from that barrel then dump the water on the contestant's crotch—I mean briefs. By the way, do the water pouring over the tarpaulin. We don't want a flood on stage. The contestants have their undies doused, so we can better evaluate the *worthiness* of the contestant and his ability to win the $500 prize. As bucket man, you get up to two votes for each contestant. In case of a tie, you choose the winner. Oh, I almost forgot, *you* need to look inside each man's briefs before you drown them. Make sure there's nothing fake!"

How the hell did I get myself into this? "Okay. Let's get started!" Joe said, hoping to cover his embarrassment.

The emcee called for the first contestant.

With a large number **1** written on his bare chest, Buc walked barefooted onto the stage. He stopped at the barrel where shy Joe poured a bucket of water inside Buc's briefs, which Buc held away from his abdomen.

The emcee chided Joe. "Joe. You have to make sure everything's legal. *You* open the briefs, inspect the contents, and *then* you pour the water."

Buc walked back to the barrel.

Joe felt terrified. His heart thumped against his breastbone as the rest of him tingled with nervous excitement. He pulled Buc's briefs away from his hairy abdomen and glanced inside. "Seems legal."

77

The crowd laughed and one man yelled, "Better do a manual inspection, Joe!"

Buc marched around the stage humping his crotch at customers, walls, and the ceiling. Through his wet briefs, Buc grabbed his cock to indicate where it began and ended. He indicated its diameter by flashing an open OK thumb-and-forefinger sign then marched offstage to applause, whistles, and cheers.

Pointing at the crowd, the emcee said, "All right guys, mark your score cards. Remember, top score is ten points per man. The lowest is one, but I'm sure we have *no* 'ones.' Our next contestant, number 2, is Bill. Let's give Bill a big hand. He loves hand jobs."

Bill walked to the barrel and paused. Joe pulled the man's briefs open and peered inside. Mouth dry from nerves, Joe managed to say, "There's a monster in there!" *Can't believe I said that.*

"Joe . . . don't try swaying the audience vote," the emcee said. "Just tell us if he's legal."

"He's legal," Joe said, pouring a bucket of water on Bill's crotch.

Bill marched around the stage, imitating Buc's routine.

"Thanks, Bill," the emcee said. "Now you tops and bottoms mark your score cards.

Our next would-be-winner is Tom, number 3. Put your hands together for Tom."

Tom had so much chest hair the number **3** could barely be seen on his chest. He waved to the crowd and walked to the wet area where he opened his briefs for inspection.

Grasping the humor in his job, Joe felt more confident. His heart rate had slowed and his palms no longer sweated. He peered inside. "There's so much hair down there I'm not sure he has anything."

Tom blushed, but the crowd roared and clapped.

Joe looked Tom in the eyes. "Sorry, man. This is cold."

Another bucket of water found its target and the parade of wet flesh began. The emcee then asked the audience to record their score.

"Our next contestant, number 4, is Bruce," the emcee said. "Give Bruce a big Cincinnati welcome."

Bruce walked on stage. He appeared shocked on seeing Joe as the bucket man. "Oh my God," Bruce exclaimed. "I didn't think you'd be here."

Stunned, Joe said, "I didn't expect to see you." *Hope he doesn't think I came here looking for him?*

"Well, for the time being, you have a job to do." Bruce opened the top of his briefs for the mandatory inspection.

Joe filled his bucket then looked inside Bruce's scanty briefs. Joe was quiet for a moment.

The emcee yelled, "Don't tell us you can't find anything, Joe."

The crowd laughed as Joe's face warmed with a blush.

"Everything's legal," Joe said, giving the OK sign. He stared Bruce in the eye. "Sorry, Bruce. It's cold." Joe emptied his bucket on Bruce's crotch.

Bruce marched around the stage, wearing little more than a smile, doing the required moves. He presented a much more polished program than the other contestants' performances.

As Bruce prepared to leave the stage, he whispered to Joe "Let's have a drink after the contest."

For a split second, Joe asked himself, *How could he offer me a drink after I just drowned him? What the Hell, it's a free drink?* "Uh . . . okay."

The fifteenth contestant pranced off the stage, concluding the contest. Joe helped the emcee collect score cards.

"Contestants, take a seat back stage for a few minutes," the emcee said. "Joe, come with me," the emcee said, heading for the back of the stage. "Let's tally the scores."

In a small back room, the emcee spread the score cards on a table. "Write the scores on this tally sheet as I read them."

With counting completed, Joe said, "The winner is Bruce by ten points."

"Well, let's go announce the winner."

The contestants, still wearing wet briefs, were asked to stand in a line at the back of the stage.

The emcee pointed his microphone at the DJ and said, "Kill the music, please." The emcee waited as most of the customers gathered near the stage. "We have a winner, but first give Joe, our bucket man, a big round of applause for keeping the contest on the up and up and the contestants wet."

The room filled with applause and yells of appreciation and envy.

The emcee said, "Joe, tell us . . . who is the winner?"

Joe took the microphone, smiled, and then read from a card. "The winner of the Mister Wet Briefs Contest of 2010 is . . . Bruce from Cincinnati!"

The boisterous crowd applauded and chanted, "Bruce. Bruce. Bruce."

Bruce took a step forward and bowed.

The emcee pulled an envelope peeking from the top of his leather jock strap. He sniffed it then held it over his head. "Will Bruce come forward and receive his prize of *$500.00*?"

Bruce waved to the crowd, accepted the envelope, hugged the emcee for a second, and then posed for cell phone photos.

Bruce hugged Joe, but his embrace lingered.

My, he awfully friendly, Joe thought.

Bruce whispered in Joe's ear, "With this money, I can

afford to buy dinner. Thanks to your help."

Shocked, Joe asked, "What do you mean my help? You won fair and square by ten points." *Damn, hope he doesn't think I threw the contest for him.*

"Well, thanks anyway. I'll get dressed. Wait for me at the bar."

"Uh . . . Okay."

Joe waited at the bar. *I've never been so torn. I wanna be here, and then, I don't. Shit here he comes. Be polite.*

Congratulatory comments and slaps on the back continued as Bruce pushed his way to Joe's position at the bar.

"Want a beer, Mister Wet-Briefs winner?" Joe asked.

"Sure. As long as you let me buy."

"Why not? You're the big winner?" *Shit. I shouldn't have said big.*

The men pulled their barstools closer to the bar, sat down, and then drank their beers. Joe glanced at Bruce. "On stage, I couldn't help but notice you have some strong looking thighs."

"Well, I used to be a gypsy. A professional dancer."

"Wow! A professional dancer."

"I've always had good legs, and . . . They've held up over the years." "What kind of dancing did you do?"

"I studied classical ballet, but I also danced contemporary stuff, often with a group." Bruce sipped his beer. "Late in my career, I did some solo stuff and did a few road tours with some Broadway shows."

"*Broadway*. When did you quit?"

"A year ago."

"Why quit? What happened?"

"It's a tough life," Bruce said, putting down his beer. "I got tired of traveling, always tired, always aching. I had had enough. I decided to return to Cincinnati, start a business, have

81

fun, and put down roots. Cincinnati happens to be my hometown, so here I am."

"I bet it was a hard life . . . all that moving around, never at home—or for long."

"You're right." Bruce gripped Joe's thigh. "Even though you're wearing pants, I couldn't help noticing you have big thighs too. Work them much?"

"Some, but I've always had big legs. They got bigger when I played football . . . in high school. Since then, I've worked them some but . . . not as much as I should. Hell, after seeing all those young, well-built guys in the parade, I realized I'd been ignoring my workouts too long.

"What do you say we get out of here," Bruce said, looking at his watch. "It's almost breakfast time. I know a restaurant up the block that's open all night. It's quiet and the food's good."

"Uh . . . sure," Joe said. "Just have to get something the bartender is keeping for me." Joe called to the bartender, "May I have my case?"

"Coming up," the bartender said, retrieving Joe's case. "I put my number inside. Give me a call sometime. We can talk about my bandana color."

The all-night restaurant buzzed with the murmurs of tipsy men. Bruce chose a corner table under a pretentious, dirty crystal chandelier. The tablecloth had a wine stain peeking from under a salt shaker as if someone tried to hide it.

An older, tired-looking waitress in need of new hair dye, handed out menus. "You men want coffee?"

"None for me," Bruce replied, "I'd like a glass of wine. A Merlot."

"Me too," Joe added.

Appearing surprised, Bruce said, "So, you're a wine

lover?"

"I'm no expert, but I like Merlots. They're not too sour or too sweet. Besides, their grown near my home, and they're cheap."

"I've drunk wine all over the world, but I have to admit, I like America's wines the best—especially Merlots." Bruce looked toward the sound of shuffling feet off to his left. "And here comes our wine."

"Where all have you traveled?" Joe asked.

"I've been to England, France, Italy, Germany, Monte Carlo, Spain, Portugal, China, Morocco, Mexico, Japan, Greece, Russia several times, and Amsterdam a few times."

"Gosh. I've never been out of the country. A family can tie a guy down."

"You should try travel sometime. It helps one learn about, and appreciate, other cultures . . . different ways of doing things. It's an education you can't get from books." Bruce tasted his wine. "Not bad."

"Yeah. Tastes pretty good," Joe said. "I guess all that traveling had to do with your dancing?"

"Mostly, but I've traveled for pleasure."

"Earlier you mentioned a business. What kind?"

"A gift shop with flowers. I've never been good with flowers, but I have a guy who is. The gift business gives me an excuse to travel when *I* want to. I go to gift shows held around the world—places with lots of fun and cultural opportunities."

"And you?"

"Dad and I run a plumbing and bath shop. Just the usual sinks, faucets . . . pipe stuff."

Bruce chuckled. "I'll bet you have the best plumber's crack in the business."

Joe smiled. "Hell, it's trademarked. If I find a woman looking at my ass, I pull my pants lower and raise my prices."

"Ah, a paid *stripper*. What do you charge a guy who looks at your ass?"

"Hmmm." Joe stared into his wine. "I've been wondering about that . . . stuff. As a kid, I thought about women a lot. Well, there was *one* boy in high school. I had a fascination for the guy, but I never thought of having sex with him. Now my trainer, that's another story. I think *he* wanted to have sex with me. He got way too close to my crotch when doing my rubdowns."

"How did you meet your wife?"

"What?"

"You told me you had children. Remember?"

"Oh yeah. We met in high school. I *think* we fell in love, but that was years ago. Sometimes, I wonder if I ever loved her. I mean *really* loved her. Our families kinda pushed us into marriage. Don't get me wrong, she's been a good wife. Gave me two great sons who I love." Joe sipped his wine. "She takes care of the house and looks after the kids, but things changed. She's become a prude. Now days, I think there is more respect than love between us."

Joe remembered meeting Maria, a sweet, unassuming local girl.

His parents thought Maria would be a good wife and encouraged their relationship. Her German parents helped play matchmaker. With considerable coercion, he and Maria lived together. Much to Joe's surprise, she turned out to be a nymphomaniac. Months later, they married, but her sex drive soon waned.

"Respect's important," Bruce said, fingering the salt shaker.

The waitress served the men's food. "Will there be anything else?"

"No, thanks," Bruce said.

Joe shook his head.

Bruce took a deep breath. "Why did you come to the bar?"

"Ha. I went to bed, but I couldn't sleep, so I went to a pawn shop to buy a trumpet for my son. He wants to learn to play. By the way, that's what's in the case—a horn, not a mobster's machinegun. Leaving the shop, I wasn't sleepy and didn't wanna go back to the hotel. Suddenly, I heard music in the distance. I thought it came from a regular bar until I got there."

"Why didn't you talk with that young bartender? He was interested in you."

"Nice kid. Certainly had a strong chest for a guy his age."

"Yeah, nice to look at."

"Why did you enter that contest?"

"It's a great way to meet men—not just the contestants, but the customers. Gives them an excuse to talk, and don't forget, the money is good. But so much for me. What kind of guys interest you?"

"Hmmm. I'm . . . well . . . I'm trying to come to terms with who I am or might be. Am I, or am I not, into women kinda thing. You know?"

"A lot of men, even married with children, do some self-questioning." Bruce tapped Joe's hand. "Sooner or later, the real person bursts through. But things take time. Their own time. Go with the flow, but above all else, *don't* beat yourself up."

"Good advice, Bruce, but it's difficult not to."

"How's your wine?"

"Great. Why?"

"Do you like Chardonnays? Chardonnay wine?"

Joe shrugged. "Can't say. I think I had some, but I don't remember if I liked it or not. Why?"

"I have one at home. A really good one. Would you like

to try it?"

Joe stared at the table for a moment. He opened his mouth to speak, but Bruce said, "Don't worry. I just want to share a bottle of fine wine—a wonderful Chardonnay."

"What the hell. Why not?" Joe mumbled, his mouth half-full of Merlot.

"Let me get the check," Bruce said, waving to the waitress. "I won the prize money."

"How can I refuse such an offer from a major contest winner?"

The receptionist at Bruce's condominium nodded toward the guys, grinned, and then said, "Good morning, gentlemen."

"Good morning," Bruce said, heading for the rear of the lobby. He whispered to Joe, "The desk guy is gay."

Joe whispered, "I'm beginning to think the whole city is."

The elevator opened and the men stepped inside.

Joe said, "This is the biggest, fanciest elevators I've ever seen. Even has a fancy chandelier and an oriental carpet."

Bruce moved beside Joe and said, "Oh, I've always thought it was small. Crowded."

Joe laughed but did not move away.

The elevator opened at the twenty-third floor—the penthouse level.

Bruce opened his apartment door. The entire city lay spread out under the apartment's twelve-foot high windows. He switched on the lights.

"Wow! This is a cool place," Joe said. "You must be a *very* rich man."

"Far from it. I inherited the place—all 3200 square feet."

"Inheritance eh? That's a great way to get things except

somebody has to die."

"My gay great-uncle left it to me. I didn't know him well, but he had no other relatives."

Joe, busy eyeing the apartment, almost did not hear Bruce as he held out a wine bottle and said "Joe, come, take a look at this Chardonnay. Have you ever had it before?"

"What? Uh, I don't think so," Joe said, taking the bottle.

"It's a good one. I've been saving it for a very special occasion."

Joe chuckled. "I know I'm special but—"

"The special occasion is my winning Mister Wet Briefs 2010."

"How could I forget. You're a celebrity."

Bruce took two wine glasses from a cabinet then handed Joe a corkscrew. "Open it will you? I have to make a pit stop. Be right back."

From deep within the apartment, Bruce yelled, "Look under the sink. You'll find an ice bucket. Fill it with ice and water from the frig door and then take everything to the coffee table near the window. Make yourself comfortable. I'll be right back."

Moments later, Bruce returned, tying the sash of a black-silk robe. "I couldn't stand that wet underwear another second. Let me pour you a glass of wine."

Bruce poured a small amount of wine into each glass. "Okay. I want you to watch and follow my lead."

Bruce held his glass toward a table lamp. "Note the color. It should be clear and a pale yellow. Now, swirl it. Stick your nose in the glass and sniff the aroma. Snobs call the aroma the *head* or *bouquet*. See if you can identify any fruit or berry scents. Now, take a mouthful and chew it. Let it rest on your tongue a few seconds. Notice the taste in different parts of your mouth and then swallow. Note the aftertaste . . . the *finish*. A good wine leaves wonderful aftertastes all over your tongue."

Joe followed each step. "I've never done this smelling, chewing, tasting stuff, but I understand the steps. I like this. Feels like there's oil or maybe butter in it. Is it expensive?"

"Let's just say most people wouldn't buy it to drink with popcorn."

Bruce took another taste, and then both men sat down on the leather sofa.

Bruce put his right foot on the coffee table and stared at the city. "I never tire of that view." The robe slid from his leg, revealing a muscular thigh.

Joe tasted his wine then said, "You have killer legs. How do you work 'em?"

"This part?" Bruce stood, untied his robe, and let it fall to the floor as he flexed his thigh.

"Uhhhh," Joe said, shocked at Bruce's sudden naked-ness. "I just wanted to see your thigh, not get *naked*!"

"Joe, you've seen naked men before. Hell, you looked down my crotch and drowned it. I'm naked all the time here. I like it. Does it bother you?"

"Yes. No. I mean . . . I don't know. *What's happening?* Oh god, I don't know what I mean? Yes, I've seen naked men before but not alone. Not with a stranger and in his house."

"Forget the rest of me. What do you want to know about legs?"

"Their size, the cuts, the quad heads. Just the results of your workouts. That's all." Joe looked away, picked up his glass, sipped some wine, and then paced in front of the sofa as he rubbed his shaved head. "Hell! I just wanted to know about your workouts. Your thighs."

"Relax. See those quads?" Bruce pointed to the area above his kneecap. "Those take full extensions, toes pointed back toward the head—and heavy weights."

"Oh God," Joe said. "Why does this happen to me?" He rolled his eyes and tabled his drink. "As a guy who works out, I'm interested in leg *workouts*. I like suggestions on how to do it better, but you're standing there naked as if nothing's wrong."

"Joe, there's *nothing* wrong. Maybe in your mind but not here. Would you be more comfortable if I dressed?

"I don't know what I want." Joe stopped pacing. He took a sip of his wine and looked at Bruce. "Are you comfortable being naked like that?"

"I'm comfortable, but I spend all my time here being naked."

Bruce sat on the far end of the sofa. "No reason for you to be upset. You already checked me out."

"Well, that was different . . . making sure the rules were followed."

Bruce shook his head. "Lots of guys wanted to look in my shorts, but *you* got, shall we say, the *honor*."

"Maybe I'm being crazy." Joe slumped onto the opposite end of the sofa. *Damn. Damn. Damn.* He shrugged and waved his hands in the air. "What the fuck! Stay naked if you want."

Bruce slid four feet away from Joe. "Aren't you ever naked at home?"

"Maria's against it. We barely get naked to make love—then the lights have to be out. She also says the boys shouldn't see their father naked if their mother is around. She's raising a couple of wimps. I know the boys are going see naked guys at school, maybe in the bushes, but somewhere." Joe shook his head and sighed. "I've been sleeping naked at the hotel. I dig the feeling. I've even thought of running naked in the woods near my house, but I haven't. Not yet?"

Bruce shrugged and tilted his head. "Well. What a great time to let your hair down—your imaginary hair. This is a non-judgmental house. Cut loose. Let go. Get naked."

Joe stared into the night. *Do I dare?* Suddenly, he raised his glass then gulped the last of the wine. "What the hell." With a flourish of hands, he removed his shoes and socks. He stood, smiled, and then dropped his pants.

"Now that's a nice set of thighs," Bruce said.

Joe stepped out of his pants then draped them over the sofa. Unhurried, he unbuttoned his shirt then let it fall from his shoulders.

Bruce chuckled. "Oh God. I should put on some stripping music."

Joe folded his shirt, then place it over his trousers. He turned his back, stepped out of his briefs, and then kicked them onto the sofa. He kept his back to Bruce for a moment.

"Oh my. A shy plumber," Bruce said.

Joe turned to face Bruce.

"Bravo!" Bruce said, staring at Joe's cock and balls.

"Is this what you wanted? Me naked."

"I won't lie, Joe. It is, but isn't it what you wanted?"

"Well, this is me—all me—naked me."

"So? How do you feel?"

"Okay," Joe said, turning around. "I feel good."

"Come," Bruce said. "Let me show you my city."

"Where're we going?"

"The terrace. I'll fill your glass."

"What? Aren't you afraid somebody might see us— naked?"

"Don't worry. We're high up. I do it all the time."

Bruce filled their glasses then opened the French doors leading to the terrace. He walked to a low wall twenty feet away, and then watched Joe's crotch as he slowly crossed the terrace.

A cool breeze flowed over the expansive space.

"Wow! That breeze feels good," Joe said. "I wouldn't have thought it'd be so cool up here. Strange though, the floor is warm."

"It's like this almost eight months a year," Bruce said, waving the breeze toward Joe. "It comes off the river every night about this time. Many nights, I switch off the air conditioning and sleep out here or sleep inside with the windows open."

"Must be nice, sleeping naked," Joe said bending over the wall to peer below.

"How do you feel?" Bruce asked.

"Good. I mean I feel free. Like a bird ready to fly off this terrace."

"Come, let me show you my place. I have things I've collected during my travels. I keep them in my art gallery. I know that sounds a bit pretentious, but I had to do something with the space."

"Lead the way."

The men traversed the wide living room lined with mirrors opposite the terrace doors. They passed the formal dining area featuring a modern crystal chandelier, a glass topped dining table resting on a twelve by eighteen-foot long oriental carpet. They then passed two large abstract paintings.

Bruce led the way into a darkened room. He switched on several rows of track lights revealing four walls of artifacts. "I collected these things." He turned 360 degrees. "These paintings and carved figures are from many countries. That bright red feather hat is from Africa." Pointing, he said, "There are a few bronze figures, and these are my two favorite tapestries."

"My god!" Joe exclaimed. "This is like a museum."

"Thanks." Bruce turned to admire an ivory carving of an African woman. "I like sharing the collection with people who appreciate it. Come the office is next."

The men entered an adjacent room. It had a masculine ambience with dark wood paneling. The space contained a Rococo desk, two overstuffed English wingback chairs, and another desk, but a modern one, facing the cityscape. It held a computer and phone.

"Now, this looks like a man's room," Joe said, dragging his fingers over the Rococo desk.

"Thanks. It's a great place to work. Now, let me show you the media room. Others would call it a TV room, but in this building, they're called *media rooms*."

Joe chuckled. "It's the same in the country."

Bruce admired oil paintings and lithographs as he and Joe strolled along a long hall at whose end stood a large antique, hand-carved wooden door.

"My god, that door is something else! Where'd you get it?"

"I think it came from Indonesia. My uncle installed it."

Bruce pushed the wide door open to reveal the media room.

Joe stepped inside the sound-dead space. "Wow. This is a real movie house."

"Well, kind of," Bruce said, admiring the regal red and gold looking space while pointing out its features. "The walls, floor, and ceiling are padded and heavy drapes keep out the light. I don't have a real movie projector, but there's a digital DVD projector that fills that screen. It's great for porn."

Joe sat on one of the plush red recliners and said, "Bambi and Lassie too, I guess."

"Not yet," Bruce said. "Let me show you the guest bedroom."

The bedroom, decorated in a modern Italian motif, had an *en suite* bath with a marble tub and a shower.

"Love that shower," Joe said. "Wish I had one."

The master bedroom had twelve-foot-tall windows on adjoining walls and a California king size bed that sat atop a platform. Off the room-sized walk-in closet stood the master bath with marble covered walls and floor. The jetted tub would hold four people, the steam-shower an army.

"My god. You live like a king!" Joe said.

"Not quite. I never use the tub. It takes too long to fill and would be a waste of water, but I have partied in the shower."

"Bet those showers were orgies, weren't they?"

"They were fun. Well, now how about we go back to the terrace. I'll refill your glass."

"Sounds good."

Bruce stopped in the kitchen and watched as Joe leaned over the terrace wall to explore the scene below.

"That's quite a vista," Bruce said, returning to the terrace with wine.

"Which part?" Joe asked, scanning the panorama.

Bruce chuckled, "You, you crazy guy. A *real* plumber's crack."

"I almost forgot I was naked, but now you're making fun of me."

"Oh, no! I could look at that butt all day, or should I say all night? Come, sit with me," Bruce said, patting a chaise.

Joe meandered to the chaise. As he sat down, Bruce placed his hand, palm up, under Joe's descending butt.

Startled by its touch, Joe said, "That's a no-no."

Bruce smiled. "Can't blame a guy for trying—can you?"

"Let's just enjoy the night and the Chardonnay—okay?"

"Sure." Bruce patted Joe's thigh then rested his hand there.

Quiet, Joe looked at Bruce. "What are tops and bottoms? Anything like with straight people?"

Bruce chuckled. "Need an education, eh? Well, a gay 'top' is someone who likes doing various things *to* another guy—could be a woman I suppose. A 'bottom' is a guy who

93

likes various things *done* to him."

"Like what?" Joe asked.

"A bottom might say, 'tie me up, fuck me,' or 'beat me.'"

"Oh, I get it," Joe said. "A top would say '*I* wanna tie you up, *I* wanna fuck you' or '*I* wanna beat you.'"

"You got it."

"Could different colored bandanas signal the same information?"

"Could," Bruce said. "You saw guys wearing them in the bar?"

"Yeah." After a few moments of silence, Joe said, "I should get back to the hotel. Got things to do in the morning."

"You *could* spend the night. I'd make breakfast and then send you along. I promise you'll be safe. Don't worry about oversleeping."

Joe grinned. "Thanks, but I can't."

Bruce must have sensed Joe needed time and space. "Of course. I hope our paths cross again. May I give you my phone number? If you're in town, or want to get away, give me a call."

"Uhh . . . Maybe."

Joe dressed as Bruce watched his every move. "Damn. You look better without those clothes."

"You never stop do you, Bruce?"

"Don't blame me for having good taste in men, Joe."

The men shook hands, and then Joe left.

In his hotel room, Joe contemplated his actions, the evening, and Bruce's hospitality in his "castle-in-the-sky." *He's an interesting guy. I like him.*

Joe's alarm rang with the subtlety of thunder. He roused himself and prepared for checking out. Wanting Maria to know he would soon be leaving Cincinnati, he opened his cell phone and searched for his home number. He then pressed the call button. The phone rang a few times, and then a male voice answered, "Hello."

"Who is this?" Joe asked, head swirling with confusion.

"This is Mark, who's this?"

"Mark? *Shit!* Sorry. I pushed the wrong number. I meant to call home. Sorry if I interrupted anything."

"No. Nothing. Nice to hear from you. Did you have a rewarding time at the kitchen show?"

"Everything went well, thank you. And you?"

"Not bad. Made a little money and some contacts for future business. Where are you?"

"Getting ready to check out."

"Had breakfast yet?"

"Uhh . . . No. I planned on getting something after I called Maria."

"I'm ready for breakfast. Why not join me? I'll pick up the check. Give us a chance to talk."

"Thanks, but I shouldn't."

"Joe, I've offered hospitality *and* a free breakfast. How could anyone say no to such an offer? You don't want to convey a warped view of Ohioan hospitality do you?"

"You do know how to twist things. Uhhhhhh. I guess there's no harm in having breakfast."

"Fine. How about I meet you in the restaurant in fifteen minutes."

"That'll work."

Joe called Maria and then headed for the restaurant.

To the hostess, he said, "I'm joining a friend back there."

Mark stood and extended his hand. "Morning, Joe. Nice to see you."

Mark held Joe's hand a long time before the men sat

down.

A waiter arrived and asked, "Coffee?"

"Yes, please," Joe replied.

The waiter pointed his pot toward Mark. "Yes, thank you. Warm it up."

For a few seconds, the men sipped their coffee in silence.

Mark stared over his cup into Joe's eyes. "You look a little tired."

"Didn't get much sleep," Joe said, putting down his cup.

"Out having a good time?"

"Not really. And you?"

"I had a client last night."

"A client dinner?"

"No," Mark chuckled.

"What kind of work do you do?"

Mark set his cup down, glanced skyward, and then took a deep breath. "Well, let's just say the 'service' industry. My formal education was in architecture. That's what attracted me to Los Angles. I joined one of the large firms doing cutting edge architecture, but they had me doing 'scut' work. I hated it, but the pay was good while I considered my options. One day, a friend took me to a model's audition. To make a long story short, I was hired, but I had a lot to learn—mostly about whom I had to sleep with to get ahead." Mark sipped his coffee, and then stared at the wall for a moment. "I mean women *and* men. Soon, I discovered I didn't have to model to earn money. People would pay me to escort them to all kinds of events or just be naked with them. You know, a boy-toy. Eye candy. I had to be sexually available to old men, old ladies, rich young guys, rich lonely housewives, and so on."

Shocked speechless for a moment, Joe finally said, "A lot of guys would dig being paid to fuck women, but how did you feel?"

"Strange, at first, but I've never been one-hundred percent straight. I can't say I liked playing the role of a gigolo, but it paid well—too well to ignore the money and benefits."

"And the guys?" Joe asked. "What about the men?"

"Can't say I hated every experience. Some I didn't like. Some I loved, but it can be exhausting—being *on* for hours at a time. Trying to please. A guy doing this kind of work has to accept being thought of as a *thing* with parts. But hell, it pays the bills and gives me a lifestyle I couldn't otherwise afford." Mark leaned across the table. "Don't tell anyone, but I don't pay taxes. It's a cash business. I do a little architectural work as my front, but I own my house, a BMW and a Jaguar. I buy the best clothes, and I get lots of gifts." Mark held up his wrist. "This watch—it's a Rolex and eighteen carat gold. It was a gift from a grateful, but lonely, housewife." Mark held up his other wrist. "This bracelet, twenty-two carat gold, was a gift from a sheik."

"I can see how you would be successful in the *service* industry. You're tall, good looking, and built like a brick shit-house, but did you ever consider yourself a prostitute?"

Mark's head jerked back. "Hey. That's a little harsh. Yeah, the thought has crossed my mind, but I put it aside. Who wants to admit he's a whore?"

"My apologies, but whatta you going to do when you get older, and God forbid, you aren't as big . . . or muscular?"

"I don't think about that—not now, but I know I need to save for retirement. I've been thinking about raising my fees, because there aren't retirement homes for poor gigolos. Are there?"

"Hell, there's gotta be at least one somewhere." Joe sipped his coffee.

"Whatta you charge?"

"My minimum is two hours. For that, I charge $1,000

plus expenses."

Joe spewed his coffee. "A thousand dollars! That's five-hundred dollars an hour. Hell, I don't make that on a good day of sweating pipes."

"Maybe you should give up pipes and become an escort."

"Not me. I'm having trouble sorting all of this . . . sex stuff." Joe paused, tilted his head, and looked Mark in the eyes. "Why didn't you hit me up for money the other night? Did you know I couldn't afford your services? Was I . . . charity work? Are you going to hit me up for money now?" Joe looked at his watch. "Gonna charge me for seventeen minutes of breakfast time?"

"Don't be silly. Believe me, there are times, and guys, whose mind and body I find attractive. You're one of those guys. This is one of those times. A gay guy would be crazy not to want to know you. I dig you, man."

"You mean I'm charity work?"

"Well, a kind of charity, but you're the one extending charity—to me. Not the other way around."

"Have you ever had a *special* guy friend, Mark?"

"I've had two men in my life. One for three years. We grew apart, but we're still friends. The other guy died in a motorcycle accident. He didn't believe in wearing a helmet—it interfered with the *freedom* of the open road."

"Sorry to hear that."

Each man took a sip of coffee.

Mark stared into Joe's eyes. "So, I'm in the service industry and you're in . . .?"

"I'm in the service industry too—plumbing."

"A plumber?" Mark asked. "Fixing pipes and drains?"

"Yep."

"That's surprising. I've never met such an intelligent

plumber. You like Merlots, classical music, and play a trumpet. That's not your average plumber, my friend, *but* you are the most *handsome* one I've met."

"With flattery like that, who knows what it'll get you."

"Everywhere I hope."

Breakfast arrived. Conversation ceased as Joe watched Mark enjoy his meal.

Mark asked, "Did you give any thought to the talk we had?"

Joe put down his cup. "I've had a lot of troubling thoughts. Something strange is happening. What'll happen to me—to Maria, my sons, and the rest of the family? I don't want to ruin their lives, but I don't want to ruin mine either." Joe leaned back. "I feel like I'm caught between a rock and a hard place. Being with you was a first, and . . . Thinking about that, I remembered my first sex with a girl. I liked it and wanted more. I liked sex with you, but I'm scared as shit to even thinking of having sex with another man."

Mark rubbed his leg against Joe's. "If you think you didn't do something right the first time try again. Practice makes perfect."

"God, I remember your hands—everywhere."

"These hands are free—I should say *available*—this morning."

Joe rubbed his forehead. "That's sooo tempting." *Too tempting.*

Mark chuckled. "This is your last chance before returning to Maria."

Joe stared at his wedding band while rotating it on his finger. "Interesting argument."

"I'd hate for you to deny yourself," Mark said, staring into Joe's eyes, "meaning *me* giving you a massage."

"Gotta admit you got *great* hands. I've never had a

massage like yours."

"You have no idea how great they are. You were, shall we say, *drunk* during the last one."

"Are you training to become a used-car salesman?" Joe asked. "Your pitch is . . . hard core."

Mark leaned forward. "In the sales world, a job isn't done until the sale is made. In my case, I'm selling nothing. Everything is free. How could a customer, like you, walk away from a free deal like me?"

The do-not-disturb sign swung on the doorknob outside Mark's room. He half-closed the drapes, blocking the brilliant sunlight.

Joe stood a few feet into the room feeling confused. *I said I wouldn't do this again.*

Mark took Joe's hand and led him to the side of the bed, kissed him on the forehead, and then unbuttoned his shirt while pulling the shirttail from his pants. As the last button yielded, Mark rubbed his hands over Joe's hairy chest and nipples.

Joe sucked air. *That feels good.*

Mark kissed Joe on the forehead then pushed his shirt off his shoulders. Mark stooped to remove Joe's shoes and socks.

Joe asked himself, *Am I just going to let this happen?*

Mark opened Joe's pants and let them fall to his ankles. Mark slipped his hands behind the waistband of Joe's briefs and pushed them down. They fell to the floor, leaving Joe naked, cock erect.

Stoic, Joe suddenly smiled and unbuttoned Mark's shirt. Mark smiled and kissed Joe on the forehead. His lips lingered there as Joe continued unbuttoning the shirt. Joe's tongue explored Mark's nipples, knowing they longed for attention.

Mark pulled Joe's head against his chest, reveling in the pleasure of Joe's mouth.

After feasting on Mark's chest, Joe loosened Mark's belt, unbuttoned his pants then pushed them down. As usual, Mark wore no underwear.

Mark kicked off his pants, picked up Joe, and then placed him on the bed.

Soon the prostitute and plumber lost themselves in sexual revelry. Mark swallowed Joe's cock to its roots. Lost in Mark's oral pleasure, Joe fell back onto the bed, engulfed by the warming sensations generated by Mark's hot, talented mouth. As Joe neared climax, his body begged to scream its pleasure. His legs stiffened, and he moaned louder and louder as both men increased the speed of stimulating the other's cock. Soon, both men neared climaxing. Each attempting to muffle their screams of ecstasy.

"Oh . . . God," Joe yelled. He went limp and panted. "Wow. That was . . . wonderful."

"Ditto," Mark said.

After a brief rest, Joe glanced at his watch. "Two hours and we're still here."

"Yeah, but spent."

"I gotta get out of here," Joe said.

"Me too. Sorry we didn't have time for other fun things."

"There's more?"

"You'll see—next time."

Chapter Nine

Joe stopped his "Vet" on the shoulder of the highway, put the top down, and then took off his shirt, so he could tan and enjoy the fresh air. His hand moved over his bruised and tender left nipple. *Damn! Can't let Maria see this.*

Joe exited Interstate 70 and turned right onto the country road that would return him to the simple life of a small town plumber. Flashbacks of the weekend intruded on his thoughts. He knew he had changed. *What is to become of me?*

Three hours later, Joe stopped the car five miles from home and donned his shirt in preparation to drive onto his driveway where domestic reality waited.

As he exited the car, his sons raced to tackle his legs. They laughed and yelled, "It's daddy! Daddy's home!"

Shuffling along like Frankenstein, Joe dragged a giggling boy from each leg.

The kitchen storm door suddenly burst open, and Maria darted out, drying her hands on a dishtowel. "Welcome home, honey!"

Joe gave her a kiss on the mouth and stared into her eyes. "I've missed you."

"We've all missed you," she said. "What do you have for the boys?"

Joe suddenly realized he didn't have John's trumpet. He whispered, "I have small gifts, for now. I have to go back to Cincinnati in a few days to pick up John's gift. It needed cleaning and polishing. He'll be happy with it when he gets it."

Inside the house, Joe removed two small packages from his travel bag then held them behind his back.

"Okay boys, the first to pick a hand is . . . Paul."

Paul chose the right hand. Joe held out a red package. Paul grabbed it and ripped it open.

"Okay, John, you get the other one."

Both boys shrieked with excitement on finding additions to their electronic games.

"They love them," Maria said.

"Don't worry, hon. You weren't left out." Joe handed her a small, blue box. "It's something you've wanted for a long time."

"Oh, I'm so excited," Maria said, hugging Joe.

She opened the box then cried. It contained an "S" shaped pendant with small glistening diamonds.

"It a journey of life pendant, Joe said. "I saw it in a hotel shop and knew you'd love it."

Maria kissed him on the lips. "It's beautiful. I'll have to give you a *special* thank you tonight—after the boys are asleep."

"Great." *I think.*

Joe went to the family room, put his feet up, read his mail, and then watched TV while holding Maria's hand. As evening approached, he turned his attention to his sons, playing with their new games. *God! I can't imagine losing them.*

At seven o'clock, everyone gathered around the kitchen table for supper as jazz played in the background.

After the meal, Joe gathered the plates and took them to the sink.

John helped as he asked, "Daddy, why don't we have a dishwasher?"

"We will, son," Joe said, looking at Maria. "In a few days."

"Do you mean that?" Maria asked, looking surprised.

"Yep. At the show, I got a deal on the latest thing since electricity, and I bought it. We'll have it in two weeks."

"Oh, Joe, I'm so happy." Maria hugged Joe's waist as he placed dishes in the sink. "Thank you, honey."

Joe grinned. "You're welcome. I just hope I can find

time to install it."

Maria slapped him on the back, "Yeah, and the cobbler's children go barefooted."

As the boy's bedtime approached, Joe helped them put away their books then carried the boys to the bathroom. "Take your bath and brush your teeth."

With the boys in bed, the house grew quiet.

Joe climbed into bed where Maria waited in the glow of a candle on the bedside table. She placed her head on his chest and stroked the inside of his thigh.

Joe whispered, "I know you've been alone for a few days, but I'm beat."

"Sure," Maria whispered. "It was a long, tiring drive."

Joe kissed her on the forehead.

"Sleep tight sweet prince."

"You too, princess."

Joe stared at the dark ceiling. *I don't know if I want sex with anyone anymore.*

As Joe entered his shop's showroom the next morning, Barbara looked up from her invoices. "Well, look what the dogs dragged in."

"And I *feel* like I've been dragged."

"Too much partying at that *business* affair?"

"Not quite," Joe said, rubbing his eyes. "Just not much sleep."

"Your dad's in the office . . . on the phone."

Joe looked through the mail as Don entered the show-room. The men hugged for a second.

"How did the trip go?" Don asked. "Didn't bust the budget did you?"

"Just on hookers!" Barbara shouted.

Joe winked at his father. "Dad, you need to fire that

woman."

"If she doesn't start putting out, I might have to fire her. Come on back to the office. As the fat cats say, debrief me."

Joe spent half an hour informing his father what he had seen at the show. They spoke about clear-glass basins, chromo-lighted shower heads, and Maria's dishwasher. Joe told his dad about the trumpet.

"That horn is a hell of a good idea, son. John will love it."

Joe informed his father that Matt wanted to sell his plumbing business.

"Sounds like a good idea. Let's talk about it."

Don and Matt met several times to discuss price and other details. Several weeks later, they completed the deal. The new shop gave Don and Joe a larger market and less competition.

Joe stretched his business wings. He enjoyed managing the new shop, for it gave him the opportunity to show his father he could be as good a manager as his dad. Joe supervised two plumbers, one helper, a stockman / assistant manager, and a part-time secretary. He felt like a capitalist in that he performed fewer jobs and made more money than he had earned working in Smithville. However, the new shop, twenty-three miles from Smithville, required Joe to rethink his priorities. The commute and managing the new shop cut into his gym time, but he did get in a workout every other day while traveling to, and sometimes from, the new shop.

Financially, things were going well, but psychologically, Joe had a sense of crumbling inside. He needed a counselor. Someone to help him sort out the man stuff. Maybe his preacher could help.

Hoping counseling would help sort his problems, Joe

arrived at the church with dread in his heart. *I gotta do it. I can't go on like this.*

He knocked on the door to the minister's study.

"Come in," the minister said opening the door. "How're doing, Joe?"

"Not so good or I wouldn't be here."

"Well then, let's talk. Have a seat."

"This is confidential ain't it?"

"Absolutely!"

"Uh . . . *How do I start?* I've been having troubling thoughts . . . about having sex outside my marriage."

"Have you acted on these thoughts?"

"Uh . . ." Joe rubbed his hands together and stared at the floor. "Yes."

"I see. Do you know why you ignored your vows to Maria?"

"I think I do."

"Was it a physical attraction thing or was it emotional?"

"Ninety-nine percent physical—lust, I guess."

"In one way that's good. There's no emotional attachment . . . at least not yet."

"No. No attachments."

"Joe, first of all, you must stop seeing the other person. God will forgive you if you pray for his forgiveness. Secondly, you must look inside yourself, evaluate why you find the other person attractive. Then, you must look for those qualities in Maria. I'm sure they're there. All you have to do is look. Have you told her?"

"No. Afraid to."

"It's probably best you don't but don't stray again. Let's pray."

Joe left the church feeling somewhat happier but angry the minister had not pushed him for more disclosure. He had shared his burden with someone, but he had received no help with his problem.

The next day, Joe visited his Dad to discuss work problems then said, "Dad, the boys and I are going fishing this weekend at Ridge's pond. Wanna join us?"

"I'd love to, but I need to stay with your mother. She's not feeling too well."

"Maybe, next time," Joe said as Don looked through his inbox.

That night, feeling duty bound, Joe initiated love making with Maria. It took a while for him to become aroused, but fantasies helped. Joe believed everything went well for Maria, but he often caught himself reliving his encounters with Mark while trying to satisfy her.

The next morning, the boys were excited about the up-coming fishing trip. Joe sneaked up behind Maria as she prepared a picnic lunch. He placed his arms around her waist and kissed her on the neck.

"God!" Maria shrieked. "You scared me."

"Sorry. Sure you don't wanna come with us and put worms on the boys' hooks?"

"You know I don't like fishing or worms. Stella and I are doing a day-out-with-the-girls thing."

"Great. I don't want you being alone while we're having fun. Who knows, we might catch dinner."

"Those pond fish are so small it'd take a car full to feed our cat."

Joe walked to the family room and yelled, "Guys, quit horsing around and gather your stuff."

"Look," Maria said, opening the picnic basket for Joe's inspection. "There's milk and water for the boys, sandwiches, and fried chicken. I put beer in the cooler for you."

"Thanks, hon."

Joe helped the boys load the car then headed for the pond. He turned on the radio. "Hey guys, whatta you wanna hear?"

John yelled, "Trumpets! Trumpets!"

Joe scanned the CD screen, selected Wynton Marsalis, and then smiled, watching John play the "air trumpet."

"Go get them, son!" Joe shouted. "You play a mean horn."

Joe parked in the shade of overhanging trees near the edge of the pond.

Yelling with delight, the boys got their rods from the trunk and ran to the pond. Joe took out a small bucket and shovel—his "worm-extraction equipment."

"Boys," Joe yelled, "let's dig some worms."

Paul grabbed the shovel and ran deeper into the shade. "I'll dig, daddy."

"Okay, but do you remember where I told you to dig the last time we were here?"

"Dig where the ground's wet," Paul said, pointing toward a pile of leaves, "under leaves."

Joe felt a flash of pride. "Okay. See what you can find."

The shovel's long handle proved difficult for Paul to wield, so Joe grasped the upper end and helped Paul turn the wet earth. The ground, softened by recent rain, offered little resistance.

In seconds, Paul found wiggling prey. "Look, daddy!" Paul shouted, "Worms!"

"Don't just stand there, son. Get them. John, help your brother gather worms."

Joe tossed a handful of dirt in the bucket, and then the boys dropped their wiggling prey on top.

"Okay," Joe said, "let's go fishing. Remember, push the worm on the hook in a zig zag fashion so it can wiggle and attract a fish."

John raised the tip of his rod over his shoulder then swung it toward the lake. The reel whirred as the float and worm-baited hook flew through the air then splashed into the water twelve feet from the shore.

"Great cast, son."

Joe and Paul cast their line and waited for nibbles.

Joe stared at the water lost in thought. *Did I enjoy those encounters too much? Why did I do it? Am I crazy?* He shook his head then went to the car and turned on the CD player. Watching his sons fish, he felt grateful for the gift of fatherhood. *God, I love these kids.*

The sun slowly stole the shade, and the guys' fishing spot grew hot. So far, there had been no nibbles. The guys reeled in their lines and checked their worms.

Frowning, Paul said, "Mine's dead."

"So is mine," John said.

"Mine is still wiggling," Joe said.

The boys threaded fresh worms on their hooks, cast their lines, and then waited.

After twenty minutes, Joe asked, "You guys hungry or want a drink?"

"I'm hungry," Paul said, rubbing his belly.

The boys followed Joe to the car where their food waited. He handed a foil packet to each child. "Use this wet-wipe to get the worm off your hands before touching your food."

Suddenly, Paul's reel whirred, and his float plunged below the surface. He ran to the pond as Joe yelled, "Grab your rod!"

Paul grabbed his rod as Joe called instructions. "Quick! Raise the tip then reel in some line then you lower the tip and reel again." Joe superimposed his hands over Paul's hands. Four hands tried to bring in the fish, but the line suddenly went limp and the float bobbed to the surface.

Joe tousled Paul's hair. "Darn. It got off the hook, but it must have been a big one from the way your rod bent."

"Hey, John," Paul said, with pride, "daddy said I caught a *big* one."

"Okay, guys, let's finish eating then we'll move to a shady spot."

Within an hour of moving to another location, sunlight flooded the new fishing area.

Joe wiped sweat from his brow. "I don't know about you guys, but I'm thinking the fish aren't interested in worms. Maybe the water is too hot. Whatta ya say we go swimming?"

"Yeah! Let's go swimming!" Paul shouted.

"But daddy, we don't have swimsuits," John said, frowning.

Joe shrugged. "If it's just us guys, we don't need swim-suits,"

"I know 'bout that," Paul said. "It's skinny dipping. My friend, Tommy, talked about it. Mom says we shouldn't do it."

"Well, mom's not here. It's just us guys. So who wants to go swimming?" Without waiting for an answer, Joe yelled, "Last one in is a monkey's uncle!" Joe stripped then dived into the pond, surfaced, shook water from his face, and called to the stripping boys. "Hurry, before the water gets hot."

The boys stripped, then dived in and swam toward their father, standing chest-deep in the water.

Joe placed a hand on each boys' head, gave it a push under the surface, and then swam away. The boys resurfaced, laughing, and swam in pursuit of their dad.

"Come on!" Joe yelled. "See who can get to that log first."

Paul yelled, "I can beat you, John."

Joe winked at John and yelled, "Slow down, John, you don't want to get a *cramp*."

John must have understood his father's unspoken message, because John slowed his pace.

Paul overtook John, but he looked winded. John shortened his strokes, so his intentional slowing did not appear obvious. Paul maintained his lead, while John faked tiring.

Appearing very tired, the boys approached the half-sunken log where Joe waited.

"Faster, Paul," Joe yelled. "John is catching up. Faster! Stretch your arms, son. Stretch!"

Paul stretched his short arms as far as he could, and with one last heave, and a kick, he touched the log.

Joe pulled him close then gave him a hug. *I can't risk losing this.*

"I won, Daddy. I won," Paul yelled.

"You certainly did," Joe said.

The exhausted boys draped their arms over the floating log.

Joe caught his breath as he rested. "Guys, I think we've had enough sun. Better head for shore. If you guys get sunburned, your mother will shoot me."

"Ah, do we have to, daddy?" Paul asked.

"Yep," Joe said. "See if you can beat John again."

"I'm rested now," John said, looking at Paul. "You can't beat me again."

The second race started. John swam as if a shark chased him, passing his brother and Joe. Spent, he crawled from the water just as Joe and Paul reached shore.

"Paul, take my hand," Joe said. "I'll help you out."

Paul stood on the shore, shivering.

"You guys wait in the sun while I get the towels."

Joe returned with several small towels. "These are work towels, but they're clean."

Paul looked up at his father. "Daddy, why do you have hair on *your* private parts and I don't?"

Surprised, Joe thought a moment. "Well son, see that small sac there?" Joe pointed at Paul's scrotum. "Inside are two small marble-like things. As you grow, those 'marbles' will get bigger. At a certain size, like those 'log rollers' you use in marble tournaments, they'll make a chemical that goes directly into your blood. Those chemicals will cause hair to grow on your chest and private parts—just like daddy's."

Paul stared at the ground for a moment. "Okay."

Wished I could have talked liked this with my dad. Joe whispered to the boys. "Don't tell your mother we went swimming or she'll fuss. Especially don't tell her we went *skinny dipping*. We won't get to come back."

"Okay, daddy."

The boys looked tired.

On the way home, John fell asleep against his father's side.

Joe looked at his sons. *I'm so lucky. Fuck that gay stuff.*

Chapter Ten

Joe needed to return to Cincinnati to pick up John's trumpet and the fixtures he purchased during the convention.

Entertaining the thought of seeing Bruce, he shook with anxiety and experienced a warm flush of happiness. He wondered if the encounter would drive him in one direction or another? Did he want it to? How would Bruce react?

Ten days after the fishing trip, Joe's cellphone rang as he drove to the new shop.

"Hello. Joe here."

"Hi, Joe, it's Bruce. Remember me?"

"Sure. Been thinking of calling you. I need to get my trumpet. Sorry, but the night I left your place I had a lot on my mind."

"I can imagine. I didn't want to call at what could be an inopportune time, but enough time has passed that I thought I should—just in case you had forgotten about the horn."

"Thanks, but I haven't forgotten about it *or* you. I've been trying to get up the courage to—"

"To what, Joe? Get naked again?"

"Nah. Just what to do regarding . . . me. You know what I mean."

"Your *situation*? Yeah. What's happening?"

"Something . . . but I'm not sure what. I get cold sweats just thinking of it. I look at my sons and say nah. Then later, I wonder why not."

"Like I said, you have time for the journey, no matter the destination. Enjoy the trip. Now, back to the horn. Do you want me to ship it to you?"

"Thanks, but that's not necessary." *God no! I don't wanna give my address to anyone.* "I gotta go back to pick up some plumbing stuff. Maybe I could pick it up then."

"That's fine. When are you coming?"

"Not sure, but in a few days, I'll give you a call when I know. Okay?"

"That's fine. I'm going to a gift show in New York this weekend. Any chance you could join me. I'd love to show you the Big Apple.

"Thanks but that's impossible."

"Well, I look forward to seeing you in Cincinnati."

"Great. Talk to you soon. Bye."

Joe closed his phone then stared into space. *Why didn't I ask him to ship it? That way I could pick up the shop stuff and avoid him, or I could meet him in a public place. Damn. I've got to face this shit. I'll get the horn and leave. Snatch and go. Nothing more.*

The sudden blast of a car horn brought Joe back to reality. His slow driving had impeded traffic. He waved to the car to pass as he contemplated his future.

Joe interrupted Barbara's eating a doughnut to ask, "Is dad in the back?"

"He's in the storage shed."

Joe walked through a back workshop then exited the front building. He strolled across the backyard, took a mental inventory of several items scattered around, and then entered the storage shed.

"Hi, Dad."

"How you doing son? Anything interesting at Dave's place?"

"Nah, just a leaky pipe. Dad, I'm going to pick up the stuff I bought at the bath show. How would you like to go with me?"

"Don't much care for big cities. Besides, I need to stay near your mother. Why don't you take Maria?"

"Maria doesn't like trips, and then there's the boys to look after."

"I'm sure she could find someone to watch them while the two of you go."

"I've been thinking of going Saturday afternoon and staying over to hear a jazz group that night. There's a trumpet player I'd like to hear. Maria wouldn't want to do that, so I don't know what to do."

Don finished storing wrenches and knives. "Here's what. Tell Maria about picking up the plumbing stuff *and* the band. Tell her you wanna stay to hear the music. Ask if she would go with you. If she says yes, there's no problem. If she says no, she'll probably say go without her."

Joe wanted Don or Maria to go with him, so he wouldn't have to face a certain situation, but then he thought of Bruce. *Shit!* "I'll think about it, dad; right now, I gotta get over to Roy Miller's place. See you later."

Joe had finished arranging tools in his van when his phone rang. The number on the screen looked familiar, but he couldn't remember to whom it belonged.

"Hello."

"Joe, this is Mark. Mark from Cincinnati."

"Mark? Oh yeah. How are you?" *Shit! I've been trying to forget you.*

"Better now that I've heard your voice."

"What's up?"

"I'm coming to Cincinnati next weekend. I thought I'd give you a call on the chance we might get together."

"That's not a good idea, Mark."

"Joe, it would be good for you and *definitely* good for me."

"Oh yeah?"

"Absolutely," Mark chuckled. "You know you want to see me—all of me."

"Strange. Not long ago, the boys and I went skinny dipping at a local pond. We had a great time, but I kept thinking about us two running around there naked."

"Invite me and we'll do it."

"What have you been doing with yourself?"

"Oh, the usual stuff. All work. No play . . . thinking about my *big* plumber friend in Ohio."

"Me? You have all that sex, and you think about me?

"Like I told you, Joe, you're unique. As for my work—it's business, nothing more. You know, a good paying gig, nothing more."

"Mark, maybe, I'll call." *Maybe.*

"There you go with those maybes. When it comes to men, you know I usually get what I want, and I *want* you. But, okay. Here's hoping you call. Bye, Joe."

Why did he call now? What the hell is to become of all this . . . me?

Joe arrived home in time for a family supper.

"Anything unusual today, Maria?" Joe asked.

"No, thank God, but tomorrow, I'm meeting with the PTA planning committee. We need to raise money for school projects."

"What projects?"

"Band uniforms and the senior-class trip. Kids are bigger today, and the old uniforms don't fit. The new ones cost twice as much. Think your dad would sponsor a few?"

"I'll ask," Joe said. "How'd you like to go to Cincinnati next weekend?"

"Why would we go to Cincinnati?" Maria asked, a look of puzzlement enveloping her face. "Why should I go? I have a lot to do with this fund raising. There's a deadline to meet."

"There're two reasons. I need to pick up your dishwasher. I also want to hear a band that's playing Saturday night. I thought you might wanna go shopping while I pick up the plumbing stuff." He winked. "I also need to pick up a certain noise maker."

"The trip might be nice," Maria said, "but I'm not comfortable leaving the boys. Besides, your dad might need help with your mother, and you know I'm *not* a jazz fan. You go. Enjoy the music. You'll only be gone one night. The boys and I will be fine."

"I don't like leaving you here."

"I don't wanna go to Cincinnati now. I'll be fine."

Maria, you're such a stick in the mud. "Boys, will you take care of your mother while I'm away?"

"Okay, daddy."

Joe went to bed, wondering if he should tell Mark about the trip, and how would he go about picking up the trumpet.

He awoke with a solution to his quandary. *I've got to see where this shit ends. I'll ask Bruce about visiting him Saturday. See if he'd like to hear some jazz and then see if Mark is free on Sunday.* Joe went blank for a moment. *This is nuts.*

Later that morning, Joe mustered the courage to call Bruce.

"Bruce. Joe here."

Bruce chuckled, "Joe who?"

"Okay, wise guy. I'm calling to let you know I'm coming to Cincinnati next weekend. I wondered if you'd like to go with me to a jazz concert Saturday night?"

"I'd love to *and* I'd love seeing you again. What time?"

"Eight. And it lasts about two hours."

"Have you made hotel arrangements?"

"Not yet."

"Why not stay with me. You'd save a lot of money."

"Uhhhh . . . okay but . . . do I have to leave my clothes at the door?"

"You know this is a clothing *optional* house. How about we get something to eat before the concert?"

"Sure."

"There's a place nearby, and the food is good. They have something for everybody, even for your sensibilities. How about meeting at my place for a drink before we head out?"

"Sounds good. Guess I should get to your place around four thirty."

"When you arrive, tell the desk guy you're here to see me. I'll alert him."

"Okay. See you next week." *Is this too crazy?*

Later that day, Joe called Mark.

"Joe," Mark said. "I wondered if I'd hear from you."

"Well, I have to go to Cincinnati next week. Are you free Sunday morning?"

"Watch how you use that word *free,* Joe."

"You know what I mean . . . *cheap*."

"For you, I'm not free or cheap just *reasonabl*e."

"Remember, I'm just a poor plumber."

"I'm sure we can negotiate a payment plan. Maybe you could clean my pipes."

"I do have this twelve-foot long—"

"Don't say another word. I like surprises. Sounds like a hell of a deal."

"Will you be staying at the Markham?" Joe asked.

"How'd you guess?"

"How about I meet you there for Sunday lunch?"

"Sounds good. Noon in the restaurant."

Joe adhered to his resolution to get to the gym on a

regular basis. Having finished work early on Friday, he decided to have a workout without his firehouse buddies. He completed his upper body exercises then headed for the shower. While waiting for the water to get hot, he did a few poses and observed his physique reflected in a mirror. *I can't believe how my pecs are growing.* He turned sideways. *Chest is thicker too.*

Joe dressed then headed for home.

"Hi, honey," Joe said. "Where're the boys?"

"At school—doing extra work."

"Don't tell me they're having trouble with their studies, not after all the time I've spent helping them with their homework."

"God no," Maria said. "The state gave us money for after school studies. The boys are learning Spanish."

"That's good given the influx of Latinos."

"Joe . . . you're gaining weight, or I should say you're getting bigger."

"Thanks for noticing, honey. I've been working out a lot. It helps me clear my mind."

"It seems strange, you exercising after working all day."

"Lifting is relaxing. Sure, I sweat a little, but it's a diversion. Some people like yoga, others like a stiff drink, but lifting works for me."

"Well, keep it up. You're looking good, honey."

Chapter Eleven

Saturday morning, Joe had a mix of emotions regarding Bruce and Mark. Anxiety, fear, and worry about consequences vied for space in his crowded brain, but he wanted to know more about the sexual things hinted at by Mark. While Joe felt an emotional tug for Bruce, he expected a less salacious experience with the former dancer than with Mark.

Instead of driving backroads, Joe took the interstate to shorten travel time to Cincinnati's warehouse district. This would also allow more time with Bruce. *This may be crazy, but I've gotta see where all this takes me.*

Dock employees helped Joe quickly load his purchases for the shop as well as Maria's dishwasher. It was now noon and Joe had two hours of free time. He decided to visit the pawnshop where he had purchased John's trumpet. He didn't want to give John his trumpet in the damaged case.

Joe heard a voice from the backroom of the pawnshop. "Be right there. Have a look around."

Seconds later, the shop owner entered the showroom and stared at Joe. "I know you?"

"Yep. I bought a trumpet."

"For your son."

"That's right. I'm back for a case. You might recall mine is kinda beat up. I'd like a better one."

"Not sure what's here, but let me look."

From the backroom, Joe heard noises, including one thud. "Damn it," the shop owner said.

Hope that noise wasn't my case.

A few minutes later, the owner yelled, "Found one!"

The shopkeeper returned then handed Joe a black

leather-covered case. "The owner pawned his horn *and* this case. Unfortunately, he couldn't afford to redeem both. Now the case is unclaimed so . . ."

Joe opened the case. The velvet lining appeared to be a more regal blue than in the case he owned. He inspected the chrome latches and the edges of the case. This one had fewer signs of wear.

"What's the price?"

"Let's see . . ." The shop owner pushed his visor back and rubbed his forehead. "I can let you have it for . . . $40.00."

Joe thought for a moment. "Make it $25.00, and I'll take it."

"Uhhhh . . . Okay," the owner said, frowning.

Joe left the shop smiling. He placed the case in the rear of his van and noted the time, three o'clock. He had no interest in just driving around or sitting in a dark bar. *I'll call Bruce about arriving early?*

Joe rang Bruce's doorbell. From inside the apartment, Joe heard movements and sensed someone staring at him through the peephole in the door. Suddenly, the door opened.

"Hello," Bruce said, naked and smiling.

Shocked, Joe said, "My god!"

"Don't looked so shocked. Come in. I told you I'm nude most of the time."

"Yes, but greeting someone at the door . . . naked?"

"Hope I didn't shock you too much."

"Well, you gotta admit it's unusual?"

"Give me a hug." Bruce whispered in Joe's ear, "Want me to get dressed?"

"No! You're too built." *Did I say that?* "It's just a shock—that's all," Joe said, keeping his eyes above Bruce's crotch.

"Come out to the terrace. I've been sunbathing. It's such a beautiful day I couldn't resist working on my tan." Stepping into the bright sunlight, Bruce said, "I poured a glass of that Chardonnay you enjoyed. It's on the table."

Joe sat at the table and Bruce stretched out on a chaise. Joe, facing the sun, squinted as he chatted with Bruce.

"You don't have sunglasses do you?" Bruce asked.

"No. I didn't think I'd need them."

"Let me get you a pair."

Joe shaded his eyes with his hand. "That'd be great."

Bruce left then returned with two pairs of sunglasses. "Pick one."

Joe selected the solid black frames and slid them on while Bruce went to his chaise.

"Joe . . . You're starting to sweat. Why don't you enjoy the sun with me?"

Joe took a sip of his wine. "You ordered this sun so there'd be an excuse to get me naked."

"Oh shut up. Enjoy your wine and the sun!"

"I think I will get some sun." Joe said, unbuttoning his shirt.

Bruce interrupted. "Would you stand over here, so I can watch without the sun being in my eyes?"

"It'll cost you." *Am I ready for the consequences?*

"What's the cost . . . another glass of wine?"

"Maybe more."

Winking, Bruce said, "We'll see but don't take so long."

Joe dropped his brief and faced Bruce. *Naked feels good.*

"Bravo," Bruce said, clapping.

Joe bowed then walked toward an empty chaise beyond Bruce's lounge. As Joe squeezed by, Bruce cupped Joe's balls in his palm. Though Joe knew he shouldn't, he felt a flash of pleasure as Bruce cradled his balls. His head battled his heart.

125

Maybe I shouldn't be so willing.

"I'll take a pound of those 'apples,'" Bruce said as Joe stretched out on a chaise.

"These 'apples' aren't for sale, but I might *give* you some."

"Ah. Produce . . . right from the farm."

"You calling me a farm boy?"

Blocking the sun from his eyes, Bruce said, "Yes and a hell-of-a-big-one. You've grown since I last saw you. Your pecs and biceps are bigger. You must be working out a lot."

"A lot more recently. I used to workout a lot, but I got lazy. One day I woke up and said, 'Joe, you're flabby. You're gonna be a ball of blubber.' On one pride float, I saw a *huge* guy. His pictures are in all the muscle magazines. Seeing him and those well-built kids on all those floats got me to thinking about the gym. So yes, I've been working out—a lot. Thanks for noticing."

"Ha. You're difficult to ignore, Joe."

"I can't take more of this sun without sunscreen. Can you loan a poor farm boy some lotion?"

"Okay, but only if I can rub it in."

"In what?"

"Skin."

Bruce reached under his chaise and got a bottle of sunscreen. "This has UVA and UVB protection."

Joe removed his sunglasses and lay face down on the chaise. "Does it have PFB—protection from Bruce?"

"Of course not," Bruce said as he straddled Joe's lower back.

"Back down a little will ya. Your weight is a bit much for my low back problems."

"That's *not* my bodyweight you're feeling."

"My god, man. I know they're big, but that's some

126

weight."

"And proud of it," Bruce said, rubbing sunscreen on Joe's back.

"You're not the only guy I know with such weighty matters."

"What?" Bruce asked and stopped rubbing. "I thought you were a virgin."

"Almost. I was with a man—once—a big son-of-a-bitch from Los Angeles. Nice guy, a *huge* guy, muscular as hell. He had a hell of a heavy package." *Why the Hell did I admit that?*

"I've got to hear more."

"It happened a longtime ago, and . . . I don't wanna talk about it."

"Okay, but you have to tell me sometime."

Joe looked back at Bruce and frowned. "Hey buddy, watch where you're rubbing that stuff! Leave my plumber's crack alone."

Bruce chuckled. "It *is* alone—with me."

Bruce moved lower on Joe's legs and rubbed lotion on the back of his thighs. "Man, these thighs are big."

"Thanks for noticing. Been working them hard."

Bruce oiled Joe's calves then tapped his butt. "Turn over and I'll do your front."

Joe turned onto his back and placed his forearm over his brow to protect his eyes from the sun. "I'm leery of men sitting over my crotch with a hand full of oil telling me he's going to do my front."

"Don't worry." Bruce touched Joe's mid-pubic area. "I'm only going to here."

"Good," Joe said. *Shit! There I go again.*

Bruce poured oil onto his palms then rubbed them together. Smiling, he rested a palm on each of Joe's pecs. "Your pecs are *hard*."

"That's not the only thing hard."

Bruce looked at Joe's crotch.

"Not that," Joe said. "It's this lounge."

"Sorry, but I'm not moving until I'm through with your front." Bruce rubbed oil onto Joe's hairy pecs and then placed one finger on each nipple and opened his mouth as if preparing to eat them.

"You're such a tease," Joe said covering his nipples with his hands. "I can't afford to have one bitten off."

Bruce glanced at a wall clock. "Hey, look at the time. I hate to say this, but we need to shower and get out of here."

"Hell, I was just getting comfortable."

"It's better to leave wanting more but don't worry. You're spending the night."

God, I hope I'm not making a mistake.

Joe watched Bruce's lithe, muscular body move with the grace of a willow tree moving in a slow breeze as he led the way to the shower.

Standing outside the shower, Joe watched Bruce adjust the water flow in the six-person shower then duck under the water.

"Get in, Joe. It's big enough for two."

Joe watched Bruce's biceps move soapy hands over his chest. His discerning stare lasted a second before he joined Bruce. Joe ducked his shaved head under the water as Bruce handed him a bar of soap. Bruce rubbed his suds-covered torso against Joe's. Staring into each other's eyes, they embraced. Their hands explored the other's body, and then each man freed a hand to find the other's cock. Suddenly, Bruce backed away, cradled Joe's face in his large hands, and said, "We have to stop this if we're to get to dinner on time."

"This is the second time you get me worked up, and then you stop." *That was feeling so good.*

"You wanna skip dinner and that jazz thing?" Bruce asked, wiping water from his eyes.

"I think I'd have more fun here. Let's cook a steak or something and listen to jazz on CDs or the radio? I think the jazz thing was an excuse to see you again—even if I do need to get that trumpet."

"Sound good," Bruce said and turned off the water. "I'd love having a *naked* Joe cooking in my kitchen. I *might* even allow an apron—at the appropriate time."

Bruce stepped out of the shower then handed a towel to Joe.

"Turn around," Joe said, taking the towel. "I'll dry *your* back."

Bruce turned his back, and Joe dried the back down to Bruce's butt where he lingered a moment then turned Bruce and dried his legs up to his crotch.

"Let me return the favor," Bruce said.

Joe turned and Bruce dried him from his shoulders to his feet.

Is he going to do anything else.

Bruce dried Joe's chest, abdomen, and crotch, then crouched to dry the left leg followed by the right. As Bruce stood, his mouth reached Joe's crotch. Without saying a word, Bruce swallowed Joe's cock.

Joe moaned. *Oh, God, that feels soooo good.*

Acting from instinct, Joe grabbed Bruce's head and pulled it closer. Bruce held the cock in his throat for a moment then withdrew it, so the head could be stimulated. "Oh Yeah," Joe said. He dropped his head backward and moaned, holding Bruce's head as if it might escape. Bruce's lips toyed with the tip of Joe's cock. He said, "Yes. Yes. Yes." His body stiffened. "That feels good." Bruce continued his magic. "Geeeez. I'm close, Bruce."

129

Joe's knees began to buckle as he slumped against the shower wall. Bruce pulled Joe's butt forward to lock his knees and prevent his collapse. Just then, Joe erupted, yelling, "Aaaahhh. . .!" Bruce dined until he had drained Joe who kept saying "Stop. Stop."

"That literally left me weak in the knees," Joe said, catching his breath. "I never felt anything like that—not standing up."

"Come, lie on the bed," Bruce said, pulling Joe into the bedroom then throwing back the bedcovers.

Joe spilled himself onto the bed face up. Bruce lay beside him, stretching his right arm over Joe's hairy chest. Bruce said, "Rest a bit."

Joe maneuvered his right hand under Bruce's abdomen then found its way to his crotch where he cradled Bruce's soft parts. Without the slightest manipulation, Bruce's cock grew hard.

Bruce's hands moved to Joe's flank then pushed him onto his stomach.

Joe, shaking inside, rested his chin on his folded forearms. *Now what?*

Bruce sat on Joe's muscular backside where dancer's cock met plumber's crack. Bruce spread a warming lubricant onto Joe's ass. Joe held his breath then flinched as Bruce maneuvered his cock inside. Joe moaned and sucked air from the discomfort he fought to overcome. *I don't know if I can do this.* He sucked in a deep breath then exhaled.

"Relax," Bruce whispered as he plumbed Joe's depth. "Relax. That's it."

Joe succumbed to Bruce's intrusion. *That's beginning to feel better.*

A minute later, both men began a slow rocking motion that became the stride of a steed and jockey racing for the finish line. Chest and back sweat eased the friction between the broad body parts. Joe's hips responded to Bruce's pleasuring. After the first few minutes, the sex felt better than Joe had expected.

Within minutes, Bruce moaned, shuddered, and then fell limp on Joe's back, saying, "Wooo horsey."

Exhausted, Joe lay motionless on the bed of first-experiences. "When you started, I didn't think I could take it, but after a while it felt okay . . . even good. I've never experienced anything like that."

Rolling onto the bed, Bruce whispered, "Maybe next time it will be more fun for you."

"Are you saying I'd do it again because you think I'm gay?"

"Joe, you wouldn't be the first man *or* father to realize he's gay."

A wave of shock move through Joe. "What are you're saying?"

"I'm not labeling you. You're just a hell of a guy that I like being around . . . having sex with."

"Okay. We did it. I did it. This could be just an experiment for me. It could also be a country boy kind of passing fling for you. Maybe you like having sex with married men, but I've never questioned my sexuality until now." Joe looked away. "No one has ever called me *gay*." Joe stared at Bruce. "I'll never forget how the word *gay* killed a classmate of mine."

"Killed him? How?"

Thinking back in time, Joe said, "Billy was his name. A group of creeps at school were always picking on him—hitting him—calling him queer. One bully called him queer and fag in the cafeteria when it was packed with kids. The bully hit him in the face, knocking him down. Billy must have gotten sick to his stomach with fear and embarrassment. He threw up. He got up, left, and never came back. His parents sent him to a private

131

school. It was a year before he returned to Smithville. Lots of guys hounded him. One day, he paid for his lunch and headed to a table. A bully intentionally tripped him. He fell and his food flew everywhere. The bully stood over him threatening him, calling him 'faggot . . . gay faggot.'"

"Billy curled up on the floor and cried. The bully yelled louder and louder. Billy called for help, but no one helped him. I'm sorry to say I didn't either. He grabbed a knife that had fallen from his tray then stabbed himself . . . in the chest. I guess he thought he had stabbed himself in the heart, but he didn't. An ambulance came, but Billy died from a collapsed lung. He died because of that creep, and *nothing* happened to him!"

"I'm sorry, Joe. Were you guys close?"

"He wasn't a friend-friend just someone I knew. I think I saw some of me in him. I felt sorry for him.

Bruce fell back on the bed and stared at Joe. "Come here," Bruce said and pulled Joe into an embrace. "Time takes care of everything."

Chapter Twelve

Twenty-three floors below, a car's alarm awakened Joe. He scanned the bedside clock—8:07 p.m.—then looked outside. The sky had grown a dark blue splashed with reddish pink clouds.

As Joe stirred, Bruce awoke.

"What time is it?" Bruce asked, rubbing his eyes.

"Too late for the concert." Joe sat up and stretched his arms. "That's okay. I have no regrets."

Turning onto his side, Bruce said, "You know you don't need an excuse to visit me."

"I guess not, considering the hospitality I've received."

"Hospitality, my friend, will cost you."

"Oh yeah?"

"You have to cook me a steak—*Naked*!"

Joe chuckled. "Okay, but I didn't know steaks needed to be stripped nak—" Joe laughed so hard he could not finish saying naked.

"Funny," Bruce said, heading for the bathroom. "Let's shower then you can cook the steaks while I supervise. We'll have *dessert* later."

"I'll need an apron, but I promise I won't wear it until the grease starts flying."

Bruce and Joe showered then headed for the kitchen.

Bruce searched the refrigerator. "Where are those steaks?"

Watching the search, Joe crossed his arms and leaned back against a counter edge. He crossed his legs, pushing his cock and balls forward, so they rested high on his thighs. He became lost in thought.

Kissing Joe on the forehead, Bruce said, "God, you're beautiful. Penny for your thoughts."

"I'm glad I met you. There's something about you that I like, but I can't put my finger on it."

"Well, so far you've put your finger on my everything, so what is it? Maybe my thighs?" Bruce looked at his own thighs. "You seem to like legs. God knows *your* thighs make a wonderful frame for your crotch."

"Yeah, I like legs. God knows I like your body, watching you move—naked—always naked. Don't ever stop being naked, but something about you is different. You're a *real* person. More so than many people I've met." *Where am I going with this shit?*

"Thanks. Seems we have a mutual admiration society." Bruce unwrapped lettuce. "I hope you become comfortable being naked. You have killer legs, a big, beautiful chest, and I like your shaved head, but inside, you're a straightforward, uncomplicated man of integrity.

"I have a feeling we'll get to know each other better."

"Me too, but would you mind cutting the lettuce while I cook the steaks. I don't want you damaging anything or covering up with an apron."

Joe chopped arugula as Bruce prepared the griddle. He must have felt drawn to Joe's butt, because he rubbed his crotch against it and hugged Joe's waist. He gave Joe a short, firm squeeze, a brief grinding motion against his butt, and a kiss on the neck. Yielding to the kiss, Joe inclined his head, welcoming more attention as the men enjoyed the moment.

I liked that, Joe thought.

Dinner ready, Bruce played a jazz CD for background music. The men sat opposite each other at the glass-top table in the dining room. An ornate mat, on which stood a crystal vase filled with roses, blocked the men's view of each other from the lap to the chin so Bruce pushed the vase and mat aside.

"I'm glad you moved that," Joe said. "The flowers

134

blocked my view of your face."

"That's not the only thing it blocked. I couldn't see your crotch."

Joe scooted forward, spread his thighs, and let his package dangle over the edge of his chair. "How's that?"

"Wow. Thanks."

"Okay," Joe said, "but don't forget my interests." *Damn, I did it again.*

Bruce slid forward letting his package dangle then smiled.

Each man's lower body could now be seen through the table top. The guys also had space for their feet to explore the other's legs, thighs, and crotch during dinner.

With dinner finished, Bruce said, "Let's clear the table then have Port on the terrace."

Joe helped load the dishwasher. That reminded him of Maria's dishwasher and the fact he hadn't called home.

"Bruce, I hate to have family things intrude, but I promised I'd call home."

"No problem. Use my office phone if you want."

Joe took his cellphone from his pants then went to the office.

"Hi, honey," Joe said. "How are you?"

"Fine."

"And the boys?"

"We're fine. How did everything go in Cincinnati?"

"Nothing exciting here. I had a quick drive to the city. Got the van loaded with shop stuff *and* your dishwasher. I got the trumpet and traded for a better case than the original one. Had dinner at a little place then enjoyed some great jazz. I've just left the music place and I'm headed for bed."

"Glad you had a good day, but your mom isn't handling her chemo very well.

"Wish I could do something to help her. I've got to see her when I get home. Any mail?"

"Just bills and junk mail. Nothing important. When do you think you'll be home?"

"Between four and five I guess."

"Okay. Drive carefully."

"I will. Kiss the boys for me and get a good night's sleep. See you tomorrow. Love you. Bye."

"Night, Joe."

Joe closed his phone and walked toward the terrace. *Joe, you'd better think about what you're doing here.*

As Joe stepped onto the terrace, Bruce said, "Stop, right there. I want to admire you, and I don't mean just physically. I'm glad you called home. That shows character and respect. I hope you didn't have to tell too many lies."

"Actually, I didn't tell a single lie. I chose my words with care. However, they might be open to interpretation."

"Good for you. Now sit down. I poured a glass of Port for you."

"I don't think I've ever had any."

"Well, it's a wine. Some are sweet; some are dry. Some in between. I prefer the slightly sweet ones—as a desert wine."

After a sip, Joe said, "Hey, this ain't bad. I like it."

"Good. It costs $75.00 a bottle."

"You're kidding!" Joe said, examining the bottle. "It's so small."

"I didn't want to tell you the price until you tasted it. As I've told you, you have good taste. After all, you choose *me* and my place to spend the evening."

"Hell. I'm getting a college education by hanging out with you."

"Yes, but you don't get credit until you pay the tuition."

"Tuition?"

Bruce grinned. "Nakedness is currency in this house."

"Nakedness! Guess I'll go for a doctorate."

Bruce slid toward the end of the lounge, making space for Joe then patted the cushion.

Joe sat down and propped his head against Bruce's chest. "Do you mind?"

"Not at all." Bruce hugged Joe and caressed his head.

The men sat in silence for a while. Nothing disturbed the moment except occasional street noises far below.

"Strange," Joe whispered. "I don't remember when I've felt so at peace." *Why can't all life be this tranquil?*

"Not running from anything are you?"

"No." Joe sat up and looked at Bruce. "Why'd you ask?"

"Just curious."

Time seemed to slow as Joe luxuriated in Bruce's quiet company.

Drinking the last of his port, Bruce said, "Perhaps we should get to bed."

"You're right. I have to head home early."

"When do you need to leave?"

"Eleven should be fine, but please, don't let me forget the trumpet."

"Promise. Now, let's get to bed."

Joe followed Bruce to the master bedroom where its platform bed awaited.

"Which side do you prefer?" Bruce asked.

"I sleep left. Maria likes the right."

"Great, I sleep on the right, but sometimes I travel from one side to the other."

Joe got into bed. Lying on his side, he pulled the sheet to his chest then looked at Bruce. "I like the idea of sleeping naked beside you."

"My pleasure." Bruce kissed Joe on the forehead. "Sleep

tight even though there's not much night left."

Joe turned face down and stretched his arm over Bruce's chest. "Let me keep it there for a minute. I wanna feel you under my hand."

"Okay," Bruce said, turning off the bedside light. "Good night."

Joe stared into the dark. *Am I willing to give up my boys . . . Maria? Do I have to? I'm afraid to answer that question.*

Sunlight streamed into the bedroom, reflected off an ornate mirror, and flooded the bed where Joe awakened. In the distance, he heard Bruce moving things about. *I'm not dreaming. I'm really here, and I did all that stuff.*

Joe took a quick shower then wrapped the towel around his waist. The aroma of coffee wafted through the apartment, enticing him to follow it to its source.

The sound of Joe's bare feet on marble floors had reached the kitchen.

Bruce's turned to greet him. "A Towel?" Bruce exclaimed. "I can't believe you're wearing a towel."

"Wasn't sure *you'd* be naked."

"What," Bruce said, pulling Joe's towel off. "I'm always naked. Now shut up and give me a hug."

The men embraced then Bruce kissed Joe on the forehead.

"Sit here," Bruce said, patting a counter stool. "I'm making Russian omelets."

"What's that?"

"Do you like omelets or fish?"

"Sort of, but don't tell me you're making a fish omelet?"

"No, silly! I'm going to put something on the omelet that has a slight fishy taste. Do you like sour cream?"

"Yep. On baked potatoes."

"We'll have that too. Well, sort of. Do you like champagne?"

"We had it at our wedding."

"Ours is just slightly sweet. I'll add orange juice, and then, we'll have a drink called a Mimosa."

Joe smiled. "Is this part of my education?"

"It's gourmet 101 with three credit hours—that's because you're naked. Help me with the sour cream?"

"What do I do?"

"Spread a half-cup over each omelet. I'll get the caviar."

"Caviar?"

"Yes. Have you ever had it?"

"Never."

"Mine isn't the expensive stuff. It tastes a little like fish but different. A slightly salty taste. If you don't like it, don't eat it."

Food preparation completed, Bruce placed breakfast on the dining table along with the Mimosas and croissants.

"Have a seat," Bruce said. "I propose a toast. Here's to many more naked breakfasts."

Joe rubbed his foot on the inside of Bruce's leg. "I'll drink to that." Joe sipped his drink. "A Mimosa eh? It tastes great. It's another first for me. I like it."

After a few hours and several Mimosas, Joe needed to take his leave.

"Needless to say, I wish you had more time," Bruce said, "but I understand obligations. I hope I've treated you so well you'll want to return."

"I don't remember when I had such a good time—a super evening and a great breakfast. I'll never forget this. Don't know how I can ever repay your hospitality."

Smiling, Bruce said, "Oh yes you do."

"What?"

"Several hours of naked time."

Joe chuckled. "Think you can afford my rates?"

"Well, as we say in the gay world, you'll have to take it out in *trade.*"

"What the hell does that mean?"

"That's for your next class."

As Joe reached for his underwear, Bruce implored, "Please, slow down. I can't bear the thought of you wearing clothes. I need some lingering images of that body."

Joe smiled, did a quick muscle pose, and then began to dress. Respecting Bruce's request, he took ten minutes to don: two socks, his underwear, shirt, pants and shoes. His cock and balls were last to vanish behind his zipper. *Never thought I'd be so brazen.*

"Thanks. I enjoyed the show, but don't forget the horn."

Bruce walked to the hall where the horn case waited. He and Joe grasped its handle. Their hands remained in contact for a few seconds before Bruce let go. He kissed Joe on the cheek, opened the door, and bid him goodbye.

"Thanks for everything," Joe said, then smiled.

"Call often and come back soon."

"Time will tell. Bye."

From his van, Joe looked skyward and saw Bruce waving from the terrace. Joe returned the wave and then drove away. *Wish I didn't have to leave.*

Chapter Thirteen

While driving to Mark's hotel, Joe relived the previous eighteen hours and asked himself if what he had done was crazy? *Was all this just plain stupid?*

He parked his van in the back of the self-parking area of the hotel garage. He wanted to reduce the chance someone he knew would see the van with its identifiers.

His heart pounded as he headed to the hotel breakfast room.

When the elevator door opened, he spotted Mark in the far corner of the dining room, and headed there, wiping his sweaty palms on his trousers

"God, you're looking good this morning," Mark said, shaking Joe's hand.

"Looking pretty good yourself. How's business?"

"Oh, I made some money. My, but it looks like you have put on some muscle since I last saw you. Are you lifting more?"

"Yeah. I decided to get in shape—before I'm too old."

"Yeah. Like thirty-three is old. With your genes, bone structure, and height, you should give thought to *serious* body-building."

"That takes time and . . . giving up foods and family fun. Why would I wanna do that?"

"First, you'd feel better about yourself. You'd look even more fantastic, and you'd have more sex appeal for women *and* men. Hell, you might make some money with that body."

Joe laughed. "Doing what? Selling myself in Smithville,"

"Don't knock it. You could make a good living as an escort."

"I *don't* wanna sell myself, but I know it wouldn't hurt to do more lifting."

"Too bad I don't live closer. I'd coach you. Now, changing the subject, would you like breakfast or lunch?"

"Neither, thanks. I ate earlier, but I'd like coffee."

Mark motioned for the waiter and then detailed Joe about recent travels and his search for a larger house. He wanted room for a home gym and space to store his new Harley "Hog."

Mark finished brunch and then looked Joe in the eye. "I've had a tough time getting you out of my head. You keep popping into my stream of consciousness when I least expect it. I've dreamed of you. Gosh damn it guy, you've impressed me."

Joe felt his face warm from blushing. "It's nice to know I've impressed someone."

"Well, you have *my* attention. I've met guys from all over the world, and *no one* has impressed me like you. You're drop dead gorgeous and hung like few men I've ever met."

Joe leaned on the table and looked into Mark's eyes. "I'm a simple, uncomplicated, country boy. Gosh damn it, I'm a plumber. A guy who makes a living using his hands and breaking his back. You know, the old salt-of-the-earth kinda guy. Most of the guys you meet are rich, educated, handsome, CEOs, movie directors, well-traveled, movers and shakers, and probably full of themselves. Well . . . I'm different. Maybe that's what you find attractive about me."

"You're right to a certain extent, but there's more to you than variations on the word *simple*. You're different in a nice way. Not a bull shitter. You're a genuine, honest guy. Intelligent and wise beyond a college education. Plus, you have a body that I find difficult to ignore or keep my hands off."

"I'm just me, Mark. I like that you like me, because I'm intrigued by you, your mind, your body, and shall we say, your

142

profession. As for the body and sex thing, you could have any guy you want. Why bother with me?"

"Hell, I don't want somebody like me. Sure, you're a man, you have a cock, hell of a nice chest, killer legs, *and* your body is appealing, buy you're different in other ways than just being another bodybuilder. I can't identify the *it* I like about you, but it's there. Hell, I have lots of body-building friends, but they're not you. Speaking of body-building, I want to show you something in my room."

"What is it?"

"Something special. Very special."

"I'd like to see it, but, I know I shouldn't. If I go, I'll . . . no, we'll, wind up naked. I'd like that, but I keep wondering where is all this . . . taking me. Don't forget, I'm a family man. I shouldn't even be here."

"So? A visit can be just a visit."

Joe sighed. "So. What should I see?"

"Something special. Well, special to me. I'd like to share it with you."

"Okay but only a minute—to see this . . . thing you have. That's all"

Mark hung the Do Not Disturb sign outside his door then opened the drapes and pulled the sheets over the bed.

"Earlier, I had a Mimosa," Mark said. "There's some champagne and orange juice left. May I make one for you?"

Joe looked at his watch and smiled. "Well, it's after twelve o'clock—somewhere."

Mark prepared the drinks and handed one to Joe. Mark raised his glass in a toast. "Here's to long life and good times."

"To long life and good times," Joe said. "Now, what's this thing you wanted me to see?"

Mark removed a four by eight-inch blue velvet-covered

box from his carryon bag. He opened the box and turned it for

Joe to see inside.

"It's a medal," Joe said. "For what?"

"I won *third* place in California's Mister Muscle Contest. Third place!"

"Wow! Congratulations, Mark. You would have won first place if I was a judge."

"Not really. I didn't do anything to prepare."

"You won third prize and did nothing special?" Joe asked with disbelief.

"In my kind of business, a guy has to stay in tip-top shape. Can't sell what you don't have. I think *one* judge had the hots for me, but winning took more than his vote. I'm proud I won third place."

Joe hugged Mark. "Congratulations, man."

Mark hugged back.

Mark looked into Joe's eyes. "I'm glad you decided to come today. Been thinking about you—a lot."

Joe loosened his hug and slid his hands onto Mark's muscular butt.

"So, you want to rub my butt?" Mark asked then smiled.

Joe said, "That wouldn't be a bad way to spend part of Sunday, would it?"

"Nope," Mark said, dropping his pants.

"You still don't wear underwear."

"I told you, I don't like underwear. Too confining and bad for business. Hey, don't just stand there, get out of those clothes."

Mark stripped then jumped onto the bed as Joe removed his underwear.

"You've got a hell of a body, Joe. I've missed it. Turn around. Slowly. . . Wow! Your chest is *so* much bigger, and those thighs—deadly!"

Joe crawled onto the bed then nibbled Mark's right nipple.

"You haven't forgotten anything have you, big guy," Mark said, pulling Joe onto his torso.

"No. I remember everything you taught me."

Joe straddled Mark's abdomen, looked into his eyes and tweaked his nipples. "Feels good doesn't it?"

Mark yielded to the obvious erotic pleasure he derived from Joe's handiwork. A moment later, Mark re-turned the pleasure. Both men became lost in hedonistic joy.

Mark freed a hand to tug Joe's balls.

Joe uttered a loud "Ahhhh . . . That feels so good." *Wish Maria would do that.*

Mark squeezed and tugged Joe's globes.

"Don't stop," Joe murmured, leaning backward. *Can't believe how good that feels.*

Tightening his grip, Mark did a half sit-up and nibbled Joe's nipples.

Joe pulled back an inch or two. *I know I shouldn't be doing this, but it feels so good.*

Marked looked puzzled at Joe's reaction. He tweaked Joe's nipples again.

Joe whispered, "Damn, that feels good."

"Feed me buddy, feed me," Mark murmured, nibbling Joe's other nipple.

Astride Mark's rock-hard abdomen, Joe rocked back and forth. Mark's cock rubbed Joe's lower belly. Wresting Mark's mouth from its nipple feast, Joe pushed Mark back on the bed then raised his ass off Mark's abdomen. Taking lube from the bedside stand, Joe applied some to Mark's cock then accepted the intruder. *I know this is going to feel so good.*

A chorus of moans filled the room as Joe nibbled Mark's

145

nipples. Mark thrust his hips against Joe's reciprocating butt that gripped the promising fullness of Joe's turgidity. Like a hammock caught in wind gusts, the men moved back and forth maximizing the other's pleasure. The tempest built with Joe thinking, *I want it. I want it.*

Joe fucked Mark's fist faster and faster as he sensed Mark's approaching climax. Suddenly, Mark's hips reached for the ceiling. Joe squeezed his butt for a moment before both men shot their load. Mark took a load on his chest as Joe slumped onto Mark's chest. Mark stopped thrusting. The sweating men were sated and exhausted.

Still coupled, Mark whispered, "You never cease to surprise me."

Joe panted, "Sometimes, I surprise myself." *Damn, I did didn't I?*

"Glad you did."

"Something in me wanted you—all of you."

"And *Man*, you got me," Mark said. "Strange, I hadn't remembered you having such large nipples so wonderfully framed by that curly chest hair."

"Strange. Maria recently commented on my nipples. I don't know if she approves or disapproves, but God knows, she never worked them like you. I have a new target for sexual fun—thanks to you."

"Happy to oblige. My hands and mouth are at your disposal. Anytime. Just call. Come, let's shower."

"I'll soap your back if you'll soap mine," Joe said.

"I might be tempted to do more than that."

"Not today, good buddy. Not today."

The men showered, dried off, and then headed for bed. Mark added champagne to Joe's Mimosa then stretched out "spread eagle" and stared at Joe's face half-buried in a pillow.

"Joe, you should take your workouts more seriously.

146

You have great potential. I can see you becoming a huge guy.My competition."

"I've thought about getting bigger, but I don't like that extreme stuff—all those veins."

"Wishing won't do it. It takes hard work. 'No pain. No gain.'"

"Who knows," Joe said and winked, "one day I might be bigger than you."

Suddenly, Mark sat up, rolled Joe onto his back, and then straddled his upper chest. With the weight of his knees, Mark pinned Joe's arms to the bed. "You're getting too big for your britches, farm boy."

Joe, feigning a struggle, said, "Just you wait." *Now what?*

"You're going nowhere. Not until you've finished with these . . ." Mark pushed his balls into Joe's mouth. "Try swallowing those. Remember what your mother said, 'never speak with a full mouth.'"

Joe moaned his enjoyment of the meal of shaved scrotum and balls. After a minute of fun, Mark gave Joe a breather.

"Whoa! Whatta mouthful," Joe said. "Now I see why guys shave their balls."

"They get shaved for lots of reasons. Avoiding a Mouthful of hair is one. Another is they have a wonderful softness to them."

"I've noticed. They're soft and fun to play with—in and out of my mouth."

With a stern look, Mark said, "One of these days, we have to shave yours."

"Never thought about it." Joe dragged his hand over his hairy pecs. "I have considered shaving my chest. I can't see it very well with this hair." Joe looked into Mark's eyes. "I

147

haven't, because Maria would suspect something crazy was going on, or the guys at my gym would think I'm getting too big for my britches."

"I don't know what you know about the rules, but if you enter *any* physique contest, you'll have to shave more than your chest."

"Yeah, I know. How does that go?"

"Well, some dudes shave themselves. That's okay, if you don't have a hairy back. Other guys get their wives or girlfriends to do it. Some guys shave each other at a kind of shaving party."

"That's wild."

Mark stared at Joe's crotch. "Looks like you're getting turned on by all this shaving talk."

"It sounds hot. I can't imagine what it'd be like hav-ing someone getting you totally naked. When I first shaved my head, I got a little . . . turned on, but I ignored it."

"Think you'd get turned on if another person shaved your head?"

"Never thought about it."

Mark slapped Joe on the arm. "Shit, you get turned on in more ways than I would have ever imagined for a country boy."

"Well, we country boys know something about life even if we've never done certain things.

"In time, there will be other things to try."

"You're going to make me guess aren't you?"

"Yep," Marks said. "We can explore more but for now—guess."

"Is this your way of trying to keep me coming back?"

"Maybe. Speaking of which, when can I see you again?"

"Hell, I shouldn't be here now, but I'm exploring . . . finding out about myself. I'm a man with children and a wife.

Besides, this sneaking around is bothering me. What would become of me if anyone found out?"

"Joe, you wouldn't be the first man *or* father to realize he's gay."

Joe's felt a wave of shock move through him. "Are you calling me *gay*?"

"I'm not labeling you anything. You're just a hell of a guy that I like being around . . . having sex with."

"Okay. We did it. This might just be a passing thing, a country boy fling. Maybe you like married men, but . . . my sexuality is in question." Joe looked away. "I've never heard anyone call me g*ay*?" Joe stared at Mark. "That word destroyed a classmate of mine."

"How?"

Joe repeated the story he had told Bruce then stared at the ceiling.

"Sorry about your friend," Mark said. "Were you guys close?"

"No, just someone I knew."

"In your story, you mentioned Smithville, Ohio. Is that where you're from?"

"Did I say that?"

"You've been hiding part of your identity," Mark said then smiled. "Don't worry. I won't tell anyone in Smithville about us."

"What are you hinting at?"

"Joe, I confess. I told some people—about you."

Standing erect, Joe glared at Mark. "God, Mark! What have you done?"

"Don't worry. I mentioned you to two friends. A guy like me can't meet a guy like you and keep quiet. I had to share my happiness with someone, so I told two California friends. They'd like to meet you."

149

"That can't happen, Mark. I can't just up and fly off across the country even if I wanted to—which I don't, and I can't have gay visitors. This is Ohio. This is where my family lives. It's the asshole of the world, but its home—my home."

"Perhaps I could visit for a weekend . . . stay in a nearby motel. We could see each other while you're on an alleged emergency job or while you're supposedly at the gym. You do get emergency calls don't you?"

"Yeah, but why come to Smithville?"

"You must be a Taurus. You're the most bull headed guy I've ever met. I told you, I like being with you."

"I can't understand why a *professional* guy like you wants ta hang out with a plumber."

"Let's start with handsome, well built, killer legs, big pecs, big nipples, big cock, big balls, sensitive nipples, hairy chest, a great mouth, a shaved head, sexy. Stop me when you've heard enough. Bind all that together with mister-wonderful-glue and the result is you—*Joe*. Unique. I've never met anyone like you—*ever*."

"*If* I believed that bullshit, I'd understand why someone like you would wanna see me, but I *don't*. Let's just say we had sex and let it go at that."

"If that's what you want," Mark said, shaking his head. "I'll have to live with it, but I usually get what I want. Besides, I have great plans for us."

"Not *too* big, I hope, because I'd hate to disappoint you." *Oh God, what have I gotten myself into?* Joe glanced at the bedside clock. "I gotta start home."

"I know. I know."

Joe reached for his underwear, but Mark grabbed them and refused to surrender the briefs. Once returned, Mark snatched them again. The men continued snatch-and-grab until the game ran its course then Joe was allowed to dress.

Chapter Fourteen

Joe kept replaying his weekend as he drove to Smith-ville. He felt amused, puzzled, sad, and anxious. He had many unanswered questions about himself, his marriage, and the new male relationships. He contrasted his experiences and weighed the differences between the hot sex with Mark and the more affectionate sex with Bruce. How would they affect his future? Would either man fit into his life? Should they? To still his troubled mind, he tuned the radio to a jazz station and increased the volume to loud, drowning out road noises and troubling thoughts.

Joe threw himself into his routine of fixing leaks and opening drains, and daily workouts. Every once in a while, he had two workouts a day and drank a protein mix with meals, hoping it would help build bigger muscles.

He spent an hour each day instructing John on trumpet playing. They often practiced in the kitchen where Maria watched with pride. John had learned to purse his lips and create a good embouchure to produce pitch-perfect notes—most of the time. The accuracy of his valve fingering lagged a bit, but he kept trying.

One evening, Joe reached to assist John and strained a shirt-sleeve seam so much it ripped.

Maria said, "Joe, if you get any bigger you won't have any clothes. Those workouts are paying off, but you're spending a lot of time at that gym."

Joe sipped his beer then placed it on the table. "At that kitchen show, I saw a kid who had to be all of twenty, and he was as big as a *barn*, and I don't mean fat. His muscles had muscles. Right then I said, 'Joe, you're thirty-three.'" Joe's speech accelerated as he spoke. "I could've looked like that, but

I said, 'Look at yourself. You're almost over the hill.' I didn't like that feeling. 'Gosh *damn it*,' I said, 'I can do it. I can still do it.' So, I'm doing it. I'm giving myself a last chance to be what I wanted to be. Call it an early mid-life crisis, but I gotta do it."

"Okay, honey. Relax," Maria said, putting a dish in the cabinet then looking at Joe. "You're getting worked up. I've heard about men and this kind of situation. Sooner or later, every married woman does. I worried something other than the usual midlife crisis might be happening. I was afraid I might have competition—another woman."

Joe put his arms around Maria's waist and then kissed her on the forehead. "Why would you think there's another woman?"

"You're not here very much, Joe. You seem distant—almost cold toward me."

"Well, here's *not* another woman. Even if I wanted one, and I *don't*, there wouldn't be time."

"Well Joe, there's almost no time for me."

For a moment, Joe stared at the counter. "Honey, I'm sorry. I *promise* I'll make it up to you."

"At times, I miss you, Joe. We don't do much, but I like having you around."

Guess I've I been ignoring my duties. "How about we get away for a weekend? We can go wherever you want."

"What would we do with the boys?"

"I'll leave that part to you. Get someone in your lady's group to baby sit a few days, and then you tell me where you wanna go. I'll cover that part. Deal?"

Three weeks later, Maria announced, during breakfast, she had made arrangements for a friend to babysit the boys, so she and Joe could go to Cincinnati. She wanted to shop, see the road show *Cats,* and eat at a fancy restaurant.

Shocked, Joe dropped his fork then knocked over his coffee cup while grabbing for the fork. "Are you *sure* you wanna go there?"

"It's close. We can drive, and it won't cost much. We could stay at that hotel where you stayed during the kitchen show. You said it was nice and close to shops and The Playhouse. I'd like to see something upbeat, like a musical.

"Honey, if that's what you want, we'll do it." *Shit! Cincinnati.* "I'll get the tickets and make the reservations."

"Don't worry," Maria said, smiling. "I've been working on this with your dad and Barbara. We have tickets for *Cats* this Friday night. We'll be staying Friday and Saturday nights at The Markham Hotel. Dad and Ted will cover for you at the shop."

"Wow! You work fast, woman."

Joe felt pleased Maria had made a decision but worried about staying at the Markham because of his experiences there. What if the staff or a maid said something about seeing him and the big guy? What if Mark had business there while Joe and Maria were there?

A junior manager welcomed Joe and Maria to the Markham Hotel. "Haven't you stayed with us before, Mister Wertz?"

"I have." Joe felt his face warm red. Like a hamster on an exercise wheel, Joe's heart raced. *Oh god. What else does he remember? Maybe me and Mark—together?*

"I thought I recognized you. Welcome back." The manager smiled. "We have the penthouse unit you reserved. I trust you will find it to your liking."

Maria smiled at Joe. "I hope you don't mind. We have so little luxury in our lives. I reserved the penthouse, but it's just for two nights."

"That's fine, honey." Joe kissed Maria on the cheek.

"Whatever you want."

The manager rang a bell. A bellboy approached the couple. He took the bags and escorted them to the penthouse floor. Joe's heart almost stopped as they walked toward the room where he had spent time with Mark. The bellboy opened the door, and Maria stepped inside.

In the hall, Joe stood frozen like Lot's wife.

"Please sir," the bellboy implored, gesturing for Joe to enter.

"Come in," Maria said. "The room is *beautiful*."

Joe, fearful of appearing too familiar with the room, asked the bellboy for a tour of the space, gadgets, and services. Afterwards, he tipped the bellboy who left wishing the couple a pleasant stay.

"This is *beautiful*," Maria said, rushing to the window then holding her clasped hands on her breasts. "Look at the city. You can see the end of Kentucky." She looked at Joe, "We're going to have a *wonderful* time."

Joe looked in the mini-fridge and saw a bottle of champagne. He held it toward Maria. "Would you like a drink?"

"Oh, yes. I remember having it at our wedding."

If I hadn't had it with Bruce, I wouldn't have remembered it at the wedding. Does this mean she wants a honeymoon weekend?

Maria sat in one of the wingback chairs that faced the panorama.

Joe opened the champagne then filled two glasses. He gave one to Maria then sat in the wingback opposite Maria.

Maria kicked off her shoes. "Thank you, Joe. We should do this more often."

Joe toasted. "Here's to a wonderful weekend."

Maria raised her glass and smiled. "To a *wonderful*

weekend." She tasted her drink. "Hmmm. This tastes good."

"After *Cats*, what do you want to do for dinner?"

"Let's go someplace nice. Maybe that revolving restaurant I've heard about."

Scratching his scalp, Joe said, "It's in the Winter Hotel. I'll call the front desk. They can make a reservation for us. How about 10:30?"

"Great." Maria said, enjoying her champagne.

Joe replayed his experiences in the room. He felt joy and panic—fearful his skull would split open and spill the secrets he kept from Maria.

Twirling her empty champagne glass, Maria said, "This stuff is good, but it makes me woozy." She looked at the bedside clock. "I got up early this morning. Think I'll take a nap. Wake me at seven will you?"

"Remember, *Cats* is at eight," Joe said.

"Don't worry, I'll have plenty of time to get ready."

Joe felt tension flee his body, knowing Maria wanted a nap. He didn't have to worry about performing for her.

At seven o'clock, he nudged Maria. At first, she seemed uninterested in getting up, but Joe forced her awake. She rushed to get ready for the evening.

Joe knew the time it would take for her makeup ritual and requested a taxi in advance for the trip to the theater. The hotel clerk assured Joe it would be waiting for them at 7:30.

After seeing *Cats,* the couple made their way to the revolving restaurant on the penthouse level of the hotel. They sat at the outer edge of the revolving floor where a waiter, in formal attire, handed them menus and inquired about drinks.

"Maria, this is a special occasion. Let's have some champagne?"

"I really shouldn't."

"Ah, just a little . . . to celebrate the weekend."

"Okay, but just one glass. Oh, look at the menu, Joe. They have Lobster Thermidor. That's what I want."

Joe closed the menu. "Think I'll have crab-stuffed shrimp."

The waiter presented the bottle of champagne. Joe sampled it then nodded his approval. He then toasted Maria and the weekend.

Maria raved about the views, décor, and the attentiveness of the staff. She did not, however, protest the refilling of her glass. At one point, she took her glass and strolled along the perimeter of the revolving floor, observing the city.

"Maria, you don't have to walk around the room. It revolves."

"I got tired of sitting, Joe. Needed to stretch my legs."
She's drunk!

Maria returned to her chair as waiters placed platters, topped with silver domes, on the table. On cue, the waiters lifted the domes with a pretentious flourish.

"Enjoy your dinners" the waiters said.

"What a beautiful lobster," Maria said, "and your shrimp look delicious."

"What do you want to do tomorrow?" Joe asked.

"I don't know. Let's decide in the morning."

Because of her staggering, Joe helped Maria through the Markham lobby.

In their room, Joe stripped and helped Maria unzip her dress. He then kissed her neck.

She tilted her head as if to ask for more but said, "Not tonight, honey. I'm too tired and drunk."

Joe wondered if she put him off because she suspected

something. *Hell, I'm going to sleep naked no matter what.* He had a restless night thinking of the time he had spent with Mark in the same bed he and Maria now shared.

The next morning, Joe woke first. Naked, he made coffee and opened a container of orange juice.

Maria awoke to the aroma of fresh coffee. "Morning, Joe."

"Good morning, hon. Did you sleep well?" *Maybe I shouldn't be naked? She might think I want sex?*

"Like a baby," Maria said, walking to the bathroom. She returned smiling and sat on the bed.

"Coffee or oj?" Joe asked.

"Oj."

Joe approached the bed and held out a glass of juice.

Maria took it, looked him in the eye, and patted the bed. "Come sit with me."

Joe sat beside her on the edge of the bed.

Maria stroked his inner thigh. "I had a *wonderful* time last night. I hope you'll forgive me for drinking too much."

"There's nothing to forgive." Joe kissed her forehead. "We had a good time."

Maria continued to stimulate Joe's inner thigh. For a moment, her caress felt like one of Bruce's, or maybe Mark's. He thought of them and questioned his future with Maria. Despite his mental turmoil, Maria's caress and nature took over. He became aroused enough to satisfy her needs.

Maria, eyes closed, seemed lost in revelry.

Joe performed as images of sex with Mark and Bruce intruded. He forced himself to see Maria's face in instead of theirs but accepted his genital sensations as if produced by the men.

Joe had heard married couples often fantasized about

other people while having sex with their spouse, but images of men invaded Joe's fantasies.

Joe slowed his thrusting, hoping Maria would climax before him or they would climax together. Maria's moans became quiet yells then exploded as she quivered and wrapped her legs around Joe's waist. Stimulating her clitoris, Joe neared climax. With a few full cycle thrusts, he yelled, "AAAHHH . . . He collapsed on Maria's sweating breast as if dead. He barely breathed then panted.

Maria and he gave in to post-coital fatigue as he rolled onto the bed to relax.

After showering, the couple returned to the window and surveyed the city.

Joe asked, "What would you like to do today?"

"I'd like to shop then get a massage, a facial, and a mud thing, or whatever."

"Anything special you'd like to shop for?"

"Nothing special. Just look around those quaint shops and see what's available. I *promise* not to spend a lot of money."

Joe reached for a pamphlet on the bedside table. "Check this out. There's a shopping village not too far from here, and it has lots of interesting shops."

Maria scanned the brochure. "Looks good. Let's do it."

The shopping village had the ambiance of old Europe and funky warehouse chic. Maria and Joe window shopped at a unique store with items from Thailand, Italy, Africa, Mexico, Morocco, and Holland. You name it and the store had it. The couple entered the shop where a man, back turned to customers, worked behind the counter.

Without looking back, the clerk said, "Be right with you. Please, look around."

That voice sounds familiar, Joe thought. *It can't be—*

"Joe, look at this," Maria said, examining a tray.

Joe stood transfixed as the clerk turned and stared at him.

Shocked, Joe stared at Bruce and said, "It's lovely, Maria." *This can't be*. Feeling terrified, Joe pointed to Maria, and mouthed, 'Wife.'

Sensing the gravity of the moment, Bruce said, "Good morning, sir. Welcome to my shop. My name is Bruce. I'm the owner."

Joe extended his hand. "Hi. I'm Joe, and this is my wife, Maria."

The men shook hands, Joe's grip firm and lingering as he stared into Bruce's eyes.

"Joe," Maria asked, "do you feel all right? You look flushed."

"Think I'm coming down with a cold."

"Where are you folks from?" Bruce asked.

"We're Ohioans," Joe said. "Here for the weekend. Trembling, Joe looked around. "You have a lot of unusual stuff."

"Thanks for noticing. I take great pride in my stock. Please, have a look around."

Joe winked and asked, "Can you recommend a place for lunch?"

"There's the Village House right down the street. It has a great menu."

"How does that sound, Maria? We could do lunch in the village, and then you could go to that hotel spa. I'd like to go to that big hardware store at the edge of town while you do your beauty thing."

Still exploring the shop, Maria said, "That's fine, I know spas aren't a guy thing, and your back seems okay so you don't need the hot tub. You go to your hardware store. I'll be fine."

Bruce smiled at Joe as Maria explored the far end of

159

the shop.

Joe mouthed, 'Can you get away this afternoon.'

Bruce whispered, "Wild horses couldn't keep me here."

"Your place around two."

"Great."

Maria completed her tour of the shop, then she and Joe went to the Village House.

Heart pounding with excitement about seeing Bruce, Joe had difficulty eating. After lunch, he almost ran to the taxi that would take them to the Markham.

Joe felt instant relief when he learned the hotel spa could accommodate Maria. He would have time to visit Bruce.

Chapter Fifteen

Joe sprinted from the visitor parking lot into Bruce's condo lobby.

"Good afternoon, Joe," the clerk said. "You're expected."

Joe hurried to an open elevator. With a trembling finger, he pushed the PH button then unbuttoned his shirt down to the waist.

Joe rang Bruce's apartment bell. A split second later, the door opened. Naked, Bruce smiled then said, "Get your ass in here."

They hugged.

"How fucking wonderful to see you," Bruce said, closing the door.

"It must have been fate that brought us to your shop. I couldn't believe it—you standing there so damn handsome—even in clothes."

"Why didn't you let me know you were coming?"

Joe shrugged. "Blame Maria. I didn't know we were coming until the last minute. She said, 'We're going to Cincinnati.' I was resigned to not seeing you, but the gods had other plans. No way did I think we'd wind up in your shop. I feel uneasy about sneaking away, but what the hell? She'll enjoy the spa."

Bruce grabbed Joe's shoulders and shook him. "I can't get over how much *bigger* you are. Bruce's gaze narrowed. "You spending *all* your time in a gym?"

"Almost. Maria is starting to complain, but the gym keeps mc sane. Domestic life, *straight* domestic life, is getting to me, but at the same time, it holds me back. I just hope I don't hurt Maria too much. God, I hope she doesn't suspect." Smiling, Joe asked, "Mind if I get comfortable? I'm dying to rub your body all over mine."

"Hell no! Let me help."

Joe stepped out of his shoes then removed his socks. The marble floors felt cool to his feet. He allowed Bruce to unbutton his silk shirt then pull its tail from his pants. The shirt then fell from Joe's shoulders.

Bruce nibbled Joe's left nipple then the right one.

"Oh god, I've missed that," Joe whispered. *Keep going.*

Bruce unbuckled the belt hugging Joe's thirty-two-inch waist and six-pack. His zipper relented to Bruce's manipulations, and his pants fell to the floor, allowing the "welcoming-committee-of-one" to escape underwear prison and greet its host as Joe stepped from his trousers.

Bruce stepped back and scanned Joe's body. "Damn, man, you're so big."

"You gonna let me stand here all day in these damn underwear?"

"Yes, I mean—no. I want *you* to take them off. There's something hot about watching a man peel off his underwear—like presenting a gift."

Joe smiled then did his interpretation of a Chippendale stripper.

Bruce grinned with delight as Joe's twists and turns exposed more and more of his butt." Impatient, Bruce used his big toe to snare Joe's briefs and pushed them to the floor. He stepped out of his underwear as Bruce stepped back to peruse Joe's muscularity. Bruce then took possession of his prize.

"I don't think I've ever seen or felt you so *excited*," Bruce said, smiling.

Joe grinned. "What are you gonna do about it?" *Make it disappear some place.*

"You'll see."

Tugging Joe's balls, Bruce pulled him into the bedroom.

Backing him to the foot of the bed, Bruce put his index finger between Joe's hairy pecs then pushed him back onto the bed.

Joe squirmed to the middle of the mattress then crossed his arms over his chest, pretending to protect himself as Bruce feigned a swan dive onto him.

Bruce straddled Joe's lower abdomen then said, "You have *no* idea how thrilled I was to see you in the shop. I've thought about you a lot. Hell, I've even dreamed about us. Sometimes your head is resting in my lap and my hand is caressing your chest. We just look at each other. Ah, such sweet dreams."

Oh Bruce. What's happening between us—to me?

Bruce kissed Joe's forehead. Joe sat up, took Bruce's head in his hands, and kissed him on the mouth—a long, lingering kiss. The men's tongues explored the other's wanton void as their bodies met, melding into one writhing mass. Joe and Bruce fell onto their sides as the kiss continued. Low level moans grew louder until each man needed a breath.

"Wow!" Bruce said, surprise ringing in his voice. I hadn't expected such a *wonderful* kiss—not yet.

"Why not?"

"I don't know if I should answer.

"Please. Do."

"I've never tried to kiss you—on the mouth—even though I've wanted to."

"Why?" Joe asked, frowning as Bruce pushed Joe backwards and sat over his pelvis.

"Well . . . I was afraid to kiss a man who is questioning his orientation. You might have found it to be too . . . much. Maybe offensive. I've read that when a guy goes from questioning his sexuality to, in some cases, deciding he isn't straight—or is gay—the last vestige of his perceived heterosexuality to go is his inhibition to kissing a man—on the mouth. Kissing can happen out of lust, sexual passion, or love, or both, but it reveals a lot about a man. Straight men don't do it. Soooo, are you crossing a threshold?"

"Damn if I know, but I liked it." *Definitely liked it!*

Joe and Bruce exchanged a deep kiss as erections beckoned. Bruce moved from just sitting across Joe's abdomen to stroking his cock while kissing his chest then diverting his attention to nipples.

Joe moaned as Bruce shared his expertise in the "nipple arts." Tweaking and biting them sent Joe to sexual heaven. "Keep it up, please . . ."

Bruce's mouth and tongue explored Joe's rock-hard abdomen, his belly button, his lower abdomen, and then his crotch. Toying with Joe's erection, Bruce swallowed Joe's balls and stimulated them with his tongue. Then, trapping Joe's nuts with his lips, Bruce gave them a steady tug.

Joe moaned. "Oh god . . . that's . . . that feels so . . . ahh. Stroke me nearer the head."

Joe had experienced similar sensations when Mark had used his hands in the same way, but Bruce now combined several skills Joe had never experienced.

Wanting more stimulation, Joe grasped Bruce's cock-encircling-hand and moved it faster. Joe's free hand explored Bruce's crotch. Each shaved part touched, caressed, stroked or tugged caused Bruce's pleasure moans to grow louder. He slid onto Joe's crotch then mounted his cock. Urged on by Joe's thrusting, Bruce rode to pleasure-land, eyes closed and fucking his own fist. Returning to reality only long enough to find one of Joe's nipples, he tweaked it to Joe's delight.

For a minute, Joe tweaked Bruce's nipples then he stroked Bruce's cock. The pace of each man's activities quickened as moans morphed into grunts and inhaled hisses. Bodies sweated and stiffened as the pair neared climax. Racing full speed, they exploded. Bruce drowned Joe then thrust his arms forward, slowing his fall onto Joe's wet chest.

Both men caught their breath.

"God, you're good," Bruce said.

"I owe it all to you."

"You're a quick learner. Hope that load wasn't too hot."

"Let's say I'm an eager learner who appreciates heat, and I want my college credits."

"How'd you know my balls would like what you did?" Bruce asked.

"I didn't, but I thought I'd return the favor." Joe grinned. "Seems I made the right decision."

The men showered, and Bruce suggested they head to the terrace.

"Gin and tonic?" Bruce asked, stopping in the kitchen as Joe headed for the terrace.

Drinks in hand, Bruce walked on to the terrace to find Joe stretched out, face up, on the double wide chaise, cock semi-erect.

"Hot damn," Bruce said. "Too bad they don't make a you in a blowup doll."

"Too bad I can't do this more often."

"Yep. We have to work on that."

Bruce and Joe sat butt-cheek to butt-cheek. Each took a sip of his drink then Joe stretched out and laid his head in Bruce's lap. "How about I stay here 'til . . .?"

"That'd be fine with me, but Maria might miss you."

"Oh shit. I forgot. I'd better check in. Can I use the cordless?"

"Sure. I'll give you some privacy if you'd like."

"No. Please stay," Joe said.

Bruce handed the phone to Joe.

165

After dialing, Joe waited. "Operator, please connect me to the spa?"

"My pleasure, sir. Transferring."

"Day spa. How may I help you?"

"This is Joe Wertz. My wife, Maria, is there. I'm calling to ask when she'll be leaving."

"One second, sir . . . she just started a mud wrap that will take two and a half hours. May I give her a message?"

"Yes, please. Tell her I called. I'll see her at seven."

"My pleasure, sir."

"Thanks. Goodbye."

"Hallelujah!" Bruce yelled. "I have you for several more hours."

"I'm the one who should be yelling."

For a moment, Joe stared at several squawking birds flying overhead.

"What are you thinking?" Bruce asked.

"Strange how things happen." Joe scanned the horizon. "Who would have thought I'd be running around naked in another man's house? Especially when the other man is naked, and we're twenty-three floors up—outside." Joe looked at Bruce. "It's hard for me to believe I've had sex with a guy—and enjoyed it. It's beyond my . . . I've done things I never imagined even in my wildest dreams."

"How do you feel?"

"Hard to say. I grew up in a strict Lutheran home. Even thinking of sex was a sin. Jerking off was a sin. Having sex with someone who wasn't your wife was a sin, and having sex with a man would send you directly to hell. No short cuts. No get-out-of-hell card."

"Are you a God-fearing man?"

"I'm a believer, but I don't believe everything I've been taught. Since meeting you, I've read books about religion and

166

being gay. I liked Bishop Spong's books. They presented a different view on things I learned as a child. Some books I read were written by preachers or priests, and they didn't think a guy had to go to hell if he was gay. However, I might be in hell, if Maria, or dad, found my books or heard of my experimenting."

"Well, as you can see, we're not in hell."

"Not yet, but I'm not dead. If Maria suspected anything, I'd be dead. She'd probably *kill* me or at least try. And my *father?* He'd die, but only after he killed me. I don't know why, but he's so antigay. Mom wouldn't like it, but she'd still love me because I've given her grandsons, but then my boys are too young to understand." Joe took a sip of his drink then looked at the terrace floor. "There're times when I ask myself, 'Where is this taking me? What'll happen to my marriage and my family?' I lose a lot of sleep over this shit."

Bruce looked away for a moment. "Shakespeare once wrote 'some people protest too much' meaning there is something hidden inside themselves that they hate and project onto others. They condemn the thing and the person who is perceived to harbor the hated trait instead of confronting *it* in their own life. Maybe your father had, or wanted a gay thing, and for whatever reason, didn't or couldn't go through with it. Now he's ashamed for doing it or thinking of it. He may unconsciously hate himself for what he did or wanted to do. Now, he projects or transfers his self-hated onto gay people. Hating gays may be his way of compensating for self-hated."

"Bruce, you're one smart guy. I don't know about that psychology stuff, but I know dad doesn't like gay people. He makes no bones about it. I'm concerned he'll brainwash my sons."

"Over the years, I've known a few men, some married some with children, who one way or the other, realized they weren't straight. Each handled it differently."

"Like what?"

"Some kept it a secret—all their lives. Others were discovered one way or another. Some decided to tell their wives and families, and some stayed in denial never having man sex again."

"What happened to the guys whose family found out?"

"Again, there were several outcomes." Bruce paced in front of Joe. "In some cases, divorce happened immediately. That can be nasty if children are involved. One wife I knew tried to keep the father from seeing his children." Bruce paused to sip his drink. "I've known families, with grown children, where the wife was mentally devastated, but the children accepted the situation. Some children turned their backs to their gay father, especially if there was a nasty divorce or the wife suffered significant mental or financial ruin."

"Oh God. And the others?"

"Some families stayed together, with the husband promising to never stray again. Sometimes the wife accepts the situation and permits her husband an occasional dalliance. Those wives probably needed a stable domestic life no matter what had happened, or the wife couldn't bear having people know of *her* problem. Some wives blamed themselves for *driving* their husband gay. Such a wife wouldn't want that news getting out. Sometimes a wife can't acknowledge she made a mistake by marrying a gay guy." Bruce shook his head. "With divorce, there may not be enough money for her to survive on her own, so she makes emotional and social adjustments. So . . . all kinds of things can happen."

Joe grimaced. "You forgot to mention the case where the husband is murdered."

Bruce walked to the edge of the terrace then looked at the street below. "There're several ways to evaluate situations like yours." Bruce looked at Joe. "First, consider who will be nurtured, and who will be harmed? I think it would be difficult, and sad, for a man to deny his true identity forever. Some people commit suicide because they can't tolerate the psychological stress that comes from hiding their homosexuality. For some, it can be a painful, impossible task."

"I'm beginning to understand why," Joe murmured, staring at the floor.

"It's hard for a man to hide being gay while trying to be true to his wife or girlfriend. The pressure can break a man. As time passes, a wife or lover lose out on what is *expected* of her man, even *required*, in the give and take of marriage or a serious relationship. Philosophers say '*truth* is the first loss in a love relationship gone bad.'"

"I can see that."

Bruce sat beside Joe then stared at the sky. "Some guys say they're bisexual, and I believe such people exist but not nearly as many as alleged. In my opinion, most so-called bisexuals can't be honest with themselves."

Joe nodded. "I can understand the hurt part, but what about the nurturing part?"

"You want the whole lecture, eh? Well, a guy can hurt himself and others through denial, but honesty can be liberating *and* nurturing to one's self and others." Bruce gripped Joe's hand. "What if your Maria expected to live her entire life with you and made long-range life plans only to discover her plans will never happen because she discovered her man was gay—maybe went his separate way. Would that be fair?" Bruce rubbed Joe's arm. "Wouldn't it be better for her to know her man's secret life? She could then decide whether or not to restart *her* life plans with another man with whom she knew she had a future? Can you imagine the hurt a woman would feel if after, say thirty years of living together, she wasn't loved—just tolerated out of fear or for financial or social reasons?"

169

"Yeah, but it takes *guts* to be that upfront," Joe said, rubbing his head.

"Guts? Of course, it takes guts. But some would say such a man was selfish if he denied his wife the same choices he had secretly made for himself."

"Ouch. That hurts, Bruce." Joe paced, rubbing his palms. "You're talking about betrayal. I hate to admit it, but I guess I'm guilty."

"Well, life is what it is."

Joe paused and faced Bruce. "Were you ever married?"

"No, thank God! In high school, I dated a girl mostly because I thought I had to—social pressures. Everyone thought we'd get married. I felt pressure to propose to her, but thank God, I got a scholarship for college and moved away. We had some contact after that, but over time, the relationship cooled and then died. Hallelujah. She married someone else."

Joe thought for a moment. "I've had thoughts like that, but then I say, 'Joe, you have two wonderful sons.'"

"I know you love them, but if you had never had sons, you probably wouldn't have thought much about kids—you can't miss what you never had. Some gay guys want children and either adopt or have a lesbian help out through artificial insemination. I've often wondered if guys go through that parenting stuff because of guilt or to satisfy their parent's expectations for grandchildren. I'm not saying the guys don't love those children, but they may not be having children for the right reasons."

"You're a tough man, Bruce."

"Maybe."

Sitting down in a chair at the far end of the terrace, Joe shook his head. "What the hell am I gonna do?"

"Only time will tell."

Joe sipped his drink. "As Kermit the frog said, 'it's not

easy being green.'"

"Enough of this serious shit." Bruce pointed to Joe's glass. "How's your drink?"

"I could use more ice."

"Coming up. On second thought, how about you get the ice? I want to watch your butt and then your jostling crotch as you come back."

Joe grinned as he took slow, deliberate steps toward the door. He over accentuated the shifting of his weight from hip to hip. Grinning, he looked back at Bruce, smiled and then disappeared into the apartment.

Minutes later, he stepped onto the terrace, carrying a glass of ice. He made sure his cock and balls had room to swing as he sported a toothy smile. "How is this?"

"Oh God, yes! I'll even take some ice."

Bruce patted his chair cushion. "Come sit . . . With all that time you're spending in the gym, are you thinking of contests or just trying to please *me*?"

"To please you of course, *and* maybe enter a contest. I've been thinking about entering a competition. You know what they say, 'if you got it, flaunt it.' Whatta you think?"

"Depends on what you're flaunting and why."

Joe sighed. "I think I'm having a mid-life crisis—at age thirty-three. Maria and me, we don't talk like we used to . . . maybe because of my situation. I didn't talk about lifting, because Maria doesn't care for it—not 'til lately. Marriage, children, and work interfered with my earlier bodybuilding plans, but ever since I saw the pride parade, I've thought of being what I wanted to be when I was eighteen. So . . . yeah, I'm thinking about physique competitions."

"Then, *go* for it."

"I'd have to shave my chest."

"Hell, that's nothing."

"You wouldn't mind?"

"It grows back. You'd have to shave your pubic hair as well, even your balls, if you wear those smaller posing trunks—which you should. You don't want ball hairs sticking out."

"Shit. Hadn't thought of that. If I did, Maria would suspect something for sure."

"Make her part of your plan. Let her know you're thinking of entering a contest and tell her you'll be temporarily losing some body hair. Don't mention shaving your crotch. Just say body hair. If she doesn't mind, you might get her to do the shaving."

"God, NO! I *don't* want her shaving me. She can't shave her legs without needing a blood transfusion. *IF*, I do enter a contest, maybe *you'd* do the honors—the first time."

"I'd be honored."

Looking at his watch, Joe said, "I hate to say this, but I gotta get, or Maria will kill me. She hates tardy people, including me."

"Sorry you can't stay longer, but I'm glad we had this time."

"I'm the one who's happy." Joe slapped Bruce on the back. "Let's keep in touch."

In the foyer, Joe put on his underwear, but as the waistband reached his crotch, Bruce pulled the briefs down. "I need a moment more to admire that bod."

Chapter Sixteen

Sipping champagne in their room, Maria glowed as she regaled Joe with the details of her spa day. "I feel like a new woman."

Joe felt less guilty, knowing Maria had had a good day.

That evening, the couple dined at a swanky restaurant then took a long walk. Back at the hotel, Maria let Joe know she wanted nothing but sleep.

Joe also had much on his mind, but sex with Maria was not one of them. Sleep eluded him. He wondered how much longer he could bear the weight of his secret.

Four months later, Joe continued to receive longing phone calls from Bruce. Joe wanted to visit him but resisted, showering more attention on his sons. Despite his busy routine, Joe never missed trumpet practice with John.

In the meantime, Joe had found a gym near his new plumbing shop. He struck up a friendship with two guys as serious about workouts as he. He threw himself into his lifting routine with the intensity of a top gunner. Even his dad commented on his muscular size.

One Friday morning, Joe received an unexpected call.

"Joe, it's your old friend, Mark. How are you?"

"What a surprise. I'm fine. What are you up to?"

"I'm in Cincinnati, seeing a longtime client. I was wondering if we could get together this weekend."

"Sorry Mark." *Glad I have an excuse.* "I'm taking my boys fishing Saturday."

A long silence followed, and then Mark said, "Hmm. Maybe I could go fishing with you."

"I don't think so, Mark. How'd I explain you to the boys, and we wouldn't have any private time—even if I wanted it."

"I'd settle just to *see* you. Come on. Think about it. Say yes. Pleaseeee."

Shit! "I'll think about it." *Don't think I can do it.*

"Deal. I'll wait for your call, but don't make me come out there and get you. Okay? Bye."

Joe could not concentrate on work. Thoughts of Mark whirled in his head. Over and over, he mulled ways to reject the invitation and then how to accept it. Most of the acceptance plans were rejected, but he finally decided on one that would allow him to see Mark then called him.

"Mark, it's Joe."

"I know. Your name came up on my screen. What have you decided?"

"I shouldn't, but I wanna see you. Here's my plan. Get your GPS and find where Ohio's rural road 13 intersects rural road 128. At that intersection is an abandoned farm. In the back is a large pond. The boys and I fish and sometimes swim there. Be at the gate at noon tomorrow. I'll tell the boys you're a friend from my gym. Please, keep everything simple, low keyed. I don't want them thinking something weird is going on. You'll need to bring a fishing rod. Oh yeah, don't be surprised if my boys stare. They've never seen a really tall guy and certainly not one built like you. Secondly, you better not be damn pedophile."

"Joe, you know I like boys—thirty-three-year-old boys. The plan sounds good, but how will I get you naked?"

"I have a plan."

"Okay. Looking forward to seeing you—*all of you*—tomorrow."

"Please, don't pull up in a Rolls Royce or anything fancy. I'd have trouble explaining it."

"Will do. I mean I won't. Well, bye until tomorrow."

That night, Joe told Maria that a gym-friend would be

joining him and the boys on Saturday's outing. He invited Maria to join the group, believing and hoping she would decline. She did.

Next morning, the family prepared for the outing. Maria prepared sandwiches and fried chicken for lunch, along with milk for the boys.

The boys giggled as they watched Joe hide towels in the car's trunk where he had packed extra beers.

Joe squirmed on his seat as he drove to the pond. Palms sweating, he shook inside as he thought about seeing Mark.

Turning onto Route 13, he saw a grey Chevrolet parked at the farm's dilapidated gate. It had been opened.

As Joe stopped at the gate, he saw Mark's head resting on the headrest. Joe tooted his car horn. Mark waved, and Joe drove through the opened gate. He motioned for Mark to follow. He did then closed the gate as Joe waited a hundred feet ahead. Joe led the way along an almost non-existent, overgrown road that wound its way through tall trees to the three-acre pond.

"Is that your friend, daddy?" John asked.

"Yep. His name is Mark. He's a nice man. Remember to be polite."

Mark pulled alongside Joe's car parked in the shade. The boys jumped out of the car and ran toward the pond. Joe and Mark grinned while walking toward each other. They engaged in an exaggerated manly hug followed by back slapping and hand shaking.

The boys approached Mark with slow, measured steps.

Joe corralled his sons at his knees. "Boys, I want you to meet my friend. This is Mister Mark. He's the tallest and strongest man I've ever known. Behave yourself or I'll have him take care of you. Understand? John, shake hands with Mister Mark."

"Howdy, Mister Mark," John said, extending his small hand while using the other to shield his eyes from the sun as he stared skyward into Mark's face

Mark offered his meaty index and middle fingers. "Nice to meet you, John. How are you?"

"Fine."

Joe turned to his other son. "Okay, Paul, shake hands with Mister Mark."

This time, Mark extended his index finger toward Paul.

Craning his neck to look skyward, Paul said, "Howdy, Mister Mark. How big are you?"

"Well, hello, Paul. Do you mean how tall am I?"

"Yes, sir."

"I'm six feet nine inches tall. How tall are you?"

Turning to Joe, Paul asked, "Daddy, how tall am I?"

"You're going on six feet."

Smiling, Paul turned to Mark. "Dad says I'm goin' on six feet."

The adults laughed.

Mark moved beside Joe, slapped him on the back, and let his hand slide onto Joe's butt where it lingered for a moment.

Joe patted his sons on the shoulder. "Okay guys. It's time to go fishing."

"Let me help unload the car?" Mark said.

Mark and Joe's hands touched often as they passed rods, beers, the worm bucket, and food.

Joe whispered, "Careful with the hands, Mark. I have a plan."

"Good. I don't know how much fishing I can take."

The men carried their fishing gear to the edge of the pond. Joe and then the other guys took off their shirts.

Paul looked at Mark's massive chest. "Mister Mark, are you Mister Marvel's brother?

"No, but I've met him."

Paul yelled to his brother. "John. Mister Mark knows Mister Marvel!"

Mark and Joe chuckled over Paul's excitement.

Joe got sunscreen from the trunk, then rubbed it on the boy's backs, faces, back of their arms and legs.

"Rub it on your chests and the front of your arms and legs," Joe said, pouring oil into each boy's hands.

Smiling, Joe turned to Mark. "Will you rub oil on my back?"

Mark rubbed oil on Joe's shoulders, his back, and then inside the back waistband of Joe's shorts. Startled, Joe pulled away and frowned. Mark withdrew his hand and grimaced.

"Thanks for oiling *all* my back," Joe said, sounding perturbed.

Handing the oil to Joe, Mark turned his back. Joe oiled Mark's shoulders then moved his hand down Mark's back until it reached the waistband of his shorts. Dropping the bottle of oil, Joe said, "Damn! I dropped it." Joe pushed his hand inside Mark's shorts and grabbed his ass while using the other hand to pick up the bottle.

Mark chuckled.

The guys drowned lots of worms, resulting in one nibble on Paul's line. Fish were seen swimming beneath the red and white float that bobbed over Paul's hook, but none took the bait.

After rebaiting their hooks several times, the sun had stolen their shade. The group stood under a searing sun.

"Daddy," Paul asked, "I'm hot. Can we go swimming?"

"Yeah, can we go swimming?" John asked.

"Mark, how'd you like to join us in a swim?"

"Last one in is a monkey's uncle," Mark said, unbuttoning his shorts.

The race to strip resembled people hurrying to remove

burning clothes. The boys finished first. They dashed into the water, ignoring the adults.

Joe and Mark scanned each other's body.

Joe noted Mark's cock stiffening. "For god's sake, get in the water," Joe said in a loud whisper.

"I'm not the only one," Mark said, glancing at Joe's crotch. "I can't help myself. It's nature."

Mark stood pubic hair deep in the water then dunked himself to cool off. "The water feels good. Come in, Joe."

Joe dove into the pond. "This feels great." He submerged his growing boner then admired Mark's body. Beads of water, sparkling like jewels, outlined every oiled, muscular curve of his ripped, shaved body from the waist up. *I can't believe a man can be so hot.*

Joe cupped his hands then yelled to his sons. "Listen up guys. Why don't you have a race? Mark and I will swim to the log we used last time? Paul, you swim first, and I'll time you. After Paul, it'll be your turn, John. All right?"

"Okay, daddy," the boys yelled.

Joe and Mark swam toward the log three hundred feet away. This gave them a chance to talk. With every stroke, they touched a part of the other's body.

"Joe, if you touch me one more time, I'll get the world's biggest periscope."

"Glad I can help," Joe chuckled. "Just keep it suberged. I'll check your submarine parts later."

The men reached the log, dived beneath it, and then resurfaced on its other side. Joe propped his elbows on the log; Mark followed his lead, causing the log to bob beneath them.

This is a beautiful place," Mark said, scanning the grove.

"Yeah. We're lucky to use it."

Joe yelled, "Paul, on the count of three swim as fast as you can. One . . . two . . . three."

As Joe started his stopwatch, Mark grabbed Joe's balls. The grope startled Joe into a yelp heard across the county. John must have thought his father had shouted encouragement to Paul and joined in the vocal support.

Mark dived then sucked Joe's cock.

God, that feels good. Joe enjoyed the attention for a moment then took Mark's chin and pulled him to the surface.

"I was just starting to have fun."

"God, Mark, we gotta be careful! I told you about our limitations." Joe grinned then said, "I didn't want you to drown."

"Okay." Mark said, treading water.

Halfway to the log, Paul lost steam, and his pace slowed.

Joe yelled encouragement. John, still on shore, added his voice to the cheering.

Mark moved behind Joe and rubbed his short pubic hair against Joe's butt.

"God that feels good, but where's the bait?"

Mark rubbed his cock deeper between Joe's butt cheeks. "Here's the bait. Want it?"

"Yes. No. This is *not* the time or the place." Joe looked at his stopwatch then yelled to Paul, "A few more yards, son. Swim faster."

"I'm trying daddy, I'm trying," Paul mumbled, gasping for air.

Joe stroked Mark's cock and unintentionally completed an underwater demolition project. Climaxing, Mark yelled and exited the water like a submarine surfacing during an emergency.

"Damn," Joe said, "I didn't realize you were so close."

"What can I say? You did it."

"I know *you* liked it, but I feel cheated," Joe said.

"The day's young," Mark said. "Who knows what's to come. Pardon the pun."

Paul stretched his arm, touched the log, and Joe stopped

179

his watch. "You're fast, son. You finished in eleven minutes and thirteen seconds."

Mark lifted fatigued Paul from the water and sat him on the bobbing log, facing John who waited on shore.

Joe looked at Paul. "Whatta you say for that lift, son?"

"Thanks, Mister Mark."

"You're welcome, Paul. That was quite a swim.

You're going to be a great racer."

"Last time, I beat John didn't I, daddy?" Paul looked at his father for confirmation.

"Yep, you did, son, but John is looking stronger today. You may have to give up your title."

"That's okay, daddy. Why don't we let him win? I don't wanna win *all* the time. That wouldn't be fair.

"We'll see, son."

Mark smiled. "Joe, you have wonderful kids."

"Thanks. I love them dearly." Joe then yelled, "John, are you ready?"

"I'm ready."

"Okay, on the count of one . . . two . . . three!"

John swam with all his might as Paul cheered him on.

Mark sneaked a fast underwater tweak of Joe's nipple then grabbed Joe's crotch.

"Wow!" Joe said.

"Are you okay, daddy?" Paul asked.

"I'm fine. I think a fish nibbled my toe." Joe looked at Mark. "Fish, you'd better stop nibbling."

Mark nodded. "I'll get that dang fish." He dived then swallowed Joe's cock and tugged his balls.

Joe shuttered. He took Mark's chin and pulled him to the surface.

Mark said, "I killed that fish."

Joe sneered. "I hope he doesn't come back."

As John approached the log, the guys cheered. In two lunging strokes, John touched the log. Joe announced John's swim time—eight minutes and forty-eight seconds.

"You win," Paul said, grinning.

"Thanks, daddy," Paul whispered, probably thinking his dad had under reported John's swim time.

John hung onto the log, catching his breath.

"Boys, why don't you guys swim around while I and Mr. Mark discuss gym stuff."

The boys swam toward shore, stopping a few times to dunk each other while yelling and laughing along the way.

Joe looked at Mark. "I don't know what I'd do if the boys found out their dad played around. If it got out, they'd never be able to go to school—not where we live. Bullies would hound them for having a queer dad."

"Maybe you should start a low-keyed educational program. Let your boys know gay people are okay."

"I can't do that—not now, and don't you."

Mark shook his head. "Don't worry. I won't say a word."

"It's *actions* that worries me. We have to be careful."

Suddenly, Mark pulled Joe beneath the surface and kissed him, Joe kissed back then resurfaced.

"I've been waiting for one of those," Mark said.

"What?" Joe asked.

"A kiss."

The boys were beyond the point where they could see actions below the log, allowing Mark's and Joe's hands to explore the other's body. They engaged in intense, crotch grabbing and mutual nipple-play.

"God, I'd forgotten how much I liked that nipple stuff," Joe said, "especially the way you do it."

Mark tweaked Joe's nipple and tugged his balls.

"You've got a day to quit," Joe said.

Mark added to Joe's pleasure through intense nipple-tweaking and ball-tugging as Joe pleasured himself. "Damn, that feels so good."

"Joe. Don't jerk off—not here. I'll take care of that later."

"But I wanna cum."

"I know but wait, please."

Mark swam a few feet away then looked at Joe. "I hadn't mentioned it before, but you're getting bigger. I mean above-the-waist bigger."

Joe bounced his pecs. "Glad you noticed. Been working out twice a day with two friends who push me. I'm pleased with my progress. I'm thinking about entering a contest."

"Great. Let me know the date, time, and place. I'd like to see how you do."

Joe grabbed Mark's crotch then pulled him under the water. Mark returned the favor. The submerged men kised then surfaced.

Mark said, "On my way here, I noted a small motel. Could we get together there tonight?"

"I can't be seen at a local motel. Everybody around here knows me."

"It's one of those places where the office is out of sight of most of the rooms. I could get a room on the private side and drive you there. I'd pick you up from a spot of your choice. Tell Maria you have an emergency plumbing job, or you're going to the gym or whatever. You still do plumbing don't you?" Raising his eyebrows, Mark stared at Joe. "Pleaseee?"

"I'd like to, but it's crazy doing stuff close to home. Let me think about it."

Joe floated on his back, spewed water from his mouth like a statue in a French garden. He glanced at Mark. "We should get back to shore. See what the boys are doing. You make sure you aren't *up* to anything."

"Don't worry. The periscope is down."

The men swam close to shore then treaded water near the beach.

The boys used towels from the trunk to dry off but remained naked, wading and looking for tadpoles.

Joe watched his sons explore the shore. "Look at them. I love their innocence. Bible thumpers have yet to teach the boys that naked is bad. They're just enjoying the sun, the water, and nature—having fun. Oh, to be a kid again."

The men waded out of the water.

"I'll get our towels," Joe said.

Mark stopped drying. "Can't say I'm not taking note of *your* nakedness, my friend. God, what a body you're developing."

Ignoring Mark's comment, Joe said, "I bring the boys here for several reasons. Gives us a chance to be father and sons and me a chance to get naked without Maria yelling. The boys and I don't tell her we skinny dip."

"This place also gives *me* the opportunity to be naked with you."

"Yeah, but I wish we were alone."

"Give some thought to the motel idea."

"I'm thinking."

Joe stopped drying and stared at Mark. "Put on our shorts and shoes then follow me."

"Boys, Mister Mark and I are going to the old farm house. I need to inspect things and report any new problems to the owner. Promise you'll stay right here 'til we get back. If you need me, blow the horn. Okay?"

"Okay, daddy," John said without looking up from the water.

"Joe, are you going to leave your sons here—alone and naked?"

"Don't worry. This isn't LA with a predator behind every tree. We're miles from another person. They'll be fine."

Joe led the way past overgrown remnants of an asphalt driveway. Ten minutes later, the men reached a dilapidated two-story house whose white paint had grown greyish black due to mold. All the window glass had been broken and several shutters hung from one rusty hinge. The metal roof over the front porch had rusted through.

"This was home for a farming family of eight," Joe said, surveying the ruin. "The only surviving child, a man now age eighty-four, lives in a nursing home in Smithville. He's given us permission to use the pond. After each visit, I look around the property and report its condition." Joe pointed to a fifteen-by-fifteen-foot square doorless wooden shed. "That's the old smoke house. Its floor is still intact."

The men stepped inside the tree-shaded building, taking a few moments for their eyes to adapt to the light-starved space.

Mark took a deep breath. "I think I can smell the hams that used to hang in here."

"God only knows what that smell is," Joe said, grabbing Mark's right nipple. He tweaked it for a second then, with his other hand, grabbed Mark's crotch.

Mark gripped Joe's nipples. "I see why you brought me here, you dirty old man."

Each man lingered in the pleasure generated by the other's hands.

Mark kissed Joe. He kissed back. The men's French kiss stole the other's exploring tongue while wanton lips tried to engulf the other's head.

Mark released Joe's nipples then pushed his shorts down. Mark kissed his way across Joe's chest, his nipples, and then his abdomen. Tugging Joe's balls, Mark's swallowed his cock.

"God, that feels good," Joe murmured.

Joe moaned as Mark swallowed his cock. Mark wanted every inch of Joe and swallowed with such energy he seemed intent on exsanguinating him. Joe grasped Mark's head and held it on course. The dilapidated smoke house rattled with sexual excitement. The moans of the men mimicked a winter wind blowing through the walls shielding them from nature's eye.

Joe's body straightened then stiffened. He stifled a scream of pleasure and gripped his abdomen while experiencing a pleasure he had never before felt as he climaxed.

Mark's hungry mouth lingered in place, draining all Joe had to give while enjoying the pleasure he had given and received.

Joe took several long, slow breaths and then went limp, leaning against a timber. "Wow!" he exclaimed. "I've *never* experienced anything like that."

"Me neither," Mark said, standing. "I owed you that from the pond."

"And I'd like to return the favor?"

"You can but not now. I'd prefer to have sex with you on a motel bed. I don't want you getting splinters in your belly."

"Neither do I, but we should get back to the boys."

"Okay, but do me a favor?" Mark asked.

"What?"

"Don't put your shorts on until we get near the far edge of the farm house. I want to admire that butt as you walk. It's too hot to be covered out here."

"Alright. As a special favor this one time."

Joe led the way, making sure his ass moved as expected. Every other step, Mark pinched or slapped Joe's muscular butt.

As the men neared the farmhouse, Mark hugged Joe's waist and pulled him backwards against a hard cock.

"Do *me* a favor," Joe asked. "Rub your pubes against my butt. I love that sensation."

Mark rubbed his bare crotch against Joe's hard butt. Mark's cock slid between Joe's butt cheeks. "We'll settle matters tonight," Mark whispered then kissed Joe's neck.

At the fishing spot, Joe's boys were still naked. They searched for lost treasures in the pond's shallow water. Clapping his hands, Joe yelled, "You've had enough sun. Time to get dressed and head home."

"Do we have to," John whined.

"Yes. Get dressed now. Your backs are red enough."

Mark and Joe dressed then gathered the fishing gear.

Each boy shook Mark's hand and said their goodbyes. Joe and Mark went through a series of manly gestures, chest and shoulder bumps, and then hugs.

Leaving for the motel, Mark led the way off the property and waved goodbye.

Their plans called for Mark to phone Joe, alleging a plumbing emergency. This should prevent raising Maria's suspicion. They planned to meet at 7:00 p.m. near the intersection of two rural routes where truck drivers often stopped to nap. From there, Mark would drive Joe to the motel.

Chapter Seventeen

Joe's family gathered around the kitchen table where Maria presented them with a pizza dinner. "Hope you guys don't mind pizza, but I got home too late to cook."

"Pizza's fine," Joe said, taking a bite.

The boys told their mother about fishing and their disappointment at not catching any. They made no mention of Mister Mark or skinny dipping.

As time passed, Joe grew anxious about the planned rendezvous. He questioned his sanity and whether or not he should risk meeting Mark.

Wolfing down a slice of pizza, Joe stared at his watch held under the edge of the table—6:23. After what seemed like a month, his watch read 6:30. Joe held his breath waiting for the phone to ring. Nothing. He looked at his watch at 6:34, then 6:38 and then 6:41. Still no call. He wondered if Mark had gotten cold feet. Joe peeked at his watch—6:43. No call.

"Joe, don't you like the pizza?" Maria asked. "You're not eating."

"It's a little greasy and doesn't sit well on my stomach."

At 6:46, a call to the shop phone switched to Joe's home phone. Maria answered, listened for a second, and then handed the phone to Joe. "Somebody needs a plumber."

Joe took the phone and listened.

"Sorry, my phone died," Mark said. "I couldn't find my charger until now. I didn't want to use the motel's phone and have its number come up on your phone and create problems. Can you still meet me?"

"Certainly, sir. I'd be happy to help, but there's a surcharge for afterhours service." Joe listened for a while then said, "Very well, sir. I can be there in twenty, twenty-five minutes. Fine. Be there shortly."

Turning to the family, Joe said, "A plumbing problem. A wet one. I'll see you guys later. Boys mind your mother 'til I get back."

Joe raced to the rendezvous spot. He scanned the shadows of the lot and saw Mark's grey Chevrolet parked far in the back.

Joe parked in the shadows created by the full moon then locked his doors. Hugging the tree line, he made his way past several cars and idling eighteen wheelers with sleeping drivers. On reaching Mark's car, Joe got in, and then the car sped off for the motel.

"Glad you could get away," Mark said, gripping Joe's thigh then his crotch.

"I'm shaking like a leaf," Joe said. "I've never sneaked out like this."

"Take a deep breath—relax."

Joe unbuttoned Mark's shirt then reached inside for Mark's nipple, and tweaked it with near-accident-causing pleasure for Mark. "You have an hour to let go."

Mark groped Joe's crotch.

"Wait," Joe said, unzipping his fly to allow Mark's hand inside his pants.

"I can't believe you're so *up*," Mark said, gripping Joe's throbber then pulling it through the opened fly.

"Hell, I was about to burst out of my pants.

Nearing the motel, Mark dimmed his car lights. Joe slouched in the front seat to avoid possibly being seen.

Mark's car crept to the back row of rooms and then stopped in front of a first floor door.

"Wait a couple minutes then come in," Mark said.

Mark entered his room and left the door ajar and lights off.

Minutes later, Joe darted into the room and closed the door. Mark turned on the bedside lamp to reveal himself, sitting naked on the bed.

Eyeing Mark's chest, Joe chuckled, "Damn, how'd you know what I wanted for Christmas?"

"Santa knows everything, little boy. Come here, you big son-of-a-bitch."

Mark stood then hugged Joe as if he hadn't seen him in years.

"Thanks for being naked. I never get tired of seeing that huge chest. The rest of you ain't bad either."

"Likewise, I'm sure. Now, you get naked."

Observing Joe's every move, Mark asked, "Have you noticed as your chest grows, your nipples move closer to the lower outer edge of your pecs?"

Joe looked at his nipples. "Oh."

"I love the way your chest hair curls around them, but that nipple location begs for a mouth. Come here."

Mark pulled Joe close then nibbled and tongued his nipples.

After a few seconds, Mark looked Joe in the eye and said, "You wouldn't believe I'm really a leg man."

Before Joe could reply, Mark kissed Joe's massive right thigh near his erect cock.

Mark's lips and tongue found their way to Joe's cock. He reveled in the pleasure soon joined by Mark's tugging on Joe's balls and ass play.

Moaning, Joe grabbed Mark's head and whispered, "Take it easy. I'm too hot."

"Okay." Mark patted the bed. "Come, lie beside me."

Crawling over Mark, Joe's balls swung near Mark's face. He grabbed the low hanging nuts and used them to pull Joe's butt onto his chest.

Joe stared into Mark's face and smiled. Joe then lay beside Mark who continued to hold Joe's balls.

"Guess I'm caught," Joe said.

The men lay parallel to each other, manipulating the other's balls. Suddenly, Joe sneezed, giving Mark's balls a sharp tug.

"Now that's what I like," Mark said. "Love that tension."

"That didn't hurt?"

"No. They *like* rough handling."

"Really?"

"Yeah."

Mark moved Joe's thumb and index finger into a circle around Mark's balls and then placed his hand over Joe's hand and pulled it hard, stretching Mark's balls.

"Got it," Joe said, stretching Mark's balls.

"God, that feels good."

"It doesn't hurt?" Joe asked.

"I love it. You can do that all you want, and If you don't want to, do it anyway. I love it, and I've noticed you like your balls stretched too."

"A bit."

"Want to try something different?"

"Maybe . . ."

"Remember, I told you there are lots of things to try. Now is a good time to experiment."

Joe scrunched his face. "Okay. I guess. What the hell? I'm game for whatever you're thinking about. I know you won't kill me."

"Stand up and close your eyes."

Joe stood beside the bed eyes closed. "Now what?" He heard rummaging sounds in what he presumed to be Mark's travel bag. Sounds of jingling metal ensued.

"Keep your eyes closed."

"Okay, but I hope you're not going to chain me to the bed and leave me here."

"We can try that later," Mark chuckled. "No, this is something else. Bear with me, but keep your eyes closed."

Joe felt his balls being manipulated and sensed something cool and firm being placed around them. He detected the faint smell of leather.

"Okay. Open your eyes," Mark said, looking at Joe's crotch. "It's a 'parachute.'"

Joe stared at a small leather "parachute." A hole in its top allowed his balls to dangle inside the chute. The conical piece of leather had two chrome snaps that keep its shape. Dispersed around the lower edge of the chute were three, six-inch-long small-gauge chains connected to a one inch metal ring below the chute.

"Now what?" Joe chuckled. "I can't use it to jump out of a plane."

"Bear with me. Put on this mask."

"What?" Joe asked. *Now what have I gotten myself into?*

Mark held out a black sleeping mask. "I want to keep everything a surprise."

Joe donned the mask. "Maria has one of these, but hers is pink silk."

Mark did more rummaging while stroking Joe's cock.

"That stroking feels good, but are you doing something with the chute?"

"Shhhh. Just savor the sensation. Tell me what you think?"

Joe felt something heavy pulling down on his balls as Mark continued to stroke his cock. "That's feeling good."

"Let's establish a baseline for what you like—okay?"

"I guess." *Whatever he's doing I like it.* Joe felt a

stronger pull on his balls. He moaned with pleasure. "I can't believe how good that feels. How about more of whatever that is?"

Mark heeded the request, but Joe now squirmed.

"Whatever that is, it's too much."

"Shall I back off a little?"

"Yeah. A little."

"Done. How is that?"

"Hmmm. Feels good, but I'm not sure if it's the ball tension or your talented hand."

"Probably both."

"Can I look now?"

"Sure. Take off the mask."

With disbelief, Joe eyed the apparatus dangling from his balls. "Are those fishing weights?"

"Yep, plain old fishing weights."

"I can't believe you hung all that on my balls."

"The point is you like stretched balls. Learn to know what you like and go for it. Now, try walking slowly but keep your legs spread."

Joe took a few steps, watching his weighted balls swing back and forth. He looked at Mark then smiled. "I dig this. Do you ever wear weights?"

"Yeah," Mark said. "I have another chute. Let me weight up and join the party."

Mark snapped a chute on his balls then added more weight than Joe wore. Mark moaned his pleasure and caused his weights to swing in a small circle.

"Damn!" Joe said. "Your balls can take a lot of frigging weight. Gives new meaning to the term *weightlifting.* Man, I love the way your nuts stretch. Look at 'em. I didn't know nuts could stretch so low."

Sounding officious, Mark said, "Technically my balls

don't, but my spermatic cord does."

"What the fuck is that?" Joe asked. "Never mind. I love the feeling."

Glad you like it but enough talk. Give me a kiss."

The men engaged in a passionate kiss to the sounds of colliding weights rising from their crotches.

Joe backed away and tugged at his chute. "I like the sensations, but the weight is a bit much."

"You've handled a lot of weight for your first time. It took a long time before I could wear weights for long periods—sometimes an hour."

Pointing at Mark's balls, Joe said, "You've worn that much for an hour?"

"Yep, but sometimes I get so hot I beat off right away. Let's take this stuff off. We can wear it later."

"No," Joe said, "I'd like to leave the chute on but with less weight. What other tricks do you have in that bag?"

"Up for more, eh?"

"You're the teacher. Teach me." Joe wondered if any straight guys ever did this or did he like the ball toys too much.

"How about some nipple toys?" Mark asked.

"Uh. Okay. Do I have to close my eyes?"

"Just for a minute."

Eyes closed, Joe again heard rummaging and the rattle of chains.

Mark kissed Joe's right nipple then tweaked it.

"Love it," Joe moaned as Mark attached his surprise.

"Wow," Joe exclaimed, jerking his head back.

"Keep your eyes closed." Mark repeated the foreplay with the left nipple then attached another surprise.

"That's different," Joe said. "I like it. Can I look?"

"Okay."

Joe stared at a fourteen-inch length of small-caliber

chain suspended from a clamp that gripped each nipple. The clamps had black rubber tips and a pressure adjustment screw. "Cool," he said.

"I can adjust it so there's more pressure if you'd like."

"Okay. Do it."

Mark tightened each clamp a quarter turn.

"Wow!" Joe said. "Okay."

Mark stroked Joe's cock and said, "It's even better if I rub *this*."

"Slow with the hand but tighten the clamps a little more," Joe said. Panting, he dropped his head backwards. "Oh, God. I can't believe how good that feels. It sends shocks from my chest through my belly to where you're rubbing."

Mark tightened the clamps another quarter turn.

Joe moaned then said, "A little more."

"How about I pull on the chain?"

"Okay."

Mark gave the clamps a quarter turn then tugged the center of the chain.

"Oh God! I love it. I love it, but I can't take any more. Get them off."

Mark released the clamps.

"Awww!" Joe yelled. "Damn! That hurt."

"Don't worry. You'll be a little sore, but it soon goes away. Next time we'll add weights to the chain and see how your nipples like that."

"Weights?"

"Yep, but let's take a break."

Joe crawled onto the bed and adjusted his ball weights. "I can't believe there's so much pleasure locked inside me."

"All you need is a teacher to let it out."

"I know you have other goodies, but I'm afraid to ask what they are."

"Don't worry. There's time for *all kinds* of new things."

"I don't know if I like the way you said that."

"Oh, shush. Roll over and I'll rub your butt—I mean your back. The other stuff I mentioned requires toys too big to get into a bag."

Mark sat on the back of Joe's thighs then grabbed a bottle of lotion. He poured a dab onto his hands then rubbed it on Joe's back.

"That feels great. Keep it up, man."

Mark massaged his way to Joe's butt. Both hands lingered on the right cheek then kneaded it before moving to the other cheek. "You have a *killer* ass, Joe."

"Glad you like it."

"Like it? I love it. It's the softest hard ass I've ever felt and the only plumber's crack that has interested me." Mark slapped each butt cheek. "But yours is no crack. It's reminiscent of a path through a French garden or a proud Venetian canal."

Feeling Mark's hot cock against his ass, Joe squirmed his butt. He lifted his hips to take pressure off his balls squashed under his ball weights. As Joe adjusted his hips, Mark rubbed lotion on his cock then guided it along the plumber's crack. Joe uttered a low whine, stiffened, and then moaned with ecstasy. Mark had entered Venice.

The men rocked to and fro as Mark plumbed the depth of Joe's expectations. Sometimes, Mark pulled his cock free then teased Joe's ass. "Fuck it," Joe moaned, his butt moving upward in search of Mark's cock. Recoupled, Joe moaned, "More. More." The slapping sounds of crotch on butt vied with moans and grunts of pleasure.

With a final burst of energy, and sweating profusely, Mark yelled. He stiffened and then trembled as he climaxed. He collapsed on Joe's back as Joe squirmed his butt and tightened his ass to maximize Mark's pleasure.

Exhausted, Joe said, "God, I love having you inside."

Mark whispered, "Wish I could get closer, my friend."

A hush settled over the room.

Mark broke the quietude. "Let's try out the motel's shower, and then have a beer. I stocked the mini-frig."

"Sounds good."

The men showered then returned to the bedroom where Mark opened two beers. Joe reattached his chute and took a gulp of beer. Naked, Mark and Joe fell spread eagled on the bed. Each exhaled a long, slow sigh.

Joe began to chuckle.

"What's so funny?" Mark asked.

"This room. I mean the way it's done up—if you can call it that. Reminds me of the house we just bought. Right out of the sixties—or so I'm told. We're still stripping foil wallpaper."

"I assume you mean you and Maria?"

"Yep."

"How's the chute feeling?"

"Good, even if it's not swinging."

"Which contest do you think you'll enter?"

"I haven't decided yet but something small. After all, I'm not Mister America."

"But you're well on your way, my friend."

"I've put on some size, but the thing that worries me is posing. I've been looking for how-to-tapes, but I haven't found any."

"Then you haven't looked in the right places." Mark fluffed his pillow. "Goolge professional bodybuilders. Most of those guys sell videos showing their posing routines. Many have *special* DVDs on posing. Hell, you can get DVDs where the guys pose naked. Everybody knows they aren't *instructional*— just soft porn for guys, or gals, who want to see big naked men. Unfortunately, most of the pros use steroids, and that stuff causes their balls to shrink. Some guys pad their briefs just to look normal on stage."

"Really? Just to win a contest?"

"For some guys, it's more than winning a contest. The huge guys make big bucks getting naked for people or doing endorsements."

"Yeah, like the protein powder I buy. Some of the pro guys' pictures are on the label."

"That's just one thing," Mark said, turning onto his back. "*Some* of the straight *and* a lot of the gay winners discover they can sell their bodies to the highest bidder—men and women. Getting it on with a huge man, even with small balls, can be a turn on for 'Johns' *or* gals. They pay big bucks to fondle a big guy—handle his body."

"I can't imagine anyone paying to handle me."

"Just be aware. Even if you *don't* win first place, some-one will try to buy you, your body or your . . . whatever. Contests provide new faces and possible contacts for perverts wanting to do strange things. Don't be surprised if a stranger asks to photograph you. Some requests can be an opener to get you naked—and more. If you *do* pose for a stranger, never, never pose naked. You might find your picture being sold on the internet."

"Sounds like you're trying to discourage me from competing."

"Not at all. Just telling you to be aware. If you want to prove yourself by competing, then do it, but remember why you're working so hard and giving up so much—family time included. Well, so much for that. Have you done any posing?"

"In the gym—when I'm alone. There's a big mirror and lighting. It's a good place to practice."

"Well then, let's see what you got."

"Here?"

"Why not? You'll never get a better judge or more friendly advice. Give it a shot."

"Should I take the chute off?"

"Not if you like it."

Adjusting his chute and weights, Joe did a posing routine. He felt he didn't do a good job because of the way Mark made strange faces, but Joe waited for the critique.

Mark said, "Play up your strengths, downplay your weaknesses. You have killer legs, a definite strength. Show them. Your chest's thick and strong. Show it."

Joe attempted several more poses.

With Mark's input, Joe's posing improved.

Mark continued to coach. "Keep it up, big guy. Turn your chest more to the audience—I mean me."

Joe turned and struck his pose.

"That's it. Tighten those biceps, your pecs—tighter. Flex them with all you got. Work your forearm back and forth. Make that bicep work. Ball it up, man." Mark moved to a chair and continued his critique. "When you show off your 'six pack,' bend at the waist. Tighten the abs and then try to stand up while holding that slightly bent, *flexed* position."

Joe did as instructed.

"That's it," Mark said, praising Joe's efforts.

"Wow!" Joe huffed. "This posing stuff is hard work."

Mark clapped in appreciation of Joe's efforts. "You bet it's hard work, but good posing can add points to your score—bad posing will cost you. Let me get my camera. I'll take some shots so you can see what you look like from an audience's view point. Okay?"

"Sure."

Mark dug through his bag then pulled out a digital camera. He asked Joe to pose in front of the burgundy drapes.

Joe practiced the techniques Mark had taught him.

Naked and still wearing his 'chute,' Joe focused on movements which flowed from pose to pose.

Mark took several photos in rapid succession. "It's like a dance, Joe. Feel the rhythm. You're a musician, hear a melody in your head and match your posing to it. Mentally choreograph your posing to the beat of the music. Before going on stage, ask the emcee to play music that best suits your routine. Better yet, take your own disc."

Mark took photo after photo until Joe slumped with exhaustion. "That's enough."

"Okay, rest. Drink your beer, and we'll screen the photos on my laptop."

"Great, but this chute is getting to be too much."

"Let me unsnap it."

Unsnapped, the apparatus fell to the floor with a thud.

"Whew. That's better."

Mark booted his laptop then pushed the camera's memory card into the computer's card slot.

Joe sat on the bed and watched as Mark pointed to parts of pictures where Joe had posed correctly and where he hadn't. "These are a big help—even if I'm naked *and* wearing a chute." Joe laughed and slapped Mark's thigh. "Don't sell them on the Internet."

"Here. Take the memory card," Mark said. "Look at the photos when you have time. Note where you're doing things right and the shots where everything is wrong. You decide what needs changing and then do it."

"Gosh darn, Mark. It's getting late. I'd—no we'd— better get going."

"Joe, I can't let you just leave. It wouldn't be hospit-able."

Mark pushed Joe back onto the bed, spread his muscular thighs, and then fell to his knees between Joe's legs. With one hand, he gripped Joe's balls and delivered a mouthful of pleasure to his cock. Ball tugs plus skillful tongue twirls had Joe squirming.

Joe clutched his abdomen as his hips lifted off the bed. "God, that feels good." He panted and moaned, holding his breath longer and longer. With his pelvis reaching for the ceiling, Joe uttered a muffled yell and shuddered. He moaned as if he had entered heaven, and then the room went quiet as death.

"Damn," Joe said, panting. "I can't believe I've experienced that sensation twice in one day. You must have had a *special* college course for that mouth work."

"Just years of observation, my friend. Guess you're ready to head home, huh?"

"Yeah, better get going. Maria will worry. I've been gone too long."

"Okay. Let's get you home."

As the men walked in the shadows toward Mark's car, Joe heard footsteps behind him.

"Good evening, gentlemen," a woman said.

"Shit," Joe muttered.

Joe then Mark faced the voice.

The woman walked closer. "Well, good evening, Joe. What're you doing here?"

"Irene, do you own this place?"

"Yep, for about a year now."

Joe gestured toward Mark. "Your guest dropped his ring down the drain and couldn't get it out. He found my twenty-four-hour ad in the yellow pages and called me. 'Said he had to leave early in the morning and needed to get the ring out tonight.' He offered a bonus *and* he came and got me. Now he's taking me home."

"Thanks for being so helpful, Joe, but I wish Mark had called *me* first."

"Madam," Mark said, "I didn't want to upset you, and I didn't want a plumbing truck pulling up to your motel and you thinking I'd wrecked the place. I just wanted to get my ring, and I did with Joe's help."

"Irene, I did a quick off and on of the elbow trap. Everything is like before."

"Thanks, Joe," Irene said. "Have a good night. Say hello to Maria for me."

Shaking in his socks, Joe entered Mark's car. "That was a close one," Joe whispered. "Maria and Irene are friends. I'm surprised I hadn't heard she bought this place, but don't let anyone say you're not quick on your feet, Mark. That was a good story."

"I've been in some embarrassing spots in my checkered life. I have to be resourceful, if you know what I mean, but you did well yourself."

Mark pulled into the shadows of the parking lot where Joe's car waited. "I want you to know I had a wonderful time meeting your boys and sliding all over you at the pond."

"I've never had such a wild day. My nipples will remember it for a long time. So will my balls. By-the-way, thanks for the coaching."

"When can I see you again?"

"Hard to say. You know my situation—the risks like Irene. Who knows what could have happened there. I don't dare do this again. Let's talk once in a while . . . see what happens. Time will tell."

"I hear you, but I want you to know I dig you, man. I want to see you again, soon. Remember, I don't like hearing *no*." Mark squeezed Joe's thigh. "Good luck with your workouts. You're doing great. Keep me posted about the contest. Okay?"

"Will do. Thanks and goodnight."

Chapter Eighteen

A beautiful fall morning dawned over Smithville. Joe's kitchen buzzed with activity as he read the newspaper and enjoyed his first cup of coffee. He ignored Maria's favorite country song on the radio, but his ears perked up when he heard the announcer mention Smithville. He turned up the volume.

"Maria, come listen."

The announcer continued, "As part of his reelection campaign, President Plant will tour local farms and businesses throughout the day. He's expected to visit Smithville's Main Street in the afternoon next Wednesday."

"This is the day we've been waiting for," Joe said, "but I'm surprised the government didn't tell us earlier. Sure you don't want to come, Maria?"

Maria placed Joe's breakfast on the table. "I have no interest in meeting a windbag."

Joe dabbed toast in his egg yolk. "Well, I'm taking the boys. I'll get them at school."

After a morning workout and completing a number of small plumbing jobs, Joe dressed in clean work clothes, picked up his sons at school, and then headed to the Smithville shop. He wanted to be there well ahead of the president's planned visit.

An hour later, the president's motorcade pulled onto Main Street. Joe, Don, Barbara, John, and Paul waited in the shop's parking lot.

The town's few remaining shop owners lined the streets, hoping to speak to the president.

Minutes later, a motorcade of four black SUVs stopped in front of the Wertz's plumbing shop.

Surrounded by Secret Service and media, the president stepped out of his car, waved to the cheering crowd, and then pushed his way toward the plumbing shop. He stopped to shake hands, pose for photographs, and chat with locals. When he stepped onto the Wertz's parking lot, he pointed to its business sign. "Ladies and gentlemen, look at that. A father and son business."

Joe, John, Paul, Don, and Barbara, waited in front of the shop's main door flanked by two secret service men.

As the president got closer, Don and Joe took a step forward.

The president said, "Wertz and Son. It's great to see family values are alive and well in Smithville." The president faced Don. "Are you the shop owner?"

"I am."

The president shook Don's hand.

"Mr. President, I'm Don—Don Wertz. This is my son, Joe, and his sons John and Paul. This lady is Barbara, our secretary."

The president shook everyone's hand then stood in the middle of the group for a photo.

"Thanks for coming out to greet us," the president said. "Don, how are things in the plumbing business and the local economy?"

"Not too bad, Mr. President," Don said, speaking just above a whisper.

Joe couldn't hold back. "Mister President, things are tough. People are losing their jobs." Joe waved his hand toward the street. "As you can see, lots of stores are closed. We've just expanded our business, and we're having trouble getting a loan to carry us over a rough spot. America needs you, *or someone,* to help the little guys. We're all for family values, sanctity of marriage, and that stuff, but we need help—real dollars and cents help—not just words. We need *real* help. Our town is dying."

The crowd cheered as cameramen moved in for close-ups of Joe.

"Now, that's what America needs," the president said, clapping and flashing a false looking camera smile. "We need more men like you, Joe. Someone to speak up and keep politicians on the straight and narrow. God-fearing, family-loving spokesmen. Joe, do you have any other words of wisdom?"

"Mister President, I'm afraid of that other guy. Don't go the route he's going or you'll not get Smithville's votes."

"Joe, rest assured I'm not going to." The president looked Joe in the eye. "You seem to have your finger on America's pulse, and you aren't afraid to speak up. Maybe we can talk later . . . get your drift on how things are going. Could we do that?"

"Absolutely, Mr. President!" Joe felt shock on hearing the request. *Can't believe he's asking me.* "Anything to help."

"Well, thank you, Joe, for taking time to educate us on the needs of Middle America. You *will* hear from us. John, Paul, do well in school. Don, good luck with your business. Have a great day Barbara."

The president walked a hundred feet along the street, greeted a few more locals, and then left town.

The gaggle of TV and press guys returned to the shop to interview Joe. After thirty minutes of questioning him about politics, the economy, and his religious affiliations, the press left him and his friends to catch their breath.

That evening, Joe and his family sat in their den, waiting for the local TV news to begin. The station used several preview photos of Joe with the president throughout the program preceding the news. Not until near the end of the news broadcast did the station air Joe's story.

"Look, there's daddy," Paul yelled and pointed to the

TV. "Daddy's on TV!"

Joe moved to the edge of his recliner and held his breath.

"They've held the best till last," Maria said.

The station presented a photo of Joe and the president shaking hands.

"I can't believe you're on TV," Maria said, clapping.

After commercials, a video showed Joe talking to the president outside the shop. The editors retained little of the interview dealing with the economy. Instead, they reported Joe's religious beliefs, family values, and his thoughts about protecting the sanctity of marriage. The commentator's voice-over noted Joe's values meshed with those of the Republican Party and how Joe might become an advisor to the president.

"Damn!" Joe said. "The bastards omitted the important economy stuff."

"And they didn't show Paul and me," John said.

Maria said, "I told you guys. The media is just like the politicians. We get what *they* want us to have. They don't care about what we want."

Suddenly, Maria screeched, "Oh look, Joe, you're on national TV!"

Joe switched from channel to channel, watching the same interview on the major networks.

Minutes later, neighbors phoned to congratulate him.

Over the weeks following Joe's national TV appearances, he received numerous calls, comments, emails, and letters from admirers, and detractors. He shrugged off the attention, thinking it would soon pass.

A month later, Joe received a phone call from the office of the president's reelection campaign. "Joe, could you spend a few days, touring the Midwest with the president?"

"When do you need an answer?"

"We need you to say *yes* today. You've already been vetted from our visit to your shop."

Joe thought for a minute. "Can you call me back in an hour?"

Joe phoned his father. "Dad, can you meet me and Maria at our house right away?"

Don and Maria sat motionless on her new sofa as Joe paced, presenting the campaign manager's request. They reassured, even pressured Joe to go. They would take care of things at home.

A few minutes after the family conference, Joe's phone rang.

"Joe here."

"Joe, this is George at the president's campaign office. Please hold. I'm going to transfer you to Jim King, the president's campaign manager. Please hold."

"Hello, Joe. Jim King here. Tell me you'll join the president's tour?"

"What do I have to do?"

"What you did when you were interviewed outside your shop."

"And expenses?"

"Don't worry. We take care of everything."

"And hotel?"

"We *promise* good hotels and good food."

"I don't have any fancy suits."

"All you need is the clothes you wore when you were interviewed. Clean ones of course. You looked good in that t-shirt. I guess you work out a lot, huh?"

"Twice a day."

"We'll see to it that you get to a gym every day. Do we have a deal?"

"Okay. Anything to help America."

"Great. People are already calling you the president's plumber. I'm sending a limo for you at 5:30 in the morning. You'll be driven to Cincinnati, board a chartered jet, and then fly to the next campaign stop. I look forward to seeing you tomorrow."

"Okay. Bye."

Joe turned to Maria. "*Damn,* these guys move fast. They're sending a limo in the morning, and I'm going to fly on a *chartered* jet."

Don slapped Joe on the shoulder. "Congratulations, son."

"Wow!" Maria said. "That's wonderful. You're gonna be famous—the plumber from Smithville."

"No, Maria. People are calling me the *President's Plumber*. Can you believe that?"

"What do I have to pack for you?"

"My usual t-shirts, jeans, and work boots—clean ones. The weather's still nice, so I won't need a coat. Oh, I'll also need gym clothes."

"I'll start packing," Maria said. "Call your mother and tell her the good news."

Waiting for the limo, Joe and his household shook with excitement. Sitting at the kitchen table, he finished reading the paper, glanced at his watch, noted the half-finished painting of the kitchen walls, and then sipped his third cup of coffee.

"I can't believe I'm gonna fly in a chartered jet." he said, looking at Maria and then at his scrapping boys.

"Daddy, you gonna be famous," John said as Joe separated his scuffling sons.

"Who knows, son, but settle down."

Just then, the limo arrived.

Several of Joe's neighbors waited on their front porches

to see him off.

Exhausted from nerves and lack of sleep, Joe slumped against the car's soft, black-leather seat then fell asleep. Before long, traffic noise woke him. Peering out the window, he noted several distant Cincinnati landmarks and wondered what Bruce might be doing.

The limo pulled onto the tarmac of the Cincinnati Executive Airport then stopped alongside a jet. Its engines were running, ready for departure.

An attendant, standing at the head of the steps, greeted Joe as if he was a VIP. "Welcome aboard, Joe. Since you are the only passenger, choose any seat and buckle your seat belt."

"Belt?"

The attendant assisted Joe in securing the seat belt for his first flight.

"Thanks. The president's not on board?"

"No sir, he flew ahead on Air Force One."

Damn. I thought I'd get to talk to him on the way.

Breakfast did not sit well on his nervous stomach, so Joe declined the offer of food, wine, and liquor.

He settled into his leather lounger and peered out the window. As the plane took off, he held his breath, gripped the arm rest, and left his worries behind.

Joe's plane arrived at a location unknown to the public. He disembarked then entered a waiting limo that would take him to a briefing venue.

During the day, he met dozens of people who wanted to shake his hand.

He overheard a female campaign worker talking to Jim, the campaign manager. She said, "You couldn't have found a better blue-collar representative for middle America. Look at that chest."

209

For the first time, Joe felt uncertain as to why he had been chosen by the president. Could it be that he, a simple plumber, personified "blue collar" men, or he looked good in a t-shirt?

Joe made twenty-seven campaign stops. He gave interview after interview about his family, family values, marriage rights and, to a lesser extent, his views on the economy. He rarely spoke to the president who joined or introduced him only four times.

Joe did not mind that no one asked him what America had to do to improve its economic slump. He wished he had the answer, but he did not. Nevertheless, he wanted the issue discussed.

At every stop, photographers snapped multiple photos and took videos of him doing everything except crapping. The front page of many local and national publications displayed his picture, and TV producers found novel ways to broadcast his image. His photos became as ubiquitous as grass.

At the end of his sojourn, Joe returned home to cheering neighbors and friends. He lowered the limo's window and waved to well-wishers who lined his street.

He did not expect to hear his neighbors had planned a party for him, but he had put their small town on the map. Reluctant to go, he agreed to attend the affair.

In Joe's honor, banners, bunting, and the American flag bedecked the town's Victorian bandstand. The high school band played patriotic music, and the Lutheran Lady's Aid Society served protestant-punch.

After an hour of celebrating and listening to too many speeches, Joe felt weary. He excused himself then retreated to the comfort of his home. He didn't leave the house for several days, avoiding reporters who hung around waiting for an interview.

A week later, Joe had cabin fever and decided he needed to return to work. He exited the house, ignoring reporters, and sped away.

In his second shop, Joe noted an increased number of completed work orders. He asked Terry, his secretary, "Did my being on TV help business?"

"We've been swamped and so has your dad."

"Well, I'm tired of that TV shit. I need a break. Where should I go?"

"We just got a flyer for a trade show in LA. You could write it off *and* take the family. Universal Studios would be a nice surprise for Maria and the boys."

Taking the flyer, Joe went to his office, leaned back in his swivel chair, and stared at the ceiling. *It'd be nice to get away for a while. Take Maria and the boys. Maybe hook up with Mark.* Joe righted himself. "Better check with Dad."

The next day, Joe visited the old shop. After a hug from his father, Joe said, "Dad, I know you've been covering for me, but I'm mentally beat. I'd like to take the family to Los Angeles. I'll attend a trade show, and the family will do tourist things. The boys will love Universal Studios . . . Would you mind covering for me for another week?"

"I don't know how you politicians can do all that moving around every day. Go. Take the trip. We made lots of money while you were on TV. Your touring was good for business so go. You've earned it."

Joe chuckled. "Glad to know I'm good for something. I saved the money I got for touring. It'll more than cover our expenses."

"Want me to get Barbara working on the reservations?"

"That'd be great, Dad, but *don't* tell Maria. I wanna surprise her."

Three days later, Barbara told Joe to be ready to travel in two days. She had e-tickets for his flights, and he would stay at the Hollywood Bowl Suites.

"Looks like a great family place," Barbara said, handing Joe a printout about the hotel. "You'll have two rooms with a kitchen, a pool, airport pickup, and breakfast included. It's also close to lots of things. The reservations are for the weekend before and after the trade show. With all there is to do in LA, you might be mentally rested, but after all that touring stuff, you may be physically exhausted."

"Thanks, Barbara."

"You're welcome," she said, picking up a jelly donut. "Just relax and have a good time with the family."

Now, what about Mark?

That evening, Joe informed the family they were going to Los Angeles, and the boys would get to go to Disneyland.

Maria almost fainted. Looking ashen, she asked, "Can we afford it?"

"Absolutely. I saved my tour money. Besides, my being on TV boosted business income. We had a lot of new customers and more in the works. While you guys tour, I'll spend some time at a trade show, so much of the trip is tax deductible."

Paul raised his hand. "Are we rich, daddy?"

"No, son. Far from it, but we *can* afford a good time."

"Are we really going to Disneyland?" John asked.

"Yep, and you'll see lots of other interesting places."

Joe further surprised his family when he told them he had hired a limo from Portsmouth. "I want you guys to know how it feels to travel like what dad calls the *big boys*, even if it's just a ride to the airport."

Chapter Nineteen

Saturday morning, a black limo waited at the curb of the Wertz's home.

The chauffeur stowed the luggage, then drove the family to the airport. Joe's sons entertained themselves by watching TV and playing with the buttons and levers controlling the gadgets in the passenger compartment.

At the airport, a counter agent flashed a smile too wide to be genuine. "Good morning, Joe. I see you're going to LA. I'm happy to tell you that your family is upgraded to first class for the round trip."

For a moment, Joe felt stunned. "Wow. Thank you."

"It's our pleasure, Joe. Take these vouchers to our private lounge and enjoy breakfast before your flight."

"Thank you, Frances," Joe said, eyeing the agent's name tag. "I didn't expect this."

Maria appeared all atwitter. "What's going on, Joe? Why is she so nice?"

"Guess it has to do with me being on TV. Let's check out that lounge."

After clearing security, Joe made his way to the lounge where he presented his vouchers to the receptionists.

"Welcome, Joe. Please, enjoy our club. I'll let you know when it's time to board."

Maria, John, and Paul were google-eyed as they scanned the room. There were several plasma TV sets distributed around the lounge, a bar, a buffet area, and a phone-free room.

"Enjoy this experience," Joe said to his family. "Who knows when we'll do this again." *This looks more like a rich man's living room than a waiting area.*

Excited, Maria said, "Let's see what's on that buffet."

Just then, Joe's phone rang. He stopped to take the call.

"Joe, this is Bruce. How are you?"

"I'm fine. A little tired from that campaigning stuff but otherwise okay. Did you see me on TV?"

"I saw a lot of you. You must be worn out."

"You can say that again, but how are you?"

"Same old, same old."

"Yeah? Right now, the family and I are in the airport. We're on our way to LA for a trade show and some R&R."

"Remember, I told you I go to gift shows? Well, tomorrow I'm leaving for LA to attend a gift show. I called to see if you could go with me, but look, you're going be there anyway."

Joe walked out of ear shot of his family. "Wow. I don't know how, but I'll find a way to see you if it kills me."

"Careful. What good is a big, hot stud, if he's dead?"

"Where are you staying?"

"The Vine Hotel, in Hollywood. And you?" Bruce asked.

"The Bowl Suites in Hollywood."

"I know the place. A family spot. My hotel is two miles away."

"That's wonderful."

"I'll call when I get there. Have a great flight."

Maria got the boys settled in the hotel while Joe explored its amenities. He phoned Mark, thinking they could have a drink.

"*Joe*. Glad to hear from you."

"I'm in LA."

"What? Why didn't you tell me you were coming?"

"Hell, it was almost a surprise for me, but I'm here— with the family."

"Family, huh? That might be good for you but not me."

"Don't worry. I'll work out something. Just wanted to let you know I'm in town—at the Hollywood Bowl Suites."

"That's a good location—not too far from my new house. You've got to see it. I have lots of things to show you."

"Did you get the Harley?"

"Yep. Can't wait to take you for a ride. You sitting behind me with your arms around my waist, holding on to—"

"A good time?" Joe asked.

"Maybe more. *God,* I can't wait to see that hot bod. Are you bigger?"

"Yeah, in one place just from talking to you. Seriously, I'm a little bigger, but I'll let you be the judge of that."

"Can't wait to see you—all of you—but when?"

"My weekend's shot with family stuff, but the trade show, which drew me here, starts Monday. Maria and the boys are touring then, so we could get naked that afternoon."

"I'll try not to get too greedy about your time, but I'm anxious to see you. I could pick you up Monday, on the Harley. We could have lunch then see the new house. How does that sound?"

For a moment, Joe wondered what people might think if they saw him clinging to a man on the back of a Hog. "Uh, Okay. See you Monday at noon in front of the east entrance to the convention center."

"Great. I saw a *lot* of you on TV. Congratulations on making it so big, but please get off that family values stuff. It's *killing* me. I know you love *your* family, but there are things like gay rights that are important to other families—g*ay* families. Don't forget, yours may be *half* gay."

"I don't know why the TV people and politicians focused so much on that family stuff. I wanted to talk about financial things, but everybody else wanted to talk religion and gay shit. Oh well. Changing the subject, see you Monday."

"Monday it is."

Joe returned to his family with information about the amenities of the hotel and several brochures detailing tours.

The family took the afternoon *Hollywood Stars' Home Tour*. It required no walking and a good way for a tired family to spend their first day.

Joe had reserved Sunday for Disneyland. He reveled in seeing his sons enjoy the park's attractions. Even he enjoyed the rides. The experience reminded him of his sixteenth birthday at the Ohio fair where Maria gave him his first kiss. Today, Maria hung onto his arm as they wandered among the attractions.

Every fifty-feet, Joe stopped to shake hands with a fan and sign an autograph.

Monday, before leaving for the convention center, Joe registered Maria and the boys for the *Avenue of the Stars and Theaters Tour*. Afterwards they would visit the famous tar pits to see real dinosaur bones.

At the trade show, Joe registered and picked up his information packet. He entered the convention hall and strolled its aisles. He looked for new market-makers, shook a few hands, and autographed various objects. Anxious to see Mark, he wondered if noontime would ever come.

At the appointed time, Joe hurried toward the meeting spot. Peering through a large window near the exit, he saw Mark. He wore black slacks and a revealing grey muscle-shirt. He leaned on his black and chrome-laden Harley parked at the curb.

Joe wondered if the Harley or Mark's good looks had attracted the group gathered at the curb. Perhaps, some of them thought Mark might be a movie star.

Joe hurried to the curb. He and Mark hugged like long-lost brothers.

"Put on this helmet and we'll get out of here," Mark

said. "These people are crazy. They think I'm famous."

Joe mounted the rear seat then hugged Mark's waist as he kick-started the engine. Its roar rattled windows.

"Floor it," Joe said. "Let's go before someone recognizes *me*."

To be heard, Joe yelled in Mark's ear, "This isn't the first body part I wanted to hug."

"Just keep hugging and pretend it's something else," Mark shouted over his shoulder while threading the Hog through traffic like a drunken sailor.

"Where we going?"

"A biker place. They do a great lunch."

Joe's ride came to an end at the Road Hog Café. Mark parallel parked next to a line of Harleys then greeted several Hog riders.

Inside, Joe selected a table that overlooked the valley. Two guys, dressed in leather, kept staring at him and then Mark.

"Clients of yours?" Joe asked then grinned.

Mark looked up from his menu. "Yeah."

"Do you think they think I'm a client?"

"Maybe. Maybe not. They might think we're looking for someone who wants to buy a *ménage a trois.*"

A waiter took the men's orders and soon returned with their food. Small talk abounded, but most of it focused on Mark's visit to the fishing pond and Joe's political escapades.

"Okay," Mark said. "Lunchtime's over."

"My. You're in a rush."

"Hell yes. I want to get you naked."

Mark drove Joe through LA's nicest neighborhoods. Finally, they entered Mark's neighborhood, which he declared to be in positive transition.

"I converted this small warehouse into a modern home

with three garage spaces—all with remote-controlled doors."

Mark pulled into the motorcycle bay where Joe dismounted then removed his helmet. Mark gave Joe a long kiss.

"Wow!" Joe exclaimed. "That was hot." *Hadn't expected that.*

"Couldn't help it. I'm so glad to see you. I've missed you something *terrible*."

"Nice to see you too."

"There's so much to do," Mark said. "I want to show you the house, but I first want you *naked*, and then I'll give you a tour."

Joe chuckled. "Isn't southern California too cold to run around naked?"

"Not my California."

The guys wasted little time stripping. Each gave the other a grope, a hug, and another kiss.

Mark stepped back and eyed Joe's body.

"What's wrong?" Joe asked.

"Nothing. Absolutely nothing. I'm just admiring that big, beautiful naked bod. You *are* getting big, my friend. I mean *really* big. Your pecs are thicker than ever and that cleavage. Wow!"

Joe flexed his pecs. "Thanks for noticing. Don't forget, you're my inspiration."

"Happy to help but how is your posing coming along?"

"Well, I ordered the DVDs you suggested. When I get time, I play them on the office computer. They're helpful. Maybe I could do some posing while I'm here and get your feedback?"

Shrugging, Mark said, "How could I refuse an offer to watch a buff, naked man strut his *stuff*?"

"Maybe that too," Joe chuckled.

Mark squeezed Joe's stiffening cock. "Okay. We can

play later."

"Sounds good."

"Choo choo," Mark said, pulling Joe's crotch like a locomotive pulling a load uphill. "Come along little train."

Mark pulled Joe to the main part of the house. "It's tour time."

Chapter Twenty

Awe struck, Joe admired Mark's eighteen-foot-high ceilings. *This place oughta be in one of those fancy magazines.*

The epitome of modern design, the room had chrome, glass, brick, and acres of Italian leather furniture defining sitting areas. Castle-size antique furniture contrasted the stark lines of the contemporary decor. The walls were hung with large, colorful abstract paintings. Skylights and track lights abounded.

"You've built yourself a hell of a bachelor's pad."

"Thanks. Just wish I had someone to share it."

"With all the contacts you have, there's no reason you couldn't fill this house with big, admiring naked guys."

"There's one guy I'd like to have move in, but he's not available . . . not at the moment."

"Do you know why he won't?"

"I think so," Mark said, looking skyward.

"Isn't there something you can do. Use logic. Or better yet, turn on your charm."

"I don't want to be too bold—might scare him away. You can't force love. It just happen."

"Well, I wish you luck," Joe said. "I'm pulling for you."

"Enough of this. Let's get back to pulling on your crotch. Let me show you the pool."

Joe followed Mark toward the back of the house. They walked into a roof-less space flooded with bright sunlight. "This had once been a room, but I converted it into this atrium with a swimming pool." Stucco walls, thirty-feet high, surrounded the space. In the far corner stood a cabana containing a wet bar, rcfrigerator, gas grill, fire pit, lounges, and a shower.

"I had the roof removed to let in sunlight. It's a great place for nude sunbathing, parties and orgies." Mark smiled large. "Here, I can make all the noise I want without disturbing neighbors."

"Gosh, Mark. You got everything you need here—except a gym."

"Ah ha. Let me show you something."

Mark walked to a door beside the cabana and pushed it open. "Come in."

Joe stepped into a room containing multiple gleaming weight machines, tons of free weight, barbells, dumbbells, and every other contraption needed for serious bodybuilding. A mirror-lined wall added to the brilliance of the space.

"Wow. Is this open to the public?"

"No way. I just don't like leaving home for a workout. I have friends over from time-to-time, but this is for me. I work out here before I see a client. I need to be pumped for them. That's part of the fantasy clients buy."

"This definitely is a wow space. I'm happy for you, but like you said, too bad you don't share it with someone special."

"Well, you've seen my workout space. Would you like to see my *work* space?"

"Hmmm. I think so," Joe said, feeling unsure. What's the difference?"

Mark walked to the center panel of the mirrors lining the wall then pushed the top of a mirror. It sprung open like a medicine cabinet. Behind it, Joe saw a wooden door. Mark pushed it open to reveal a dimly-lighted room.

"Come in," Mark said, entering the space.

"Damn. A Secret passageway," Joe said as he entered and adapted his vision to the room's low light level.

"Few people, you among them, know of the connection between the gym and this room."

"What is this place?" Joe asked, scanning the room. "What's all that stuff on the walls?"

Arms extended, Mark turned three-hundred-sixty

degrees. "This is my workspace. Others call it a dungeon or place of *pain and pleasure*. Clients don't know my home is just one secret door away."

"You use this stuff on your clients?"

"Mostly clients. I've rented it to a few porn filmmakers and a few S & M partners, but it's primarily for private customers." Mark pointed to a dungeon-like wood and iron door. "Clients enter there. Its exterior surface is ordinary looking, because it opens to the street."

Walking to the right side of the room, Mark pointed to another door. "That's the client's room. In there are showers, lockers, a massage room, and a waiting area." Marked entered the room then looked back at Joe. "Don't be shy. Come in."

Mark pushed the door farther open, permitting a gush of cool air to flow past.

Joe looked around the shadowy room for a moment. "Smells like eucalyptus oil."

"You guessed it," Mark said.

Joe returned to the dungeon. "I know you travel to some of your clients, but what kinda people come here?"

"A strange mix," Mark said, fingering a wall hook. "I find it interesting that some of the biggest, most muscular guys want someone to tie them up, beat them, humiliate them, and on and on. Lots of little guys want to do the beating. Some guys want to be chained or tied and left helpless for a while. Some restrained guys get so worked up they shoot their load without any physical stimulation." Mark examined two leather restraints. "Over time, I've discovered that having a guy sit naked in the waiting area, longer than expected, gets them hot and horny. It's the anticipation, I guess. Sometimes, I play videotapes of things clients want to experience. Boy, do they get hot! I can watch them on this closed-circuit TV."

"I'm thinking you're one of those watching guys."

Kinda weird though.

Mark straightened some hanging whips. "Hell, I'm into everything."

"It's kinda hard to believe." Joe said and nodded toward one corner of the room. "Don't tell me that thing with a black cloth is a dining table."

"Not in the strictest sense even though I've eaten a few things on it. It's padded and big enough to handle two people on top. It's covered with a fabric that simulates leather but isn't damaged by liquids.

Joe dragged his fingers over the fabric. "Feels a little like a raincoat."

Mark pointed toward different areas of the table. "The rails along the sides are for restraints. These two sections can be removed from the top for *special* entertainment." Mark patted the table top. "It's good for wrestling, shaving, massages, fucking, whipping. You name it."

"This is beginning to seem a little creepy, but I better understand your business. It's hard to believe you get *paid* to use this stuff."

"Yep. I'm paid to give clients what they can't get from friends, lovers, or relatives. I also insure anonymity and confidentiality. Clients have to be referred."

Joe shook his head. "Man, I need a drink. I wanna clear my head of this room and think about you, the biggest, most beautiful chunk of muscle I know. Besides, we don't wanna *waste* that expression of interest you've grown."

Joe grabbed Mark's crotch and pulled him through the gym to the patio bar.

Joe dived into the pool as Mark opened a bottle of champagne. Treading water, he watched Mark's cock and balls swing back-and-forth as he walked along the pool's coping then place two champagne-filled glasses near water's edge.

224

Joe swam toward Mark. "I've never seen your balls from this angle. They're huge."

"Thanks. They're for our mutual pleasure."

Mark dived into the pool and swam to Joe's side. They French kissed for a long time, melding bodies. Treading water, they stroked each other's cock before returning to French kissing.

Joe pulled away. "I'd better pace myself or be spent for the day."

"Okay. I'll try to control myself—a little. What say we get some champagne?"

The men swam toward the shady side of the pool. Joe pinched Mark's ass then reached between his legs and tugged his balls.

Mark looked back and spat a mouthful of water. "Thought you said we were going to cool it."

Joe chuckled. "I didn't say I'd leave *you* alone. It was *me* getting too hot to let you continue stroking me."

"Oh yeah."

Mark sank below the surface, swallowed Joe's cock and pulled his balls while dragging Joe below the surface. A mock water battle ensued. Crotch grabbing, ass slapping, dunking, and water splashing gave way to a round of French kissing and hugs.

Water logged, Mark pulled himself from the water and sat on the edge of the pool, his feet dangling in the water. Joe swam to him, pushed his silky-smooth, muscular thighs apart, and devoured his cock.

After a minute, Joe said, "Scoot forward so I can get at your balls."

Mark scooted forward, letting his balls hang over the edge of the coping.

Joe sucked and tongued them one at a time and then, using his lips, he tugged one ball while manually pulling the

225

other. Seconds later, he pulled them widely apart.

Moaning his pleasure, Mark lowered himself backwards onto the coping, lost in revelry. "Better ease up. I'm getting close."

"I'm not even touching your cock."

"Yeah, but I'm getting hot anyway. Come sit," Mark said, patting the coping. "I want you close so we can talk."

Joe pulled himself from the water and sat at Mark's side. The guys sipped their champagne then Joe reclined his head on Mark's chest. Mark wrapped his right arm around Joe's shoulder. Joe returned the hug. Each seemed lost in the quiet embrace of the other.

"I didn't know doing nothing could be so wonderful," Joe said.

"I wouldn't exactly call this doing nothing," Mark whispered. "I'm hugging the man I love."

Except for the whir of the pool pump, silence filled the space.

Joe forced himself upright then looked at Mark. "Did you say you're hugging the man you *love*?"

"Yes. I said it. I love you."

"God. Men don't do that."

"I hadn't meant to say it, but I've loved you from the first time I saw you in those tight shorts—at that jazz bar. I've loved everything from your shaved head to your . . . everything. I've had tons of trouble trying to reconcile my feelings for you, knowing your situation."

Joe raised his voice. "Mark. We're not . . . I'm not having that kind of relationship."

"Please, don't get angry, Joe. I'm just being honest. I hadn't planned to tell you, but it slipped out. Blame it on circumstances. One reason I haven't called more often is having to hang up—to say goodbye. I want to be near you, even by phone, but talking to you and then saying goodbye is painful."

Staring at a cloud, Joe took a deep breath. "I don't know what to say. I'm not sure how I feel. I must feel something otherwise I wouldn't be here. Hell, I'm not sure how I feel about myself anymore. Maybe I'm afraid to name it. Shit. I don't know."

"You don't have to name it anything, and I'm not trying to pressure you. I'm just glad you're here."

"*Hell*, me too." Joe placed his glass on the coping. "I've had all kinds of problems facing the fact I like men, naked men. Sex with men. Men gosh damn it. *Men*! I struggle trying to get my brain around this shit. The thought of making a commitment, even to a wonderful guy like you, is mind blowing. I have sons I love very much and wonder what would happen to them. I don't know how I, or any man, could mesh. I worry about how any kind of gay relationship would affect Maria—my marriage, but above all, my sons."

"What can I say?" Mark asked, shrugging. "Give what you can. So far, I'm happy, but please don't write me off."

Joe looked into Mark's eyes then stared at the water. "I'd never write you off. Somehow, you and our experiences will forever be a part of me. An important part. You're a hell of a teacher and most important, a beautiful man, inside and out. Now, shut up and let's get drunk. Do you have more of that champagne—maybe several bottles?"

"Finish your glass and I'll refill it."

Joe downed his champagne and watched Mark walk toward the bar. He moved with the sex appeal that only a big man has—all for one admiring Joe. "Damn, I never get enough of watching you," Joe said. "Your shoulder, waist, ass ratio is unbelievable. The Greeks would have loved your classic "V" shape. You're fucking *hot,* man. At times, I just wanna eat you, all of you, and I wouldn't mind starting with that ass."

Mark turned, smiled, and then grabbed his crotch. "Don't forget this."

Mark leaned back against the bar.

Kneeling, Joe swallowed Mark's cock to its root. Looking up from the shadow of Mark's looming pecs, Joe grabbed Mark's ass and pulled it forward as if trying to stuff all of Mark's lower body in his mouth. Joe's tongue lingered on Mark's cock then he swallowed it to its roots. Sensing a rising climax, Joe retreated, leaving Mark's cock glistening in the sunlight.

"*Damn*. That felt good," Mark said.

"I know. I liked it too, but I stopped, because we don't want Mount Vesuvius erupting *now* do we? Let's cool off on those cushions."

Mark refilled their glasses then placed the champagne bottle in an ice bucket. He carried it to the pile of cushions where Joe lay spread eagle. Mark stepped over him to get to a cushion.

Joe looked up, squinting from the sun. "Why didn't you walk around instead of over me?"

"Just wanted to block the sun from your eyes."

"Then do it again."

Mark straddled Joe's legs, blocking the sun from his face. Mark chuckled. "The shadow of my balls is on your chest."

"That's the best sun block I've ever had, and look, it has a long handle."

Joe grabbed Mark's cock and jostled his dangling balls. Both guys laughed.

Mark shook his crotch to entertain Joe, then lowered himself onto Joe's chest, dropping his nuts into Joe's open mouth. Joe's tongue manipulated them while Mark moaned with pleasure. Joe tweaked Mark's nipples as Mark reached back to stroke Joe's cock.

With a stuffed mouth, Joe mumbled, "Ease up, man. I'm

close."

Mark slapped Joe's face, kissed his shaved head, and then retreated to a cushion.

Joe sat up. "Don't act like the kid who goes home with his balls because he can't play his favorite position."

"Don't worry. There'll be other *ball* games."

The men drank, swam, splashed, dived, dunked, and sunned themselves while consuming three and a half bottles of champagne. Both men were pain free.

Joe tugged Mark's balls as Mark said, "Let's go to my workplace."

Chapter Twenty-one

Mark sat on the dungeon "dining" table and invited Joe to join him. Joe, woozy from champagne, climbed on. Mark took a bottle of baby oil from under the table then rubbed a handful on Joe's chest and abdomen. Mark let his hand linger on Joe's throbber for a moment then stretched out on the table. He drained the remaining oil over his torso and pulled Joe onto his glistening body. Joe knew he should slide on Mark's torso.

"I love it," Joe said. "Your balls feel better with oil.

"Interested in my balls, eh? Then let's both enjoy them. Give them hell."

Joe gave Mark's balls a long, strong tug.

"You pull nuts like you were taught by a pro"

"I was," Joe said. "Thank you."

"Let me get a hold of yours."

Joe sat across Mark's hips, making his balls available. Mark clamped his huge hand around Joe's nuts and pulled them.

"Wow," Joe said, pleasuring himself. "You work nuts like a crap shooter."

"Wanna try something different?" Mark asked, slurring his words.

"I'm in the mood for lots of stuff."

Mark got off the table then removed a narrow section from the head end of the table top. Next, he removed a square section from its middle then leaned the sections against the wall.

"Now what?" Joe asked, lying on his side and staring at the holes.

"Lic face down but move three inches toward the head end."

Joe's pecs now hung through the rectangular opening. His cock and balls dangled through the opening in the

231

middle of the table.

Straddling Joe's legs, Mark massaged his butt. Joe moaned with pleasure as Mark's kneading grew more intense. He slid his torso and crotch over Joe's oiled back then ground his crotch on Joe's butt.

"Uuhhh," Joe moaned. "I love it."

Mark moved on to Joe's back then dragged his balls over Joe's shoulders, back, and butt.

Sucking air, Joe expressed his appreciation of Mark's bull balls. Several times, Mark flopped them on Joe's back.

"Love the sound and weight of your nuts hitting my back."

"Glad to oblige." Mark got off the table then pressed a wall button.

"What the . . .?" Joe heard the soft whir of a motor while the table rose. Standing under the table, Mark tweaked and nibbled Joe's nipples. "Wooooooow."

"Ready for more fun?" Mark asked.

"I guess," Joe said, while Mark tugged his balls.

Onto each of Joe's nipples, Mark attached a clamp. "Now comes some weight."

Joe's moans reached a crescendo.

Mark turned his oral attention to Joe's cock while tugging and squeezing his balls.

"God, what wild and crazy sensations," Joe mumbled. "Keep it up."

Mark placed a "chute" around Joe's nuts then added the weight he remembered Joe wearing at the motel. Mark lowered the table then crawled onto Joe's back. Joe wiggled his ass, begging for attention.

"I'm not sure what all you did under there, but it feels sooo good."

"Just trying to please," Mark said, spreading lubricant

on Joe's ass then mounting him.

Joe squirmed on the slippery surface as Mark probed his muscular butt. It rose and fell erratically as Joe maximized his pleasure while giving Mark the ride of his life.

Mark whispered, "You trying to buck me off?"

"No, but when I move, the weights swing. Makes my balls and nipples feel sooo good. I love it."

Mark's ride began like Ravel's Bolero but soon reached the Tempo of a Sousa march.

Grasping Joe's hips, Mark pulled them toward his thrusting crotch. "I'm getting close. Very close."

Joe's ass tightened to add stimulation to Mark's cock and his own bottom. His body movements heightened his nipple and ball swinging pleasure. As Joe panted and grunted, Mark's cock stimulated his insides.

The dungeon resonated with the sounds of an oiled crotch slapping a begging butt.

Joe wiggled his chest, accentuating the swing of the nipple weights as his groin began to contract

Suddenly, Mark stiffened, held his breath, and then roared, "God . . ." He fell on Joe's back while continuing too grunt and shake.

Suddenly, Joe had an auto-climax. He writhed, shook, and yelled, "Oh God! Oh God . . . Wow! Wow!"

"You okay?" Mark asked.

"God, I can't believe I did it. I've never come like that."

"You're luck," Mark whispered. "Most guys go their entire life without cuming like that."

"Poor bastards. They don't know what they're missing."

Mark lay motionless on Joe's spent body as both men panted from exhaustion. After a rest, Mark reached under the table and released Joe's tit clamps. Their liberation produced the anticipated pain of release. Next, he released the chute. It fell to the floor with a thud.

After a few minutes, Mark rolled off Joe then pulled a towel from a rack under the table. "Let's shower," Mark said. "Take this towel. If you have oil on your feet, wipe them. Don't want you slipping and breaking something."

After showering, the men dried each other's backs, rubbed the others butts, and then headed to the patio where they finished the fourth bottle of champagne.

Joe looked at the patio clock. "I'd better get going. Maria and the boys will soon be at the hotel. Since neither of us is sober enough to ride a Harley, I'll take a taxi."

"Okay," Mark said frowning, "but I hate to see you go. How about you lead the way to our clothes. I'll follow your butt to make sure you don't get lost."

Joe grinned like a cookie-stealing first grader. "You wanna watch my ass don't you?"

"Who wouldn't want to watch that ass—I mean your asset."

Joe gathered his clothes, and despite multiple inter-ruptions by Mark's groping hands, he managed to dress. As Joe put on his shoes, his phone rang. "Who the hell? Hello."

"Joe. It's Bruce. Just wanted to let you know I'm in town."

"I'm sorry, sir. You've reached me on my cell phone. I'm not in Smithville now. You should call the shop's main number. Someone there will help you with your problem."

"I get it," Bruce said. "Call me when you can?"

"Yes sir. Call the other number. Goodbye."

Mark frowned. "Can't escape work can you?"

"Nope. On call twenty-four seven—like doctors."

Mark, still naked, phoned for a taxi. He and Joe hugged, kissed, and groped each other until the cab arrived.

From behind the half-opened door, Mark watched Joe

enter the cab and yelled, "Call ASAP, Joe."

From the taxi, Joe phoned Bruce. "Hello, mister-beautiful dancing-man."

"Where are you, Joe?"

"I'm in a taxi. I've been to a convention party, and I'm a little drunk. Had too much wine. Where are you?"

"In my hotel. Remember where I'm staying? I'm just a few miles from your place."

"Sorry, Bruce, but I'm a little *drunk*. Can we talk later?"

"No problem. I know how trade show parties can be— too much free booze. Call me tonight? Okay?"

"Okay. I'll call when I can."

"I understand. Take an aspirin otherwise you'll have a headache in the morning."

Joe got to his hotel room just in time to welcome his family from their tour. "Hey, guys," Joe slurred. "Did you enjoy the dinosaur bones?"

"Yeah," Paul said. "You should have seen them, dad. They're humongous."

Looking exhausted, Maria said, "I've had my fill of theaters and tar pits. The boys enjoyed going through the bone lab, but we're tired."

"Sit down, honey. Take your shoes off and relax a bit," Joe said. "Do you want anything to drink? How about you boys? Milk or apple juice?"

"Joe, have you been drinking?" Maria asked.

"Yep. Too much wine at a faucet party. Don't worry, I'm alright."

"It's a little early to be drinking, but it sounds like you had a better time than I did. Think we'll take a nap. Between the tours, time zone changes, and jet lag, the boys and I are beat."

"Where do you want to eat tonight?" Joe asked.

Maria thought for a moment. "This hotel would be fine."

"Sure that's what you want?" Joe asked. "I want to go back to the show after a snack. There's a presentation about a new plastic pipe that I want to hear. It's supposed to be the greatest thing since running water. I need to know about it. They'll have food and drinks. Why don't you go with me?"

"No. We'll eat here. You go to the show without me. Right now, the boys and I are taking a nap. Wake us at six?"

Joe kissed each boy and left the room so the family could nap. He used the time to call Bruce.

"Please, say you can come over, Joe."

"Yep. How about eight?"

"Wonderful. I'm in room 2020. Don't be late."

At six o'clock, Joe woke the family, helped the boys prepare for dinner, and then escorted everyone to the dining room and got them a table by the window.

Joe waved to Maria as he hailed a taxi. He told himself, I shouldn't be doing this, but I want to.

At Bruce's hotel room, Joe rang its doorbell. Bruce opened the door two inches, peered out, and then welcomed Joe in.

As expected, Bruce wore nothing but a smile.

"How nice to see you—all of you," Joe said, grabbing Bruce's crotch.

"Give me a hug."

The men hugged for a minute and then Bruce kissed Joe's neck.

"You look tired," Bruce said. "Are you okay?"

"I'm fine. I just drank too much at that party."

"I know about those parties, unending booze, cheap

236

food, and loose women. Any of them chase you?"

"Some, but I wasn't looking for women."

"What say I give you a massage—loosen you up?"

"Sounds good—even if it's just an excuse to get me naked."

"What can I say?"

Joe stripped under the watchful gaze of his admirer.

"My God, Joe. Let me look at you."

Knowing Bruce to be a leg lover, Joe extended and flexed his right, then his left leg.

"I admire your ambition, Joe, but I can't believe the bulk you've added to your thighs since your last visit."

Joe chuckled as Bruce prodded and inspected the rest of his body.

Bruce hugged and kissed Joe. He kissed back—hard.

"Come, Joe, lie on the bed." Bruce straddled his hips then stretched out over Joe's broad back and lay still for a moment. He whispered, "You have no idea how wonderful it is to feel you under me . . . knowing you're here."

"I'm the one who's happy, Bruce. I love having you on top of me. You can't imagine how much I've missed you."

Bruce kissed Joe's shoulder. "I promised you a massage, and I'm going to give you one—whether you want it or not."

Bruce massaged Joe's calves then worked his way to Joe's basketball butt. His hands lingered on the butt cheeks before giving each a firm squeeze. With each squeeze, Joe moaned, "Ohhh. That feels great." *Maybe he'll do more.*

Bruce massaged Joe's butt with such vigor he almost melted on the bed. Bruce rested his hands for a second then directed his attention to Joe's back and shoulders.

Joe purred.

Bruce pulled his cock upward then let it strike Joe's back with a thud.

"You gonna beat me?"

"No. I think you need a nap more than a fuck." Bruce went to the sofa then sat down. He patted a cushion. "Come. Sit."

Joe forced himself off the bed then walked zombie-like to the sofa.

"Stretch out," Bruce said. "Put your head on my lap. Take a nap if you need one."

"You think I can nap with *that* poking me in the head?"

"Sorry."

Snuggling his head in Bruce's lap, Joe stared in to his eyes. "You make me feel so comfortable."

"Good. Now close your eyes. Relax."

Bruce lay his head on the back of the sofa and placed his forearm across Joe's chest. Within minutes both men fell asleep.

Bruce awoke aware his legs were "asleep." The numbness caused him to squirm. The motion woke Joe.

"God!" Joe exclaimed and rubbed his eyes. "What time is it?"

"Sorry," Bruce said. "I didn't mean to wake you."

"No problem. I'm the one who should be apologizing. I didn't mean to fall asleep."

Joe grasped Bruce's arm still resting on his chest, kissed Bruce's fingertips, then his arm up to the elbow. "I had a wonderful dream about you."

"Happy to know I can please."

Glancing at the desk clock, Joe stood. "I can't believe I've wasted time napping. I owe you *big* time." Joe lowered himself between Bruce's muscular thighs.

Bruce stopped him. "Joe, you owe me nothing and *certainly* not sex."

"Bruce, I *want* you."

"Me too." Bruce fell back on the sofa.

Joe devoted himself to Bruce's pleasure, kissing, stroking, and nibbling every inch of Bruce from navel to the underside of his balls. Using his lips, Joe tugged Bruce's pubic hair then tongue-teased his cockhead before swallowing it.

Bruce lifted his hips, moaned, and said, "I want you too."

The men engaged in a 69 horserace where stretched balls substituted for reins. Stroking, tugging, sucking, and panting, the men were hell bent on maximizing the other's pleasure. Moans and grunts melded into one long "ahhhhhh" then the sounds of shallow breathing as the only expressions of life.

Joe thought, *I'm getting too used to this.*

Bruce sat upright.

Joe lay on the sofa with his head in Bruce's lap. He looked into Bruce's blue eyes and said, "That was the most satisfying sex I've ever had."

"Ditto," Bruce said, fingering Joe's chest hair.

"I shouldn't, but I want to see you again. Is that possible?" Joe asked.

"Of course. Just say when."

"Next time, I won't so drunk. I've never done that 69 thing before. Maybe you can dream up other fun stuff."

"Depends. How wild do you want it, big guy?"

"I'm still learning so teach me."

"Okay. I'll dream up something."

"Good. Sorry, but I gotta go. The lecture I'm supposed to be attending should be over."

"Okay, but let me help you with your underwear."

Joe chuckled, "Oh! Another excuse to play with my balls?"

Crouching and holding Joe's underwear, Bruce raised the briefs, inch-by-inch, up Joe's thighs. Nearing the crotch, Bruce tugged Joe's balls while kissing his cock.

Underwear in place, Bruce looked up. "Now, that didn't hurt did it?"

For Bruce's enjoyment, Joe let his balls and cock hang out of his briefs until he had donned the remainder of his clothes. He then tucked his package inside and zipped his fly.

"Guess the show is over," Bruce said, escorting Joe to the door where they kissed.

"Until next time," Joe said.

Chapter Twenty-two

Joe rose at the crack of dawn. He tiptoed to the kitchenette and brewed coffee.

Its aroma awoke Maria. "Morning," she said, stretching. You're up early. What's on your schedule today?"

"I thought we'd enjoy the pool." Joe searched in a drawer for his trunks. "I'd like to get some sun and relax for a change."

"Are you sure?" Maria asked, a scowl crossing her face. "There's so much to do in LA. You can swim at the pond anytime. I'd like to do something besides sit around the pool worrying about getting sunburned."

"Okay," Joe said, holding up his trunks. "We'll swim for a while then you do your thing while I go to the show."

"Okay, but I'm hungry. Let's get the boys ready for breakfast."

Poolside, Joe stretched out on a chaise and rolled the legs of his trunks high on his thighs then rolled his waistband down so he could maximize his sun exposure. He didn't want Maria asking questions about a tan he hoped to get while sunbathing that afternoon at Mark's pool.

Maria pulled her chaise into the shade of a palm tree then rubbed lotion on the boys.

During a midmorning "pit stop," Joe's phone rang.

"Good morning, beautiful," Mark said. "What's happening?"

"Me and the family are at the hotel pool. I thought I'd get a tan in Maria's presence, so she wouldn't suspect anything when I show up with a tan after being at your pool today."

"Today?"

"Yep. Are you free this afternoon?"

"For you, I'm always *free*. What about two o'clock?"

"See you then."

Joe headed to Mark's place, leaving the family to spend the afternoon touring. He felt a tinge of guilt on leaving them, but he had few chances to see Mark.

Joe rang Mark's doorbell.

Moments later, the door opened. Mark wore a beach towel around his waist. His hair and body were wet.

Guess he's been swimming.

Joe glanced up and down the sidewalk. Seeing no one, he yanked away Mark's towel, leaving him wearing nothing but a look of surprise.

"Glad I wasn't wearing anything expensive. It would have been shredded with that kind of enthusiasm."

"You're welcome," Joe chuckled as he unbuttoned his shirt.

"Faster," Mark said, backing into the foyer and pulling Joe inside. "Champagne is waiting poolside."

Mark led the way to the pool as Joe left a trail of discarded clothing while walking and admiring Mark's ass.

"Your ass moves like none I've ever seen. Has it had dancing lessons?"

Mark turned abruptly. His cock and bull-balls lagged behind, but then, they caught up with his momentum and they dangled in front of his thighs.

"What are you staring at?" Mark asked.

"Your balls, man. Those suckers are hanging way low— must be the heat."

"So much for my balls. Get *yours* out."

Joe stepped onto the patio while removing his briefs.

Mark popped a champagne cork then filled two glasses.

Joe gave him a bear-hug from behind and nibbled his shoulder.

"From all that nibbling, I assume you didn't have lunch, but is that pubic hair against my ass?"

"I had lunch, and yes, it's pubic hair, and I love muscular shoulders as a fat-free dessert."

Mark turned and reciprocated the bear hug, lifting Joe off the floor.

"Oh, trying to show off are you?" Joe said. "Well two can play that game."

Joe lifted Mark, dropped him in the pool, and then dived in beside him. The men embraced and exchanged a long, passionate kiss.

"I've missed you," Mark said, pushing back his wet hair then gripping Joe's butt. "I'm going to make sure you have a memorable afternoon."

"I like the way it's starting off," Joe said, slapping Mark's butt.

Sun-time, pool-time, embracing, kissing, nipple-tweaking, ball-tugging, and cock-sucking, filled the hours. The champagne flowed. With several glasses of wine under his imaginary belt and a slippery floor, Joe staggered around the patio then bumped the half-opened door to Mark's gym.

Mark smiled then said, "Maybe we should go in?"

Slurring his words, Joe said, "I might just do that."

"Do you want a *workout* or a *work over*?" Mark asked.

"Let's see . . . How about the *workshop*?"

Mark opened the workshop door and turned the lights to dim. He took Joe's hand and led him inside. A damp coolness welcomed him. Joe steadied himself then scanned the room's black metal objects, ropes, and chains. His gaze fell on a rack of leather whips. He walked to the rack, fondled several of the toys, and then removed one having eighteen-inch strands of leather.

He shook it. "Whatta you call this?"

"Ah, you have good taste. That's a handmade, kangaroo-leather, cat-of-nine-tails."

"Yep. There are nine ends," Joe mumbled, counting the strands. "How do you use it?"

Positioning the whip in Joe's hand, Mark said, "Move your hand like this." He guided Joe's arm through several arcs of motion then Joe made several solo swings. On one swing, Joe struck Mark's ass with two or three of the tails.

"Trying to *whip* my ass, eh?"

"You want it?"

"Well, it never minded a little attention." Mark turned his back to Joe. "Just the ass, big guy."

Joe tightened his grip on the whip, raised it, and then sliced the air with the tails that struck Mark's tensed, muscular butt.

Mark sucked air. "Whew! Whip that ass like a *man*?"

"More?"

"Yeah, but let's go over there."

Mark walked to a wooden Saint Andrew's Cross on the far side of the room. He faced it then gripped a leather cuff at the top of each wooden arm. He spread his legs and stood as if his ankles were bound to the lower ends of the beams.

Mark flexed then shook his butt. "Now, let's see what you got, big guy. Lay it on me."

Joe watched Mark stiffen his body in anticipation of the whip's sting. Every muscle fiber could be seen through the skin covering his glutes.

Watching Mark prepare his body for pain, Joe wondered what else Mark might want and could he satisfy him?

Joe snapped the whip then swung it with a loud swoosh-ing sound, striking Mark's tensed ass.

Mark threw his head back and sucked air. "God! Yeah!

That's it, big guy. Another one! Harder!"

Joe gave his all, striking Mark's ass with the nine tails.

Beads of sweat ran down Mark's back as his body stiffened. "That's what I wanted. One more!"

Joe asked himself, Can I do this? He then obliged with all his energy.

Mark moaned and wiped at sweat. "Another!"

After a long pause, Joe looked at the whip then caressed the whelps forming on Mark's ass. "I don't wanna do this. I don't like hurting you."

Mark lowered his arms and rubbed his ass. "It hurts, but it's a good hurt. Sometimes, I like it a lot. Especially when *you* do it. It's like me pulling on your balls. You like it to a point, then we ease off. Same with the whip."

Grabbing Mark's balls, Joe looked into his eyes, "I'd rather pull on your balls or nibble your pecs—even if they are sweaty."

Joe walked to the patio and dived into the pool.

The men spent the rest of the afternoon lying in the sun with intermittent intimate moments and sporadic trips to the gym to exercise. Sometimes, sexual exploits found their way into the workout. More than once, Joe pushed Mark's hand off his cock. "Remember," Joe said, "we're exercising."

Mark prepared to spot Joe's bench press. Joe positioned his hands on the bar and squirmed his head on the bench in preparation to push the barbell off its supports. Instead, he raised his head, capturing Mark's nuts in an oral prison. Their entrapment occurred with such intensity Mark didn't know whether to scream or enjoy the moment.

Balls captured in Joe's mouth, Mark said, "If you're going to play like that, then take *this*." Mark squatted and squeezed his thighs on either side of Joe's face. Joe struggled to breathe and pried at Mark's thighs. Suddenly, Mark released his

245

pressure.

With speech muffled by a mouthful of balls, Joe mumbled, "I'm not letting go."

"What the hell. Two can play this game."

Mark maneuvered himself under the barbell, taking Joe's balls in a mouth-hold as strong as Joe's. A tug-of-war ensued.

Moments later, Joe exchanged ball-swallowing for cock-swallowing. Mark followed suit. The men lay on the floor engaged in a 69. In rapid succession, both men climaxed. Mark collapsed on Joe and panted.

"What a hell of a way to start the afternoon," Mark said. Recovered, he helped Joe up. The men then moved to lounges and fell asleep.

Mark's wristwatch chimed, awakening the men.

"Did you hear that?" Joe asked.

"Yeah. I have a client coming in two hours."

"How *do* you do it? How can you give so much so often? It's like your some kind of machine?"

"This client pays twice my fee to be rope-bound. He has a fetish about big guys dominating him. Thank God, I don't have to unload for him."

"I still don't know how you do it, but I guess I'd better get out of here. I wouldn't want to interfere with a working man earning a living."

"I'd love to have you around. Why don't you think about joining me? Live in LA. My clients would love having you in charge of their fantasies." Mark gestured toward the sky. "You'd make tons of tax-free money. We could provide dual attention to clients. Twice the fun, twice the pain, twice the money. And I could help you train for your contest."

"Mark, money isn't everything—at least not for me. I have a family to think about."

"Then think about the people you'd make happy. Lots of guys fantasize about two big guys working them over. Hell! We could raise our fees. Why not try it—part time—see how you like it. Our working together would give us personal time. Wow! What we couldn't do together."

Joe sat up. "I'm not cut out to do what you do, and I don't like thinking about us and a third party. Call me selfish, but that's how I feel. I know you're thinking *you* share me with Maria, but that'll change." Mark propped himself on his elbows as Joe continued. "But that still leaves my boys. You want me to just up and leave them? I couldn't do that." Joe shook his head. "I don't know when, but things will change. I just have to minimize the hurt it'll cause." Joe stood. "Oh well, you've got to get ready, and I've got to get. Will you call me a cab?"

Joe eyed Mark's physique. *God, how I dig that bod. I wish I was that big. And that cock.*

Small talk ensued as Joe dressed then waited for the cab. Mark, still naked, permitted "attacks" by Joe's wandering hands.

The doorbell rang, and the men headed for the entrance and the waiting taxi. Joe exited the half-opened door, his right hand lingering on Mark's balls. "See you soon."

On his way to the hotel, Joe phoned Bruce and told him family plans prevented their meeting that day, but he'd schedule a get together later.

Joe needed some downtime—a rest.

The next day, Joe hurried to Bruce's hotel and rang his doorbell. Joe expected him to be naked when the door opened.

"Bruce. You're dressed. What's up?"

"Nothing. I just don't want you thinking I'm predictable, but now, I want to take you to lunch. A place I *know* you'll like."

"What kinda place?"

"You'll see."

The guys dined in a trendy café in West Hollywood where Joe received lots of attention from gay diners. One customer asked for his autograph.

"I didn't think I'd be so recognized," Joe whispered.

"Let's face it, you're famous and being with you makes me look good. Thanks."

"Do you think they think I'm a rent boy?"

"Now that's rich." Bruce chuckled, "Maybe they think *you* bought me."

Lunch finished, the men were about to leave when a fortyish effeminate man approached the table. "Excuse me, Joe, but may I have your autograph? I'm a big fan. Saw you on TV— a lot."

Joe took the man's pad and pen. "What should I write?"

"To my friend, Scott, would be nice."

"You got it, Scott," Joe said, signing the pad.

Scott stared at the autograph, looked at Joe, and then asked, "Would you flex your biceps? You've got killer arms."

"No can do, Scott."

"Sorry, but I had to ask."

"Well mister big shot," Bruce said, "if you're through taking care of your public, let's get out of here."

Chapter Twenty-three

Exiting the cab, Joe released Bruce's hand and stared at a sign that read *The Pleasured Body*. "Is this what I think this is, Bruce?"

"It's one of a chain of sex shops. They have everything you can imagine. Let's go in."

The shop reeked with the smell of leather. Joe took a deep breath and glanced around the shop. Its walls were covered with items alien to a novice like him.

A salesman looked Joe in the eye and extended his hand. "Welcome, *big guy*. I'm Clark. I don't think I've met you before, but you look familiar."

"I'm Roger," Joe said, shaking Clark's hand. "I'm no one you know or ever heard of."

"Well, leather's my specialty. We have some killer leather jockstraps, and fitting is my specialty. I'd be pleased to help fit you." Wiping drool, Clark continued to eye Joe. "You'll need a good fit if it is to be comfortable." Clark pointed to a dressing room. "Undress in there then yell when you're ready. I'll bring in a variety of straps for you to try on."

"Thanks, Clark. I'll think about it." *God, what a jerk.*

Joe and Bruce walked around the expansive shop.

Bruce smelled, caressed, and admired one jockstrap after another. He even licked a pair of leather pants. He picked up a leather chest-harness, smelled it, and then held it against Joe's chest, admiring the match.

"God, you'd look hot in this, Joe."

"Yeah, but I couldn't take it home."

"If you like it, I'll buy it and keep it at my place. You could wear it there—for me."

"Uhhhh. I don't know, Bruce."

"Take it to that dressing room and get naked. I'll help

you cinch it up."

Joe glared at Bruce. "You gotta be crazy. Plus I don't have to be naked to try on a chest harness."

Mimicking Clark's effeminate speech, Bruce said, "Remember, its leather, and we want to make sure it fits well."

Joe chuckled. "I know what you're after, but I think I can get it on by myself." Joe looked in Clark's direction and grinned. "If I can't, I'll call Clark."

"Alright big boy. Back to matters at hand. Will you try it?"

"I like it, but I don't want you buying me gifts."

"Oh shut up. Try it on and *I'll* decide if I want to buy it."

Joe took the harness to the dressing room. To surprise Bruce, Joe stripped. He tightened the harness to a snug fit over his chest. The crisscrossed pieces pushed his pecs up-and-out, making his chest look twice as thick. *Damn! I like this thing.* He opened the door three inches and beckoned Bruce.

Bruce entered the dressing room. "Oh my God! I thought you'd be half-dressed, but you're naked—well, almost. That harness is hot." Bruce gave Joe a passionate kiss. "Damn, you've got to have this, Joe. Please, let me buy it for you. It would make me very happy if you wore it at my place."

"If buying it would make you happy, then . . . okay. I like it, and I'll wear it—here and in Cincinnati."

"You've made my day, big guy." Bruce leaned against the dressing room door. "I'll see if there's anything else you might like. By the way, you don't have to get dressed. No one will mind if you wander around naked—particularly Clark."

"If you don't stop groping me, I'll never get out of this thing. Now get out of here while I get dressed."

Joe found Bruce roaming in the "BALLS OF FUN" department. The department name appeared on a three-foot sign shaped like a scrotum and painted a flesh color with curly black hairs.

"What've you found?" Joe asked.

"There are lots of fun things here. Look at this." Bruce held up a chromed thick-walled short tube.

"What the hell is that?"

Bruce admired the shiny item. "It's a ball weight. They have all sizes and weights."

He handed Joe the two-inch-long tube.

"Wow, it's heavier than it looks. Pardon my ignorance but how does it work?"

"See that recessed screw? Unscrew it and this separates into two equal halves."

"Okay, now what?" Joe asked.

"First, you stretch out your balls then place one half of the weight around the back of your sac—like this." Bruce used two fingers as a substitute scrotum. "It fits between the base of your cock and the top of your balls. Place the other half over the front of your sac and then tighten the screw to hold the parts together."

"Think they'd let me try one?" Joe asked, remembering Mark's chute.

"Don't ask," Bruce whispered. "Just take one and put it on. No, take two—see which one you like best. From what I know about you, I suggest you try this one and a heavier one. Now go. Try them. Let me know if you need help."

"No thanks." Joe chuckled. "Clark is available."

Joe took the weights to the dressing room where Bruce waited outside.

"Ouch! The damn thing pinched me," Joe muttered.

"I heard that," Bruce said. "I offered to help. Make sure there's no skin between the two halves when you tighten the screw, or you'll regret it. It would be easier if your balls were shaved."

251

After several minutes, Joe opened the door and said, "Okay, Bruce. Come in."

Bruce smiled when he saw naked Joe with the weight hanging on his nuts. "I love giving second opinions to a naked man, especially when he wears ball weights so well. Your face suggests your balls love it. How does it feel?"

"It took some effort to get it on, but I like it." Joe shook his hips, causing the weight to swing. "Feels great."

Bruce smiled. "Guess you've noticed your balls not only get pulled they prevent the thing from falling off. God, it's embarrassing to have a ball weight fall off. It's like having a cock ring fall off. Not a proud moment."

"I'd like to try a heavier one?"

"Okay but give some thought to what you want to do with it. Do you want to wear it for hours or just while you're getting off. If it's for a short time, get a heavier one. If you want to wear it a long time, get a lighter one, or you could get both and do whatever you want."

"Would you get me the next heavier one? I want to see how it feels."

"Okay. I'll be back with a weightlifter's dream."

Bruce presented Joe with a heavier weight and helped him get it on.

"It feels better than the last one, but I don't think I could wear it very long. But how'd I know. Maybe I should get both. Whatta you think?"

"Both it is, but only if you let *me* buy them."

"You drive a hard bargain, guy." Joe glanced at Bruce's crotch. "Are you getting hard looking at my weight?"

"Can't help it." Bruce placed his hand over his crotch. "I want to buy the weights for you. They will be my surrogate hand for when I can't pull your balls."

"Okay, but I wanna a third one," Joe said, "one to take

home. Somehow, I'll make time to wear it."

"Good. Anything else?"

"What's that cock ring thing you mentioned? I hope it's not one of those things requiring a hole in your cock.?"

"God, no! A cock ring is a big ring," Bruce said, making an "okay" sign. "It can be metal, stone, leather, or God knows what else. It goes around your balls *and* cock and temporarily traps blood in your cock to make it bigger *and* harder."

"What?"

"I know. You want to try one. Okay. Stay here. I'll get a few."

Bruce returned with an adjustable leather cock ring, a silicone ring, and several steel rings of different diameters.

"The ring goes over your balls and then your cock. It should be a little loose when you're soft." Bruce demonstrated by placing a ring around four of his fingers. "Now, don't get a hardon after you put this on."

Bruce placed a steel ring around Joe's cock and balls and then moved the ring to the base of his cock. "It fits well but take it off. You can wear it and get hard at my place."

Joe stared at the cock ring. "Damn, Bruce! It's feeling good."

"I know, but you need to get it off and get out of here, now—unless you want a 'de-fitting' hand-job by Clark."

Joe lay naked on Bruce's hotel bed, legs spread.

Bruce worked fast, fitting a cock ring on Joe before he got hard. "Was it my manipulation or the metal that got you growing?"

"Both, I guess," Joe said, "but close your eyes while I put the harness on. And promise not to peek?"

"Okay, but hurry."

Joe went to the bathroom to don his harness.

"Why are you taking so long?" Bruce called out.

Joe returned. "Okay. Open your eyes."

Bruce's jaw dropped as silence filled the room.

Joe did a frontal double-bicep pose with his legs flexed and spread. The harness made his chest look thicker and the weight made his balls hang twice as low. The cock ring also worked its magic—Joe sported a huge erection. He grinned as he thrust his hips, causing the ball weight to swing between his thighs. He tightened his abs and caused his engorged cock to bounce.

"Whatta you think, Bruce?"

"I'm speechless. I've never seen *anything* so hot. Just want to *eat* every inch of you."

"Then have a nibble—wherever you want."

Bruce fell to his knees and mouthed Joe's cock. Joe pleasured his own nipples while Bruce tugged his stretched balls. Bruce knew the tug would add pleasure to that of the weight. He also tweaked Joe's nipples while struggling to swallow his engorged cock.

Joe pulled back. "Don't hurt yourself."

"That cock ring makes your cock so fat I can barely swallow it."

"Don't worry. What you were doing felt great."

Bruce gave the head of Joe's cock lots of tongue action.

"Oh God," Joe moaned, grabbing his abdomen with both hands as his moans grew louder.

Bruce whispered, "Quiet, buddy. Somebody will hear you."

"I'm trying."

Bruce pushed Joe toward the foot of the bed then directed him to turn around and extend his arms to support himself over the mattress. His ball weight swung toward his abdomen.

Bruce dragged his cock and balls over Joe's ass. With a

tease and a dab of KY, Bruce guided his cock inside Joe's beckoning ass as it backed toward the advancing intruder. Joe's moans of pleasure filled the room. Bruce grabbed the back of the harness and pulled Joe farther onto his cock.

Joe stroked his cock in sync with Bruce's thrusts. *Damn, his cock feels good.* The repetitive sounds of skin slapping skin echoed around the room. Bruce pushed Joe's hand aside and took over the stroking. The rhythm and the tempo of hand and hip actions increased until both men climaxed. Joe collapsed onto the bed with Bruce on his back. For a few seconds, the only sounds were heavy breathing.

"Not bad for a matinee, eh?" Bruce asked, rolling off Joe. "And don't forget there's an evening performance."

The men showered then rested.

After half-an-hour, Bruce asked, "What do you say we check out the hotel gym? Their brochure says it's well equipped and they provide workout clothes, shoes, private lockers, and individual showers."

"Okay, but give me fifteen minutes of rest."

After resting, Joe started to don his underwear. "I think I'd like to wear the lighter ball weight for my workout."

Bruce picked up the weight. "I'll help you put it on."

"Seems you're always looking for an excuse to pull my balls aren't you, Bruce."

"Not me. I just don't want you pinching anything. Now, get dressed."

"Feels good," Joe said, noting a sizeable bulge in his pants.

"People will notice that wad," Bruce said. "I'd better walk in front of you, so it won't be noticed.

On the way, Joe said, "I miss the weight's swinging. I'll be glad to get my underwear off."

"Then you had better not wear a jockstrap."

Workout completed, the men returned to Bruce's room.

"How'd you like a gin and tonic?" Bruce asked.

"Sounds good. Make it a tall one while I get out of these clothes. I want my ball weight to swing. You'd better get naked too."

Bruce stopped pouring tonic water and watched Joe strip. "Wow, It doesn't take much of a workout to get you pumped."

Joe flexed his pecs. "I pump up quick."

Bruce stripped then resumed drink preparation.

Joe approached Bruce from the rear then hugged him. Joe swung his hips, causing his weight to slap Bruce's butt crack.

Bruce glanced over his shoulder. "You're not putting *that* anywhere, big guy."

"Oh, shut up."

Bruce handed Joe a drink. "I'll take the man but not the weight. Come lie on the bed. We can watch a recording of the Mister California contest. It's one of the free things on cable. I've seen it, but I think you might enjoy it."

The recording started in the middle of the contest. Joe watched as senior-level, male contestants performed various posing routines.

"How do you think you'd do with those routines?" Bruce asked.

"I'll do some, and you rate me. Sometimes, I watch a posing DVD in my shop, so I have an idea what to do."

Bruce restarted the program to the most common of poses, the frontal double bicep pose. "Let's see you do that."

Joe executed the pose then Bruce made suggestions. The men viewed several portions of the video with Joe mimicking the poses.

"I'm happily surprised," Bruce said. "That was good. I

guess you've spent a lot of time practicing."

"Yeah. When the shop's empty, I strip and practice, using a mirror behind my door."

"With your size, and what you've learned, you're ready for a contest."

"Think so?"

"I do, and I know the judge who schedules them. I'll inquire about the most appropriate one for you, and then we'll get you enrolled."

"That'd be great. I appreciate the encouragement, but I don't want no favors from your judge friend."

"Don't worry. He won't do you, or any bodybuilder, any favors. He's a stickler for details. I've seen contestants cry after getting his feedback. Actually, he's a bit brutal—but honest."

"I don't like brutal, but I'd appreciate honest feedback."

"Enough of this posing stuff. Come, give me a kiss."

The guys kissed, body melded to body.

The guys were rolling about the bed, playing sexual games when Joe's phone rang.

"Now who can that be? I'd better get it in case it's Maria."

"Hello."

"Joe, it's me, Mark. How're you doing?"

"I'm sorry, Sir, you've reached me on my cell phone. I'm out of town now and can't be of service. Please, call the office. Someone there will help you."

"I understand, Joe."

"That's right Sir. Please call my office. Goodbye."

"Bye, Joe."

"Just can't get away from work can you?" Bruce asked.

"Not for long. I hate to do this, but it's getting late, and I'd better get going. Maria and the boys are probably at the hotel by now." Joe stood and held Bruce's hands. "I Can't tell you

257

how much I enjoyed the lunch, shopping, the new toys, and oh yeah, the sex. Take care of my playthings 'til I see you again."

"And when will that be?"

"Maybe, tomorrow. I'll call in the morning."

Bruce sat on the edge of the bed, put his arms around Joe's legs, and pulled him close. He gripped Joe's nipples with his expert fingers and then swallowed Joe's cock.

"Sorry," Joe said. "There's no time now. I've gotta go."

Chapter Twenty-four

Joe entered a taxi and settled onto the rear seat.

He phoned Mark. "I'm sorry I couldn't talk when you called. What's up?"

"I hoped you'd call to say you were coming over tomorrow, however, I got a call from a client who wants me go on a seven-day boat trip."

"Wow. Boats are nice but seven days . . . that's a long time, man."

"It's a yacht. Actually, it's more like a battleship. I don't know how he makes his money, but he pays well—all cash."

"Well, you gotta do what you gotta do," Joe said, feeling disappointed.

"Sorry, Joe, but I need the money. Once I referred a friend to fill in for me, and something happened. My client wanted nothing more to do with him. The old guy only wants me. He pays so well, I can't refuse even if it means giving up another client."

"I understand." *Guess I'm just another client, eh?*

"I get my hourly rate, times fourteen hours, times seven days—sleeping time doesn't count."

Joe did some mental calculations. "That's $98,000 a week—tax free! No one can afford to ignore that kinda money, but what do you have to do to earn it?"

"Not as much as you think. The guy is into big balls, big chests, big nipples, and he likes my butt. He says I 'tick all his boxes.'"

"Well, he didn't go wrong when he found you did he?"

"I hope that's a compliment."

"So, you run around naked all day?"

"Well, not all the time. He had a tailor make some special threads for me. They match the old dude's sexual interests. They're made of spandex. The front of the t-shirt has holes that expose my nipples. The matching shorts have a hole in the crotch so my balls hang out, and there are two holes in the back that expose my butt cheeks."

"What a waste of fabric," Joe chuckled. "I'd just keep you naked, but how do you spend your day?"

"I have to be ready for gropes at all times. Occasionally, he gets me off, but I don't have to return the favors."

"There must be a big crew, and I'm sure the man doesn't cook. So, what does the help think about you—your clothes—your job?"

"There's a crew of seven. They're not muscle guys but they are well-built. They're naked when the boat is away from shore and other boats. The only crew member not naked is the engineer. 'Clothes equal safety,' he says. The chef wears an apron while cooking, otherwise he's naked."

Joe chuckled, "Must be a lot of sun screen on board, but what about the boss man?"

"The old guy occasionally plays with a member of the crew but not often—not publicly. Some are allegedly straight, but they work for the old guy because he pays well. As for me, he wants me around all the time. I'm never to hide my balls, no matter what position I might be in."

"Sounds tedious."

"I'm with him all day. We sometimes jet ski, swim, or whatever the hell he wants, and believe me, he wants to play with my balls a lot. He's fallen asleep with them in his hand."

"And you're always in that special shirt and shorts?"

"Yep, except when I sleep, then I'm naked, but you knew that."

"What does the crew think of your special suit?"

"Who cares? They're naked, and I, at least, get to wear something even if it's full of holes. Now, for the captain. That's a different story. If you see him docking the boat, he appears to be dressed in his spiffy white and gold uniform. What you don't see is he's naked from the waist down. That guy has some loooow hangers, and he is proud of them. Loves to show them off."

"Like you," Joe chuckled.

"Yeah. He often stands at the helm with his legs spread in case the boss stops by and wants a look or a feel. But hell, he'll let anybody play with them."

"Do you wear the same suit every day?"

"Kinda. Several identical sets were made but in different colors.

Each set has the same holes."

Joe sighed, feeling disappointed. "I understand why you can't see me. With that kind of money at stake, I wouldn't see me either. I'm sure we'll get together again—sometime. Enjoy the ship. I'm sure it'll have good food and booze. Be careful though, don't get your balls sunburned."

"Joe, you know I love you. I want to be with you, but I can't get away. Not with all the expenses at the new house. I need the money."

"Like I said, you gotta do what you gotta do." *Guess money is more important than me.*

"Thanks for understanding, Joe. I'll call soon."

"When are you leaving?"

"We weigh anchor at 7:30—in the morning."

"Damn it. I won't be able to grope you again this trip."

"Sorry, Joe."

"Yeah. Me too."

The next morning, John asked, "Daddy, can we go back to Disneyland? There are things we didn't get to do."

"Whatta you think, Joe?" Maria asked. "I'd like to go

back too."

"Well then, we'll go back."

John hugged his father's leg.

Joe said, "Okay. I'll play hooky from the show tomorrow. Let's get ready to go."

While strolling throuhg the amusement park Thursday morning, Joe found an opportunity to phone Bruce.

"Bruce, I'm sorry I can't see you today. I've been roped into taking the family to Disneyland. We'll be here all day, but I'll do my damnedest to see you tomorrow if you're free."

"Sorry you'll have a good time without me, but I understand. I've seen most of the gift show, so we can get together tomorrow."

"Thanks, Bruce. I'll call you in the morning."

During Friday breakfast, Maria informed Joe she and the boys would spend the day at the Getty Art Museum.

"That's great," Joe said. "The boys need exposure to art." *And I'll get some time with Bruce.*

Maria waited in front of the hotel for the tour bus while Joe hailed a taxi.

A few blocks from the hotel, snarled traffic interrupted Joe's trip. After waiting ten minutes without moving, the driver detoured and drove away from the convention hall. Along the way, the cab crossed the path of Maria's tour bus. Maria and Joe saw each other and smiled.

Joe's phone rang. He answered to hear Maria say, "Joe, I thought you were going to the convention hall."

"I am. We got caught in traffic—had to make a detour. Hopefully, I'll get there soon."

"Okay, honey. Be careful. Love you."

"Love you too. Bye."

Joe began to shake. *What would happen if Maria had*

seen me returning to the hotel from the wrong direction or entering Bruce's hotel? Hell, even Mark's place. What the hell am I doing? What'd happen if Maria suspected something?

At the convention hall, Joe continued to think about the ramifications of Maria seeing him in the wrong place at the wrong time. He grew anxious. After visiting a few exhibits, he had seen everything of interest and phoned Bruce.

"Bruce. I've had enough of this show. Can I come over?"

"Sure. Come when you want."

The cab sped to the hotel, spurred on by Joe's request for more speed.

"Keep the change" Joe said, darting from the cab.

He rang Bruce's doorbell and waited.

As usual, Bruce answered the door naked.

"Bruce, don't take this wrong, but would you please get dressed. I wanna do some *normal* things today. Can we go to the zoo, a movie, a seaside pavilion, or—whatever. Some place Maria isn't likely to take the kids. I want us to do *normal* kinds of things. Not just have sex."

"Calm down," Bruce said, looking Joe in the eye. "Sex *is* a normal thing, but we can do whatever you want. What's with you? You're wound as tightly as a G string on a cheap banjo. Relax. I'll get dressed."

The men headed for the lobby where they scanned a rack of brochures advertising local attractions. They chose Venice Beach for its gay atmosphere and promenade. There they could stroll the beachfront and enjoy themselves without fear of confronting Maria who toured inland.

Joe and Bruce strolled the beach promenade, enjoying the sun and ocean breezes. The usual boisterous crowds of skaters, runners, dog walkers, an occasional drag queen, and gawkers filled the walkway.

After walking three-hundred feet, Joe said, "I'm sorry for my mood, but I'm tired living a double life and tired of lying. I'm burning my candle at both ends, and I'm running out of candle. I think I'm in one of those places we talked about, and I don't know what to do."

Bruce put a hand on Joe's shoulder, stopping their stroll. "Well, first of all, relax. You're still wound as tight as a G-string." Bruce pointed to a bench. "Let's sit there."

The men sat down then Joe rested his head in his hands. "God. What am I going to do?"

Bruce gripped Joe's shoulder. "Look at what you're doing to yourself and the people around you. You have to ask yourself, 'Who is most important in my life?' If not you, who? Then ask who is next most important. Make a list. Know the *reason* for each entry. What is there about yourself or the relationship with that person that bothers you? Is it money, shame, love, responsibility, aversion, a misfit, unrealistic expectations, sex, selfishness or what? We've discussed selfish-ness, but you have to be truthful. You've got to ask the hard questions and come up with *real* answers."

Joe stared at the sidewalk, saying nothing.

Following a pause in his one way conversation, Bruce said, "Joe, maybe you should talk to a psychotherapist."

Joe looked up. "Bruce, I'm not *crazy*. Just confused. Mixed up."

"No one is saying you're crazy, but talk-therapy might be helpful, and California might be just the place to do it. No one knows you here—personally that is. Let me see if I can set up an appointment for you?"

"Bruce, you're a good friend, and I trust you—completely. I'll do whatever you think best. Would you do it—

now—please? Find me someone to talk to."

"Okay. Relax!" Bruce patted Joe's thigh. "Come. Let's walk."

As the men continued their stroll, Bruce became pensive and rubbed his chin. "Ah, I've got it." Bruce took out his phone. "Now I know why I splurged on this smart phone. I'll do a Google-search. See if I can find someone near your hotel." Pointing toward a building on their left, Bruce said, "Let's get a drink at that bar while I search."

"It's a gay bar," Joe said. "Look at those guys."

"So what."

Joe selected a table in the shade of an awning then ordered drinks.

Bruce Googled psychotherapists and found four listings for psychologist near Joe's hotel.

"Waiter," Bruce asked, "may I have a pen and a paper, please?"

Bruce called a doctor's office then frowned and looked at Joe. "No appointments until next week. I'll try another one."

Bruce dialed another number. There had been a cancelation. The doctor could see Joe the next morning. Bruce jotted down the information and smiled. "You have an appointment at nine thirty tomorrow morning to see Doctor Sterns. Here's his address. Now relax. Let's enjoy the day."

Joe slapped Bruce on the back. "Thanks, man. I don't know how I can ever repay you."

"Yes you do. Don't play dumb with me."

"Come on, Bruce. Don't you think of anything other than getting me naked?"

Bruce grinned. "Okay, okay. Finish your drink and we'll talk."

They walked for a while before speaking. Soon, they found themselves at Muscle Beach.

Joe pointed toward nine guys working out. "My god, Bruce. Look at the size of those guys!"

"They look just like you, Joe."

"No way."

"You're no shrinking violet, my friend." Bruce slapped Joe's bicep. "Why don't you go say hello. I'm sure they're friendly, and you might learn something. I'll *bet* that even if they kill you they *won't* eat you. Go on! Say hello. I'll sit on this bench and wait—"

"For what—my blood to flow?"

Joe took a deep breath then walked toward the body-builders. As he made eye contact with the biggest man, Joe extended his hand. The beach guys looked at each other as if to ask, 'who is this guy.' Joe started talking, and after a minute, each guy shook his hand and looked him over. Joe continued talking. He soon got lots of back slaps and a bear hug from one guy who lifted him off the ground.

Joe glanced at Bruce and gave him a covert thumbs up.

After some discussion, Joe removed his shirt and stretched out on the bench press deck. The largest guy spotted Joe's lift. The bodybuilders clapped as Joe completed his set of bench presses then sat up. Joe rotated sets with the bodybuilders and soon worked up a sweat. One lifter shared his sweat towel.

Lost in the euphoria of acceptance, Joe realized he had left Bruce too long. He said his goodbyes to the group and walked toward Bruce.

"God! What an eye opener, Bruce." Joe let his shoulders drop. "I couldn't have done that without your pressuring me."

"Yes, I pressured you, but *you* did the work. Now, let's get some lunch."

Saturday morning, Joe took a seat in the waiting room, and completed the usual medical forms. *What am I going to tell this guy? Do I tell him everything?*

After a short time, the receptionist invited Joe to enter an office that reminded him of the décor in Mark's home. Doctor Sterns sat in a leather and chrome chair reading Joe's chart.

The doctor looked up. "Good morning, Joe. My, you're a big guy. Please, have a seat. How are you?"

"I'm well thank you, but as you can imagine, I have problems, or I wouldn't be here."

"Then, tell me what's bothering you."

After a long pause, Joe blurted, "I think I'm going gay."

"Okay, but could it be that you don't know what to *do* about it that's bothering you?"

"You know, Doc, you might of hit the nail on the head. You gotta help me."

"First, tell me about your boyhood then your adult life and then today's problems.

"Okay, but you're going to get an earful."

"That's why we're here. Start wherever you want."

Joe opened the floodgates of his memory. An hour later, he had emptied his soul. He sat motionless, feeling exhausted and wrung out. "I guess most of my problem is my relationship with Maria. I keep asking who comes first in my life? As for the kids, they're . . . young. Well. That's it, Doc. That's my story. Whatta you think?"

The doctor thought for a moment then offered his evaluation.

Fifteen minutes later, he said, "So there you have it Joe. Think about what we've discussed and do the homework I outlined for you. If you want, we can talk by phone. You can email or fax your homework for my review. However, you might want to find help closer to home. If that's the case, let me know. I'll arrange a referral. It's all in your hands now."

"Doc, you don't know how much better I feel. I'd like to

keep in touch. See how things go."

"I'm here when you need me. Take care of yourself and keep in touch."

Joe left the office smiling. He phoned Bruce. "I just had the most awesome morning with Doctor Sterns. Can I come over?"

"By all means. I'm just leaving the show. Meet me for lunch in the restaurant on the mezzanine."

"Okay. See you in thirty minutes."

Bruce chose a chair from which he could see the restaurant's elevators. Before long, Joe arrived and looked into Bruce's eyes.

"Come, sit down," Bruce said as he shook Joe's hand. "Tell me about your morning."

"That Doctor Sterns is a nice guy. I guess I didn't shock him with my story. He seemed interested. Said he'd seen me on TV. We discussed my life and the problems I'm having. He made some suggestions and gave me homework to send back and offered to help me long distance. Said he'd arrange a referral near home if I wanted." Joe took a deep breath then smiled. "Man, do I feel better. I think I have a handle on my problems, some alternatives, and a path that's right for me. The world doesn't seem to be closing in on me."

Bruce nodded understanding and said, "Good."

"I owe you a lot, Bruce. Without your help I would not be where I am now—mentally that is. Thank you, buddy."

"I'm glad you and Doctor Sterns hit it off, and I'm happy I could help. But so much for this doctor talk. Let's have lunch and decide how we should spend the afternoon."

During lunch, the men discussed Joe entering a physique contest, and Bruce informed him how to prepare for competition.

Bruce called for the check. As they waited, Bruce asked,

"So, how do you want to spend the afternoon?"

"Bruce, I'd like to spend the afternoon having wild sex."

Bruce grinned. "I think I can handle that. Can you?"

"We'll see. I could wear my new things."

"I'll think about it."

Joe grinned. "You might have to help me with the weight."

Chapter Twenty-five

Entering Bruce's hotel room, the men hugged then exchanged a passionate kiss. The lifting of stress freed Joe to let go—to enjoy his and Bruce's body as well as their growing relationship. Lips locked, they undressed each other. As pants fell, Joe grabbed Bruce's balls. Bruce returned the favor. Once naked, the men jumped onto the bed and kissed until the point of asphyxia while stroking each other.

"Take it easy," Joe said. "I want it to last all afternoon. Slow down."

"If that's what you want, but how about something new?"

"Like what?"

"Baby oil," Bruce said, retrieving a bottle from the bed-side stand. "It makes everything better."

Joe thought, *I'd better not admit knowing about oil.*

"How is this?" Bruce asked, spreading oil on Joe's cock.

"Wow. That feels good, but it makes me very sensitive."

The men lay on their backs, moving oiled hands up and down the other's cock.

Bruce said, "With that erection, you won't be able to wear your cock ring or the ball weight."

"Right now, I don't mind."

"Maybe I should let you cool off. Then you can don your toys."

"In a while. Just keep doing what you're doing."

The guys lay in silence, stroking each other.

"Whew," Joe said, "better stop for a second. It's feeling *too* good. I can't hold on forever."

Bruce sat up. "Okay. I'll fix us a gin and tonic while you cool down."

Bruce headed to the minibar, preceded by his erection.

Joe lay on his back, hands behind his head.

Bruce looked back at Joe. "You're still up."

"How could I *not* be up, when I'm looking at that ass."

"If that's the case, stop looking. Close your eyes and think of the snow-covered Arctic—naked. That should shut you down."

"But I don't want to shut down. Not like that."

"So, think about something painful."

Bruce mixed drinks then took them to the bed. Joe turned onto his belly, took his drink, and allowed Bruce to rub his butt.

"I could take that butt rubbing for hours."

"Hours, no. Minutes, yes," Bruce said.

"I'll take whatever I can get."

"I know," Bruce chuckled. "But you never know *what* you might get."

"Well, whatever it is, I hope it's yours."

After a few minutes of back and butt rubbing, Bruce said, "Okay, it's my time."

Joe put down his drink then sat astride Bruce's hips and prepared to massage his back. "I should of known you were a dancer," Joe said.

"Oh? How?"

"Ordinary guys have asses that extend down to their legs. Your legs go up to your ass. That's hot."

"I think I've heard that line before, but I'll take it as a compliment."

Joe spied a bit of wrinkled flesh peeking from below Bruce's upturned butt. He pulled at it until he got hold of the enclosed balls. Bruce spread his thighs, inviting ball play. Joe continued to massage Bruce's butt and tug his balls.

"I like that," Bruce said, "but if you keep rubbing your

crotch on me, we'll both be up, and you won't be able to wear your ring or weight."

"So, I'll stop. You wanna help me with the weight?"

"You bet. Get it from the top desk drawer. Better yet, bring both. You take the big one, and I'll wear the small one."

"You will?" Joe asked, sitting on the edge of the bed. "That's hot. I'd love to see that."

After tonguing Bruce's cock, Joe assisted him in donning his ball weight.

"Joe, you'd better hurry. You're getting hard."

"Okay," Joe said, "yours is on. Now stretch my balls while I put this piece around the backside."

Joe fumbled with his weight. "Okay, it's in place. Now, the front piece," Joe said, searching the bedcovers. "Where the hell did I put that screw?" Ah. Here it is. Okay, It's on."

"Great, but don't just stand there," Bruce said. "Spread your legs. Let's see how everything hangs."

Bruce tugged on Joe's weight then pushed it back between his thighs. Released, it swung like a pendulum.

"Damn, that feels good," Joe said. "I love the heft *and* the swinging."

"So I see. You're rock hard."

"Sorry," Joe said.

"Sorry hell. I'm happy to be of assistance."

"Swing yours, Bruce. I wanna see how much your balls stretch."

Bruce thrust his hips, setting his weight into motion. "That does feel good. I haven't worn one of these in years."

"You've worn one before?"

"Oh yeah. There isn't much I haven't done, *sexually*. Remember, I'm instructing you for college credit, so I have to be experienced. I have a doctorate."

Joe pulled Bruce close, kissed him, and then thrust his

hips. Bruce must have sensed Joe's intent and repeated the movement. Both men's weights swung back and forth. Each man squatted an inch or two, allowing the weights more space to swing. With every thrust, the weights arched higher into the men's crotches.

Joe stood erect. "Who'd have thought I'd be using a ball weight to bump crotches with a man?"

"Strange how things happen." Bruce said, kissing Joe on the forehead. "I hope you like it as much as I do."

"How could I *not* like it, especially with you?"

"We'll have to wear them to dinner some night," Bruce said.

"Yeah, but we'd have to wear baggy pant—"

"Let's do it," Bruce said. "We could go to one of those gay places where everyone does crazy things—wear harnesses, collars, butt plugs, ball weights—all that stuff—and no one cares."

"I couldn't. This is my last night in LA, and Maria will wanna go out."

"Tell you what? From what I've heard you say about her, I think I can predict her behavior. Tell her there's going to be a dinner for the closing of the show. Tell her you'd like to take her, and you'll have the hotel get a babysitter for the boys. I'll *bet* she'll tell you to go alone, and she'll have dinner with the boys at the hotel. She'll want to pack, get ready for tomorrow's flight etc., etc. Trust me. I know her."

"Bruce . . . I don't know about that."

"It will be a long time before you get another chance to see how the other half lives. These opportunities don't exist in Smithville.

Joe bit his lip for a second. "Shit. This could get complicated. I shouldn't . . . but . . . okay." *I do wanna see that place.* "I'll do it, but I'd better wait 'til she's back from touring

Pasadena. I don't wanna leave a voice mail."

"Great."

"Now, where were we?" Joe asked.

"I was about to nibble your nipples."

"Please, and swing my weight?"

Bruce nibbled Joe's right nipple and tweaked the left. Joe's cock ring had his cock engorged as never before. This enticed Bruce to rub his knee against it.

Joe moaned. "God, you never stop."

Bruce squeezed Joe's oiled cock in the space behind his bent knee and continued to stimulate Joe.

"Damn, Bruce, you're a contortionist. I dig it, but I'm getting close."

"That's okay. Let me get you off."

"Yeah. Don't stop anything. Oh, Godddddddd."

"Come on, Joe. Let it go."

"Goooooooooddddd!" Joe's yell rattled the nearby lampshade. He fell onto the bed, moaning and panting. Both men were quiet for a minute. "Wow, I didn't think a knee could do that. Sorry I made a mess."

"That's no mess. It's a thank you. There are lots of things you don't know about me—not yet, but don't worry. We have lots of time, and you're a fast learner."

Joe gathered his strength then sat up. "Earlier, you mentioned a butt plug. Tell me about that."

"How about show-and-tell?"

"Uh . . . okay."

Bruce pushed Joe face down on the bed. "Okay, big guy."

Bruce sat astride Joe's hips, rubbed his butt, and then cock-teased his ass. With the aid of KY, Bruce slid inside. Joe winced as his entire body tensed. He took a deep breath, sighed, and then went limp.

"Relax," Bruce whispered then thrust his cock.

Joe's moans revealed his pleasure.

Bruce stretched himself over Joe's broad back and whispered, "Pretend my cock is made of rubber and there's a vibrator inside. Feel that movement?"

"Yeah."

"Imagine if you were able to walk around and experience that sensation wherever and whenever you wanted. With a butt plug you can. I know. You want to try one. I'll get you one when we're in Cincinnati. I'm not taking one through airport security."

Bruce squirmed on Joe's butt.

"Now what?" Joe asked.

"I'm not through with you. Take me for a ride."

The men began synchronized hip movements. Soon, Joe sensed Bruce neared a climax, so he added extra hip and butt actions to carry Bruce to the end of his ride.

"Come on Bruce. Do it. Yeah. Faster. Faster, man."

Bruce emitted a loud moan, gave a great heave, and then fell onto Joe's back, saying "Whoa pony!"

Joe murmured, "I loved the feel of your ball weight slapping my ass. We gotta do that again."

"Sounds good, but it's shower time."

Fifteen minutes later, the guys returned to the bed and rested.

After a minute, Joe looked at the clock. "Our timing's great. Maria's probably at the hotel now. I'd better call her."

"Okay, but first give me a kiss—for good luck."

So Bruce could hear the conversation, Joe held the receiver away from his ear. He presented Bruce's suggestions and waited for Maria's response. As expected, Maria told Joe to go alone. She would hang   out with the boys and pack.

With a sigh of relief, Joe hung up.

"Hallelujah!" Bruce yelled, "We're going to have a balls-swinging dinner tonight! Let me fire up my laptop and see if I can find *the* restaurant."

After examining several websites, replete with photos, some almost pornographic, Bruce selected a restaurant.

"Okay, Joe. Get your ball weight on, we're going out.

Joe thought, *I hope this doesn't turn out to be a night-mare.*

Chapter Twenty-six

The taxi took the hand-holding guys to a seedy part of LA. A single street light strained to illuminate the gritty neighborhood.

"The Kilt," Joe said, pointing to a kilt-shaped sign hanging over a tartan decorated door in an unremarkable brick building.

"Their webpage looked interesting," Bruce said. "Let's hope the food is."

"Do you think our crotch-bulges are too much?" Joe asked, adjusting his ball weight.

"Hell no! From the looks of their webpage, we'll be the least noticed guys here."

Opening the padded front door, booming bass notes compressed Joe's chest. Red light flooded the interior like a bad Halloween version of Hades.

Six men sat at the highly-polished wooden bar. Four wore kilts. One man's kilt was hiked skyward exposing his muscular butt. Two kilt-wearing guys played with each other's cock as if they were alone on a deserted island.

The bartenders were young, muscular bare-chested guys. Three wore leather harnesses and sported tit-rings. One guy wore a dog collar and a spiked Mohawk hairdo dyed red. All wore either Scottish or Irish kilts.

Bruce and Joe had to yell to be heard over the din of the music.

"I see why it's called the kilt," Bruce yelled, eyeing a wall covered with photos of well-known men wearing kilts. "Let's get a drink."

"I see what you mean about us being conservative," Joe said as he sat down on a bar stool.

A young, bare-chested bartender, wearing a red and blue

Scottish clan kilt, extended his hand. "Hi. I'm Bill. Welcome to Kilts."

Joe and Bruce introduced themselves.

"What's it going to be, guys—beer or hard stuff?"

"Two drafts," Bruce said.

The bartender eyed Joe's and then Bruce's crotch. "How heavy are your weights?"

"Not too heavy for a long night," Bruce shouted over the din.

"I'm wearing two pounds," Bill said, lifting his kilt to reveal his weighted balls.

"Great set," Bruce said. "Come around later and I'll pull on them for you."

"How about when I bring your beers?" Bill asked, leaving to get the men's drafts.

"I like friendly bartenders," Bruce said, watching the bartender.

Bill carried the beers to the front of the bar, placed them in front of the guys, and then lifted his kilt. "Give them a tug."

Bruce looked at Joe. "Give them a tug, Joe."

Joe felt his face warm. "Me?"

"Yes," Bruce said. "Give them a tug."

Joe hesitated then grabbed Bill's ball weight and gave it a strong tug.

"Ooooow," Bill said, "Where have *you* been all my life? We gotta get together sometime!"

"Sorry," Bruce said, tapping Bill on the shoulder. "He's taken."

"Why does that always happen to me?" Bill chuckled then walked behind the bar.

Bruce motioned for Bill then asked, "How's the food here?"

"It gets high marks, but that might be because the

waiter's balls and butts are kind of exposed."

"Is there a *special* waiter we should ask for?" Bruce asked.

"Well, seeing you guys are wearing ball weights, ask for John. Not only is he hung, he wears a Prince Albert and a three-pound weight. He has *huge* low-hangers, which he's happy to show off." Bill wiped the bar. "You guys should rent a kilt. It's $20.00 for the night and makes for a fun evening. Somebody is going to want to see your weights, and a kilt makes it easy to show off. The $20.00 includes a locker. You can pay here if you want."

"How about it, Joe?" Bruce asked.

"Uh . . . I like playing with your balls, but I don't want other guys playing with them *or* mine."

"Come on, Joe, it's fun."

Is this going too far. "Okay, but this is a bit fast for me."

"Bill, here's $40.00 for the rental," Bruce said. "Where do we get them?"

Bill pointed left. "Go through that door. The locker guy will take care of you. Oh yeah. *No* underwear!"

Joe chose a green kilt and Bruce chose a red one. The guys donned their kilts then returned to their waiting beers.

Bill leaned over the bar. "Let's see 'em, guys."

Bruce slapped Joe on the back. "Let's show Bill our weights."

Joe shrugged then he and Bruce stood and lifted their kilts.

"Nice," Bill said. "Joe, you're getting hard. It's not fair keeping that thing on that side of the bar. Sure I can't meet you after work?"

"I told you, he's spoken for," Bruce said.

"Why are the hot ones always taken?" Bill asked, leaving to take a customer's order.

281

Joe shook his head. "I can't believe I'm here, no underwear, and I hiked my kilt, so some kid could see my balls."

"Fun wasn't it," Bruce said, smiling. "May I have a feel?"

"Here?" Joe asked.

"Why not? It's been an hour since I pulled them."

"Okay, but quick."

"You mean for an hour don't you?"

"No, Bruce. Just a quickie."

Joe stood and spread his legs.

"They must have warmed up," Bruce said. "They're hanging really low."

Joe and Bruce watched two muscular, bearded guys enter the bar. They waved to Bill and headed for the locker room. Minutes later, the strangers returned bare chested, wearing red kilts and tall black-leather biker boots.

"Look at the size of those guys," Joe said, "Their muscles have muscles and look at the abs on the tall one."

"They're your size," Bruce said, "but the taller guy has the thickest abs I've ever seen."

The strangers introduced themselves to the guys as Brad and Brent.

Everyone shook hands.

"I don't think I've seen you guys before," Brad said. "You from LA?"

"No, just visiting," Bruce said, "but I presume you guys are locals."

"Yeah," Brad said. "We live here—eight years. Right Brent?"

Bruce rubbed his hand over Brad's abs. "Those are the most remarkable abs I've ever seen. Hope you don't mind my feeling them?"

"Nope. Enjoy 'em," Brad said. "We love doing sit-ups

don't we, Brent? Hit 'em if you want. You won't hurt them."

"Nah, just want to feel them," Bruce said, fingering the thick muscles. "Joe, feel these."

Brad pivoted and tightened his abs for Joe's inspection.

"Wow," Joe said. "Killer abs, Brad."

"Thanks."

"How do you like your kilt?" Brent asked Joe.

"They're fun," Bruce replied. "Neither of us has ever worn one before. How about you guys?"

Puffing with pride, Brad said, "We come here just for the kilts. We love them. Would you guys mind if Brent and I have a feel under yours?"

Bruce looked at Joe. "Let's let the guys have a feel. That's why customers wear these things—here."

"Uhhhh, you go first," Joe said.

Bruce then Joe stood. Brad and then Brent felt under the guys' kilts.

Brad nodded. "Nice cocks and balls, guys. Hefty weights too. Bruce, I like your shaved balls. You guys wanna feel us up?"

Bruce felt under Brad's kilt then Brent's.

"Nice nuts," Bruce said. "What's on your balls that make them so smooth?"

"Baby powder," Brad said. "Makes it easy on your hand doesn't it?"

Joe put his hand under Brad's kilt then jerked it back as if he had received an electric shock.

"You're *naked*," Joe said. "I mean you aren't wearing a weight."

Brad chuckled. "Who said I had to wear a weight?"

Shocked, Joe said, "I thought everybody would be wearing weights."

"You're partially right," Brad said. "Lots of guys do but

not everybody. Brent and I don't always get weighted down, because we like guys to play with our balls—not a weight."

"Brad's right," Brent said, "but some guys prefer an ass rub. Other guys like their dicks rubbed. We enjoy getting our balls played with. Here, you can do whatever turns you on as long as you're *discrete*."

Bruce chuckled. "Guess that excludes the guys at the end of the bar. They oughta get a room."

"Ah, ignore 'em," Brent said. "They ain't hurting nobody."

"You guys are big," Brad said. "How often do you work out?"

"Not often enough," Joe said.

"Joe is getting ready to compete," Bruce said, "so he does the most lifting."

Brad smiled. "Brent and I have a gym set up around our pool. We work out every day—naked. Someday, we'll enter a contest, but say, why don't you guys join us for a workout this week."

Feigning disappointment, Joe said, "Thanks, but we're leaving tomorrow."

"Too bad," Brad complained. "We won't get to see you guys naked."

"Nor we, you," Bruce said.

"Hell," Brad said, "Brent and I can get naked for you guys in the locker room if you wanna check us out, or we can email our pictures—naked around the pool—couldn't we Brent?"

"No thanks," Joe said.

Brad said, "We don't mind showing off. We love it; pictures of us naked are all around the world aren't they, Brent?"

Brad placed his hand on Bruce's chest and pinched his nipple. "Nice chest."

284

"If you keep pinching that, I'll get hard."

Looking at Brent, Brad said, "We don't mind do we, Brent?"

Bruce put his hand over Brad's nipple-pinching hand as a gesture for him to stop.

"There *is* something you can do for us," Brad said.

"What's that?" Joe asked.

"Take your shirts off," Brent said. "We'd like to see your chests."

"And maybe your butts," Brent said, smiling.

"Guys, we're not comfortable doing that," Bruce said. "Bear with us will you? Joe and I are from the East Coast. We're shy. You have no idea how strange we feel just wearing a kilt, but you can rub our butts if you want."

Brad took a deep breath. "You're cool, Bruce. No problem. We understand. Well, enjoy the place. If you can't find better balls to play with, ours are available. Oh yeah, if you're staying for dinner, ask for one of John's tables. He's got killer balls and loves to share them with appreciative fans."

Brad turned to leave when Brent said, "Brad might not want to, but I'd like to feel your butts."

Bruce looked at Joe. "Let him have a go at it."

Brad and then Brent felt the guy's butts.

"Damn, Joe, you got one hard ass," Brent said, "and I like your butt-fuzz. Let's go to the locker room. I want to have a look. Feeling is not enough."

"Sorry guys," Joe said. "That's it. But thanks for the compliment."

Bruce and Joe headed toward the dining room.

Bruce chuckled, "I've never met crazier or more straightforward guys than those men. You should've felt their crotches, Joe. Their balls were huge and shaved smooth. With nuts that large, you know they didn't use steroids for muscle development."

"I freaked out when I discovered Brad was naked. I thought he'd be wearing a weight. I'm not used to feeling other guys' naked balls."

In the dining room, the muscular host wore a leather kilt and chest harness. He asked if the guys wanted a table.

Staring at the host's broad hairy chest, Bruce said, We'd like a seat at one of John's chests—I mean tables."

"Oh! John's tables," the host said. "You wanna sit on the ballplayer's side, eh? Well, right this way."

"Ballplayer's side?" Bruce asked. "What do you mean?"

"This side of the room is for guys who play with balls," the host said. "The other side is for guys into butts."

"We love balls playing," Bruce said.

The host chuckled and pulled out a chair for Joe. As the host left, he said, "Have a ball."

Within minutes, a waiter arrived. "Evening guys. I'm John. I'll be taking care of you tonight." John winked. "Care for any of our expensive *cheap* wines for dinner?"

"Two beers," Joe said.

Bruce asked, "How's everything under your kilt?"

"Check it out," John said, lifting his kilt.

Bruce and Joe stared at the longest soft cock they had ever seen.

"Wanna feel?" John asked.

John used his Prince Albert to lift his cock for better viewing. His goose egg size nuts were stretched to the edge of his kilt where he sported a three-pound chromed ball-weight.

"May we?" Bruce asked.

"Sure. They love attention."

Bruce and Joe took turns examining and fondling John's cock and balls.

"How long did it take for you to wear three pounds?"

Joe asked.

"Six months," John said, lifting his weighted balls.

"How long can you wear it?" Bruce asked. "I don't take it off except to put on a heavier one. My goal is to wear five pounds in two years."

"Ouch!" Bruce said. That must hurt."

"They like it," John said, fanning his crotch.

"Your nuts will drag the floor with five pounds," Bruce said.

"I'd love that and so would my friends."

"Good luck," Joe said.

"Thanks guys. Be right back with your beers."

As the evening progressed, other kilt-wearing customers arrived. When they passed, Bruce sometimes asked if he and Joe could feel under their kilts. Every man they asked said, "Yes."

After feeling-up three guests, two newcomers asked Joe and Bruce to stand, so they could return gropes.

Joe whispered to Bruce, "I thought the tall guy would never let go of my butt. Guess he didn't know he was on the ballplayers side of the room."

"Take attention wherever you get it," Bruce said. "Other than a bathhouse, this is the most hedonistic place I've ever seen. Uh oh. I shouldn't have said *bathhouse.* I know. You want to visit one, but there's no time this trip."

"Maybe next trip. I've heard of them. AIDS got spread in bathhouses, right?"

"Yeah, too much depravity. Some guys with AIDS didn't give a damn. Others didn't have a clue."

"That's disgusting. Oh. Look. Dinner is coming."

Dinner proceeded with periodic interruptions to feel a guys crotch or watch customers get their butt rubbed.

"Joe, I hate to say this just as the evening is getting Interesting, but we'd better change and leave. Maria will worry if you're not back soon."

"You're right, but this has been a hell-of-a-trip. You have made this a week to remember."

Joe and his family worked their way through LAX security. Joe made sure his carry-on bag went through the X-ray machine after his family's bags were screened. The screener, a muscular man, stopped the conveyor belt and stared at the images of various things inside Joe's bag.

The screener looked at Joe and smiled. "I see you've been lifting *weights*, eh?"

Joe smiled. He knew the screener had identified the ball-weight. "Gotta stay in shape."

"Sure do," the screener said and winked. "Have a *ball* at your next workout."

"Thanks." Joe took a deep breath then escorted his family to their gate.

Chapter Twenty-seven

Following the California trip, Joe received several calls from Mark and Bruce.

Mark proclaimed his love and pleaded with Joe to live and work with him in LA. Mark often discussed the money he and Joe could earn as a team.

Once, Joe received a call from Mark who entertained a Middle East sheik at a private oasis in the Jordanian desert. "The sheik is into big guys and wants a second man for a threesome. He pays well, and he'll send his jet to pick you up. Can't you get away for a few days? We'll make a ton of money, and I'd get to see you. Please, Joe, say yes."

"God, Mark, you know I can't just up and fly off. Why do you even ask? Besides, I don't dig being a prostitute."

"Ouch. I dig you, Joe, and I want to see you again. Please, try to get away for a few days?"

"No way, Mark."

"You know I don't like hearing *no* about you and money."

"Well, you'll have to get used to hearing no every now and then."

"Joe, there's not another man—is there?"

"Why would you *think* that? I gotta go, Mark."

Bruce often called Joe and reminded him how much he missed him. Every six weeks, Bruce and Joe got to spend a few hours together when Joe went to Cincinnati for supplies. Sometimes, they worked out. Joe often contemplated what life might be like if he lived with Bruce.

One spring day, Bruce called Joe. "there's a physique contest you should consider entering, and it's in Cincinnati. You could spend the night with me before the competition, and I could shave you."

That evening, Joe helped Maria place dishes on the kitchen table. "Honey, I've been thinking about entering a physique contest."

Joe held his breath, waiting for Maria's reaction.

"With the workouts you've been doing, I'm not surprised? If it's something you want to do then I want you to do what's gonna make you happy."

"*If,* I enter, I'd have to shave my body hair. How'd you feel about that?"

"Hmmm," Maria said, lowering the oven door to check on a roast. "You mean you'd have to shave your chest?"

"Yeah, and other places. Contestants have to wear small shorts. Hair interferes with the judges being able to gage a guy's build . . . his muscles."

"Well, I've never been crazy for body hair." Maria turned the roast. "I guess it's not like you're losing it forever. It grows back? Right? I wouldn't want the boys to see their father lose his body hair—forever. Who knows what that'd do to 'em?"

"Don't worry, honey. It grows *back.* Remember when I shaved my ankles for football?" Joe pulled up his pant leg. "See. It grew back."

"You don't mind wearing skimpy shorts in front of strangers?"

"It's just for a few minutes."

"Where is this contest?" Maria asked, basting the roast.

"Downtown Cincinnati."

"When?"

"In two weeks, but first, I have to send in an application."

"Anyone from around here entering?"

"Not that I know of . . . But I hope you and the boys might come?"

Maria removed her oven mitt. "What day?"

"Sunday, three o'clock, but *I'd* have to be there on Saturday."

Maria thought for a moment. "You know I don't like driving in the city. Maybe I could get your dad to drive me and the boys."

"That'd be *great,* hon. See if he'll do that. But you ask him, okay? You know how he feels about men exposing their bodies. I don't want him thinking I'm queer."

Maria adjusted the oven thermostat. "You complete the application; I'll see what I can do with your dad."

The next day, Mark made one of his many calls. Joe told him of his intent to enter a contest. Mark said he would attend even if he wouldn't have any one-on-one time with Joe.

For the next two weeks, Joe spent most of his time preparing for the contest. He worked out twice a day and began a low carb, high-protein diet to lose fat and hone his physique. He kept Mark informed of his progress, and reminded him of the contest date.

Friday morning before the competition, Mark called to say he couldn't attend the contest. He had a high-roller client that weekend. He wished Joe well and promised to call after the event.

Joe felt sad, angry, and put-off by Mark's decision. *How could he be so hot for me one day and then so cool on another?*

Friday night before the Sunday contest, Joe didn't sleep well. He dreamed about seeing himself on stage. He had finished posing, but no one clapped.

Saturday morning, Joe collected his gear and gave Maria a hand-drawn map of the contest's location. From the front door, she waved goodbye as the boys escorted him to his car. He hugged them and whispered, "If daddy had to go away for a while, would you guys visit me?"

"Yeah," Paul said. "We'd get to go places."

"Sounds like fun," John said.

Joe kissed each boy on the forehead then got in the car. Pulling out of the driveway, he waved and drove out of sight of the waving boys.

He became lost in thought. *All this lying is killing me. I don't want to hurt Maria, but I want to see Bruce. I've got to find a way to settle this.*

Bruce's condo receptionists waved Joe through to the elevators. "You're expected."

Joe rang Bruce's doorbell, shifting his weight as if standing on hot coals.

Bruce, naked and wearing a ball weight, opened the

door.

"Dancer man, you're looking weighed down."

"Just so you'd have something to play with," Bruce said, hugging Joe. The men kissed hard and long.

After they came up for air, Joe asked, "Where's my weight? I wanna get naked and hangout with you."

"Not so fast, big guy. First, get naked. I'll shave you and *then* you put on your weight."

"Why wait?"

"So you'll appreciate the ease of putting the weight on when your balls are shaved, but now, I want to play with your balls—*not* a weight."

"Well, get started." Joe unzipped his slacks and pulled out his balls.

Frowning, Bruce said, "You don't get off that easy. *Everything* has to go."

Lusting, Bruce watched Joe undress. "I never tire of watching you strip."

"And I never tire of getting naked. Now, I wanna play with *your* balls, dancer man."

Bruce slapped Joe on the butt. "Take it easy, big guy. Drinks are waiting on the terrace. I want you to lounge around a while so I can admire that bigger, naked bod."

"You think I'm bigger?"

"Absolutely! You look fifteen pounds heavier."

"Close. Twelve pounds—thanks to hard work and lots of protein powder."

"Enough of this muscle-talk. Let's go to the terrace. I'll follow your butt."

Bruce extended his hand. Joe led him to the terrace

where they sat in the sun.

Bruce took a sip of his drink. "Where do you want me to shave you."

"Start with my chest."

"No, funny guy. I mean out here, or on the bed, or wherever?"

"I guess shaving is messy, so maybe we should do it out here."

"Sounds good. When you finish your drink, I'll get the equipment and we'll get started."

"What's all that?" Joe asked as Bruce returned to the terrace.

"I have an electric razor, an extension cord, a plastic pail containing hot water, a can of shaving cream, two towels, a safety razor, and extra blades. I want you to sit on the floor between my legs. I'll start by shaving your head, or don't you want me to do that?"

"No. You can do it?" Joe said, handing a razor to Bruce. "No one else has ever shaved it."

Before the shaving began, Bruce created several shaving-cream hats on Joe's scalp then shared each new artistic shape with Joe, via a mirror. "Well, here goes," Bruce said, drawing the safety razor over Joe's stubbly scalp.

Scalp shaving proceeded without a hitch. Bruce wiped off the excess cream.

Joe felt his scalp. "Couldn't have done better myself."

"Okay, now lie on the lounge, and I'll do your chest. I'll start with the electric razor for the thicker stuff."

Chest hair fell away in thick rolls. Bruce noticed the more hair he removed the more Joe's cock grew.

"My god!" Bruce said. "Shaving turns you on."

"Can't help it. It's your getting me *totally* naked that excites me."

"Well, don't blow your gasket, big guy."

Bruce made the final swipe across Joe's chest with the electric razor then shaved his pubic hair. The next hair to go was the hair at the top of Joe's thighs and the space under his balls. Joe turned onto his belly, allowing Bruce to trim what little hair grew on Joe's butt.

As Bruce spread shaving cream in the plumber's crack, Joe moaned and tightened his glutes. "Can't you warm that stuff?"

After rubbing shaving cream over Joe's butt, Bruce used a safety razor to produce that smooth-as-a-baby's-bottom result. Joe rolled onto his back so Bruce could spread shaving cream on his abdomen, crotch, and upper thighs. He then shaved Joe's chest and around each nipple.

"God, that's hot" Joe said as Bruce nibbled the shaved nipples. "Keep doing that and you'll have me shooting all over the place."

"Then I'll stop—for now."

Bruce stretched Joe's scrotum to create a flat path over which he could safely shave the thin, sensitive scrotal skin.

"I'm glad you're doing that and not me," Joe said.

"Oh. Shaving balls isn't difficult."

"I meant the ball tugging. I love the way you handle my balls."

Shaving completed, Bruce toweled off the remaining shaving cream then admired his handiwork. He ran his fingers over Joe's skin, checking for stubble and smoothness.

"Not bad," Bruce said. "Now, it's time for you to shower."

Joe returned to the terrace and faced a smiling Bruce stretched out on a chaise. "This is the damnedest thing ever," Joe said. "I'm more naked than the day I was born. I had a full head of hair then."

"What do you think of the shaved look?"

"It'll take getting used to. Especially my chest. Not bad though. I can see my pecs better, but my crotch looks like a kid's."

"Yeah, except for the eight-inch cock and those bull balls."

"Everything feels so different without hair. I feel *really* naked."

"So? What do you think?" Bruce asked.

Joe ran his hands over his chest and crotch. "I love it, and my balls feel great. They're slick and smooth. Have a feel."

"I'd *love* to," Bruce said, "and your ass as well, but first, I want to rub baby oil on the shaved areas. It'll reduce skin irritation."

Prepared to have his chest oiled, Joe raised his arms, but Bruce oiled his cock. "Hey! You didn't shave that."

"Shhhh. Let me enjoy myself. Now, turn around." Bruce ran his fingers over Joe's butt several times. "Your ass feels like a baby's. I love it."

"I forgot to check that," Joe said running his hands over each buttocks. "Wow. Ultra-smooth. It feels so different shaved and oiled."

"Okay. You're ready for tomorrow's contest. Now, get your weight on but without my help."

"What?" Joe asked, frowning and dropping his head. "You don't want to play with my balls anymore?"

"Oh, grow up. I'll be right back with your weight."

Moments later, Bruce handed Joe a ball weight then watched as he tightened the screw securing the two halves.

"You were right. The weight is easier to put on. It even feels better, or is it the oil?"

"Both," Bruce said.

Bruce rubbed his chest against Joe's while exchanging a kiss. Catching a breath, Bruce turned Joe around and rubbed his crotch against Joe's shaved ass.

"Damn, that feels good. It's more sensitive. Do that again."

"Happy to oblige." Bruce hugged Joe then ground his crotch against Joe's ass and tweaked his nipples. Between crotch-grinding and the baby oil, Bruce made his way inside.

Each man's hip motions caused their weights to arc between their legs.

Joe pleasured himself but then leaned forward, suggesting he wanted to lie on the lounge.

"No," Bruce whispered. "I want us to have sex while standing. That way I can better work your nipples."

Joe paced his stroking to match his sense of Bruce's

impending climax. The men reciprocated the other's exaggerated hip movements at an accelerating pace. Every few seconds, their weights collided, creating a heightened feeling of ball-tugging pleasure. Joe loved the sensation accompanying Bruce's cock being withdrawn then re-inserted.

Their ecstasy moans reached a crescendo and echoed across the cityscape. Joe held his breath as his legs began to buckle, but Bruce hugged him, keeping him upright. Both men climaxed within seconds.

Struggling to remain upright while coupled, Bruce and Joe slowly laid down on a chaise with Joe's back bearing Bruce's weight.

Bruce lingered for a minute. He slapped Joe's butt and said, "You shower while I rest."

After showering and resting, Bruce ordered Chinese food. The men ate in the media room while watching Joe's DVD about posing. An hour later, Bruce insisted they get to bed early so Joe would be rested for the contest.

Joe woke the next morning, stretched, and then stared into Bruce's eyes. "I love waking up with you beside me—naked."

Bruce stared back. "Me too. How do you think you'll feel when you're *almost* naked in front of that audience *and* your family?"

"Don't wanna think about it especially since dad will be there."

"I'm sure he'll be proud of his son."

Joe turned onto his side. "Dad has recently said some nice things about my size, but he won't like my shorts. He's been kidding me about showing off my body to men." Joe sat up. "I know. Women will be there, but I hear there are usually more men than women. That'll probably make him think most of them are gay."

"Don't worry, Joe. Most of the audience is straight. Many contestants bring wives, girlfriends, sisters . . . Maria and your dad shouldn't be suspicious. Well, we have things to do, and you need to call Maria to make sure your dad still plans to drive your family to the contest."

The guys ate breakfast on the terrace then Joe paced its perimeter. "Bruce, I'm too nervous to sit around here. I'd like to get in a workout at the hall so I'll be ready for the competition. Okay?"

"Sure. Do whatever you have to do. I have things I need to do here."

Joe dressed as Bruce watched.

Bruce said, "At the hall, I'll sit to your far right in the first row. I remember Maria so I'll avoid her." He chuckled, "If you hear lots of yelling from the right side of the hall that'll be me." Bruce sighed then bit his lip. "I won't get to see you again this weekend. You'll be too busy with your family and fans, but don't worry. I'll call you Monday."

The men hugged and kissed then Bruce sent Joe on his way.

Joe checked in at the contestants' desk. He wanted to review the rules and regs, get updated instructions, and select his posing music.

In the locker room, he changed into his posing

briefs and found another man with whom he could reciprocate the oiling of the other's back. Finding an unused wall mirror, Joe rehearsed his posing routine.

An hour later, the short and medium height men's competitions concluded.

Joe sized up his competitors and paced in the wings as he waited for his group to go on stage. *What have I gotten myself into? These guys are huge.*

The muffled voice of the emcee, not heard well backstage, rattled Joe's nerves as the presenter announced, "Ladies and gentlemen. The tall man competition is the next and last contest."

"Here we go," Joe muttered, taking his place in the line of contestants. *God help me.*

The audience yelled and applauded as the almost-naked competitors strutted like gladiators onto the stage.

Joe inhaled the scent of baby oil, wafting from the glistening muscular bodies. *Bet it fills the auditorium.*

The contestants smiled and flexed their muscles, attempting to elicit crowd approval and prejudice judges' decisions before the formal posing started.

Maria whispered to Don, "I've never seen Joe looking so good."

"He's big," Don said, nodding, "but he looks weird without his chest hair."

Pointing to Joe, John spoke to the man sitting next to him. "That's my daddy! He's the tallest, biggest, strongest man in the world!"

Maria muffled a laugh on hearing John.

In the row behind her, a man said, "I think you're right, son."

"He certainly is," Maria mumbled. "Paul, can you see daddy okay or do you wanna sit on my lap?"

Standing on his seat, Paul said, "I see daddy okay."

Squinting from the bright stage lights, Joe saw Bruce sitting in the first row, but the darkness at the back of the auditorium prevented him from seeing his family. *Hope they made it.*

Shifting his weight and shaking his arms, Joe watched the contestants complete their posing routines. As his time approached, he shifted his weight more and more, shaking tension from his arms and hands. *Now I know about stomach butterflies.*

"The next contestant is number 80," the emcee announced. "Number 80, you're up."

That's me. Joe took a deep breath, stepped under the posing lights, shook his limbs, and waited for the music to start.

As Joe waited, the audience roared and clapped. He felt embarrassed. The music started and he began his routine with a well-executed frontal double-bicep pose. He remembered Mark's advice. ". . . move slowly, smoothly from pose to pose. Show your best parts and work them hard. Make the crowd want more, and give it to them. Bounce your pecs for the guys and tighten your butt for the women. Men like biceps so give them your cantaloupes. Work them."

Amazed, Don said, "*Where* did he learn that posing

stuff?"

"At the gym, I guess," Maria said, "but he never talked about it."

"Where'd he get those sissy-blue shorts?"

"I think through the mail."

"Gosh damn," Don said, "he's showing his *everything* to these people."

"Oh, Don, relax. It's just a contest between men."

"I wonder how many queers are here to gawk at these guys—Joe included?"

"Don. That's your son," Maria retorted. "He's just being a man. Give him some respect for God's sake."

Joe finished his routine. The crowd roared their approval, stomped their feet, and refused to let him leave the posing spot. He bowed and waved to the crowd three times before stepping alongside his competitors. His feelings of fear dissolved into relief and pleasure.

The last man completed his routine then the contestants left the stage.

The contestants and audience awaited the judges' decisions.

Thirty minutes later, Maria wondered why it was taking so long to get a decision.

An audience member yelled, "What's taking so long? Who's the winner?"

The audience clapped in unison and yelled as another ten minutes passed.

The emcee picked up the microphone, walked to the front of the stage, and then announced, "Ladies and gentleman, third place in the big man's contest goes to Joe . . ."

Maria held her breath when she heard "Joe." She thought her husband had won third place.

"Joe . . . Green," the emcee announced.

A polite round of applause rose from the audience.

"The second-place winner is . . . Joe . . . Wertz."

Maria turned to Don, "I hope Joe is happy with that."

"I hoped he'd win first prize, but second ain't bad," Don said.

Many in the audience clapped, but most people booed.

The emcee readied himself for the last announcement. "Ladies and gentlemen, the first place winner is . . . George . . . Wood."

Some of the crowd clapped, but many booed.

The contestants took their trophies and started to leave the stage when the emcee announced, "Would the contestants please return to the stage. Ladies and gentlemen, please stay where you are."

A collective buzz filled the auditorium.

"There has been a computation error," the emcee announced. "The first place winner is *not* George Wood! The winner is *Joe Wertz!*"

The audience erupted with applause and shouts of approval. Many audience members rushed the stage to congratulate Joe.

"Yeah! Joe won," Maria yelled. "He won!"

John and Paul jumped up and down, yelled, clapped, and then hugged their mother and grandfather.

"Daddy won! Daddy won!" Paul yelled to everyone

around him. "My daddy is the biggest, strongest man in the world."

When the ruckus died down, the emcee addressed the audience, "Ladies and gentlemen, would you believe the man who won first prize has never before competed in a physique contest? Look out Schwartzenegger here comes Joe!" The emcee waited for the audience's roar to subside. "If you haven't recognized him, our winner is Ohio's favorite son—the one and only *President's Plumber*!"

The audience clapped with abandon as they yelled in unison, "Joe! Joe! Joe!"

"I'm so happy for Joe," Maria said, hugging Don.

Joe glimpsed Bruce, clapping as if the Cincinnati Bengals had won the Super Bowl. He waved to Joe then walked toward the exit, disappearing into the darkness.

Joe's heart sank.

With the adulation of the crowd, Joe left the stage. Backstage he received a round of applause and congratulations from fellow contestants. Many of them asked for his autograph as he pushed his way to the locker room.

He showered, dressed, and then looked for his family in the designated waiting area.

Joe's sons hurled themselves at his legs as he hugged Maria and then his dad. Joe picked up his sons, held them to his chest, and then kissed each on the cheek.

"Daddy, where's your trophy?" John asked.

"I get it in a few weeks. They have to engrave it."

Having to pick up his trophy later would give him a chance to see Bruce.

Excited, little Paul yelled from his father's arms, "And then, and and. . . then, uh . . . I can show it to my friends. My daddy's the biggest, tallest, strongest man in the *world*!"

Bystanders laughed at Paul's excitement as Joe stood him on the floor.

"We're very proud of you," Maria said, hugging Joe and kissing him on the cheek.

"Very proud, son," Don said, slapping Joe on the back.

The next day, all the Ohioan, and a few national, newspapers published pictures of Joe and the story of Joe, *The President's Plumber,* winning the contest.

Joe's handlers at the Republican Campaign Office saw the press photos. They met to discuss how they might use Joe's publicity to their advantage. A week later, the national campaign office manager asked Joe to do another tour with the president. This time, his per diem would be tripled.

Joe discussed a second tour with Maria and Don.

"We could use the money," Maria said. "Do it."

"It'd be another shot-in-the-arm for the business," Don said.

A week later, Joe joined the tour. His new clothes, paid for by the tour manager, exploited Joe's physique. In photos and on TV, the muscular spokesman became an icon. His image spread worldwide.

Tour officials and the press agreed. Joe's

appearances helped attract larger than expected crowds at rallies, making him a celebrity.

Joe continued to workout while touring. He gave interviews in gyms as TV cameras zoomed in for close-ups of his chest, biceps, and shaved head. People scampered to be photographed with him and get his autograph. He had his share of ass pinches, gropes, and ass rubs, but not all were from women.

He had verbal offers to do motivational speaking, modeling, sponsor products, write a book, run for elected office, do a TV ad for gym equipment and for protein powder, but contracts failed to appear.

Mark saw Joe on national TV news and phoned him.

"How're you doing, Mark?"

"Guess you saw my name on your cell screen?"

"You guessed it."

"You seem to be doing well for yourself."

"Yep," Joe chuckled. "I make money with my clothes on."

"Why didn't you tell me you won your contest?"

"Ahh, just a local thing. Not an important one like you won."

"Joe, I'm sorry I haven't called lately. You know how business can be. I've been traveling a lot but not back East. I'm sorry I couldn't be at your contest, but it would have been nice if you'd told me you won."

"Mark, *you* said you'd call me. Remember? I gave you the date, time, and place."

"Forgive me. From what I see on TV, you're in Cincinnati a *lot*. Too bad you can't visit LA."

"Travel? Nah. I've got three more days doing tour stuff, and then, I can go home."

"Man, I miss you terribly. I'd like to see you. What say I come to Cincinnati? Surely, you can find an hour or two for us."

"Mark, you know I don't have the same feelings you say you feel about me. Don't you think it'd be better if you found a special guy in LA rather than me?"

"What can I say, Joe. I love you. I want to see you. Need to see you! Tell you what. I'll come to Cincinnati. Let's see if we can get together on your terms. Okay?"

"That's a bad idea, Mark."

"It'll be good for you—me—for both of us."

"I don't have time to breathe much less see you."

"Joe, Joe, Joe. You *know* I love you, and you like me."

"Mark, I'm seeing a guy that I kinda like."

"Joe! He *couldn't* be right for you—not like me."

"He and I have more in common than we do, Mark."

"That *can't* be true, Joe."

"Mark. Face reality. You need to move on."

"But Joe, I want *you* in my reality."

"Mark, I don't fit your lifestyle—or your reality."

"We can find compromise. There's always room for compromise."

"What? Seeing weird guys for sex—no way, Mark."

"Damn it. Give me a chance, Joe."

"You helped me out of the closet, so I owe you, but I can't say I love you when I don't."

"You're just confused, Joe. You *do* love me!"

"Don't make this hard, Mark. Please. You've got to move on."

"Joe, think about my proposal. I'll call when I get to Cincinnati. We can take it from there, big guy. Remember, I don't like no's."

Chapter Twenty-eight

Mark took a "red-eye" flight from LA, arriving at 9:22 a.m. in Cincinnati. He called the Republican campaign office to inquire about the President's Plumber's speaking schedule. Mark learned Joe would speak at 2:00 p.m. in a park near the Republican Campaign Tour Office.

At noon, Mark phoned Joe. Joe did not answer the call.

Five minutes later, Mark phoned again. Joe ignored his phone.

Five minutes later, Mark phoned again.

Mary, a tour member and one of Joe's handlers, asked, "Not answering your phone, Joe?"

"It's someone I don't want to talk to."

Mary chuckled, "I know what you mean."

Mark kept calling, but Joe ignored the calls.

Joe started a call when his phone rang again. *Damn! Maybe I should take it.* Cupping the phone with his hand, Joe said, "Mark, I told you we can't get together."

"All I want is an hour, Joe."

"Mark! Listen carefully. I do *not* want to speak to you again! Do I make myself clear? Let's not let this get ugly."

"Joe, don't *yell* at me. I need to see you. I *love* you!"

"Mark, I do *not* love you, and I do not want to see you. Bye!"

Shaking inside, Joe busied himself with office affairs and then was driven to the park to give his two o'clock speech. His voice broke a few times after he thought he saw Mark at the edge of the crowd.

After Joe had answered the last question from the crowd, bodyguards drove him to a secret place where he got into his car then headed to Bruce's apartment.

Joe had a key to Bruce's apartment and let himself in.

He had begun to undress when Bruce, naked, walked in from the terrace and gave him a hug then a kiss.

"Saw you on TV," Bruce said. "Seems reporters aren't interested in the economy anymore."

Joe shook his head. "All they want is for me to talk about the Bible and gay marriage. I'm sick and tired of their stupid questions. Whatta they think I am—a preacher? I'm ready to quit this stupid tour! If it wasn't for the money *and* the contract, I'd be gone."

Joe threw his underwear on a chair.

"*Relax*," Bruce said. "Go lie on the bed. I'll get some lotion then I'll give you a back rub."

"Sounds good."

Joe threw himself, face down, on the bed, arms folded in front of his head.

Entering the bedroom, Bruce said, "I love that butt."

Joe twitched his glutes. "Don't fuck it. At least not yet. You can rub it *if* you first rub my back."

"Deal."

Bruce returned with oil then straddled Joe's hips, kissed his shoulder, and started the promised backrub.

"You have no idea how much I needed a backrub. An ass rub would feel good too."

"What's bothering you?"

"Things . . . Demands. Schedules. *People*."

Considering what you've been doing, I thought we'd have dinner in tonight. Is that okay?"

"Good. I don't wanna go out or see anybody—other than you."

"There. That's enough rubbing for now. Take a nap. I'll wake you at drink time."

After an early dinner, the men lounged on the bed in the

master bedroom, awaiting the evening TV news. Cradling Joe's head in his lap, Bruce caressed Joe's chest. His fingers lingered over each bit of chest stubble.

Joe purred with pleasure.

The television announcer said, "Stay tuned for a recorded press conference concerning revelations about the President's Plumber."

Bruce stopped caressing Joe's chest. "What's that about?"

Joe lay pensive for a moment. "Hell if I know . . . just have to wait and see."

Bruce stared into Joe's eyes and shrugged.

After the first commercial break, the local news anchor said, "We now go live to Leslie Arrow, on location, for breaking news."

"Thank you Harry. I'm Leslie Arrow outside the Cincinnati Republican Party's Campaign Tour Office where Mark Hanlan held a press conference that will set most Republicans, and the world, on their heels. Mister Hanlan disclosed shocking information about the President's Plumber."

"Oh my god!" Joe yelled and sat up. "Don't do this, Mark. Don't do this!"

"Who the hell is Mark Hanlan?"

"Please, wait a minute, Bruce?"

Bruce leaned back against the headboard.

Leslie continued, "Because our tape reveals adult material, some content has been blurred. Discretion is advised. Let's roll the tape."

The video showed Mark standing on the steps of the tour office before twenty reporters, multiple microphones, and several TV cameras. He wore tailored casual clothing that revealed every inch of his muscular body and ample crotch. He started to speak but stopped to clear his throat.

"My name is Mark Hanlan—spelled H A N L A N."

"I am a professional escort and model. Most of my customers are men—men from around the world. I earn my living by helping them attain secret sexual desires away from the prying eyes of homophobes. For many months, I have had a consensual, commercial free, sexual relationship with the man called the President's Plumber."

"Fuck! Is that true?" Bruce asked, shaking Joe's shoulder.

Joe said nothing as Mark continued. "Joe is *not* who or what you think he is. He has pretended to be a man with family values that are above reproach. He is misleading himself, his family, *and* the American public about his moral and sexual values.

"The President's Plumber traveled to California to see me and have sex. I visited him near his hometown of Smithville, Ohio. I've met his sons—great boys. I, Joe, and his sons spent a wonderful afternoon fishing and skinny dipping in a pond near their home."

"Oh God," Bruce exclaimed, staring at Joe. "Say it isn't true, Joe. Say he's lying."

Joe stared at the TV screen.

Gasps emanated from the reporters as camera crews jostled for better positions to photograph Mark.

Mark extracted a sheaf of glossy color photos from an attaché case then waved them over his head. "Here are some adult-type photos of Joe that *I* took when I secretly visited him in an Ohio motel in Smithville."

The TV camera moved in on a blurred nude photo of Joe. "These will prove my case. I believe Joe has a male lover here in Cincinnati. I wish them well in their relationship." Mark paused a moment. "Joe refused to see or speak to me today, so I'm sorry to tell him, via television, he may have the AIDS virus." Mark took a deep breath. "I have recently learned I do. Joe, his Cincinnati lover, and his wife should be checked for the virus. That's all I have to say. I will not be taking questions." Mark placed three piles of photos on the building steps. "These photo copies are for the press. Thank you."

The television picture switched to the female announcer. "There you have it, Harry. This is Leslie Arrow reporting from the Republican Campaign Tour Office in Cincinnati. Now, back to Harry in the studio."

Bruce pressed the off button on the TV remote then slumped onto the bed. A crushing silence filled the room.

Joe hung his head in his hands and wept in waves of despair. "Shit! Shit! What have I done? God, I'm ruined. Damned."

Bruce took a deep breath, shrugged, and turned his palms to the sky. "Joe . . . I don't know what to say. How long have you known this . . . Mark Hanlan?"

Through sobs, Joe stuttered, "I met him the same week-end I met you . . . last year."

Silent, Bruce looked at Joe with a befuddled gaze. "Is he the guy you once said you didn't want to talk about?"

The apartment became as quiet as a corpse.

"Yes," Joe whispered, wiping tears. "He's the guy."

"And you saw him after you left my apartment? And you . . . lied about going home when you left me?"

Sobbing, Joe said, "Yes."

"And you and the boys went skinny-dipping?"

"Yes . . . for an hour or so. One weekend."

"What the fuck were you thinking, exposing your kids to a naked fuck buddy—a lover?"

"I wasn't thinking. I shouldn't have done it."

"You were seeing him *and* me while you were in LA?"

"I was experimenting, but I didn't love you then."

Bruce stared at the ceiling. "When you said you were with your family, were you with him?"

"Part of the time. But I'm finished with him. He's trying to—no, he is destroying me. Partly because of you, but mostly because I did not want to see him again. He's jealous. He wanted me to live with him in LA and join him in his sex business. I said *no*. Told him I didn't love him, and I'd fallen for you, but I never mentioned your name. I swear! No one else knows about us."

"Well, my lobby man knows. Had you decided to tell your family?"

"Believe me," Joe mumbled, "I've been working on a plan—not that it matters now."

Feeling like a ruined man, Joe sobbed. "I never wanted this, Bruce. Believe me. I just wanted us to get on with our lives but look at the mess I've made. Maria has to know by now. She and dad always watch the evening news." Joe sobbed for a moment then regained his composure. "My boys can't go to school again—*ever*. They'll be harassed by *so-called* friends. I've ruined my life and the family's. This could kill mother." Joe burst into tears. "Dad's probably yelling about how I've let him down—how I've *disgraced* the family—ruined our business." Tears running down his cheeks, Joe looked at Bruce. "I know nothing about the virus thing. I thought Mark was clean. I knew I was. I hope to hell you, me, and Maria are okay. Oh, Bruce. I'm so sorry."

Bruce wiped his tears with the sheet. "Joe, I feel betrayed by someone I loved. How could you do this to me—to us? Even worse, I may be infected with HIV because of you!"

"Oh god, Bruce, I don't know what to say . . . the AIDs thing. We can't . . . You *can't*, have it—not because of me!"

"And Maria . . . what about *her*, Joe?"

314

"God, I don't know. I was planning to tell the family about . . . me . . . my secret life. Believe me. I want to stop all the lying. I wanted to live with you. I knew I could find work here and continue to see my boys. I wanna see them grow up. I wanna take care of them." Sobbing harder, Joe said, "Maria? I don't know what'll become of her. My dad? Guess he'll just do whatever he has to do."

"Well, Joe, seems Mark Hanlan has forced you out of the closet. God only knows what else will happen now."

"Please, don't hate me, Bruce."

"Joe . . .You're not the first man to hurt me, but I'll get over it. We might be able to work out something about our relationship, but right now, I think you should go."

A hush filled the room. Feeling desperate, Joe lifted his head and stared at Bruce. "Please don't make me leave. Not now. Where would I go. I don't wanna see anybody—not Maria, my family, not anyone."

"Joe, I—no we—need some alone time."

"Please, Bruce. Please. Let me stay."

"Go home, Joe. Confront Maria, your boys, your mom and dad. Get it over with. You have to start there. Go home."

Joe dressed. The usual ass slapping and ball groping didn't happen. No one laughed. There were no smiles.

Joe moped out the door with no idea where he would go.

He ignored the lobby clerk and forced himself to his car. He looked up at Bruce's terrace but saw no one.

Joe sat in his car for a long time, sobbing. "God help me. Please . . . God help me." *What have I done . . . Where do I go?*

Chapter Twenty-nine

Maria stared in disbelief at the TV. "What did he say about Joe?" *Am I dreaming?* "He was swimming naked with the boys? It can't be true. There must be a mistake. Joe can't be involved in something like this." Maria paced. "Shit!" *Where are the boys?* "Boys! Where are you? Get in here—now!"

John and Paul walked into the den, looking as though they were murder suspects. Maria turned off the TV.

"We're just playing Xbox," John said. "We ain't done nothing."

Maria stooped and look her sons in the eye. "I want you guys to tell me the truth. Did you and daddy go skinny dipping with a big man at the pond?"

Paul looked at John who put a finger on his lips. Paul smiled then said, "Mister Marvel's friend. He's a friend of daddy's."

"Oh God!" Maria said, slapping her forehead. "Did you guys go swimming without swim suits?"

Paul stared at the floor and put his hands in his pockets. "Daddy said we're not supposed to tell."

John smiled. "Mister Mark's a nice man. Really tall. He helped Paul in a swimming race."

"Did Mister Mark do anything to you guys that he shouldn't do? Anything bad?"

"No, mama," Paul said. "He's a nice man."

"Real nice," John said.

Maria slumped onto the sofa. Tears welled as she shuddered. "Go play."

"What's wrong, mama?" John asked.

"I got something in my eye. I'm okay. Go play with your games." Maria sobbed. *I can't believe Joe did gay stuff. Not my Joe.*

Grabbing a tissue, she wiped her eyes wondering what to do. Joe had spent a lot of time in Cincinnati but now she wondered if he had done that because he had a gay friend—a gay lover? *Has he been lying to me? Why? Oh God, have I done anything to turn him gay? I've got to know.* She scanned the room. "Where in the hell did I put that damn phone?"

Driving slowly, Joe meandered around Cincinnati. After two hours of self-bludgeoning mental anguish, he drove through the old factory area of the city then headed west.

He entered a dingy, dimly-lighted bar on the far west side of town. No one seemed to recognize him or care he had joined their depressing company. The elderly, disheveled bartender showed more interest in his own drinking than serving customers.

Joe yelled for a double whiskey with a Coke chaser. He dispatched the drink in three gulps. "Two more," he yelled.

An androgynous looking street lady of ancient vintage, reeking of urine and beer, waddled past Joe and went to the jukebox. She wore two caps, and despite the warm weather, several old coats and multiple pairs of pants. After searching several pockets, she found a coin then inserted it in the antiquated jukebox. Its faded bubbly neon lights were difficult to see through years of accumulated grime.

The twangy voice of Tommy Wynette filled the bar singing "Stand By Your Man."

Joe sobbed loudly.

The street lady crept to his side. She patted him on the back and, in a gravelly voice, said, "There, there, Sonny. Lots of people get jilted." She hiccupped. "Don't you worry none. It'll all work out."

Joe downed his drink then yelled, "Bartender, bring me a double! For the road!"

After tossing several bills on the bar, Joe took his new drink to his car awkwardly angled across two parking spaces. As he opened the car door, his phone rang. He stared at its screen. "Maria. Can't talk to her now."

Not knowing where to go, Joe drove through the city until he felt the need for another drink. He stopped at a liquor store where he bought a liter of whiskey. He took several gulps of his anti-despair elixir then gunned his car into traffic. *I don't wanna, but I gotta go home.*

Intoxicated, he found his way to the interstate then the state road that would take him home. He knew he weaved all over the road, so he slowed his speed, hoping not to attract unwanted attention.

His cell rang. He didn't recognize the number but answered, "Yeah."

A strained voice asked, "Joe Wertz?"

"Maybe," Joe mumbled.

"Joe, this is Mary. Mary from the campaign tour office. We won't be needing your services anymore." The line went dead for several seconds. "Joe, tell me the story isn't true."

"Maybe."

"Are you okay?"

"Maybe."

"Joe. This is Mary. Say something!"

"Bye."

Sobbing, Joe pulled off the road. "God help me. Please, God help me. What am I goin' to do?"

Joe's phone rang again. *Maria. Not now.*

Between sobs, he gulped mouthfuls of whiskey and soon fell asleep. His head fell on the horn, startling him awake. *Where am I?* It took minutes for Joe to orient himself. After downing another drink, he started the car and pulled onto the road.

Ahead, he noticed a liquor store and drove onto its

parking lot. With a bang, his car bumper rested against the store steps. Hanging on to the car door, he steadied himself then staggered inside.

The owner asked, "Ain't you that Joe guy on TV?"

"Hell if I know what you're talking about. I want two bottles of cold champagne to go."

Joe slammed money on the counter, and the owner handed him the bagged champagne bottles.

"Better be careful driving, young man."

"You betcha!"

Joe drove ten miles an hour in a fifty-mile-per-hour zone, thinking his slow weaving along the road would not attract attention. Instead of thirty minutes, it took him three hours to get to Smithville, but he made it without incident.

Crossing the town line, he finished his first bottle of champagne and recalled the first time he drank champagne with Bruce.

Darkness shrouded Main Street as Joe neared his shop. The combination of too few mercury and sodium-vapor streetlamps gave an eerie glow to the empty street. The boarded-up storefronts made the village feel like a ghost town.

Joe parked outside his darkened shop. "God give me mercy."

For the first time, he felt abandoned—alone. He slapped the steering wheel. "Damn!" His thoughts became verbal as he cried out, "Dad, please . . . please . . . forgive me! I've tried so hard to be a good son. I'm sorry I let you down. Please, can you find it in your heart to forgive me? Please . . . Dad, forgive me!"

Joe's phone rang. He put his fingers in his ears and shook his head. "No."

Five minutes later, his phone rang again.

"It's her." *Damn. Damn.* Joe answered, "Yeah."

"Joe!" Maria yelled. "Where are you? I've gotten calls

from your dad, Mister Mark and a lotta hateful people about that TV thing. Are you coming home?"

"Maybe."

"Are you drunk?"

"Maybe."

"Joe! Come home. We *need* to talk."

"Maybe."

"Did you hear me? We have to talk!"

"Maybe. Bye."

"Joe. *Don't* you hang up."

"Maybe. Bye."

Joe's periodic sobbing fractured the silence smothering Main Street. His shirt and trousers were soaked with tears and spilled champagne.

"John. Paul. What've I done to you guys? Please forgive me. I know what your friends are going to say, and I'm sooooo sorry. Please forgive me. Forgive me. Mark, *why* did you do this? Damn it! *Why*?"

Joe swilled the last of his whiskey then left the car. Clutching the second champagne bottle, he staggered toward the shed behind the main shop where he remembered storing a rolled up sleeping bag.

At the shed, he struggled with key and lock alignment. After several attempts, he unlocked the door. Summer heat had stirred the acrid smell of grease and solvents stored inside.

Spying a rickety chair, Joe eased himself onto its seat then battled the wire cage securing the cork in the champagne bottle. After repeated attempts, he loosened the wire then threw it into a corner. Pop! The cork flew across the room causing warm champagne to spew across the room. Joe rushed the hemorrhaging bottle to his mouth. The hot bubbles felt sharp on his tongue. He winced and gulped three mouthfuls.

Balancing himself on the chair, he scanned the room,

looking for the sleeping bag. Stilling his bobbing head, he blinked several times to clear his vision. He saw the sleeping bag sticking out of its black plastic wrapper on a top shelf. *I need the ladder to get it.*

Shaking and staggering, Joe struggled to position the ladder against the flimsy shelf then climbed to the sleeping bag. He yanked it forward causing it to topple to the floor. He tried to catch it mid-flight but failed. He too almost fell to the floor twelve feet below.

"Damn it! I can't do anything right," Joe said, weeping.

Months earlier, the rolled sleeping bag had been securely tied while he and John had been on a Cub Scout camping trip. Joe had taught a class on knot tying and had demonstrated his skills by securing this sleeping bag with multiple knots. Now, he struggled to untie them. He stopped often to take a swallow of warm champagne and cry. Many attempts later, the knots yielded, and he unrolled the sleeping bag on the shed floor.

He kicked off his shoes then removed his socks. Undressing, he fumbled with each piece of clothing. After losing a struggle with shirt buttons, he ripped the shirt open then pulled it off his shoulders, but he couldn't get the buttoned sleeves over his hands. The shirt dragged the floor as he stumbled around the shed, shaking his arms to dislodge the sleeves and free his hands.

Next, he struggled with his zipper, moving it half-way down. He then tugged at the hook at the top of his trousers, but he pulled in the wrong direction and wondered why it would not open. Exhausted, he slumped onto the chair and stared at the hook. "Ah, it moves that way."

Joe opened the hook then stood. His pants fell toward the floor, but they stopped at knee level. Using his left hand to steady himself on the chair, he stepped on each pant leg, freeing his feet from his pant legs.

After struggling with his underwear, he tore them away.

A remnant of the elastic waist band remained around his waist.

Joe caught a glimpse of himself in a shard of mirror leaning on a shelf. "Who the hell do you think you are *mister muscle* guy?" He placed his face against the mirror. "A fucking *loser* that's who!" He shook his fist at his reflection. "Son of a bitch! Just look at you, Mister *fuck up*!"

Joe slumped onto the chair, scrunching his balls. He pulled them free then hung his head and wept. Tears, falling onto his thigh, coalesced into a rivulet that streamed down his right leg. The coarse rope used to tie the sleeping bag, lay bunched beneath his bare foot, irritating it. He managed to pull it free then draped it over his thigh, wicking away his tears.

Howls of despair shredded the night as the wails of a broken man filled the shed. Head held in his tear-washed hands, Joe prayed, "God please help me. Forgive me."

Joe reached for the champagne. Sobbing, he took a gulp then set the bottle down. He dropped his head, leaned forward on his chair, and released a deluge of tears. When his eyes had nothing more to give, he forced himself upright. He staggered toward the ladder, dragging the rope on the floor. Ignoring the cold of the metal rungs on his feet, he climbed the ladder.

Maria paced in her living room, wringing her hands and crying. Picking up the phone, she thought, *Should I call him again? No. I'll call Don . . . see what he knows.*

"Don. It's Maria." She sobbed. "Have you heard from Joe?"

"No. Have you?"

"I spoke to him a few minutes ago. He's drunk. He hung up on me. Damn him!"

"Did he say where he was?"

"No."

"Did you hear any background noises to hint where he

might be . . . like a bar?"

"Nothing."

Don took a deep breath then became quiet. "Maybe he's in his car or worse. He's driven off the road somewhere. I was thinking about calling the police. Sergeant Taller is probably working the night shift. I'll ask him to watch for Joe and his car. It could be off road. God only knows where he could be if he's drunk."

"Don, I'm worried."

"Me too. Mother's shaking in her rocker. She's been crying ever since she saw that damn TV thing. She keeps asking if that Hanlan guy was telling the truth, and then she says, 'It's all a lie.' I can't console her, and I can't tell her Joe's missing. I don't know what to do. I mean he's still my son."

"You want me to come over?"

"Thanks, Maria. Just take care of the boys."

Don called 911 and spoke to the dispatcher. She transferred Don's call to Sergeant Taller.

"George, this is Don Wertz. How're you doing tonight?"

"I'm fine Don. What can I do for you?"

"George, I'm concerned about Joe. That damn TV show has me so upset I don't know what to do, but God, I love that boy, and I want him back—no matter what."

"How can I help?"

"I haven't heard from him, and I don't know where he is, but Maria spoke to him a while ago. She thinks he's drunk. It's possible he's in his car somewhere . . . maybe off the road. Maybe hurt. I was wondering if you could cruise around town and the back roads; see if you can spot him."

"Sure thing. I'll call if I see anything. I'm sorry you have to deal with that TV stuff, but I'll keep an eye out for him."

"Thanks, George. I owe you one, buddy."

"Don't mention it, Don. Over and out."

Don exhaled a long sigh and for a moment stared into space. He then phoned Maria.

"Maria, I called George Taller. He's gonna keep an eye out for Joe and his car."

"Thanks, Don. I'm so worried I don't know what to do."

"Why don't you and the boys come here. If Joe needs me tonight, I wouldn't want to leave mother alone."

"Okay, Don. I'll get the boys ready and come over."

Don's phone rang as Maria's headlights shined in his front room windows.

"Mother," Don said. "Maria is here."

Don opened his phone.

"Don, it's George. When you called, I was cruising around downtown. I noticed a car parked kinda haphazard in your parking lot. It looks like Joe's."

"Are you there now?"

"Yep, just pulling beside it now. Hold on a minute . . . Don, the car's empty, and the doors are unlocked."

"See any lights inside the shop?"

"No. It's dark."

"Maria has just pulled in my driveway. I'm gonna get her settled in, then I'll drive there and have a look around."

"Okay, Don. Sorry. Gotta—"

"There's a lot static, George. I didn't understand you."

"It's my radio. I gotta get to the Hamilton's. Mike's beating his wife again."

"Okay. George, I'm much in your debt."

"Hope everything works out all right."

"Thanks."

Don hung up then went to Maria's car. He helped Maria unload her sons and their bags and said, "George found Joe's empty car at the shop."

"God, I hope he's alright."

"I'm going to look for him. Why don't you go in and see to mother? See if you can calm her down. She's been crying over that TV show."

"Okay, Don. Call when you get there."

"Will do. Put the boys to bed upstairs."

Lois sat in her rocking chair, staring into space. She looked at Maria and burst into tears. "I can't believe what those TV people said about Joe. It can't be true. Say it's not true, Maria?"

"I don't know what to believe, Mother, but we need to find him. Don's gone to the shop to look for him. Don's police friend said he saw Joe's car parked there."

"Oh God! I hope nothing's happened to him."

"Don thinks he's in the shop—drunk. He's on his way to check on him now."

Don screeched to a stop beside Joe's car. Walking around it, he looked for anything to suggest an accident but found nothing. He saw several empty wine and whiskey bottles on the front seat and the floor.

"He's drunk. He's Gotta be inside."

Don unlocked the shop's front door and turned on the lights. He looked everywhere he thought Joe might hide or sleep. As Don searched, he glanced out a rear window and noted a light in the shed. *Bet he's in there.*

The last of Joe's tears dripped from his chin. With unsteady moves, he climbed the ladder then sat on the top rung, staring at the sleeping bag below. Fumbling with the rope, he made a large slipknot loop then surveyed the rafters. To steady himself, he grasped the rafter over his head. He tossed the loose end of the rope over the joist then tied several knots to hold it in place.

Sobbing, he dropped his head in his hands. After a few seconds, he wiped a tear, took a deep breath, and then stood at attention as he had done when commanding his Cub Scout troop. He took another deep breath, placed the loop of rope over his head then cinched it around his neck. Arms at his sides, he wobbled back and forth, staring straight ahead. Swaying, he held his right foot eighteen inches in front of the left one as if ready to take a step. He took a deep breath, leaned forward, and walked.

Don knocked on the shed door. "Joe. You in there? Joe! Are you in there?"

Don opened the door and saw the sleeping bag and ripped clothes scattered on the floor. Just then, he heard a noise behind him and turned to see Joe hanging by the neck. His twitching feet were striking the ladder.

"Joe!"

Don's Army field training kicked in. He grabbed a knife from the workbench and raced up the ladder. He had cut halfway through the rope when the remaining strands broke, and Joe fell to the floor. His legs continued to twitch.

Don scurried down the ladder, dropped to his knees, and with trembling hands, pulled the rope from Joe's cyanotic neck. Don had just started mouth-to-mouth resuscitation when Joe gasped an agonizing breath, coughed, and then opened his eyes.

Looking skyward, Don said, "Thank you God!" He slapped Joe and asked, "How could you do this?"

Don pulled Joe to his chest, hugged him, and wept. "Thank God, you're alive." Don rocked back and forth, hugging Joe and crying. "Thank God you're alive."

The deathlike blueness that discolored Joe's face

drained away, and he became more alert.

"Why are you here?" Joe muttered. "Why'd you stop me?"

"You're my son," Don mumbled, through tears. "I love you no matter what."

"Nobody can love me—not after what I've done. Leave me to die."

"Stop that. You've got everything to live for—your mother, Maria, your sons."

"They can't love me. I've hurt 'em too much."

Don took Joe's head in his hands and stared into his eyes. "Joe, I need you. Your mother needs you. We love you no matter what. You're our son."

Joe struggled to sit up and clutched his throat. A bruise grew under the chafe marks caused by the rope.

"Thank God you didn't break your neck."

"I need a drink," Joe muttered, reaching for the champagne bottle.

"Oh no you don't. Let me have that bottle."

Joe grabbed the bottle and took a gulp. Mid swallow, he vomited. In a half-panicked, pained voice, he whispered, "I can't swallow. Throat hurts like hell."

"Gotta get you to Doc Wilson's—make sure you didn't damage anything."

"No."

"You will, damn it, because I'm taking you."

"Doc won't see me. Not with all I've done."

"He's a *doctor* for God's sake. He'll see you. Let's get you dressed."

Don examined Joe's torn shirt, shredded underwear, and ripped pants. "Shit. You can't wear these. Put your shoes on. I'll get mother's blanket out of the trunk."

Don returned with the blanket, wrapped it around his

staggering son, and then led him to the car. He attempted to buckle Joe's seatbelt, but Joe blocked Don's hand. "I don't need no seatbelt. I ain't afraid to die."

"You're gonna wear the damn belt," Don said. "Shut up. I'm gonna buckle it!"

Joe attempted to get out of the car, but Don pushed him back then buckled the seatbelt.

Speeding to the private clinic, Don phoned Doctor Wilson who said he'd be waiting.

Don called Maria. "I found Joe. I'm taking him to Doc Wilson's to make sure he's okay."

"Whatta you mean okay?" Maria yelled. "Is something wrong?"

"Maria . . . He tried to hang himself, but I got to him in time. I think he'll be alright, but I want doc to examine him."

"Oh, God! No, no."

"Maria, calm down. He's going to be alright. We're almost at doc's now. I'll call you later. Tell mother he's okay—just drunk."

Chapter Thirty

Joe waited in the examination room while Doctor Wilson talked to Don into the hall. "I don't think there's anything to worry about, but I'd like to keep him overnight. I want to make sure his bruised voice box doesn't cause any breathing problems. We'll also do a suicide watch. I don't think he'll have trouble sleeping, considering what he's had to drink. Pick him up in the morning . . . around ten o'clock. We'd better schedule psychiatric help for him. He, you, and Maria are going to need a lot of help to get through this."

"Thanks, Doc. See you in the morning."

Looking anxious, Maria and Lois stood as Don entered his living room.

"How's Joe?" they asked, each grabbing one of Don's hands.

"He's fine, just drunk. He's spending the night at Doc Wilson's place to make sure everything's okay. I'll pick him up in the morning."

"Thank God," the women said.

"Maria, would you bring a full set of Joe's clothes here in the morning? He vomited all over his. They're ruined. I'll take the clean ones to the hospital, but I'd like to have a talk with him here before taking him to your house."

Maria half nodded. "Whatever you think best."

"All right then. Everybody, let's get some sleep."

Don drove Maria to the Smithville shop. "There," he said, "You drive Joe's car home, and I'll go on to Doctor Wilson's." *Can't let her see the mess in the shed.*

When Maria saw the trash in Joe's car, she covered her gaping mouth with a quivering hand. Shaking her head, she made room on the driver's seat to sit down then drove home.

Don collected Joe's wallet and cell phone in the shed then tossed Joe's ruined clothes in the shop dumpster. Just then, Joe's cell phone beeped.

Don looked at the phone. "A voice mail. Wonder who called."

As Don retrieved the message, the phone rang. Don answered, "Hello."

"Thank God you finally answered," the caller said. "I was afraid you had done something stupid."

"Who is this?" Don asked in a gruff voice.

"Who's this?" the caller asked.

"This is Don, Joe's dad. Who're you?"

"I'm a friend. A *real* friend. How is Joe?"

"I see you're calling from Cincinnati. You're not that Mark fella are you?"

"Hell no. I'm a *true* friend. I'm Bruce. How is Joe?"

"How well you know Joe?"

"Let's say we're very good friends. Mister Wertz, how is he?"

"Are you the guy that Mark fella mentioned—a gay lover?"

"Mister Wertz, please! How is Joe?"

"Answer me! Are you Joe's lover?"

"I was. I hope I am. For God's sake how is he?"

"For now, he's okay, but thanks to you queers, he tried to hang himself."

"Oh, God! No! Where is he? I need to see him."

"Oh no you don't. Not after how he's reacted to you queers."

"Mister Wertz, I can understand how you feel, but believe me, I have *no* ill will for Joe. It may shock you to hear this, but I love him, and at one time, he loved me. I hope he still

332

does."

"I'm old enough to know I can't live somebody else's life—my son's included, but I hope he gets over this shit and makes up with Maria. He needs to get on with his life. Leave Joe alone."

"Mister Wertz, I know you're upset, and I know your son's going through a tough time but denying his situation isn't helpful. Joe needs help not abandonment or denial. You and he need to talk."

"I'm not abandoning him. I'm trying to protect him— from queers like that son-of-a-bitch Hanlan guy."

"I see I can't change your mind or Joe's situation, but I hope you'll tell him I called, and that I'm concerned about him."

"Enough of this shit—stay away from my son."

At the clinic, Don jostled Joe's clothes onto one arm, so he could shake Doctor Wilson's hand.

"How'd he do last night, Doc?"

"No problems, Don. He slept well and drank four ounces of juice this morning. Swallowing will be painful for a week or so, but I don't anticipate other problems. Here's a prescription for pain pills. They should get him through next week. If the pain persists, let me examine him. I should warn you that his neck bruises will get worse, but they'll fade over time."

Don breathed a sigh of relief. "Thanks, Doc."

"Joe and I had a talk this morning. He told me he had seen a psychologist when he was in California. Said he planned to stay in touch with the therapist, but if you note any unusual behavior, let me know right away."

"He told you he saw a shrink in California?"

"You didn't know?"

"I had no idea."

"Well, you guys have a lot to discuss." Doctor Wilson

gripped Don's shoulder. "Give him time, Don. Don't push. Most importantly, be a good listener. Try to put *your* feelings aside as both of you work through this. You have to accept he is a changed man."

"We'll work on it, Doc. Can I take him now?"

"Surely. Go on in. He's a little anxious about seeing you, but he's expecting you."

Don shook his head. "He's not the only one feeling nervous."

Wearing a hospital gown, Joe sat on the edge of the bed, staring at the floor.

"How you doing, son?" Don asked quietly.

Joe remained silent.

"Joe? You alright?"

"Yeah," Joe murmured, without looking up.

"I heard you drank some juice this morning."

"Yeah. Hurt like hell."

"Doc says that'll go away. You ready to go home?"

"I don't have a home."

"What're you talking about?"

Joe continued to stare at the floor. "Nobody wants me. Not now."

"There are lots of people who want and love you."

"They won't when they know everything." Joe looked at his father. "Even I ran from the truth."

Don pulled Joe's head against his chest, hugged him, and then stooped to stare into Joe's downcast eyes. "Joe, you're my son. Your mother and I and Maria and John and Paul love you. I don't know how, but we'll get through this—together. Everything'll work out the way it's supposed to." Don stepped back and said, "Let's go see your mother." Don held up Joe's clothes. "I brought these for you. Let's get you dressed then get out of here."

Joe dressed at a snail's pace then moped toward the car. He sat motionless in the passenger's seat, staring at the floor as Don started the car and drove away, saying nothing.

At Don's home, Don exited the car then opened Joe's door.

Joe sat motionless.

"Joe. Go in and see your mother. She's worried sick. Seeing you is the only thing that'll make her feel better."

Almost in a whimper, Joe said, "I don't know what to say. I've hurt her something terrible." Joe fought back tears as he looked heavenward. "God, forgive me." He surrendered to the weight of his emotions and sobbed. "How could I have been so stupid? I'm sorry. So sorry."

Don pulled Joe from the car, hugged him, and then took his hand, tugging him toward the house. Don led Joe to the living room where his mother sat in her rocking chair, staring at the floor.

As Joe entered, she raised her head. It took a moment for her to realize Joe was home. Her sad eyes widened as a smile crept across her pale, withered face. With a bony hand, she grasped Joe's arm and cried. "Joe, Joe. You're all right. Thank God. My prayers have been answered."

Weakened from rounds of chemotherapy, the withered woman pushed herself up from her chair and shuffled closer to Joe. Don watched them embrace as they hadn't in years. She wept tears of unbounded happiness.

"Mom, I'm sorry I hurt you and dad." He looked her in the face. "Please, forgive me."

"Joe, we love you no matter what. You're our son—my son. I love you."

Lois Wertz grew weak. Joe helped her into her chair. She pulled a handkerchief from her pocket and wiped her eyes as she mumbled, "Thank you, Jesus for getting my boy home."

Don took Joe by the hand then led him to the kitchen as he had done when Joe was five-years old. Don recalled the many times he had taken Joe to the kitchen table to eat foods he didn't like.

"Sit down, son. You probably can't eat, but do you want anything to drink?"

"No," Joe whispered.

"Son . . . What's been going on?"

Joe glanced at his father then stared at the floor. "Dad, let's just say I've been mixed up a long time . . . about who I am. I never talked about it. I couldn't, and I don't wanna talk about it now."

"Okay, son."

Joe looked at his father as Don sat down. For a moment, Don said nothing. "Maybe I haven't been the best father, but I've always loved you. I still love you, and I'm here for you. Anytime. No matter what or who you are."

"Thanks, dad." Joe put his head in his hands and sighed. "I didn't mean for things to go like this." He glanced at his father. "I'm sorry for the hurt I've caused you and mom. I hope you will forgive me."

Fighting tears, Don smiled and nodded.

Joe shook his head. "I don't want to, but I have to talk to Maria. Would you drive me home?"

"Sure, son."

On the way to Joe's house, neither man spoke. A car filled with so much emotional pain had no room for conversation.

Don pulled into Joe's driveway.

Both men exited the car. Don gave Joe a hug and kissed him on the cheek. "Take care, son. I'll call you."

Don drove away, leaving Joe standing in the drive-way.

Maria opened the front door and yelled, "Joe, you're home. Thank God you're okay."

In a hoarse voice, Joe said, "Hello, Maria. Are the boys here?"

"No. They're at Wanda's for the day."

"Good. I don't know what I'd say to them."

"Joe, your neck is bruised."

Joe shook his head. "Maria, it's a long story of hurt. I'm sorry."

"What do you mean *sorry*, Joe? "Maria's voice grew louder and angrier. What about me? Your family?"

Joe shook his head. "I don't know where to begin."

"How about starting with the truth, Joe? The *truth*. Have you been doing—gay things?"

Joe stared at the ground then looked up. "Maria, I . . . yes. *Yes*!"

Maria stood erect, her arms stretched downward, fists clinched. "God, Joe. How could you do this to me—to us? And taking your sons swimming naked with that man from the TV show. Why?"

Joe shook his head as he stared into space, searching for an answer. Kicking at a stone, he said, "Ever since I was a boy, I've felt strange. Different. I wasn't sick, nervous, or depressed just confused about how I felt about guys. I didn't have a name for . . . *it*. I had certain interests in class-mates that I had been taught I shouldn't have." Joe walked in small circles. "I told myself it was a passing thing, but it never passed. Later, it was for men. I didn't know there were other people like me . . . people who could help me understand what was going on."

"So you've know about this all along?"

Joe nodded. "You came into my life, and we had

337

children. I pushed *it* to the back of my mind, but it never went away. At the kitchen show, I went to a bar to hear a jazz band and then got drunk. I met a guy there. A nice guy. I wound up experimenting."

"Was the *nice* guy that Mark fella on TV?"

"Yeah. He opened my eyes. I became aware of . . . things."

"What things?"

"Stuff buried deep inside, gnawing at me forever. Stuff I *had* to admit to myself."

"And . . .?" Maria asked, mouth puckered as if she had sucked a lemon.

"After that, I was different. Inside, I felt different. I was aware. Then I met another guy. We experimented. No. *I* experimented. He *was* what I had thought about but couldn't admit to myself even though part of me wanted to."

Maria choked back tears. "Then what that guy on TV said is true?"

"I'm sorry, Maria." Joe took Maria's hand then led her to the front steps where they sat down.

Maria dropped her head in her hands and cried. "Why? Why'd you do it?"

Fueled by rage, she suddenly stood and pummeled Joe's head.

After several blows, Joe grabbed her wrists and stared her in the eyes—red and weeping. "I don't know why I did it, but I never meant for things to end like this. When that show aired, I was humiliated. I wanted to die. That would end my pain, my humiliation, my anger, my sorry, my having to confront my family—everything—but dad stopped me."

Maria fell to her knees. She buried her head in her hands, washed with tears. "Joe. What's to become of us?"

"I wish I knew. I know we have to work things out, but

where they'll wind up I'm not sure. I'm going to talk to a mind doc. Doctor Wilson said you and me should see one together."

Attempting to control her anger, Maria looked up. "Joe, you know I love you. I'll do whatever it takes to get through this. I want to keep this family together. We can do it, but what about the boys? They're gonna hear stuff. We can't stop it."

"First, I need to tell them I love them then tell them the truth—in a way fit for their age."

"Good," Maria said, weeping, "because I don't want to . . . I don't know how."

Joe and Maria rejoiced in the news they tested negative for the AIDs virus.

For three months, Joe attended counseling sessions. Sometimes, Maria went with him. He did so more to make sure he would be allowed to share custody of his children if the marriage ended.

Joe and Maria slept in separate rooms. They tried to lead normal lives for the sake of their sons, but the emotional strain leaked through the parents' defenses.

After the first week of couples-counseling, the therapist recommended their sons get counseling. They needed it to help them understand and deal with verbal attacks of peers.

As couples counseling progressed, Maria realized their future as a couple needed to change. With that realization, counseling became less frequent. At first, the couple discussed temporary separation, but their conversations soon switched to discussions about permanent separation.

Joe and Maria prepared their sons for the breakup. They received lots of love, attention, and the assurance their relation-ship with both parents would not change.

Joe stopped shaving his head and grew a mustache,

hoping his new look would allowed him to interact with society without being identified as the president's *gay* plumber.

He had taken over the second plumbing shop just as he joined the first campaign tour. In fast succession, there had been the LA visit then another tour. This resulted in his having little facetime at his new shop, leaving him with little community exposure to worry about.

His secretary and assistant plumber were young and accepting of gay people. Nevertheless, he and Don agreed to remove the Wertz name from the new shop.

"I know you must feel awful about changing the name," Joe said to his father. "It's not like I'm not your son, but I'll do my best to make it up to you. The shop will be profitable, I promise."

"No matter what happens, son, we'll get through it together."

Joe and Maria agreed that their sons should go to a school in a town east of Smithville. Maria moved there, established residency, and took a part time job. Joe remained in the old house, paying alimony and child support. In exchange, he got to regularly see his sons, strengthening parental bonds and becoming a better father.

Over the months following the TV incident, Joe received many voice mails from Bruce, reiterating his undying love. Joe never returned the calls, but he listened to and saved them. He never stopped loving Bruce, but he needed time to resolve his personal and domestic affairs before permitting himself to think of the future.

One day, after a long, hard day of work, Joe returned home. He showered, and for the first time decided not to dress. He thought of Bruce—naked Bruce. Joe wondered if he should call him. He wondered if or how Bruce had changed? What would Bruce think about his new look? Joe kept thinking, *Should I?*

      With a shaking finger, Joe dialed Bruce's number.

      "Hello," Bruce said.

      "Bruce."

      "Who's calling?"

      "It's me, Joe."

      "Joe? Joe wh— Oh, my God, Joe."

      "Yep. It's me. How are you?"

      "I'm fine, just shocked. God, it's good to hear your voice. How are you?"

      "I'm feeling better, but the last six months have been hell. I hope you'll forgive me for not answering your calls. I just couldn't. I wasn't ready."

      "And your marriage?"

      Maria and I divorced—on friendly terms. She and the boys moved to a nearby town for the kids' sake, but I see them often. I'm living alone in the old house."

      "I hope I didn't make a nuisance of myself with so many voice mails?"

      "Not at all. Even though I didn't answer, I listened to them. Saved 'em all."

      "Really?"

      "Yeah. I'm glad you kept calling. I liked hearing your voice."

      "Are you still plumbing?"

      "Yeah, but I only work out of the new shop."

      "Are you still working out?"

      "I didn't for a long time, but I've started again. How is everything at your gift shop?"

      "Business is good. Had to hire a second guy."

      Joe chuckled. "So you're becoming a capitalist like me."

"Yeah. It's good to be king. Anything else change in your life?"

I let my scalp hair grow, and I've grown a mustache. It's a bit of a disguise. It's harder for people to recognize me.

"I guess your body hair has grown back?"

"Yeah. I'm as hairy as ever."

"I can't imagine you with hair—I mean on your head and lip."

"You might not recognize me."

"Will I get a chance?"

"I was wondering if we could have dinner sometime. I could come to Cincinnati."

"Oh, God! Of course. I'd love to see you. We can do whatever you want. When can you come?"

"How about this weekend?"

"Wow! Absolutely! How about arriving around noon Saturday? I'll leave the shop early."

"Okay. See you then.

For two days, thoughts of Bruce intruded on Joe's consciousness, causing him problems with simple tasks—errors in addition, forgetting phone numbers and appointment times.

Saturday morning, Joe shook with anxiety as he drove to Cincinnati. *God, I hope this goes well.*

Joe parked in a visitor's spot then looked up at Bruce's terrace.

Bruce waved.

Joe waved back then walked to the reception desk and addressed the familiar clerk, "I'm expected at the penthouse."

The clerk apparently did not recognize Joe camouflaged by head hair and a mustache. "Go right up, sir. He's expecting a visitor."

Joe rang Bruce's doorbell and waited. In seconds, Bruce

opened the door.

Joe gasped. "My god, Bruce, you're dressed."

"Damn, Joe! You're looking great. Hair and all." Bruce grabbed Joe's hand. "Get in here. Give me a hug."

Joe and Bruce exchanged a long, tight hug.

"Nice to see you, Bruce, but I gotta say I didn't expect you'd be dressed."

"I didn't want you to think I expected any funny stuff."

"I don't know about funny stuff, but I'm disappointed you're not naked. I know you don't wear clothes at home."

"I can get naked, if you want."

"Only if you want to," Joe said then grinned.

Bruce smiled. "You know I don't like undressing alone."

Joe felt his face warm with a blush. "Okay. I'll join you."

"Deal."

Both men undressed under the gaze of the other. Naked and aroused, they hugged, kissed, and tugged each other's balls as if the men had never been apart.

"I've missed you," Joe said, looking into Bruce's eyes.

"I've missed you too, and I'm sorry for sending you away that awful night."

"Yeah. That night was hell."

Bruce took Joe's hand then pulled him toward the terrace. "Come. I have your favorite champagne waiting on the terrace. We've got a lot of catching up to do."

The End

Brad Barham has also published *Men Who Loved* and *Hiding From the Blind.*